SMART DRAGONS, FOOLISH ELVES

SMART DRAGONS, FOOLISH ELVES

EDITED BY
ALAN DEAN FOSTER
AND MARTIN HARRY GREENBERG

ACE BOOKS, NEW YORK

Ace Books are published by The Berkley Publishing Group,
200 Madison Avenue, New York, New York 10016.
The name "ACE" and the "A" logo
are trademarks belonging to Charter Communications, Inc.

PRINTED IN THE UNITED STATES OF AMERICA

Contents

◆

Introduction

◆

HUMOR AND FANTASY have had a long and happy marriage. Every society has felt the need now and then to leaven heavy doses of religion and mythology with laughter, lest the populace feel too oppressed by the gods. Not only did healthy injections of humor help to lighten the life loads of otherwise impoverished peoples, it served to humanize the vast unknowables of existence. Believing that Zeus, or Odin, or Shiva could find themselves on the cosmic whoopee cushion every now and then just like Uncle Cheng probably made the night seem a little less dark, the vastness of space and time a smidgen less overbearing.

So the people told funny stories; sometimes respectfully, sometimes not. Clearly the gods had a sense of humor, because including them in amusing tales did not result in imminent destruction and devastation. No matter how serious the religion or mythology, some irreverent soul always found room for a good laugh.

Today only the parameters have changed. The universe is better understood and therefore less threatening, but we still find space in religion for humor. The mythologies are different, though. The old gods repose comfortably in the Valhalla Retirement Home, having been replaced by computers, satellite communications, and psychoanalysis. Science, not mythology, rules the day.

Yet much of the old hangs around, having slipped comfortably into new clothes. Human concerns are still universal. Many of the stories in this collection would make sense to readers of a hundred or even a thousand years ago. It would do our ancestors good to know that their offspring can still laugh and smile at themselves.

Fantasy can be much more than escapism. Like the Arabian Nights, the imaginative tales in this collection often have points to make about the human condition: about love and truth, greed and lust, children and reality, what is really important in life and what is peripheral or over-rated. The best stories are the ones that can make us think as well as smile. That's as true of fantasy fiction as it is of stand-up humor.

Fantasy is a tool that enables the writer to go beyond the constraints of everyday life to make a point. The vehicle can be ethnic mythology, puberty, Roman history, love, beer, a grand quest or a tiny afterthought. The humor can be contained in a quick punchline or an elaborate buildup. A story can make us laugh out loud or simply smile knowingly. Humor can be light, dark, and every shade in between, depending on what setting the toaster has been left on.

I like to believe that in addition to making us laugh or smile, each of the stories in this collection has something to say to us. Laughter lingers longest when it also makes a point. We usually remember the stories that cut deeper than those that merely anesthetize.

Some of the authors in this collection are noted for their humorous fiction. Most are not. Quite the contrary, they are famed for the dark and serious, or expansive and adventurous, or the biting, or the poetical. But not humor. Not for making the reader grin and chuckle. Those are the ones I particularly prize.

Because there's laughter in all of us, even in long-faced, somber authors charged with explaining the Meaning of It All to desperate read-ers. Sometimes it's a little slow manifesting itself, is all. The reason is that genuinely amusing fiction is the toughest kind to write. Succinctly put, "Funny is hard."

Keep that in mind as you put aside your casual evening's reading of Proust or Solzhenitsyn and dig into something really serious. Like this book. If it makes you smile, then it's done its job. If it makes you think, you've received a bonus. Take two stories, drink plenty of liquids, and stay in bed.

That done, have you heard the one about . . . ?

—Alan Dean Foster
Prescott, Arizona

SMART DRAGONS, FOOLISH ELVES

---◆---

How nice to be able to open a collection of the extraordinary with a quite ordinary tale. After all, what could be more ordinary than buying a car? Cars are unremarkable utilitarian objects that we deal with every day of our lives.

Still, it would be a fairly simple matter to concoct a story about a remarkable car. One that kills, like Stephen King's *Christine*. Or one that metamorphoses into a starship, as in the movie *The Last Starfighter.* But once you've tossed out the punchline, so to speak, where's your story? No, no. Better to keep it simple, ordinary, unspectacular.

Robert Silverberg has been writing simple, ordinary stories about everyday situations and events for a long time now. It's the ease and skill with which he brings off whatever he wants to try that's spectacular. This quiet little story, for example. You have to take it . . .

---◆---

As Is

ROBERT SILVERBERG

"As IS," the auto dealer said, jamming his thumbs under his belt. "Two hundred fifty bucks and drive it away. I'm not pretending it's perfect, but I got to tell you, you're getting a damned good hunk of car for the price."

"As is," Sam Norton said.

"As is. Strictly as is."

Norton looked a little doubtful. "Maybe she drives well, but with a trunk that doesn't open—"

"So what?" the dealer snorted. "You told me yourself you're renting a U-Haul to get your stuff to California. What do you need a trunk for?

1

Look, when you get out to the Coast and have a little time, take the car
to a garage, tell 'em the story, and maybe five minutes with a blow-
torch—"

"Why didn't you do that while you had the car in stock?"

The dealer looked evasive. "We don't have time to fool with details
like that."

Norton let the point pass. He walked around the car again, giving it
a close look from all angles. It was a smallish dark-green four-door sedan, with the finish and trim in good condition, a decent set of tires, and
a general glow that comes only when a car has been well cared for. The
upholstery was respectable, the radio was in working order, the engine
was—as far as he could judge—okay, and a test drive had been smooth
and easy. The car seemed to be a reasonably late model, too; it had
shoulder-harness safety belts and emergency blinkers.

There was only one small thing wrong with it. The trunk didn't
open. It wasn't just a case of a jammed lock, either; somebody had fixed
this car so the trunk *couldn't* open. With great care the previous owner
had apparently welded the trunk shut; nothing was visible back there
except a dim line to mark the place where the lid might once have lifted.

What the hell, though. The car was otherwise in fine shape, and he
wasn't in a position to be too picky. Overnight, practically, they had
transferred him to the Los Angeles office, which was fine in terms of
getting out of New York in the middle of a lousy winter, but not so good
as far as his immediate finances went. The company didn't pay moving
costs, only transportation; he had been handed four one-way tourist-class
tickets, and that was that. So he had put Ellen and the kids aboard the
first jet to L.A., cashing in his own ticket so he could use the money for
the moving job. He figured to do it the slow but cheap way: rent a
U-Haul trailer, stuff the family belongings into it, and set out via turnpike
for California, hoping that Ellen had found an apartment by the time he
got there. Only he couldn't trust his present clunker of a car to get him
very far west of Parsippany, New Jersey, let alone through the Mojave
Desert. So here he was, trying to pick up an honest used job for about five
hundred bucks, which was all he could afford to lay out on the spot.

And here was the man at the used-car place offering him this very
attractive vehicle—with its single peculiar defect—for only two and a
half bills, which would leave him with that much extra cash cushion for
the expenses of his transcontinental journey. And he didn't *really* need a
trunk, driving alone. He could keep his suitcase on the back seat and
stash everything else in the U-Haul. And it shouldn't be all that hard to

have some mechanic in L.A. cut the trunk open for him and get it working again. On the other hand, Ellen was likely to chew him out for having
bought a car that was sealed up that way; she had let him have it before
on other "bargains" of that sort. On the third hand, the mystery of the
sealed trunk appealed to him. Who knew what he'd find in there once he
opened it up? Maybe the car had belonged to a smuggler who had had to
hide a hot cargo fast, and the trunk was full of lovely golden ingots, or
diamonds, or ninety-year-old cognac, which the smuggler had planned to
reclaim a few weeks later, except that something unexpected had come
up. On the fourth hand—

The dealer said, "How'd you like to take her out for another test
spin, then?"

Norton shook his head. "Don't think I need to. I've got a good idea
of how she rides."

"Well, then, let's step into the office and close the deal."

Sidestepping the maneuver, Norton said, "What year did you say
she was?"

"Oh, about a 'sixty-four, 'sixty-five."

"You aren't sure?"

"You can't really tell with these foreign jobs, sometimes. You know,
they don't change the model for five, six, ten years in a row, except in
little ways that only an expert would notice. Take Volkswagen, for instance—"

"And I just realized," Norton cut in, "that you never told me what
make she is, either."

"Peugeot, maybe, or some kind of Fiat," said the dealer hazily.
"One of those kind."

"You don't *know?*"

A shrug. "Well, we checked a lot of the style books going back a few
years, but there are so damn many of these foreign cars around, and some
of them they import only a few thousand, and—well, so we couldn't quite
figure it out."

Norton wondered how he was going to get spare parts for a car of
unknown make and uncertain date. Then he realized that he was thinking of the car as his, already, even though the more he considered the
deal, the less he liked it. And then he thought of those ingots in the
trunk. The rare cognac. The suitcase full of rubies and sapphires.

He said, "Shouldn't the registration say something about the year
and make?"

The dealer shifted his weight from foot to foot. "Matter of fact, we don't have the registration. But it's perfectly legitimate. Hey, look, I'd like to get this car out of my lot, so maybe we call it two twenty-five, huh?"

"It all sounds pretty mysterious. Where'd you get the car, anyway?"

"There was this little guy who brought it in, about a year ago, a year last November, I think it was. Give it a valve job, he said. I'll be back in a month—got to take a sudden business trip. Paid in advance for tune-up and a month's storage and everything. Wouldn't you know that was the last we ever saw of him? Well, we stored his damn car here free for ten, eleven months, but that's it, now we got to get it out of the place. The lawyer says we can take possession for the storage charge."

"If I buy it, you give me a paper saying you had the right to sell it?"

"Sure. Sure."

"And what about getting the registration? Shifting the insurance over from my old heap? All the red tape?"

"I'll handle everything," the dealer said. "Just you take the car outa here."

"Two hundred," Norton said. "As is."

The dealer sighed. "It's a deal. As is."

A light snow was falling when Norton began his cross-country hegira three days later. It was an omen, but he was not sure what kind; he decided that the snow was intended as his last view of a dreary winter phenomenon he wouldn't be seeing again, for a while. According to the *Times,* yesterday's temperature range in L.A. had been sixty-six low, seventy-nine high. Not bad for January.

He slouched down behind the wheel, let his foot rest lightly on the accelerator, and sped westward at a sane, sensible forty-five miles per hour. That was about as fast as he dared go with the bulky U-Haul trailing behind. He hadn't had much experience driving with a trailer—he was a computer salesman, and computer salesmen don't carry sample computers—but he got the hang of it pretty fast. You just had to remember that your vehicle was now a segmented organism, and make your turns accordingly. God bless turnpikes, anyhow. Just drive on, straight and straight and straight, heading toward the land of the sunset with only a few gentle curves and half a dozen traffic lights along the way.

The snow thickened some. But the car responded beautifully, hugging the road, and the windshield wipers kept his view clear. He hadn't expected to buy a foreign car for the trip at all; when he had set out, it was to get a good solid Plymouth or Chevvie, something heavy and sturdy to take him through the wide open spaces. But he had no regrets about this smaller car. It had all the power and pickup he needed, and with that trailer bouncing along behind him he wouldn't have much use for all that extra horsepower, anyway.

He was in a cheerful, relaxed mood. The car seemed comforting and protective, a warm enclosing environment that would contain and shelter him through the thousands of miles ahead. He was still close enough to New York to be able to get Mozart on the radio, which was nice. The car's heater worked well. There wasn't much traffic. The snow itself, new and white and fluffy, was all the more beautiful for the knowledge that he was leaving it behind. He even enjoyed the solitude. It would be restful, in a way, driving on and on through Ohio and Kansas and Colorado or Arizona or whatever states lay between him and Los Angeles. Five or six days of peace and quiet, no need to make small talk, no kids to amuse—

His frame of mind began to darken not long after he got on the Pennsylvania Turnpike. If you have enough time to think, you will eventually think of the things you should have thought of before; and now, as he rolled through the thickening snow on this gray and silent afternoon, certain aspects of a trunkless car occurred to him that in his rush to get on the road he had succeeded in overlooking earlier. What about a tool kit, for instance? If he had a flat, what would he use for a jack and a wrench? That led him to a much more chilling thought: what would he use for a spare tire? A trunk was something more than a cavity back of the rear seat; in most cars it contained highly useful objects.

None of which he had with him.

None of which he had even thought about, until just this minute.

He contemplated the prospects of driving from coast to coast without a spare tire and without tools, and his mood of warm security evaporated abruptly. At the next exit, he decided, he'd hunt for a service station and pick up a tire, fast. There would be room for it on the back seat next to his luggage. And while he was at it, he might as well buy—

The U-Hall, he suddenly observed, was jackknifing around awkwardly in back, as though its wheels had just lost traction. A moment later the car was doing the same, and he found himself moving laterally in a beautiful skid across an unsanded slick patch on the highway. Steer in the direction of the skid, that's what you're supposed to do, he told himself, strangely calm. Somehow he managed to keep his foot off the brake despite all natural inclinations, and watched in quiet horror as car and trailer slid placidly across the empty lane to his right and came to rest, upright and facing forward, in the piled-up snowbank along the shoulder of the road.

He let out his breath slowly, scratched his chin, and gently fed some gas. The spinning wheels made a high-pitched whining sound against the snow. He went nowhere. He was stuck.

The little man had a ruddy-cheeked face, white hair so long it curled at the ends, and metal-rimmed spectacles. He glanced at the snow-covered autos in the used-car lot, scowled, and trudged toward the showroom.

"Came to pick up my car," he announced. "Valve job. Delayed by business in another part of the world."

The dealer looked uncomfortable. "The car's not here."

"So I see. Get it, then."

"We more or less sold it about a week ago."

"*Sold it?* Sold my car? *My car?*"

"Which you abandoned. Which we stored here for a whole year. This ain't no parking lot here. Look, I talked to my lawyer first, and he said—"

"All right. All right. Who was the purchaser?"

"A guy, he was transferred to California and had to get a car fast to drive out. He—"

"His name?"

"Look, I can't tell you that. He bought the car in good faith. You got no call bothering him now."

The little man said, "If I chose, I could draw the information from you in a number of ways. But never mind. I'll locate the car easily enough. And you'll certainly regret this scandalous breach of custodial duties. You certainly shall."

He went stamping out of the showroom, muttering indignantly.

Several minutes later a flash of lightning blazed across the sky. "Lightning?" the auto dealer wondered. "In January? During a snowstorm?"

When the thunder came rumbling in, every pane of plate glass in every window of the showroom shattered and fell out in the same instant.

Sam Norton sat spinning his wheels for a while in mounting fury. He knew it did no good, but he wasn't sure what else he could do, at this point, except hit the gas and hope for the car to pull itself out of the snow. His only other hope was for the highway patrol to come along, see his plight, and summon a tow truck. But the highway was all but empty, and those few cars that drove by shot past him without stopping.

When ten minutes had passed, he decided to have a closer look at the situation. He wondered vaguely if he could somehow scuff away enough snow with his foot to allow the wheels to get a little purchase. It didn't sound plausible, but there wasn't much else he could do. He got out and headed to the back of the car.

And noticed for the first time that the trunk was open.

The lid had popped up about a foot, along that neat welded line of demarcation. In astonishment Norton pushed it higher and peered inside.

The interior had a dank, musty smell. He couldn't see much of what might be in there, for the light was dim and the lid would lift no higher. It seemed to him that there were odd lumpy objects scattered about, objects of no particular size or shape, but he felt nothing when he groped around. He had the impression that the things in the trunk were moving away from his hand, vanishing into the darkest corners as he reached for them. But then his fingers encountered something cold and smooth, and he heard a welcome clink of metal on metal. He pulled.

A set of tire chains came forth.

He grinned at his good luck. Just what he needed! Quickly he unwound the chains and crouched by the back wheels of the car to fasten them in place. The lid of the trunk slammed shut as he worked—hinge must be loose, he thought—but that was of no importance. In five minutes he had the chains attached. Getting behind the wheel, he started the car again, fed some gas, delicately let in the clutch, and bit down hard on his lower lip by way of helping the car out of the snowbank. The car eased forward until it was in the clear. He left the chains on until he reached a service area eight miles up the turnpike. There he undid them; and when he stood up, he found that the trunk had popped open again. Norton tossed the chains inside and knelt in another attempt to see what else might be in the trunk; but not even by squinting did he discover anything. When he touched the lid, it snapped shut, and once more the rear of the car presented that puzzling welded-tight look.

Mine not to reason why, he told himself. He headed into the station and asked the attendant to sell him a spare tire and a set of tools. The attendant, frowning a bit, studied the car through the station window and said, "Don't know as we got one to fit. We got standards and we got smalls, but you got an in-between. Never saw a size tire like that, really."

"Maybe you ought to take a closer look," Norton suggested. "Just in case it's really a standard foreign-car size, and—"

"Nope. I can see from here. What you driving, anyway? One of them Japanese jobs?"

"Something like that."

"Look, maybe you can get a tire in Harrisburg. They got a place there, it caters to foreign cars, get yourself a muffler, shocks, anything you need."

"Thanks," Norton said, and went out.

He didn't feel like stopping when the turnoff for Harrisburg came by. It made him a little queasy to be driving without a spare, but somehow he wasn't as worried about it as he'd been before. The trunk had had tire chains when he needed them. There was no telling what else might turn up back there at the right time. He drove on.

Since the little man's own vehicle wasn't available to him, he had to arrange a rental. That was no problem, though. There were agencies in every city that specialized in such things. Very shortly he was in touch with one, not exactly by telephone, and was explaining his dilemma. "The difficulty," the little man said, "is that he's got a head start of several days. I've traced him to a point west of Chicago, and he's moving forward at a pretty steady four hundred fifty miles a day."

"You'd better fly, then."

"That's what I've been thinking, too," said the little man. "What's available fast?"

"Could have given you a nice Persian job, but it's out having its tassels restrung. But you don't care much for carpets anyway, do you? I forgot."

"Don't trust 'em in thermals," said the little man. "I caught an updraft once in Sikkim and I was halfway up the Himalayas before I got things under control. Looked for a while like I'd end up in orbit. What's at the stable?"

"Well, some pretty decent jobs. There's this classy stallion that's been resting up all winter, though actually he's a little cranky—maybe you'd prefer the bay gelding. Why don't you stop around and decide for yourself?"

"Will do," the little man said. "You still take Diner's Club, don't you?"

"All major credit cards, as always. You bet."

* * *

Norton was in southern Illinois, an hour out of St. Louis on a foggy, humid morning, when the front right-hand tire blew. He had been expecting it to go for a day and a half, now, ever since he'd stopped in Altoona for gas. The kid at the service station had tapped the tire's treads and showed him the weak spot, and Norton had nodded and asked about his chances of buying a spare, and the kid had shrugged and said, "It's a funny size. Try in Pittsburgh, maybe." He tried in Pittsburgh, killing an hour and a half there, and hearing from several men who probably ought to know that tires just weren't made to that size, nohow. Norton was beginning to wonder how the previous owner of the car had managed to find replacements. Maybe this was still the original set, he figured. But he was morbidly sure of one thing: that weak spot was going to give out, beyond any doubt, before he saw L.A.

When it blew, he was doing about thirty-five, and he realized at once what had happened. He slowed the car to a halt without losing control. The shoulder was wide here, but even so Norton was grateful that the flat was on the right-hand side of the car; he didn't much feature having to change a tire with his rump to the traffic. He was still congratulating himself on that small bit of good luck when he remembered that he had no spare tire.

Somehow he couldn't get very disturbed about it. Spending a dozen hours a day behind the wheel was evidently having a tranquilizing effect on him; at this point nothing worried him much, not even the prospect of being stranded an hour east of St. Louis. He would merely walk to the nearest telephone, wherever that might happen to be, and he would phone the local automobile club and explain his predicament, and they would come out and get him and tow him to civilization. Then he would settle in a motel for a day or two, phoning Ellen at her sister's place in L.A. to say that he was all right but was going to be a little late. Either he would have the tire patched or the automobile club would find a place in St. Louis that sold odd sizes, and everything would turn out for the best. Why get into a dither?

He stepped out of the car and inspected the flat, which looked very flat indeed. Then, observing that the trunk had popped open again, he went around back. Reaching in experimentally, he expected to find the tire chains at the outer edge of the trunk, where he had left them. They weren't there. Instead his fingers closed on a massive metal bar. Norton tugged it partway out of the trunk and discovered that he had found a

jack. Exactly so, he thought. And the spare tire ought to be right in back
of it, over here, yes? He looked, but the lid was up only eighteen inches or
so, and he couldn't see much. His fingers encountered good rubber,
though. Yes, here it is. Nice and plump, brand new, deep treads—very
pretty. And next to it, if my luck holds, I ought to find a chest of golden
doubloons—

The doubloons weren't there. Maybe next time, he told himself. He
hauled out the tire and spent a sweaty half hour putting it on. When he
was done, he dumped the jack, the wrench, and the blown tire into the
trunk, which immediately shut to the usual hermetic degree of sealing.
An hour later, without further incident, he crossed the Mississippi into
St. Louis, found a room in a shiny new motel overlooking the Gateway
Arch, treated himself to a hot shower and a couple of cold Gibsons, and
put in a collect call to Ellen's sister. Ellen had just come back from some
unsuccessful apartment hunting, and she sounded tired and discouraged.
Children were howling in the background as she said, "You're driving
carefully, aren't you?"

"Of course I am."

"And the new car is behaving okay?"

"Its behavior," Norman said, "is beyond reproach."

"My sister wants to know what kind it is. She says a Volvo is a good
kind of car, if you want a foreign car. That's a Norwegian car."

"Swedish," he corrected.

He heard Ellen say to her sister, "He bought a Swedish car." The
reply was unintelligible, but a moment later Ellen said, "She says you did
a smart thing. Those Swedes, they make good cars too."

The flight ceiling was low, with visibility less than half a mile in
thick fog. Airports were socked in all over Pennsylvania and eastern
Ohio. The little man flew westward, though, keeping just above the fleecy
whiteness spreading to the horizon. He was making good time, and it was
a relief not to have to worry about those damned private planes.

The bay gelding had plenty of stamina, too. He was a fuel-guzzler,
that was his only trouble. You didn't get a whole lot of miles to the bale
with the horses available nowadays, the little man thought sadly. Everything was in a state of decline, and you had to accept the situation.

His original flight plan had called for him to overtake his car somewhere in the Texas Panhandle. But he had stopped off in Chicago on a
sudden whim to visit friends, and now he calculated he wouldn't catch up

with the car until Arizona. He couldn't wait to get behind the wheel again, after all these months.

The more he thought about the trunk and the tricks it had played, the more bothered by it all Sam Norton was. The chains, the spare tire, the jack—what next? In Amarillo he had offered a mechanic twenty bucks to get the trunk open. The mechanic had run his fingers along that smooth seam in disbelief. "What are you, one of those television fellers?" he asked. "Having some fun with me?"

"Not at all," Norton said. "I just want that trunk opened up."

"Well, I reckon maybe with an acetylene torch—"

But Norton felt an obscure terror at the idea of cutting into the car that way. He didn't know why the thought frightened him so much, but it did, and he drove out of Amarillo with the car whole and the mechanic muttering and spraying his boots with tobacco juice. A hundred miles on, when he was over the New Mexico border and moving through bleak, forlorn, winter-browned country, he decided to put the trunk to a test.

LAST GAS BEFORE ROSWELL, a peeling sign warned. FILL UP NOW!

The gas gauge told him that the tank was nearly empty. Roswell was somewhere far ahead. There wasn't another human being in sight, no town, not even a shack. This, Norton decided, is the right place to run out of gas.

He shot past the gas station at fifty miles an hour.

In a few minutes he was two and a half mountains away from the filling station and beginning to have doubts not merely of the wisdom of his course but even of his sanity. Deliberately letting himself run out of gas was against all reason; it was harder even to do than deliberately letting the telephone go unanswered. A dozen times he ordered himself to swing around and go back to fill his tank, and a dozen times he refused.

The needle crept lower, until it was reading E for Empty, and still he drove ahead. The needle slipped through the red warning zone below the E. He had used up even the extra couple of gallons of gas that the tank didn't register—the safety margin for careless drivers. And any moment now the car would—

—stop.

For the first time in his life Sam Norton had run out of gas. Okay, trunk, let's see what you can do, he thought. He pushed the door open and felt the chilly zip of the mountain breeze. It was quiet here, ominously so; except for the gray ribbon of the road itself, this neighborhood had a darkly prehistoric look, all sagebrush and pinyon pine and not a trace of man's impact. Norton walked around to the rear of his car.

The trunk was open again.

It figures. Now I reach inside and find that a ten-gallon can of gas has mysteriously materialized, and—

He couldn't feel any can of gas in the trunk. He groped a good long while and came up with nothing more useful than a coil of thick rope.

Rope?

What good is rope to a man who's out of gas in the desert?

Norton hefted the rope, seeking answers from it and not getting any. It occurred to him that perhaps this time the trunk hadn't *wanted* to help him. The skid, the blowout—those hadn't been his fault. But he had with malice aforethought let the car run out of gas, just to see what would happen, and maybe that didn't fall within the scope of the trunk's services.

Why the rope, though?

Some kind of grisly joke? Was the trunk telling him to go string himself up? He couldn't even do that properly here; there wasn't a tree in sight tall enough for a man to hang himself from, not even a telephone pole. Norton felt like kicking himself. Here he was, and here he'd remain for hours, maybe even for days, until another car came along. Of all the dumb stunts!

Angrily he hurled the rope into the air. It uncoiled as he let go of it, and one end rose straight up. The rope hovered about a yard off the ground, rigid, pointing skyward. A faint turquoise cloud formed at the upper end, and a thin, muscular olive-skinned boy in a turban and a loincloth climbed down to confront the gaping Norton.

"Well, what's the trouble?" the boy asked brusquely.

"I'm . . . out . . . of . . . gas."

"There's a filling station twenty miles back. Why didn't you tank up there?"

"I . . . that is . . ."

"What a damned fool," the boy said in disgust. "Why do I get stuck with jobs like this? All right, don't go anywhere and I'll see what I can do."

He went up the rope again and vanished.

When he returned, some three minutes later, he was carrying a tin of gasoline. Glowering at Norton, he slid the gas-tank cover aside and poured in the gas.

"This'll get you to Roswell," he said. "From now on look at your dashboard once in a while. Idiot!"

He scrambled up the rope. When he disappeared, the rope went limp and fell. Norton shakily picked it up and slipped it into the trunk, whose lid shut with an aggressive slam.

Half an hour went by before Norton felt it was safe to get behind the wheel again. He paced around the car something more than a thousand times, not getting a whole lot steadier in the nerves, and ultimately, with night coming on, got in and switched on the ignition. The engine coughed and turned over. He began to drive toward Roswell at a sober and steadfast fifteen miles an hour.

He was willing to believe anything, now.

And so it did not upset him at all when a handsome reddish-brown horse with the wingspread of a DC-3 came soaring through the air, circled above the car a couple of times, and made a neat landing on the highway alongside him. The horse trotted along, keeping pace with him, while the small white-haired man in the saddle yelled, "Open your window wider, young fellow! I've got to talk to you!"

Norton opened the window.

The little man said, "Your name Sam Norton?"

"That's right."

"Well, listen, Sam Norton, you're driving my car!"

Norton saw a dirt turnoff up ahead and pulled into it. As he got out, the pegasus came trotting up and halted to let its rider dismount. It cropped moodily at sagebrush, fluttering its huge wings a couple of times before folding them neatly along its back.

The little man said, "My car, all right. Had her specially made a few years back, when I was on the road a lot. Dropped her off at the garage last winter account of I had a business trip to make abroad, but I never figured they'd sell her out from under me before I got back. It's a decadent age, that's the truth."

"Your . . . car . . ." Norton said.

"My car, yep. Afraid I'll have to take it from you, too. Car like this, you don't want to own it, anyway. Too complicated. Get yourself a decent little standard-make flivver, eh? Well, now, let's unhitch this trailer thing of yours, and then—"

"Wait a second," Norton said. "I bought this car legally. I've got a

bill of sale to prove it, and a letter from the dealer's lawyer, explaining
that—"

"Don't matter one bit," said the little man. "One crook hires another crook to testify to his character, that's not too impressive. I know
you're an innocent party, son, but the fact remains that the car is my
property, and I hope I don't have to use special persuasion to get you to
relinquish it."

"You just want me to get out and walk, is that it? In the middle of
the New Mexico desert at sundown? Dragging the damned U-Haul with
my bare hands?"

"Hadn't really considered that problem much," the little man said.
"Wouldn't altogether be fair to you, would it?"

"It sure wouldn't." He thought a moment. "And what about the
two hundred bucks I paid for the car?"

The little man laughed. "Shucks, it cost me more than that to rent
the pegasus to come chasing you! And the overhead! You know how
much hay that critter—"

"That's your problem," Norton said. "Mine is that you want to
strand me in the desert and that you want to take away a car that I
bought in good faith for two hundred dollars, and even if it's a goddam
magic car I—"

"Hush, now," said the little man. "You're gettin' all upset, Sam! We
can work this thing out. You're going to L.A., that it?"

"Ye-es."

"So am I. Okay, we travel together. I'll deliver you and your trailer,
here, and then the car's mine again, and you forget anything you might
have seen these last few days."

"And my two hundred dol—"

"Oh, all right." The little man walked to the back of the car. The
trunk opened; he slipped in a hand and pulled forth a sheaf of new bills, a
dozen twenties, which he handed to Norton. "Here. With a little something extra, thrown in. And don't look at them so suspiciously, hear?
That's good legal tender U.S. money. They even got different serial num-
bers, every one." He winked and strolled over to the grazing pegasus,
which he slapped briskly on the rump. "Get along, now. Head for home.
You cost me enough already!"

The horse began to canter along the highway. As it broke into a
gallop it spread its superb wings; they beat furiously a moment, and the
horse took off, rising in a superb arc until it was no bigger than a hawk
against the darkening sky, and then was gone.

The little man slipped into the driver's seat of the car and fondled the wheel in obvious affection. At a nod, Norton took the seat beside him, and off they went.

"I understand you peddle computers," the little man said when he had driven a couple of miles. "Mighty interesting things, computers. I've been considering computerizing our operation too, you know? It's a pretty big outfit, a lot of consulting stuff all over the world, mostly dowsing now, some thaumaturgy, now and then a little transmutation, things like that, and though we use traditional methods we don't object to the scientific approach. Now, let me tell you a bit about our inventory flow, and maybe you can make a few intelligent suggestions, young fellow, and you might just be landing a nice contract for yourself—"

Norton had the roughs for the system worked out before they hit Arizona. From Phoenix he phoned Ellen and found out that she had rented an apartment just outside Beverly Hills, in what *looked* like a terribly expensive neighborhood but really wasn't, at least, not by comparison with some of the other things she'd seen, and—

"It's okay," he said. "I'm in the process of closing a pretty big sale. I . . . ah . . . picked up a hitchhiker, and turns out he's thinking of going computer soon, a fairly large company—"

"Sam, you haven't been drinking, have you?"

"Not a drop."

"A hitchhiker and you sold him a computer. Next you'll tell me about the flying saucer you saw."

"Don't be silly," Norton said. "Flying saucers aren't real."

They drove into L.A. in midmorning, two days later. By then he had written the whole order, and everything was set; the commission, he figured, would be enough to see him through a new car, maybe one of those Swedish jobs Ellen's sister had heard about. The little man seemed to have no difficulty finding the address of the apartment Ellen had taken; he negotiated the maze of the freeways with complete ease and assurance, and pulled up outside the house.

"Been a most pleasant trip, young fellow," the little man said. "I'll be talking to my bankers later today about that wonderful machine of yours. Meanwhile here we part. You'll have to unhitch the trailer, now."

"What am I supposed to tell my wife about the car I drove here in?"

"Oh, just say that you sold it to that hitchhiker at a good profit. I think she'll appreciate that."

They got out. While Norton undid the U-Haul's couplings, the little man took something from the trunk, which had opened a moment before. It was a large rubbery tarpaulin. The little man began to spread it over the car. "Give us a hand here, will you?" he said. "Spread it nice and neat, so it covers the fenders and everything." He got inside, while Norton, baffled, carefully tucked the tarpaulin into place.

"You want me to cover the windshield too?" he asked.

"Everything," said the little man, and Norton covered the windshield. Now the car was wholly hidden.

There was a hissing sound, as of air being let out of tires. The tarpaulin began to flatten. As it sank toward the ground, there came a cheery voice from underneath, calling, "Good luck, young fellow!"

In moments the tarpaulin was less than three feet high. In a minute more it lay flat against the pavement. There was no sign of the car. It might have evaporated, or vanished into the earth. Slowly, uncomprehendingly, Norton picked up the tarpaulin, folded it until he could fit it under his arm, and walked into the house to tell his wife that he had arrived in Los Angeles.

---◆---

Ah, that elusive, sneaky, somehow slightly *dangerous* Mr. Sheckley has gone and done it to the reader again. A Sheckley story is always a joy to read because you never quite know what to expect. Of all the authors in this collection, the one I envision actually cackling with a soft manic glee as he bends over the keyboard is Robert Sheckley.

The curse is a mainstay of modern as well as traditional fantasy. There are funny curses, and horrendous curses, liberating curses and damning curses. Then there is the IRS. Another mainstay is the wish, whether conveyed by genie, accident, malapropism or telegram (does anybody actually get telegrams anymore?).

Put the two together in the hands of a quiet riot name of Sheckley, dump them on an ordinary *schlemiel*, and you end up with . . .

---◆---

The Same to You Doubled

ROBERT SHECKLEY

IN NEW YORK, it never fails, the doorbell rings just when you've plopped down onto the couch for a well-deserved snooze. Now, a person of character would say, "To hell with that, a man's home is his castle and they can slide any telegrams under the door." But if you're like Edelstein, not particularly strong on character, then you think to yourself that maybe it's the blonde from 12C who has come up to borrow a jar of chili powder. Or it could even be some crazy film producer who wants to make a movie based on the letters you've been sending your mother in

17

Santa Monica. (And why not; don't they make movies out of worse material than that?)

Yet this time, Edelstein had really decided not to answer the bell. Lying on the couch, his eyes still closed, he called out, "I don't want any."

"Yes you do," a voice from the other side of the door replied.

"I've got all the encyclopedias, brushes and waterless cookery I need," Edelstein called back wearily. "Whatever you've got, I've got it already."

"Look," the voice said, "I'm not selling anything. I want to give you something."

Edelstein smiled the thin, sour smile of the New Yorker who knows that if someone made him a gift of a package of genuine, unmarked $20 bills, he'd still somehow end up having to pay for it.

"If it's *free*," Edelstein answered, "then I *definitely* can't afford it."

"But I mean *really* free," the voice said. "I mean free that it won't cost you anything now or ever."

"I'm not interested," Edelstein replied, admiring his firmness of character.

The voice did not answer.

Edelstein called out, "Hey, if you're still there, please go away."

"My dear Mr. Edelstein," the voice said, "cynicism is merely a form of naïveté. Mr. Edelstein, wisdom is discrimination."

"He gives me lectures now," Edelstein said to the wall.

"All right," the voice said, "forget the whole thing, keep your cynicism and your racial prejudice; do I need this kind of trouble?"

"Just a minute," Edelstein answered. "What makes you think I'm prejudiced?"

"Let's not crap around," the voice said. "If I was raising funds for Hadassah or selling Israel bonds, it would have been different. But, obviously, I am what I am, so excuse me for living."

"Not so fast," Edelstein said. "As far as I'm concerned, you're just a voice from the other side of the door. For all I know, you could be Catholic or Seventh-Day Adventist or even Jewish."

"*You knew*," the voice responded.

"Mister, I swear to you—"

"Look," the voice said, "it doesn't matter, I come up against a lot of this kind of thing. Goodbye, Mr. Edelstein."

"Just a minute," Edelstein replied.

He cursed himself for a fool. How often had he fallen for some huckster's line, ending up, for example, paying $9.98 for an illustrated two-volume *Sexual History of Mankind*, which his friend Manowitz had pointed out he could have bought in any Marboro bookstore for $2.98?

But the voice was right. Edelstein had somehow known that he was dealing with a goy.

And the voice would go away thinking, *The Jews, they think they're better than anyone else.* Further, he would tell this to his bigoted friends at the next meeting of the Elks or the Knights of Columbus, and there it would be, another black eye for the Jews.

"I do have a weak character," Edelstein thought sadly.

He called out, "All right! You can come in! But I warn you from the start, I am not going to buy anything."

He pulled himself to his feet and started toward the door. Then he stopped, for the voice had replied, "Thank you very much," and then a man had walked through the closed, double-locked wooden door.

The man was of medium height, nicely dressed in a gray pinstripe modified Edwardian suit. His cordovan boots were highly polished. He was black, carried a briefcase, and he had stepped through Edelstein's door as if it had been made of Jell-O.

"Just a minute, stop, hold on one minute," Edelstein said. He found that he was clasping both of his hands together and his heart was beating unpleasantly fast.

The man stood perfectly still and at his ease, one yard within the apartment. Edelstein started to breathe again. He said, "Sorry, I just had a brief attack, a kind of hallucination—"

"Want to see me do it again?" the man asked.

"My God, no! So you *did* walk through the door! Oh, God, I think I'm in trouble."

Edelstein went back to the couch and sat down heavily. The man sat down in a nearby chair.

"What is this all about?" Edelstein whispered.

"I do the door thing to save time," the man said. "It usually closes the credulity gap. My name is Charles Sitwell. I am a field man for the Devil."

Edelstein believed him. He tried to think of a prayer, but all he could remember was the one he used to say over bread in the summer camp he had attended when he was a boy. It probably wouldn't help. He also knew the Lord's Prayer, but that wasn't even his religion. Perhaps the salute to the flag. . . .

"Don't get all worked up," Sitwell said. "I'm not here after your soul or any old-fashioned crap like that."

"How can I believe you?" Edelstein asked.

"Figure it out for yourself," Sitwell told him. "Consider only the war aspect. Nothing but rebellions and revolutions for the past fifty years or so. For us, that means an unprecedented supply of condemned Americans, Viet Cong, Nigerians, Biafrans, Indonesians, South Africans, Russians, Indians, Pakistanis and Arabs. Israelis, too, I'm sorry to tell you. Also, we're pulling in more Chinese than usual, and just recently, we've begun to get plenty of action on the South American market. Speaking frankly, Mr. Edelstein, we're overloaded with souls. If another war starts this year, we'll have to declare an amnesty on venial sins."

Edelstein thought it over. "Then you're really not here to take me to hell?"

"Hell, no!" Sitwell said. "I told you, our waiting list is longer than for Peter Cooper Village; we hardly have any room left in limbo."

"Well. . . . Then why are you here?"

Sitwell crossed his legs and leaned forward earnestly. "Mr. Edelstein, you have to understand that hell is very much like U.S. Steel or I.T.&T. We're a big outfit and we're more or less a monopoly. But, like any really big corporation, we are imbued with the ideal of public service and we like to be well thought of."

"Makes sense," Edelstein said.

"But, unlike Ford, we can't very well establish a foundation and start giving out scholarships and work grants. People wouldn't understand. For the same reason, we can't start building model cities or fighting pollution. We can't even throw up a dam in Afghanistan without someone questioning our motives."

"I see where it could be a problem," Edelstein admitted.

"Yet we like to do something. So, from time to time, but especially now, with business so good, we like to distribute a small bonus to a random selection of potential customers."

"Customer? Me?"

"No one is calling you a sinner," Sitwell pointed out. "I said *potential*—which means everybody."

"Oh. . . . What kind of bonus?"

"Three wishes," Sitwell said briskly. "That's the traditional form."

"Let me see if I've got this straight," Edelstein said. "I can have any three wishes I want? With no penalty, no secret ifs and buts?"

"There is one but," Sitwell said.

"I knew it," Edelstein said.

"It's simple enough. Whatever you wish for, your worst enemy gets double."

Edelstein thought about that. "So if I asked for a million dollars—"

"Your worst enemy would get two million dollars."

"And if I asked for pneumonia?"

"Your worst enemy would get double pneumonia."

Edelstein pursed his lips and shook his head. "Look, not that I mean to tell you people how to run your business, but I hope you realize that you endanger customer goodwill with a clause like that."

"It's a risk, Mr. Edelstein, but absolutely necessary on a couple of counts," Sitwell said. "You see, the clause is a psychic feedback device that acts to maintain homeostasis."

"Sorry, I'm not following you," Edelstein answered.

"Let me put it this way. The clause acts to reduce the power of the three wishes and, thus, to keep things reasonably normal. A wish is an extremely strong instrument, you know."

"I can imagine," Edelstein said. "Is there a second reason?"

"You should have guessed it already," Sitwell said, baring exceptionally white teeth in an approximation of a smile. "Clauses like that are our trademark. That's how you know it's a genuine hellish product."

"I see, I see," Edelstein said. "Well, I'm going to need some time to think about this."

"The offer is good for thirty days," Sitwell said, standing up. "When you want to make a wish, simply state it—clearly and loudly. I'll tend to the rest."

Sitwell walked to the door. Edelstein said, "There's only one problem I think I should mention."

"What's that?" Sitwell asked.

"Well, it just so happens that I don't have a worst enemy. In fact, I don't have an enemy in the world."

Sitwell laughed hard, then wiped his eyes with a mauve handkerchief. "Edelstein," he said, "you're really too much! Not an enemy in the world! What about your cousin Seymour, who you wouldn't lend five hundred dollars to, to start a dry-cleaning business? Is he a friend all of a sudden?"

"I hadn't thought about Seymour," Edelstein answered.

"And what about Mrs. Abramowitz, who spits at the mention of your name, because you wouldn't marry her Marjorie? What about Tom Cassiday in apartment 1C of this building, who has a complete collection of Goebbels' speeches and dreams every night of killing all of the Jews in the world, beginning with you? . . . Hey, are you all right?"

Edelstein, sitting on the couch, had gone white and his hands were clasped tightly together again.

"I never realized," he said.

"No one realizes," Sitwell said. "Look, take it easy, six or seven enemies is nothing; I can assure you that you're well below average, hatewise."

"Who else?" Edelstein asked, breathing heavily.

"I'm not going to tell you," Sitwell said. "It would be needless aggravation."

"But I have to know who is my worst enemy! Is it Cassiday? Do you think I should buy a gun?"

Sitwell shook his head. "Cassiday is a harmless, half-witted lunatic. He'll never lift a finger, you have my word on that. Your worst enemy is a man named Edward Samuel Manowitz."

"You're sure of that?" Edelstein asked incredulously.

"Completely sure."

"But Manowitz happens to be my best friend."

"Also your worst enemy," Sitwell replied. "Sometimes it works like that. Goodbye, Mr. Edelstein, and good luck with your three wishes."

"Wait!" Edelstein cried. He wanted to ask a million questions; but he was embarrassed and he asked only, "How can it be that hell is so crowded?"

"Because only heaven is infinite," Sitwell told him.

"You know about heaven, too?"

"Of course. It's the parent corporation. But now I really must be getting along. I have an appointment in Poughkeepsie. Good luck, Mr. Edelstein."

Sitwell waved and turned and walked out through the locked solid door.

Edelstein sat perfectly still for five minutes. He thought about Eddie Manowitz. His worst enemy! That was laughable; hell had really gotten its wires crossed on that piece of information. He had known Manowitz for twenty years, saw him nearly every day, played chess and gin rummy with him. They went for walks together, saw movies together, at least one night a week they ate dinner together.

It was true, of course, that Manowitz could sometimes open up a big mouth and overstep the boundaries of good taste.

Sometimes Manowitz could be downright rude.

To be perfectly honest, Manowitz had, on more than one occasion, been insulting.

"But we're *friends*," Edelstein said to himself. "We *are* friends, aren't we?"

There was an easy way to test it, he realized. He could wish for $1,000,000. That would give Manowitz $2,000,000. But so what? Would he, a wealthy man, care that his best friend was wealthier?

Yes! He would care! He damned well would care! It would eat his life away if a wise guy like Manowitz got rich on Edelstein's wish.

"My God!" Edelstein thought. "An hour ago, I was a poor but contented man. Now I have three wishes and an enemy."

He found that he was twisting his hands together again. He shook his head. This was going to need some thought.

In the next week, Edelstein managed to get a leave of absence from his job and sat day and night with a pen and pad in his hand. At first, he couldn't get his mind off castles. Castles seemed to *go* with wishes. But, on second thought, it was not a simple matter. Taking an average dream castle with a ten-foot-thick stone wall, grounds and the rest, one had to consider the matter of upkeep. There was heating to worry about, the cost of several servants, because anything less would look ridiculous.

So it came at last to a matter of money.

I could keep up a pretty decent castle on $2000 a week, Edelstein thought, jotting figures down rapidly on his pad.

But that would mean that Manowitz would be maintaining two castles on $4000 a week!

By the second week, Edelstein had gotten past castles and was speculating feverishly on the endless possibilities and combinations of travel. Would it be too much to ask for a cruise around the world? Perhaps it would; he wasn't even sure he was up to it. Surely he could accept a summer in Europe? Even a two-week vacation at the Fontainebleau in Miami Beach to rest his nerves.

But Manowitz would get two vacations! If Edelstein stayed at the Fontainebleau, Manowitz would have a penthouse suite at the Key Largo Colony Club. Twice.

It was almost better to stay poor and to keep Manowitz deprived.

Almost, but not quite.

* * *

During the final week, Edelstein was getting angry and desperate, even cynical. He said to himself, I'm an idiot, how do I know that there's anything to this? So Sitwell could walk through doors; does that make him a magician? Maybe I've been worried about nothing.

He surprised himself by standing up abruptly and saying, in a loud, firm voice, "I want twenty thousand dollars and I want it right now."

He felt a gentle tug at his right buttock. He pulled out his wallet. Inside it, he found a certified check made out to him for $20,000.

He went down to his bank and cashed the check, trembling, certain that the police would grab him. The manager looked at the check and initialed it. The teller asked him what denominations he wanted it in. Edelstein told the teller to credit it to his account.

As he left the bank, Manowitz came rushing in, an expression of fear, joy and bewilderment on his face.

Edelstein hurried home before Manowitz could speak to him. He had a pain in his stomach for the rest of the day.

Idiot! He had asked for only a lousy $20,000. But Manowitz had gotten $40,000!

A man could die from the aggravation.

Edelstein spent his days alternating between apathy and rage. That pain in the stomach had come back, which meant that he was probably giving himself an ulcer.

It was all so damned unfair! Did he have to push himself into an early grave, worrying about Manowitz?

Yes!

For now he realized that Manowitz was really his enemy and that the thought of enriching his enemy was literally killing him.

He thought about that and then said to himself, Edelstein, listen to me; you can't go on like this, you must get some satisfaction!

But how?

He paced up and down his apartment. The pain was definitely an ulcer; what else could it be?

Then it came to him. Edelstein stopped pacing. His eyes rolled wildly and, seizing paper and pencil, he made some lightning calculations. When he finished, he was flushed, excited—happy for the first time since Sitwell's visit.

He stood up. He shouted, "I want six hundred pounds of chopped chicken liver and I want it at once!"

The caterers began to arrive within five minutes.

Edelstein ate several giant portions of chopped chicken liver, stored two pounds of it in his refrigerator and sold most of the rest to a caterer at half price, making over $700 on the deal. The janitor had to take away 75 pounds that had been overlooked. Edelstein had a good laugh at the thought of Manowitz standing in his apartment up to his neck in chopped chicken liver.

His enjoyment was short-lived. He learned that Manowitz had kept ten pounds for himself (the man always had had a gross appetite), presented five pounds to a drab little widow he was trying to make an impression on and sold the rest back to the caterer for one third off, earning over $2,000.

I am the world's prize imbecile, Edelstein thought. For a minute's stupid satisfaction, I gave up a wish worth conservatively $100,000,000. And what do I get out of it? Two pounds of chopped chicken liver, a few hundred dollars and the lifelong friendship of my janitor!

He knew he was killing himself from sheer brute aggravation.

He was down to one wish now.

And now it was *crucial* that he spend that final wish wisely. But he had to ask for something that he wanted desperately—something Manowitz would *not* like at all.

Four weeks had gone by. One day, Edelstein realized glumly that his time was just about up. He had racked his brain, only to confirm his worst suspicions: Manowitz liked everything that he liked. Manowitz liked castles, women, wealth, cars, vacations, wine, music, food. Whatever you named, Manowitz the copycat liked it.

Then he remembered: Manowitz, by some strange quirk of the taste buds, could not abide lox.

But Edelstein didn't like lox, either, not even Nova Scotia.

Edelstein prayed: Dear God, who is in charge of hell and heaven, I have had three wishes and used two miserably. Listen, God, I don't mean to be ungrateful, but I ask you, if a man happens to be granted three wishes, shouldn't he be able to do better for himself than I have done? Shouldn't he be able to have something good happen to him without filling the pockets of Manowitz, his worst enemy, who does nothing but collect double with no effort or pain?

The final hour arrived. Edelstein grew calm, in the manner of a man who had accepted his fate. He realized that his hatred of Manowitz was futile, unworthy of him. With a new and sweet serenity, he said to himself, I am now going to ask for what I, Edelstein, personally want. If Manowitz has to go along for the ride, it simply can't be helped.

Edelstein stood up very straight. He said, "This is my last wish. I've been a bachelor too long. What I want is a woman whom I can marry. She should be about five feet, four inches tall, weight about 115 pounds, shapely, of course, and with naturally blond hair. She should be intelligent, practical, in love with me, Jewish, of course, but sensual and fun-loving—"

The Edelstein mind suddenly moved into high gear!

"And *especially*," he added, "she should be—I don't know quite how to put this—she should be the *most*, the *maximum*, that I want and can handle, speaking now in a purely sexual sense. You understand what I mean, Sitwell? Delicacy forbids that I should spell it out more specifically than that, but if the matter must be explained to you . . ."

There was a light, somehow *sexual* tapping at the door. Edelstein went to answer it, chuckling to himself. Over twenty thousand dollars, two pounds of chopped chicken liver and now this! Manowitz, he thought, I have you now: Double the most a man wants is something I probably shouldn't have wished on my worst enemy, but I did.

I've never met Harvey Jacobs. I don't *know* anyone who's ever met Harvey Jacobs. Mr. Jacobs, wherever he may be, does sadly dwell not in the land of prolificacy. For this we must all sorrow. Because Mr. Jacobs is a wonderful writer. His story is one of that rare species that when read by other members of the same persuasion is often referred to in the terms, "Gee, I wish I'd written that." No higher praise can writers bestow on a colleague than emeraldine envy. There are some who might argue that this story is more in the nature of science-fiction than fantasy. It matters not, because it is not the subject of the tale that concerns us here so much as it is the telling of it. "The Egg of the Glak" is rambling and Rabelasian, writing chock-full of mental cholesterol, fattening and filling and altogether as hearty as thick gumbo on a cold winter's night. It is not, indeed, a perfect story.

In some ways it is better than that. We readers in search of something beyond the mundane all have Harvey Jacobs to thank for hatching . . .

The Egg of the Glak

HARVEY JACOBS

To the memory of Dr. David Hikhoff, Ph.D.
May he rest in peace. Unless there is better.

A SPRING NIGHT. The campus quiet. The air soft breath. I stood at my post, balanced on stiff legs. The fountain, a gift of '08, tinkled under moonlight. Then he came, trumpeting like a mammoth, stomping, tilting, staggering, nearly sitting, straightening, roaring from the back of his mouth, a troublemaker.

"My diphthongs. They monophthongized my diphthongs. The frogs. The frogs."

Echoes rattled the quadrangle.

I ran to grab him. It was like holding a bear. He nearly carried both of us to the ground.

"Poor kid. You poor kid," he said, waving short arms. "Another victim of the great vowel shift. The Northumbrian sellout."

He cried real tears, hundred proof, and blotted his jowels with a rep tie. Oh, this was no student drunk. This was faculty, an older man.

"Let us conjugate *stone* in a time-tarnished manner. Repeat after me. Repeat or I will beat you to a mosh. *Stan, stan, stanes, stane, stanas, stanas, stana, stanum.*"

"Easy, sir," I said.

"Up the Normans," he shrieked. "They loused my language. Mercian, Kentish, West Saxon and Northumbrian sellouts. French ticklers. Tell your children, and their children's children, unto the generations. Diphthongs have been monophthongized. Help."

"I'm trying to help," I said.

"Police."

"I am police."

"Victim," he said, whispering now. "Sad slob."

How many remember what happened a thousand years ago? If it were not for Hikhoff, I would know nothing of the vowel shift, though it altered my life and fiber. For it was this rotten shift that changed our English from growl to purr.

Look it up. Read how spit flew through the teeth of Angles, Saxons, and Jutes in the good old days. Get facts on how the French came, conquered, shoved our vowels to the left of the language, coated our tongues with velvet fur.

For Hikhoff, the shift of the vowels made history's center. *Before* was a time for the hairy man, the man who ate from the bone. *After* came silk pants, phallic apology.

"From Teutonic to moronic," Hikhoff told me. "Emasculation. Drought in the tonsil garden. No wonder so many strep throats in this town of clowns."

Sounds. Hikhoff's life was sounds. The sounds that make your insides wobble. Sounds of chalk screaming, of power saws cutting wood, of forks on glass, scrapings, buzzings, the garbage disposal chewing, jet wails, dentists drilling, pumps gurgling, drains sucking, tires screeching, ambulance sirens, giants breaking wind, booms, bangs, clangings, ripping and tearing, nails scratching silk.

Softer sounds too. Music and musical boxes, bells, chimes, bottle players on Ed Sullivan, all that, all noise, but mostly noises that make you squirm. His favorite: people sounds. Body sounds, sounds of talking, squishing, words, singing, cajoling, cursing, ordering, asking, telling, excusing, insisting. That is why the great vowel shift meant so much to him.

"What those concupiscent Gauls did to me," he said. "They shriveled half my vocal cords. They denied me my voice."

Hikhoff liked to rasp and sputter. His lungs were organ bellows for rolling R's and CH's that choked to the point of dribble. He listened to himself with much pleasure. He played himself back on a tape recorder, reading from *Beowulf* or Chaucer or the *Prose Edda,* which tells of the Wind Age and Wolf Age when the Sun swallows Earth.

"Aggchrrr, don't talk from your nostrils. Nose talkers are bastards. Diaphragm. Lungs. The deepest tunnels. Use those. Form your words slowly. Shape them in your head. Let them out of the mouth like starved animals, hot smoke rings. Speak each sentence like a string of beautiful sausages. Show me a mumbler and I show you a turd. SPEAK OUT. SAY YOUR PIECE. YOU WILL NOT ONLY MAKE OUT BETTER BUT DO A SERVICE FOR THE ENTIRE HUMAN RACE."

Hikhoff. We became friends. I don't kid myself. At first he had motives, improper designs. All right, think what you think.

"A despondent, disappointed soul." "A bitter person, a cynic." "A lump of rage." "A bad influence." I have heard all that said, and worse. To me, Hikhoff was redeemer, beloved comrade. I close my eyes and there he is in full detail.

Hikhoff.

Body like a cantaloupe. Little head, big jaw. A wet mouth gated by purple lips. Heavy in the breathing. Short arms and legs. A funny machine, an engine liberated, huffing, puffing. Like the power cabs that pull trailers and sometimes go running without their loads. The amputated heart. They move on diesel oil, Hikhoff on food. Fueling always. Always belching gas. I loved him. I miss him.

"Cousin North," he once said in a mellow, huff-puff voice when he finished panting and scratching after a chase around his coffee table. "I accept your repressive shyness. Lord, god king of fishes, you are too young to know what trouble a man's genitals can give." Then, pointing at the top of his paunch, "AND I HAVE NOT SET EYES ON MINE IN FORTY YEARS."

Ah. I knew what trouble, since I was then twenty, not ten. But Hikhoff was making jolly. We had become friends when I carried him home that spring night. Now, later in the turning year, he invited me to dinner. A feast. A groaning board. While we digested, he tried to make me.

He wooed me. First, by throwing peels to the garbage disposal which he called Mr. Universe. They were swallowed, chopped to puree. Next, he wined me with Liebfraumilch. Then he chased me, the engine with legs, roaring pre-vowel shift verses about clash and calm, stimulated by, and frustrated by, my agility.

"I am sorry, sir," I said in a moment of pause. "I do not go that way."

"Alps fall on your callow head," Hikhoff screamed so storm windows rattled. But we came to an agreement. Back to normal when his pressure dropped, we talked frankly.

"Sir, Dr. Hikhoff, even if I were interested in deviations, if that's how to put it, I could just not with you, sir. You are a cathedral to me, full of stained light, symbolic content. The funny thing is that I love you, but not that way."

"Distinctions," Hikhoff said a little sadly. "If you have a change of heart some day, let me be the first to know. Wire me collect. For the meantime, we will continue to be friends. You have a good head. A good head is a rare and precious stone."

We continued to be friends. I, who had taken a temporary job as campus cop to audit free courses, stayed on to become captain of the force. I kept taking courses, and would still be.

Once each week I went to see Hikhoff and we dined. He did not fail to steam a little after the mandarin oranges with Cointreau, but he never attacked me again. He was well controlled.

We talked of life and poetry. I was writing then. He read my works, sometimes translating them into Old English. He criticized. He had faith in me, encouraged me.

I wrote of life, courage, identity, time and death. These subjects delighted Hikhoff. He was a grand romantic, full of Eden, pro-Adam, pro-Eve, pro-Snake, pro-God, pro-Gabriel, anti-the whole scene. His self-image wore a cape and carried a sharp sword. He believed in battle bloody and reunion soft. To sum it up, Hikhoff had a kind of kill and kiss vision.

The important thing was to keep the winds stirred, the debris flying.

"Churn the emotions, but do not turn them to butter," he said. "Not with drugs or booze or mushrooms that give a pastel mirage. Use life, Harold. Be a life addict. Generate your own chemicals, your own trance and dance. Hikhoff The Absolute has spoken."

Our evenings were fine for me and I hope for him. I was like his son, he said so. He was better than my father, I say so. I could have gone on that way a hundred years. But the carpet was pulled, as it usually is.

One night when we were sealed by winter, I got a call. I was not sleeping when it came, but on the edge of a dream. The dream was forming in swirls of snow. The telephone bell was a noisy bug, and I fought to crush it. Finally I got up, naked and shivering in the cold room. I knew there was trouble.

The first thought was of fire. Or dormitory suicide. It was not the season for panty raids, and rape was obsolete up there.

"Hello, yes, hello?"

"Harold North? Is this he?"

"He. Yes."

"This is Miss Linker at the Shepherd of the Knowing Heart Clinic. On Kipman Place."

"Yes."

"A patient, Dr. Hikhoff, is asking for. . . ."

The night was frozen. Ice gave a glitter, a gloss like the shine on photographs. I remember smoke coming from the sewers. It fogged the street. It was pleasure to hear the car skip and start, to think of spark plugs flaming.

By the car clock it was three. I keep my clock ahead by forty-five minutes, This is a silliness, having to do with sudden endings. I have a stupid idea that if destruction should come, I would have nearly an hour to go back and make ready.

They let me go right to his room. He was critical, a mound in the white bed with side bars pulled up. A nurse leaned over him, and he moved his tongue in and out, side to side, as if she were a canapé. He was delirious, saving words in clusters, words melted together like candies left in the sun. They gave him oxygen. He took gallons, emptied tanks.

I cried.

The nurse shook her head "no." She reached a verdict. There was no hope except for the pinpoint dot of light that always flares. He had suffered a massive stroke, an eruption. Lava poured into his system and slowly filled him with black dust.

The nurse gave me two letters. They were marked FIRST and FI-NALLY. I put the envelopes in a pocket and stayed there by the bed. I heard a train whistle which meant five o'clock. The whistle was for Hikhoff. He opened his eyes, ripped off the oxygen mask, slammed the nurse away with his fists, sat up, saw me and said, "Touch. Touch."

I took his head in my hands and held him. The round head was a basketball with frightened eyes. "I will write thick books," he said. Then the eyes went away. Hikhoff was dead.

The white room filled with his escaping soul, cape, sword, all. The window was open a crack, and out the soul went into cold air.

Hikhoff's body was cremated after a nice funeral. In his will he requested that his remains be scattered in campus ashtrays. They were not. Instead, they were sent to his family in a silver box.

They should have been used as fertilizer for a tree, an oak, something with a heavy head of leaves and thirsty plunging roots, a trunk for carving on, branches to hold tons of snow.

After the funeral I went into seclusion.

I wished for time to think of my friend and to shape him into a memory. He was easy to remember, not one of those who fades with the first season change. I could not only see him but hear him and feel the vibration of his ghost. I had him down pat.

When I was sure of keeping the memory, I read the letter marked FIRST. It was tempting to read FINALLY first and FIRST finally because I suspected Hikhoff of throwing me a curve. But I thought no, not with death in his mind. Hikhoff would do the obvious because the corrupted obvious is purified in the face of death.

Dear Harold,

When you read this I will be dead, which seems ridiculous. Know that I look forward to meeting you again in some other world. At such time I will continue the education of your shade. If there is corporeal immortality, I will persist in your seduction.

Be that as it may. There is a favor I request of you. Naturally it is an idiotic request and very demanding. You have, of course, the option to refuse, maybe even the absolute need to refuse.

In this noble hamlet, Crap-Off-The-Hudson, there lives a lady who runs a store called Poodleville. This lady, a combination of estrogen, the profit motive, and a green thumb for animals, has come into the possession of a fantastic find.

It is the egg of a Glak.

No such egg has been seen for years. It is quite probably the last and final Glak.

The egg was brought to her by a relative who served with a radar unit in Labrador. I saw it in her shop, when I went there with the thought of buying a parrot. Thank God, the egg was sitting near a radiator.

Harold, I believe that this egg is fertile.

I have since paid this lady to heat her egg. The hatch span of the Glak is seven years and four days. I sought information from our late Dr. Nagle, of Anthropology. He set a tentative date for the Glak birth *in middle April of next year.*

Harold, the Glak is officially EXTINCT; so you can imagine the importance of all this! (That is the first exclamation point I have used since Kaiser Wilhelm died.)

I do not anticipate anything happening to me before then. I never felt worse, which is a sign of excellent health. But should I be struck down by a flying manhole cover or a falling bowling ball or the creeping crud, and should you have the agonizing duty of opening and reading this letter, please do the following:

1.) Go to the Upstate Bank and Trust. You will find an account in both our names containing five thousand dollars.

2.) Contact the lady at Poodleville, a Miss Moonish. Pay her $2,500 for custody of the egg, per our agreement.

3.) Take the egg, suitably wrapped, and nurse it until the ides of April. Then you must transport the egg to the one place where the Glak is known to have thrived; i.e., upper Labrador.

4.) WARNING BELLS. While Dr. Nagle, of Anthropology, is deceased, I believe he told his son, John, of my find. I also believe, from certain twitchings of Nagle's right ear, that the old man had dreams of glory, that he fantasied a lead article in *American Scholar* entitled "Nagle's Glak." The driving, vicious ambition of anthropologists is well known. What then of their sons? Beware of the young Nagle, Harold. I have a premonition.

5.) Due to this implicit Nagle threat, I urge you to act with dispatch.

Harold, ersatz son, I know this appears to be a strange request.

Think carefully what you will do about an old fool's last testament.
If you cannot help me, shove the whole thing.

Take my money and spend it on pleasure. Throw my letters
into the garbage disposal. Sip Polly Fusee while singing "Nearer My
God To Thee." Break champagne on your head and sail on. Do
what you must do.

Harold, writing this and still to write FINALLY (to be opened
only if by some miracle a Glak is born, and born healthy) has left me
quivering. I feel as if I have swallowed a pound of lard. Thoughts of
my own death fill me with sadness, nourishing sadness.

Goodbye, dear Harold. May the things that go clump in the
night bless you.

Yours in affection,
David Hikhoff

I put down FIRST, repocketed FINALLY, blew out the candles and
sat there in the dark.

Hikhoff died in February, a month hardly wide enough to hold him.

That February was cold as a cube. It straddled Crap-Off-The-Hudson like an abominable snowman with icy armpits and a pale, waiting
face. No wonder Hikhoff chose cremation, a last burst of heat. The only
reminder that the world sometimes welcomes life came from struck
matches, steam ghosts from pipes under our streets, the glow of cigarette
tips. It was as if nobody smiled.

My decision to honor Hikhoff's request took a frigid week. In that
week I purchased a tiny glazed Hikhoff from a student sculptor who
made it in memorium. The little Hikhoff was a good likeness, orange and
brown ceramic the size of a lemon. I carried it with me like a talisman.
Morbid, I know, but it helped me make up my mind.

So, for a few hours, I owned five thousand dollars. There *was* an
account at Upstate, and a vice-president there who expected my visit. If
there was an account, there was probably an egg. And, very likely, a
Nagle. Still, I was suspicious of Hikhoff, who had a great sense of humor,
a capacity for the belly laugh, and the belly for the laugh.

There was also Harold North's choice.

Hikhoff himself, Hikhoff the far-seeing, dangled the golden carrot. I
could use the money for play. I, who lived like a hermit, had no grandi-
ose ideals of frolic. But each bill could translate into time. I could go to
Majorca; I could write until my fingers were stubs without a care.

Glak. Damn the Glak. Some of the finest creatures are extinct, have gained stature through oblivion, have won museum fame. Great green things with tails the size of buildings. Hairy fellows with pounds of chin and strong eyes. Flying dragons that dripped acid. Elephants with tusks that could spear dentists. Why not the Glak? Extinction is nature's way. Did this world need a Glak? Who suffered by its disappearance? Is anyone, anywhere, Glak deprived? There was no real choice. I had to do Hikhoff's post-mortem bidding. We had consumed too much together; I had taken so much for myself of every portion. Could I point my rump at his last request?

Yes, naturally I visited the library. Even before my trip to the bank I looked up the Glak. There was not much to be learned. A tall crane-like bird with a raucous croak resembling *glak glak*. Famed for its mating dance which involved a rapid twisting of the dorsal plume in a counterclockwise direction. Habitat the sub-arctic regions of Eastern North America. Dwindling Glak population noted in the 1850's. Classified extinct 1902.

Glak, glak. Hikhoff once said he thought maybe the vowels stayed there and we shifted. Glak, glak to tweet, tweet. Could I care less?

In the bank I looked at the five and three zeroes while patting my ceramic Hikhoff, which was stuffed in the left-hand pocket of my mackinaw. When I noticed the Upstate vice-president watching my patting hand, I took the Hikhoff and placed it on the table.

"It's a Hikhoff," I said.

"A Hikhoff?"

"The man who left me this money."

"You carry it around?"

"On special occasions."

"That's a nice sentiment. It could start a trend."

I had the money placed in a checking account.

The next thing I did was to find Poodleville in the telephone book. I called and was answered by a voice which could have been a person or an unsold beast. The voice was thin and high, air deprived.

"I am Harold North. I believe a Mr. Hikhoff suggested. . . ."

"I've been expecting your call."

"Can we meet?"

"Assuredly. The sooner the better."

Poodleville caters to a genteel clientele, even for Crap-Off-The-Hudson. The shoppe (their spelling) is located in an ancient part of the city, a residential area, a nest of strong, well-built homes, each with some land, some trees, a gate. These are the houses of people with ancestors who settled that part of the land, and of those who came later and found luck smiling. The houses are impressive. Each is a fortress, guarding special privacy. Each has seen many bitter winters.

Through the large windows of these grandfather houses, I could see splendid toys like chandeliers of crystal, paintings in gold painted frames, pewter tankards, silver samovars, thick drapes, balconies with railings, curved staircases, wooden panels. Each house was an egg in itself with its own source of warmth, cracking out life now and then which ran for a car or a waiting cab.

Bits of movement, footprints not yet covered over by the new snow, smoke trails rising from chimneys animated the neighborhood in slow motion. Winter had the streets under siege. They had a cemetery quality. I could easily imagine Hikhoff waddling behind me, a spectre spy observing my movements, enjoying the tranquility of snowbound luxury.

Poodleville had been built out of the bottom floor of a brownstone. There was hardly a suggestion of commerce, much less of the usual cluster of dogs, birds, fishes, cats, hamsters, apes and even ants. No puppies solicited behind the glass. The window was tastefully decorated with a picture of a memorable poodle champion with the arrogant snout of one who is making his mark in stud. There was also a pink leash and a stone-covered collar.

When the door opened, a bell jingled. The animals sounded off. There was a jungle smell under airwick. But even inside, the mood was subdued.

Here was my first glimpse of Elsie Moonish. She stood near the tropical fish looking at an x-ray by bluish light from the tanks. A canary sang on a shelf above her head. Three or four dogs banged their heads against bars painted in candy stripes. A myna bird slept, and near it a single monkey swung around on its perch, squeaking like a mouse.

Miss Moonish never turned. She kept looking at the negative. I assumed it was a poodle spleen or parakeet kidney that held her.

She was not what I expected from the curdsy voice, but an attractive, plumpish, fortyish lady with her hair, black with grey rivers, in a Prince Valiant cut, a desirable lady, though her legs were on the heavy side.

I wondered if she heard me come in. She must have if she had eardrums, since the warning bell rang and the animals reacted. I waited, keeping my distance. I made no sound except for a wheeze when I breathed, since I was coming down with a cold.

One wheeze got to Miss Moonish. It was a tremendous snort that sounded like it came from Hitler's sinus. I think she was waiting for it as an excuse to register sudden surprise. Even the beasts shut up, not recognizing that mating call.

"My pancreas," she said.

"Pardon?"

"I was concerned about my pancreas. But it seems to be in fine fettle. Care for a look?"

"Not before dinner," I said.

"They say I am a hypochondriac, which is to say I fear death, which I do. I love x-rays. What a shame radioactivity is harmful."

"Always complications," I said. "I'm Harold North."

"Ah. Not the other."

"The other?"

"The Nagle person."

Her myna bird woke, blinked, and said *person person person.*

"You have spoken with the Nagle person?"

"Not too long ago. Your competitor. Poor Dr. Hikhoff. I read about his demise. What was it, a cerebral artery? Beautiful man. Such a tragedy."

I noticed why Elsie Moonish spoke thinly. It was because she hardly ever inhaled. She took air in gasps and kept it for long periods. By the end of a breath her voice nearly vanished. How hard it must have been for Hikhoff to deal with her.

"All this fuss over an egg," she said. "Remarkable."

"Speaking of the egg, may I see it?"

"At these prices I would scramble it for you, Mr. North."

First Miss Moonish locked the front door of the shop, though it did not exactly seem as if the store would be swamped with customers. Then she led me back past animal accessories, foods, a barbering table covered with curly hair, to a little door. Behind the door was a staircase leading up.

Over Poodleville, on the first floor of the brownstone, the Moonish apartment had elegance, but with the feeling of leftovers. The room had high ceilings, stained glass windows, columned archways and plush furniture, all a bit frazzled. There was a rancid dignity. I was directed to a blue tubby chair with the arms of a little club fighter. I sat and waited.

She went into another room, the bedroom as it turned out, and came back with a cardboard box. It was the kind of box you get from the grocer if you ask for a carton to pack for the painters. Written in red (by lipstick) on the top it said FRAGILE. KEEP WARM. I expected more, a glass case or ebony, but there it was, an old tomato carton.

Elsie Moonish took out a pound of old newspaper, then a ball wrapped in velvet. Carefully, but not too carefully, she unwrapped the egg and there it was. Just an egg, a few inches bigger than a chicken's, dotted with violet splotches.

To make it sound as if I were in on this from the start, I said, "Uh-huh. There it is all right."

She gave me the egg and I examined it. It was warm and seemed to be in good condition. As soon as possible, I put it back in the velvet nest.

"Dr. Hikhoff sat where you are sitting," she said, "for hour after hour. He called the egg his family. He was quite involved."

"He was."

" 'There are chills in this room, drafts,' he would say. A very protective man."

"Definitely."

"Mr. North, perhaps it's time to talk business, a crass thing in face of the occasion. But life goes on."

"Business," I said. "Per Dr. Hikhoff's instructions, I have in my pocket a checkbook, and I am prepared to give you a draft for $2,500."

"Mr. North," she said, "that's sweet," fitting the egg back into its box.

"Think nothing of it."

"Mr. North, let me say that I feel like the queen of bitches, forgive the expression. But the Nagle person called this morning with an offer of $4,500, all his money in the world, and for the very same egg."

"But you promised Dr. Hikhoff. . . ."

"Mr. North, what is money to me? Time? Health? It's only that hypochondria is dreadfully costly. Doctors charge outrageous fees; it's a disgrace. Let me show you something."

She took the egg back to her bedroom and returned with a large book, an album.

"Browse this. My x-rays. Five years of x-rays and some of friends and family. There. My uterus. Fifty dollars. My coccyx. Fifteen or twenty, as I recall. Heart, lungs, the lower tract. Do you have any idea of the cost?"

Looking at her insides was embarrassing for some reason, on so short an acquaintance. If medical magazines had centerfolds, she would have done well. Her organs were neat and well cared for. After finishing a flip of the pages, I actually felt as if I had known her for years.

"Miss Moonish," I said, "I will level with you, cards on the table, face up. Dr. Hikhoff left me with a certain amount of cash. Enough to pay you, live a little, and get the Glak back home."

"The Nagle person was so insistent," she said. "Willing to risk *all*."

"I'll match his offer," I said, "though it will mean hardship. *Plus* one dollar."

"Marvelous. I'm so relieved. It's thrilling when two grown men meet in conflict. Especially the moment, Mr. North, when their bids are equal, when they have exhausted material resources. Then they are thrown back on primitive reserves. Spiritual and physical qualities. The *plus*, as you said. The *plus-plus*."

"You lose me."

"Your money, Mr. North, or Mr. Nagle's money. They add up to the same thing. So the bids erase each other. Two men yearn for my egg. Each has offered gold. Now *other factors* creep into the picture. The *plus-plus*. You know, I hesitate to give up this situation. I lead a dull life, Mr. North."

"What you said about *other factors*. What other factors?"

"The city is frozen. Everything strains under tons of snow. I will tend my shop, care for my pets, cut poodle hair, and so forth. I will eat, sleep, wait out the dull months. Despite my x-rays, I feel hollow inside at this time of year. Like an empty jug. An empty jug yearning for, how shall I put it, honey. I want honey, Mr. North, the honey *plus-plus*. Memory."

"Are you suggesting, Miss Moonish, to a total stranger, anything in any way directly or indirectly involving the possibility of what the students call 'body contact'?"

"You have a quick mind, Mr. North. You have a frankness. Being around nature, I, too, am a to-the-point person."

"Miss Moonish, I work as a campus cop. I write poems. I read a lot. I hardly have a social life. I am not exactly a bulldozer. In fact I am a sexual camel. I can go for miles without. My sex is my work. I sublimate. And I don't know you well enough."

"I find you charming, Mr. North."

"And then there is the Nagle person. A terrible amoral fellow from what I gather. Suppose, for the sake of discussion, you find the Nagle's *plus-plus more* charming."

Elsie Moonish stood up and did a slow turn, stretching.

"It's my Glak. I'm in the catbird seat. The Glakbird seat. The Glak-egg seat. I'm absolutely enraptured by the entire chain of events."

"All right, five thousand, though now I am including my own small reserve, retirement money. Five thousand dollars."

"Are you offering an additional four hundred ninety-nine dollars *not* to make love to me?"

"Yes. Yes and no. It's nothing personal."

"It feels personal. Or is it just the price of your own dear insecurity. You don't want this little competition to be decided on the basis of your . . . ability?"

"It's not that."

"It is that."

"Maybe it is."

"Find courage."

"Something is chirping downstairs, Miss Moonish. Maybe a prowler. . . ."

"You are the prowler. Prowl."

Damn Hikhoff. What is my debt to you? First a vow. Now, if you take things seriously, my most precious possession. For a Glak?

"I like involvement," I said.

"Who doesn't? Who among us doesn't? But there is a lot to be said in months with R in them for love without possession. The most painful kind of human contact. Transients welcome. Exciting, infuriating. The ultimate act, but without the owning. It teaches a lesson, Mr. North. It renews the lesson of separation. It reminds one of the magic of flesh in winter. Fusion and non-fission. It builds immunities against the terrible desires of SPRING."

All that on one exhale, and I thought she would burst from decompression.

"I'm no philosopher," I said.

"Philosophy is in the tip of the tongue," she said, "the small of the back, behind the ears, where the legs meet the trunk, inside the thighs, behind the knees, on the mountain peaks, in the valley. The demilitarized zones."

"I fear my own rust," I said. "Lust. A Freudian slip. I'm not calm."

"Come," said Miss Moonish.

Naked, Elsie Moonish was very nice, though I had a tendency to see past her skin to the insides. We stayed together for hours fusing and non-fusing, loving without possessing, beating the winter odds and strengthening the blood against spring. Our music came from the animals downstairs, and her bed could have been grass. We were in the country. Elsie was wet and ready again and again. I was a fountain of youth to my amazement. It had been so long.

"How long, Harold?"

"Two years."

"Who?"

"A coed doing a paper on police brutality."

"I hate her."

Then too soon, she said, "Now. I have reached the point where I want you to stay. So go."

"Once more."

"No."

"Plus-plus."

"Go."

We took a shower together. She soaped me and said she liked my body. I told her, soaping her, that the feeling was mutual. She said, while I dressed, that I should telephone tomorrow.

I went out into the cold shaking like gelatin, blowing steam. I would have gone back, but she locked the shoppe behind me.

Back home I saw that I had been broken and entered, ransacked.

The room was upside down. The only thing taken was the letter FIRST. Luckily I had FINALLY with me. I called Elsie Moonish right away, but got only a buzz.

A Nagle who would rob is a desperate Nagle, I thought. How would he deal with the owner of the egg? I worried for Elsie. Then for myself. He might deal very well. I never had seen the Nagle. Maybe he was a football type, a walking penis.

I sat worrying about the Nagle's secondary sexual characteristics, and would have stayed in that trance of doubt, had it not been for my cop brain which saved me. Here I was, following the rules, waiting to hear if I won the egg, while an unleashed Nagle of no principle was running loose. What a passive idiot I was. By the time I bolted into the snow, Elsie Moonish could already be inside a camp trunk on her way by American Express.

I caught a cab to Poodleville, and none too soon.

As we pulled in front of the shoppe, I saw a man hurrying along down the street. He was carrying a large parcel, too small for a camp trunk but large enough. While I paid the driver, not before, it came to me that it was the Glak box.

That very moment a window flew open upstairs from Poodleville. I saw Elsie, wrapped in a wrap, lean out, look from side to side and shout, "Glak snatcher."

I flew after the fleeing Nagle, my shoes skimming on glossy pavement. The Nagle ran, holding the Glak box before him and would have gotten away but for fate. The old part of town is as hilly as Rome. From nowhere a fat child on a sled came swooshing down the street and caught the Nagle at his ankles. His legs opened like a scissor. The egg box soared through the air. The sledder went crashing; the Nagle collapsed in a lump.

I intercepted the box in midair. Then I fell, tail down, box up, on top of the skidding sled and went with it down the Poodleville hill. The sidewalk was frozen glass. The sled broke Olympic records. The world blurred. I caught a glimpse of Miss Moonish as I went by, then saw the branches of trees and grey sky. Down and down I went, and heard the twing twing of bullets around me.

The Nagle was firing and getting close. Fortunately, the sled jumped the sidewalk and hustled along in the gutter. There was no traffic, and clear sailing. I felt a hot flash. I was hit but not dead.

Down I went, about a thousand miles an hour, toward the railroad tracks. I heard whistle and clang up ahead. The traffic blinker turned red. The zebra-striped bar that stops cars came down. I headed right for the crossing, shot under the roadblock, hit the track, saw the front of the freight, a smoky Cyclops, locked my arms on the box, left the sled, turned upside down, and came down in a snowbank with the train between me and my enemy.

Forgetting pain, I grabbed my box and climbed into an empty car.

So this is it, I thought. My body will lie here and roam the United States, a mournful cargo. I bawled. There was so much work still undone. Here I was cut at the budding.

A brakeman found me in the Utica yards. I was in the General Hospital when I woke.

"Do you have medicare?"

"Ummm."

"You are here mostly for exposure and shock. But not entirely. To state it unemotionally and simply, Mr. North, you have been perfectly circumcised by a 22 calibre bullet. Are you sure this was not some kind of muffed suicide attempt?"

"Hikhoff," I raged aloud. "If the Nagle were a more accurate shot, I would have collected your ashes, reassembled you and kicked you in the ass. I have always been intact from cuticles to appendix, and now this. What trauma you have caused."

They tranquilized me.

Soon I learned that when they brought me to the hospital, they brought my egg too. It was in a hot closet near my bed. What damage the excitement might have done to the Glak I could not know.

Poor Glak, I said in a whisper. What if you are born slightly bent? Forget it. Let the world know you have endured hard knocks. All survivors should carry scars, if only in the eyes. Be of good cheer, Glak.

Hikhoff would have enjoyed the sounds of the hospital. Pain sounds, fearsome in the deep darkness. Baby sounds full of good rage and wanting. For those sounds, my companions in the night, the vowels have not shifted. And the sounds of the loudspeaker calling Dr. this and Dr. that, and Dr. Mortimer Post when they do a dissection, and the sounds of the trays and televisions, the visitors, the wheeling carts, all these sounds would interest Hikhoff for there is the honesty of a white wall about them. Hikhoff, but not me.

Joyfully, I left the hospital an ounce or two lighter, none the worse. I carried my box with new enthusiasm. The Nagle's bullets motivated me. I had a stake in this adventure now, a small but sincere investment.

There were six weeks to endure (it was March) before the egg would pop, assuming it would pop at all, and Labrador to reach on a limited budget. And a Nagle to watch for, a fanatic Nagle who would surely pursue us. Clearly, the first order of business was to find a hideout, an obscure off-the-track place where a man and his egg would be left alone.

I searched the classifieds. Two ads caught my eye. One of them was addressed directly to it:

H.N. KNOW YOU ARE IN UTICA. ALL FORGIVEN. CAN WE TALK? AGREEMENT CAN BE REACHED PROJECT G. RIDICULOUS TO CONTINUE HOSTILE. DANGEROUS TO WAIT.

Dangerous to wait. So the Nagle had traced the destination of the train. Smart man, and a compromiser. If there had been no shooting, no tampering with my equipment, however slight, I would have answered his P.O. box. And why not? He was his father's son, acting on correct impulses. Hikhoff was not even a blood relation.

But, with soreness when I walked, I was in no mood to negotiate.

The second ad was for a room in a nice, clean, well-heated house with a good view, kitchen privileges, housekeeping, good family on a tree-lined street near transportation and churches of all denominations. The price was right. I called the number and, yes, the room was vacant.

The house was welcoming. There was a small garden where a snowman stood and even an evergreen. I rang the doorbell, self-conscious over my package, which I held in my arms since the steps looked cold. I tried to take the attitude that this was a pregnancy and that I was blooming and entitled.

The box made no difference to Mrs. Fonkle who owned the property. Probably there was a buyers' market for rooms up there.

I told her I was a scientist, but not the kind who makes bombs. I was dependable, safe, well-mannered, a person who asked only tidbits from existence, not noisy, good-natured, involved in breeding a new kind of chicken big enough to feed multitudes. Mrs. Fonkle liked, but worried over, the idea of big chickens.

"How big?" she said, and I held out my hands three feet apart.

"Some chicken," she said, laughing herself into a red face.

The first night she invited me to dinner.

The Fonkles were a mixed grill. Mrs. Fonkle had been married once to a pencil of a man, a man who lacked pigmentation. He was dead now but left a daughter behind, a girl in her mid-twenties who was pretty, all angles, intense and full of gestures.

Mrs. Fonkle's present husband, a plumber, was a side of beef, medium well. Her daughter by him was a dark, soft affair, just nineteen, filled with inner springs that pushed out.

At dinner, there were comments about science and the mushroom cloud and how the world was better before. The daughter of Husband One, Myrna by name, said, "People are beginning to realize that war accomplishes nothing."

"So how come everybody is fighting," Cynthia said.

"Two things can stop wars," I said. "First is discovering life from another part of the sky with a big appetite for all kinds of people, regardless. Second is the hope implicit in the fact that nations good at sex are bad at marching."

"Tell me, are you a married man?" Mrs. Fonkle said, handing me seconds.

"No. I have no family. I am married to my work."

"She's getting personal," Mr. Fonkle said.

"In a house where doors are left open," Mrs. Fonkle said, "I'm entitled to a few questions."

Mrs. Fonkle's house was truly a house where doors are left open.

Even me, a paranoid now, watching for shadows of the Nagle, took to leaving my bolt unclicked.

The first week went well. You could say an intimacy grew between me and the family. I had never lived so close to people.

I spent my days writing. At night I checked the egg and took walks. My Hikhoff sat on a dresser, on top of a doily, and he too seemed serene. But problems arose.

One evening, an ordinary evening, I came in from my dinner. As always, I examined the egg. It was trembling, shivering, moving. I thought *earthquake, catastrophe.* But nothing was shaking the egg. It was the egg itself moving around, rolling a little.

I put the box closer to the radiator, and the jumping slowed.

Then I did what I knew from the beginning I would have to do.

I sat on the egg.

I put it on a pillow, put the pillow on a chair, stripped to my underwear and gently sat on the egg, holding most of my weight with my arms.

The jumping, squiggling, shivering stopped completely. So there *was* a Glak in there. And it was chilly, protesting. It wanted its due, namely body heat, and who could blame it?

Look at me now, I said to my Hikhoff, a full-grown man warming eggs with his rear. Look what you did to me. Is it for this that you fed me and pissed and moaned about our feminized century? Finally you have put me into hatching position. Hikhoff, barrage balloon, how you must be laughing.

Falling in with the folksy quality of Mrs. Fonkle's, I had left my door half open. In thin PJ's, holding a turkish towel, her hair covered with a cloth to hide curlers, her feet bare, wearing no makeup on her dear bony face, Myrna came to check my health.

"Are you OK, Harold?"

"Fine," I said. "A little over-exposed. I'm sorry. I should have closed my door."

"Oh," Myrna said. She threw me her towel. I covered my kneecaps. "I could swear you made a sound, a kind of clucking."

"Chicken thoughts," I said. "I was thinking out loud."

Her entrance and my surprise must have dropped my pressure and temperature because the egg began again, jumping under me. It had a lot of energy. I had to hold tight to keep myself in the chair.

"You're catching cold," Myrna said, coming into the room.

"No, I'm fine."

The egg gave a bump. I flew up a little and could have squooshed it then and there except for a last-second flip.

"Give me your pulse," Myrna said. I gave her.

"A hundred fifteen beats a minute?"

"Normal for me. Normal."

"Something is bothering you, Harold." Myrna sat down on my bed. "Talk to me. I'm a good listener."

"Nothing," I said. "Besides, Myrna, if your mother walks by and sees you sitting there in your sleepies, what will she think? What?"

Myrna got up with her serious face and closed the door. She came back to the bed and stretched herself, her chin propped on elbows. She made herself at home.

"You are suffering," Myrna said. "Don't deny it."

"Better you should go," I said.

Myrna was very attractive in those PJ's. They were sad cotton PJ's with no class, covered with blue flowers, a thing little girls wear. When she moved they tightened around her breasts, small volcanos. They held her bottom nicely, too. For a slender lady she was well built. That long, lazy body was a winding road.

"Is it your stomach, Harold?" she said.

"No. Yours."

"Don't be a glib. Come sit here and talk to me."

"I can't move."

"Why?"

"Don't be alarmed. Don't shout. Myrna, I'm sitting on an egg. You might as well know. I'm sitting on a large egg."

"Harold?"

Like a fool I told her everything. Everything. Everything. The dam broke. I was amazed by my own need to confide. Always a loner, I dropped my guard with a thud. That is the danger of human contact. It breeds humanity.

When I finished the tale of the Glak, Myrna cried.

"I can't speak," she said. "In some ways, this is the most wonderful story I have heard since *Rapunzel*. Harold, dear Harold, my impulse is to cherish you, to hold you and give you back heat. I know it's wrong. I know that. I know your work is its own reward, and the thing you are doing for Dr. Hikhoff is beautiful and contained in itself. But I have the impulse to take you to me, to be naked with you, to recharge you with all the sun I stored up on Lake Winnapokie last summer. Bring the egg here. Let me give."

Am I made of aluminum? Myrna, Glak and Harold fell together and again the winter was kept outside.

Even the egg was radiant. If you have never seen a contented, happy, and secure egg, let me tell you it is a fine experience. Dear Myrna, half rib-cage, half air, generated fire like a coil. Her nerves practically left her skin. She gave like a sparkler.

Before going to her own room, Myrna promised to come regularly, on a schedule, and to help me with my egg and my own thawing. I felt marvelous. I had a friend, a lover, a bed partner interested only in nourishing.

The next morning, I woke rested, nicely sore as after a ball game, restored and ready for anything. I sat on the side of the bed and the egg came toward me. First, it thumped, then jiggled, did a half turn, then rolled right up to my thigh.

"Look," I said, "enough is enough. Hear me, Glak, I will do my part and take good care, but this rolling stuff has got to stop. I need time for my own pursuits."

I made a nest for the egg, using the pillow again, and put it under the blanket. Then I went to wash my face, shave, and brush my teeth.

Bright as a penny, tingling with menthol, on the way back to my room, I heard what sounded like the Great Sneeze.

It was Cynthia who stood, blowing into a handkerchief, in my room, at my bed, holding my blanket, *looking at my egg*. She was wearing a quilted housecoat over her nightgown, her long hair tumbled down, her dark face darker than usual.

"Harold," she said, "we have something to talk about."

"What are you doing home?" I said.

"I have a cold."

"Where's your mother? It's drafty in here."

"Harold, why is there an egg in your bed?"

"I didn't lay it, if that's what you think."

"I don't know what to think."

"Look, Cyn, your father is a plumber, he's got a plunger. I'm in science. I have an egg. There's a perfectly logical explanation."

Hearing my voice the egg began to turn circles. That's one smart, responsive Glak, I thought, but the incident shook Cynthia, she so young, and she cried like her sister, only wetter.

"Oh, don't weep," I said. "Please."

"A man shouldn't sleep with an egg."

"*There's* a quote from the Old Testament. Who are you to judge me?"

"It's perverse. When ma hears about what's going on in this house. . . ."

"Cyn, why, oh why should ma or pa or any lady be involved. Cyn, older people get nervous about such things. They think right away suppose it hatches and is some kind of nutty meat-eater. Cyn, please, this whole episode demands silence. If you've ever kept your cool, keep it now."

"It's wrong for a man to sleep with a big egg."

Standing there, she manufactured commandments. It was informative to watch her, though. She breathed in heaves. Clouds practically formed over her head. Her toes nearly smoked. So totally involved, so passionate, she was different by more than chromosomes from Myrna. Plumber blood shot through her pipes. Her valves hissed. You could see needles rise on gauges and warning lights flash.

I had to tell her something. You owe it to your audience. Myrna had the whole truth. It seemed somehow disloyal to tell Cynthia the same story.

"Cyn, this egg is my responsibility. A lot of lives depend on what happens in this room. Because this egg is no ordinary egg. It is an egg found in the wreckage of a strange and unidentified crashed aircraft, a UFO."

"Harold, stop."

"Cyn, on my heart. Probably the whole thing is nothing, a hoax. Maybe there really is a big chicken in there. I may even be a control."

"Control?"

"There are 42 agents like myself in 42 rooms with 42 eggs like this. None of us knows if he has the space-egg. To throw off the competition, Cyn. Standard procedure. The point is, this egg may just be the one. The thing."

"The thing?"

"Cyn, you have got to keep this to yourself."

"A thing in our house?"

"A nice thing. A vegetarian. We know that much by tests. Lettuce, carrots, parsley, like that. By computer calculations, a furry, sweet kind of beast like a rabbit. A bunny. Nice."

"Beast? Why did you use the word beast?"

"Well, a furry bunny is a *beast*, Cyn. It's still a *beast.*"

"I don't know what to say."

"Nothing. Go about your business."

"How come our house?"

"IBM selected. Strictly impersonal from a juggle of IBM cards with punched classified ads. Out of the way. Small city. Quiet. Unlikely discovery. IBM didn't figure on you, Cyn. I mean, it's obvious if this got out there could be panic."

"Harold, I do not believe you. And to me what matters is what I know, which is that you personally are sleeping with a lousy egg while youth flies."

"Where does youth come in? And what do you know about youth? You're too young to know beans about youth."

"Look at me. Do you see the bags under each eye? Do you know how sleepless I have been for a month because of you in this house?"

"Me?"

"Yes. And now you tell me about lettuce-eaters from the movies. I don't want to know anything, Harold. I hate you and I hate your thing."

The egg rolled again. Cynthia could not contain herself. She grabbed a dust pan and began to swing. I got my hand under the flat part just in time. She would have splattered my Glak all over the neighborhood.

We struggled and it was not all violence. We tangled as people do, and it came to pass that Cyn ended up with her back to me, my arms around her front, and she threw back her head so I drowned in perfumed black hair. She was a buttery girl, a pillow, who gave where squeezed but popped right back to shape. Now she stopped the battle and cried again. I turned her and comforted her. What could I do? Send her out yelling?

As we fell together onto the sturdy bed (it was maple), Cynthia tried to crunch the egg with a leg this time. I thwarted her, then put the Glak on the floor where it jumped like a madman.

Love was made that morning.

"Harold," she said near noon, at which time her mother was expected from the supermarket, "I don't care who or what you are. All I care about is that I come first and not some turkey from Mars."

"OK, Cyn, my honor. And the egg business is between us."

"Don't say between us. I'll break the bastard if you ever so much as pat it in my presence."

"I didn't mean between us, I meant between-us. Hush-a-bye. Our business."

"Hush-a-bye yourself. Make me sleepy again."

Within an hour I had swollen glands. They were heaven's gift. I would have preferred measles or mumps, but the glands would do. I needed time and Cynthia's cold, a splendid virus that made me sweat, chill and shake, gave me time.

With Myrna offering fire, with Cynthia openly hostile, competing for egg-time, and me being only one human being, I needed time, time, time.

I refused to recover. But my illness did not protect me. The sisters were stirred by helplessness. The nights were much. First Myrna would come and soon fall asleep. I pulled blankets over her. Cynthia liked the bed's far side. She blew fire in my ear. One Fonkle slept; another awoke until the weest hours. I was destroyed.

I had nothing left for the Glak. I was spent, an icicle, so cold and uncaring I could have sunk the *Titanic*. The Glak lept in deprivation and threw covers on the floor.

"Harold," Mrs. Fonkle said to me one gray morning soon after, "something is going on."

"What?" I said weakly, coughing a lot.

"A woman with daughters is a woman with all eyes. And such daughters. I think they like you, Harold."

"Fine ladies," I said. "Cute as buttons." I put a thermometer in my mouth, which was not even oral, to prevent further speech.

"And my intuition tells me, Harold, you like them. But *them* is not Myrna and *them* is not Cynthia. You follow my mind? Harold, your blanket is shaking. Are you all right?"

"Mmmm." I tried to hold down the egg with my hand.

"What is life but decisions," Mrs. Fonkle said. "A time for fun and games, a time for decisions."

I was expecting this inevitable confrontation and prepared. With the thermometer still plugged in, I dived, without warning, under the pillow. I howled. There, in readiness, was a can of Foamy. I squirted the Foamy around my whole head, mouth, face, eyes, and hair. To cancel the whoosh of the lather, I yelled like an owl. Then up I came like a sub, from the depths of the Sea of Despair. Mrs. Fonkle was torpedoed.

My wet white face, waving arms, kicking feet, jumping quilt, had a fine effect. A cargo ship by nature, hit on her water line, Mrs. Fonkle slid slowly under waves without time for an SOS.

After carrying her to her room and leaving her on her bed with a wet rag on her forehead, I went back to my own room. My thermometer was on the floor, its arrow touching the silver line at normal. I quick-lit a Pall Mall and heated the mercury drop. At 104.6 I was happy and left it in a prominent place, wiped myself clean, got back in the bed and awaited commotion.

Should all the air raid sirens and dystrophy ads and cancer warnings we go through be wasted, a total loss? How much has society spent to keep you alert, Harold North, pumping adrenaline, listening for vampires? Use your training. Deal with challenge. I lay there waiting for my next idea.

Coma. A beautiful word, and my answer. Coma.

When I heard Mrs. Fonkle rise finally, I put myself into a coma. In a self-created and lovely blue funk I lay there, smiling like Mona Lisa, stroking my egg.

Naturally enough, she called the doctor.

"And the blanket was jumping during all this?"

"Like a handball. . . ."

I heard them in the hall. Mrs. Fonkle came with him to my room. I stayed in my coma while the doctor stuck pins, took blood, gave needles, checked pressure.

Later, in a miserable mood, Mrs. Fonkle stormed back alone, pulled at my blanket while I pulled back, and she said I was a cheat, a malingerer, a fraud, a leecher.

"Dr. Zipper says nothing is wrong with you. Not even athlete's foot."

I never would have given Zipper the credit. He actually found me out.

"So, Mr. North, name the game."

"Darling," I said, "darling, darling and darling." I planted a kiss on Mrs. Fonkle's thyroid. "I hope you are on the pill," I said. "I hope at least you took precautions." I looked lovingly at her while her eyes rolled, a slot machine making jackpots.

"You never did," she said.

"I didn't. *We* did."

"It never happened."

"Old speedy," I said. "When again? Tell me. Come on. Tell."

"It never happened."

"They're not kidding when they say like mama used to make," I said.

"Pig," she said. "An unconscious lady."

How I hated myself. If I could, I would lay down on spikes, I thought. Well, maybe something in her will be flattered. Maybe she will feel good that a young man was inspired to do her some mayhem. Let her think of me as a crumb, a nibble, a K ration on the road to social security.

It was Myrna who brought supper on a tray.

"Harold," she said. "I have thought you over. In your present weakened condition this egg business is too much for you. Psychologically, I mean. You have got to think of keeping for yourself, not of giving. Darling, we are all so worried. Even mama is in a state of distraction. She served daddy three portions of liver tonight. You have got to get well. Let me take the egg. I will keep it cozy while you recuperate. Let me take it to my room, at least for the nights. Harold, please say yes."

Why not? If Myrna, who had embers to waste, said she would care for the Glak, she would care for it. This was a trustworthy lady. And my blanket would no longer bounce.

"I agree," I said. "Thank you, dear one. Thank you."

Myrna beamed. Then and there she took the box, put back the angry egg, and carried it to her bedroom. Transporting the bundle she hummed a lullabye.

"Now," she said, removing my empty tray, "use *all* your energies to heal. Save everything like a miser until you are better."

"I will save," I said, nearly crying from good feeling.

To do her duty, Myrna retired early, even eagerly. I think for the first time in her life she locked her door. When the house settled down, Myrna asleep, the Fonkles watching television, Cynthia came with dessert.

"Hello, Jello," she said.

"Hello jello to you, angel."

"Harold, I have had some second thoughts."

"At this late date?"

"Harold, that stinking egg has got to go. It's draining your strength. Government or not, I am going to bust it to pieces. I never liked it, but I lived with it. But when the time comes, that the egg hurts you and keeps you from total recovery, then it's time for a change. I want your permission to smash that egg because permission or not here I come."

"Let me think on it."

"Think fast. You know me. The first minute I catch you with your eyes closed—splat."

"I'll think fast. I must weigh personal gain against my sworn. . . ."

"I have stated my intention, Harold."

I thought fast. Not bad. Why not let Cynthia eliminate the egg, at least, *some* egg. It would remove her desperation, apprehension and combativeness. Not to mention her curiosity if she ever discovered that the Glak was already gone.

After doing with my jello what I have always done, that is, slicing around the cup and putting the saucer over it and turning the whole thing upside down so that the jello comes out like a ruby hill, Cynthia removed the dishes.

"I am going to the movies," she said. "Have your mind made up, Harold, by the time I get back. And by the way, you eat jello in the most disgusting sensual manner. I'm dying to be with you."

I kissed her nose.

What a marvelous family. Even Mr. Fonkle was roaring with laughter downstairs, so happy with the "Beverly Hillbillies."

The TV which occupied Mr. and Mrs. Fonkle with slices of flickering life was in the living room. The living room was removed by a dining room from the kitchen.

On the balls of my feet, I went down and slipped into the control center of the house. There I opened the fridge and removed three eggs. Why three? Cynthia knew the egg of the Glak was big. In fact, by then it had swelled to the size of a small football. Big eggs make big splashes.

I tiptoed upstairs walking in my own footprints. In the room I took scotch tape strips from the dresser drawers where they held paper to the wood. With what glue was left I pasted two eggs together. Praise be, there was only enough tape for a pair. I cut my pinky with a blade and speckled the pasted eggs with A-positive. There was enough left, before clotting, to dot the third too.

I waited with my egg bomb under the blanket in the Glak's former place. The third egg went under my pillow on an impulse.

The arrival of the specialist surprised me. Mr. Fonkle showed him in.

"Harold," Mr. Fonkle said, "this is Doctor Bim. Doctor Zipper called him in for consultation. It seems you are a puzzling case, a phenomenon to medicine."

Dr. Bim nodded. I replied in kind. If Zipper was sure I was faking, why this? Playing safe against malpractice, I thought, and I looked to my Hikhoff for confirmation.

"Feel well, Harold," Mr. Fonkle said. "We're in the middle of a hot drama. Excuse me."

Dr. Bim went to wash his hands, then came back and closed the door. After drying, he put on white cotton gloves.

"I never saw a doctor do that," I said.

"We all have our ways," he said. "Now to work."

Dr. Bim pounded me with hands like hammers.

"Now, close your eyes and open your mouth," he said.

I closed hard and opened wide.

"When I tell you, Harold, then look. Not before. Depress the tongue. Hooey, what a coat."

"Aghh."

"Keep the eyes closed."

"Broop."

"Now bite hard."

My mouth shut on the barrel of a gun. My eyes popped open.

"No noise," he said, and kept the gun close.

"Nagle, I presume. How did you track my spoor?"

"By checking room-for-rents in the papers on the days after you left us, Harold. By asking around. From the ZIP code on a certain letter to a certain lady who sells poodles."

"You are nobody's fool. Nobody's."

"Thank you," the Nagle said, appreciating my large heart. "It's a shame we couldn't come to a more civilized agreement. I hope, Harold, that you comprehend my motivation. Take my father, a man who spent his whole life contributing bits and pieces. Imagine, fifty years of droppings, footnotes in *American Scholar*, a few *ibid's* and some *op cit's*. Nothing to make headlines, never once. Then one day in comes your fat friend Hikhoff carrying a genuine, fertile Glak egg. 'Tell me, Dr. Nagle,' he growls in that meretricious voice of his, 'what do I have here?' Harold, at that moment, in the fading evening of my father's life, the sun rose. On the brink of shadow, my father saw blinding rays. Understand?"

"Yes. It's not hard to understand."

"Do you have any concept of what a fertile Glak egg means to an aged anthropologist?"

"A small grasp."

"Immortality. For the first time, my father begged. For what? For halfies. No more. Not fifty-one percent, just fifty. The Hikhoff-Nagle Discovery is how he put it. Hikhoff laughed at him."

"The egg was full of meaning for Dr. Hikhoff," I said.

"I swore at the funeral, Harold, that my father's memory would be based on more than just mummy swatches from the graves of second-string Egyptians. Now I fulfill my vow."

"Nagle," I said, "are you in this for your father or for your own need to up the ante on your ancestors?"

"How would you like a loose scalp?"

"Sorry. But I am vow fulfilling, too. You read the letter marked FIRST."

"And tonight I will read FINALLY."

"Impossible," I said, "that letter was lost. When I woke up in the hospital after you. . . ."

The Nagle scratched his ear. "It could be," he said. "Does it matter? What can FINALLY be except more of Hikhoff's Old English ravings. Virility of the vocal chords, which was the only place he had it."

"Have some taste," I said. "The man is among the dead."

"Let FINALLY blow along the Utica-Mohawk tracks. The egg is what matters."

"We could go partners," I said.

"Ha. You are a gutsy one, Harold. Too late for partners. Now give me the Nagle Discovery. Any hesitation, reluctance or even a bad breath and you join Hikhoff for choir practice."

He was a nice fellow, the Nagle, with a face like Don Ameche, not the killer type, but you never know.

"The egg is here under my pillow," I said.

My luck held. The Nagle had never seen the egg before. He lit up when I showed him that pink-splotched pullet, balancing it in his palm.

"Slow and easy," I said, with wild eyes.

"It's been a pleasure," he said, tucking the egg in a towel and putting it into his medical bag. "Maybe when this is over and done with, you and I can sit and play chess."

"I would like nothing. . . ."

Pong. I was hit so hard on the head I flew half off the bed. I saw ferris wheels turning at different speeds. I tumbled too, spinning like a bobbin. Then later, there was another crash. A gooshy sound, a wetness. I woke.

"Bye, bye. Poor thing," Cynthia was saying, lifting my blanket, observing the destruction.

"What, what, what?"

"Harold, it had to be this way. Even that specialist said all you needed was complete rest. Better the egg should never see light, even in the free world, than you should die in your prime."

Cynthia never noticed the Scotch tape in the goo. She was so self-satisfied.

The next days passed smoothly.

Myrna had my Glak. Cynthia had her pleasure unshared. The Nagle was accounted for, squatting on his chicken. Mrs. Fonkle avoided me like doom. Mr. Fonkle, served like Farouk by his wife, brought cards to my room and we played.

Out of respect for her promise and a sense of my need for quiet, Myrna came gently only to report on the Glak. It was hopping all the time now, making tiny sounds. She described the sounds as like chalk on the blackboard, and I knew how happy Hikhoff would be if he could hear, as maybe he could.

While Myrna warmed Glak, Cynthia warmed Harold. Her vision of recovery was not based on abstention.

My only discomfort came from Mrs. Fonkle, and it was mild. Out of suspicion, she fed her daughters garlic and Ox Tails and other odiferous, glutenous foods that made their lips stick or filled them with protective cramps. I kept Tums and Clorets at bedside.

March went like the best kind of lamb. The windows unfroze. A bird sang on the telephone line. I had to move again and make plans again.

How did Chaucer say it? APPPRRRILLE WITHE HER SHOWERRRS SOUGHT THE DRAUGHT UFF MARS HATH PIERCED TO THE RUCHT. Like that. Up I came like a crocus.

Now it came time for partings and farewells. Cynthia was easy to leave, so easy it hurt. When the month turned, she met a podiatrist of good family. Her prospects improved. When we had our confrontation, she brought knitting along. In the tense air she knitted like a factory. A sweater for him.

"I am called back to D.C.," I said. "And will be punished."

"Punished, heh?"

"Forget it. Nothing painful. Chastised is more the word."

The thought of my punishment made it easier for Cynthia to say goodbye. Really, she had never been the same since the breaking of the egg. I think she thought less of me for not breaking it myself. Who can fathom a woman's heart? While we talked, she compared me to her podiatrist, and found him better. The mystique of new weather.

"No reason to prolong this suffering," I said. "I will always remember you and what we had together and how you sustained me."

Cynthia dropped a stitch, but caught it. Her reflexes had gained from our acquaintanceship.

*   *   *

It was harder to leave lanky Myrna.

"I know you must go," she said, "I know and I won't make scenes. Do you plan to return?"

"My life is a question mark," I said honestly. "What can I say?"

"It won't be the same without you two."

"Or for me. Ever."

"Send an announcement if it hatches. Nothing too fancy. A simple card."

Mrs. Fonkle, who had taken to charitable activities, said a swift goodbye. She was full of dignity and adorable poise. Such an ego.

The air was balmy on the day I left the Fonkle home. I had a new suitcase, the pudgy executive type, and in it my Glak had room enough. The egg was practically a bowling ball now, straining to pop.

The Fonkles stood in a family group when I entered the cab. I waved and wished them well. I was full of emotion, with watering eyes. They did so well by me and mine.

We live in a time of shortening distances, except between people. How easy it is to reach the most remote corners of the imagination. A person like myself can go from Utica, New York, to Labrador for $120.35 by bus and by plane. The facts made me swoon. Utica to Labrador. We are only hours from the place where the world ends.

To reach Labrador you go first to a travel agent. You tell him you wish to visit Labrador. He does not flinch.

"Where," he says, "Goose Bay?"

"No," you say, having studied maps and folders. "Maybe the Mealy Mountains."

"We have a special on the Mealys," he says.

"Or Lake Melville," you go on, "Fish Cove Point, White Bear, Misery Point, Mary's Harbor, Chidley on Ungave Bay, Petissikapan Lake, Nipishish, Tunungayluk or perhaps Gready. I haven't made up my mind."

"Go to Goose Bay," the agent says. "From there you can go any place."

"Can I jump off to Kangalakksiorvik Fiord?"

"In the Torngat region?" he says. "Naturally."

*   *   *

By intuition I had already chosen Kangalakksiorvik Fiord as the place where my Glak would be born. Not that Canadian citizenship could not be gotten closer, but Kangalakksiorvik felt right.

"The scenic route," the agent said, stamping tickets. "By Greyhound from Utica to Syracuse leaves 10:50 AM, arrives Syracuse 12:05 PM. Leaves Syracuse 2:30 PM, arrives Montreal 10:20 PM. You have a bite, see a picture. At 4:00 AM, Air Canada flies out, and at 7:20 AM you are in Goose Bay for a total cost, including economy air fare, of $120.35 plus a little tax."

"Then?"

"Then in Goose Bay ask around, hire a charter, and zoom you are in Kangalakksiorvik. The Torngats are lovely this time of year."

From the agent's convenient uncle I bought $10,000 in travel insurance. My policies were divided between Myrna and Cynthia, deserving souls.

At long last, with my Hikhoff snug in a pocket and my Glak bag in my hand, I headed for the terminal. On the downhill slope of responsibility, time is sweet.

For me a bus ride is only slightly removed from sexual intercourse. Since a child, I am prone to vibrations, put to sleep, handed the same dream. In the dream I drift in a washtub on a silver pond. This pond is populated by stunning things, all color and light, who knock themselves out for my amusement. I look forward to this dream like a friend.

My bus dream began and expanded to include my Glak. Each time the bus bumped or took a hard curve, the pond produced a three-headed lizard who nuzzled my nose. His triple grin woke me. I reached to see if the egg was intact, then, assured, slept again.

The bus went smoothly, as did my transfer to Air Canada.

There was some worry about how my Glak would like flying, especially under someone else's power, but there was no problem. The egg did not jiggle, except for takeoff. Since there were empty seats, I belted the Glak beside me and reclined my chair. The silver pond is strictly an automotive fantasy. In planes I dream of crashing.

Here in the clouds over eastern Canada, I was allowed no repose. Behind me sat a couple who were touring the world. I had seen their luggage, a mass of labels, in the terminal. Now, on the way to Labrador, I deduced from their talk that they were running out of places. After Saskatchewan, there was nothing left.

"See there, in small print," the man said, showing a guide book. "See there, a fellow named Bjarni discovered Labrador in 986. Imagine. Bjarni the son of Herjulf. See there, he sold his boat to Leif Ericson, who later used the identical craft in his explorations."

"How do they know?"

"See there, it's in the guide. Helluland, land of stones."

"Where?"

"Fish and fur are the two major industries."

"Oh."

Labrador did not sound bad. There were trees, according to the guide, conifers, birch, poplars, spruce, lichens, moss, red azaleas, blue gentians, even white orchids. And they had chickadees, geese, ducks, lemmings, lynx, wolves, ermines, martins, otters, foxes, seals, bears, owls, red gulls, and Patagonian terns. There were some Eskimos, the ones not shot by fishermen, Algonkins, Nascapees, Englishmen and Scotch. Not bad for a bird. Activities, company, a little conflict. A nice subarctic community.

It was a foggy morning. Helluland, land of stones, fish, furs, etc., lay like a lump. Our plane began its descent. I could see no ermines or white orchids, only patches of smoke and the lights of the Goose Bay Airport. No wonder Bjarni unloaded the ship.

"Are you sure we haven't been here?" the lady said.

"See there," said the man, "it does look familiar."

Familiar it looks, like your own subconscious laid out to dry.

Goose Bay may be a fine place. I don't know. I checked my egg in the airport men's room. There was a crack in the shell, the tiniest fissure, not the kind that swallows grandmothers in Sicilian earthquake stories, more like a hairline. But it was there. If I were a first time mother, a primagravid as they say, with a broken bag of water, I could have acted no worse.

I collared the first Lab I saw and screamed at him about renting a plane to Kangalakksiorvik.

"Matter of fact, there's a plane leaving now. Pilot is by the name of Le Granf. He currently drinks coffee in the coffee place. You will know him to see him by his enormity. Also, he has one arm."

I found Le Granf in the coffee place, and there was no missing him. In a red and black mackinaw, he looked like a science fiction checkerboard. Built in blocks, head, chest, middle, legs, he was made from squares. His one arm held a pail of coffee, black.

"Mr. Le Granf?" I said.

"Yas," he said, a Frenchman monophthongizing his diphthongs, "who are you, Quasimodo, the hunchback of Notre Dame?"

"I am Harold North," I said.

"Beeg news. Vive Quebec libre."

You basically insecure vowel shifter, I thought. You son of a bitch. It's your plane.

"I understand that you pilot a plane up to Kangalakksiorvik."

"The world's puke."

"I've got to get up there."

"Why? You have a yen to bug seals?"

"Why is my business."

"True. How come this rush on Kangalakksiorvik? I got passenger for there. OK. We fit you in for a hundred dollars."

"Done."

"I swallow this sweat, we go."

Le Granf gulped the coffee and we went. We walked to a hangar in front of which sat something which must have been an airplane.

"Meet Clarette, the old whore," said Le Granf. "My saggy express. The snatch of the wild blue. You change your mind to go?"

"No."

"Stupid. My passenger is not here yet. Get in and we wait for him."

We climbed into Clarette's belly. There were four seats, two at the controls, two just behind.

"Clarette has a terrible cough," said Le Granf. "I worry for her tubes."

He pressed a button and the propeller turned. Puffs of smoke shot from the nose. The cough began, a hack.

"Phew. Not good."

I stopped noticing because Le Granf's other passenger arrived. It was the Nagle carrying a duffle bag. We saw each other head-on, and both of us made the sound of old doors closing.

"Acquaintances," said Le Granf. "Then we have stimulating conversation of the past."

I was sitting next to Le Granf, but when the Nagle came aboard, I did the prudent thing and shifted next to him in back. He put his duffle bag in the storage space and saw my executive suitcase.

"Are you armed?" I said.

"Don't make nasty personal jokes," said Le Granf.

"I was talking to my friend," I said.

"Ah."

"No, of course not," said the Nagle. "What are you doing here, Harold?"

"Same as you. Same as you."

"But I have the egg."

"You have the chicken."

"I get it," the Nagle said. "The goal-line stand. I admire your persistence, Harold."

"You have a chicken, Nagle."

"Sure, Harold. I have a chicken."

"Where is this chicken?" said Le Granf. "Include me in the discussion."

"Go ahead, tell him," I said.

Le Granf informed the tower that we were ready for takeoff by yelling out the window. Then Clarette fought her bronchitis, and slowly we were moving.

"She will rise," Le Granf said. "We will have our jollies."

She rose, after a fashion, and the Nagle told Le Granf his story of the Glak. I must admit, he presented his case objectively, as he saw it, keeping all things in proportion.

"So, well, then one has a chicken and one a Glak?" said Le Granf, after I explained the complications. "Marvelous."

I began to feel oddly ill. I got violent cramps. I had flashes. My stomach swelled. In a flash of insight, the kind Hikhoff taught me, I knew I was feeling the symptoms of labor. This condition is not unusual in emotional kinds like myself, but still it is embarrassing.

"So," said Le Granf, "tell me. Which of you poppas is the real father, that I want to know. What kind of educated man would fornicate with a feathered friend?"

"Nobody fornicated with a feathered friend," I said.

"Love is love," Le Granf said. "But a bird."

"Fly the plane," I said, doubled over with pain.

Le Granf found a bottle of brandy and passed it around.

"I have heard tell many strange tales under the Northern Lights, you bet," said Le Granf, "but two men infatuated with the same pigeon, oh boy!"

"Ignore him," said the Nagle.

"Tell me," I said, "what made you pick Kangalakksiorvik?"

"The *galakk*, I suppose, which sounds like Glak."

"I never noticed that."

"And you followed me all the way up here with nothing but the chicken story, Harold? I keep expecting you to play a trump card. Are you waiting until we land to hit me on the back of the neck?"

"Follow you? Why should I follow you? What you have there in the sack is a rooster, maybe a hen, but no Glak."

"Harold," said the Nagle, "I hope I find a friend someday as loyal to me as you are to Hikhoff."

Bouncing like an elevator, Clarette flew us to the dead heart of winter, over fields of blue ice.

The Nagle and I fell into bemused silence. Under my pains, I had thoughts of Hikhoff, out of place, out of time, out of focus, tossing vowels like darts at the passing parade. Was Hikhoff himself involved in a pregnancy, kindled by food? Could it be that he felt himself with child, some kind of child? Were Hikhoff's bellows labor pains too, for an invisible offspring? The Glak. Some son. Some daughter. *Some* product, at least, of Hikhoff's perpetual pregnancy.

Le Granf sang dirty songs about caribou and snowshoe rabbits. They helped pass the journey.

"There it blows," said Le Granf. "Look down. Nothing, eh?"

Clarette lost altitude, such as there was, as Le Granf searched for a landing place. He flew us off to the left of what seemed to be a settlement, circled, dipped, banked.

The Nagle and I grabbed for our luggage. We both had red faces, flamed by the moment of truth.

"Nagle," I said, "I feel sorry for you. You will soon stand chin deep in snow and discover at the moment of triumph that you have carried a fryer to practically the North Pole."

"Really, Harold. Do you plan to hit me?"

"No violence from me," I said. "The violence is done."

Le Granf found a spot, a clearing in the woods. Clarette settled into it as if it were a four poster, a remarkable landing, one-point.

The deal with Le Granf was for him to wait.

The Nagle's egg was as ready as the Glak's. Neither of us anticipated more than a few minutes. Outside in the absolute cold, the Nagle and I wrapped scarves around our faces. We lugged our burdens toward a place near trees.

"This is it," I said.

Like duelists, we stood back to back. We bent to our bags. Out came the Glak egg, hopping to my hands. It was hot as a muffin. More fissures lined the shell and more showed all the time. The egg was more like a web.

Le Granf stood near the plane out of decency. He could see how serious we were and hummed the wedding march.

The egg broke in my hands.

I was holding a blinking, stringy thing with stubs for wings and fat. "Hi, Glak," I said.

"Hi, Glak," the Nagle said to his chicken.

You would think my warm hands and the furnace of my affection would have meaning to a Glak barely sixty seconds old. No. Already, it strained for escape, looking at me as if I were a Nazi.

I put it gently on the frozen turf. It did what it was supposed to. It waddled, fell, slipped, staggered, stopped, stretched and said *glak* in a raucous manner.

Cheep, said the Nagle's chicken, and he said, "Did you hear that?"

I paid him no attention. My Glak, *the* Glak I should say, was examining the world. It took a step toward the forest, but hesitated.

"Come here, Glak," I said to the wasteland.

Glak. Cheep.

The Glak did not come back. It took a baby step toward the woods, then another.

I moved after it, but stopped. There, in the land of stones, I heard Elsie Moonish's dictum on love without possession, the act without the owning.

I without Glak, Glak without me. We were both our own men. Poor Glak. Already it speared looks here and there in a jerky search for its own kind. Were there any others? Would it find them? Did we do this frazzled thing a favor or the worst injustice?

"Goodbye, my Glak," the Nagle was saying. His chicken had taken a stroll, too. The Nagle began snapping pictures of it for the record. I had no use for the record, and Hikhoff had written nothing of Polaroids.

"Glak," said my Glak, more raucous than before. And there it was, Hikhoff's croak, pre-vowel shift as they come.

The Nagle snapped away at his impostor, a yellow tuft.

Then the newborns met. The Glak and the chicken felt each other out, shrugged, shivered, took a look at Labrador and walked off together into the primeval forest.

"A Glak and a chicken," I said to the Nagle, who rolled film. "Some team. Chickens, at least, are not extinct. Glaks do not yield their drumsticks so willingly. Maybe hope blooms here in the snow."

Off went the birds. What could I say? Could I give wisdom? Could I say, "Call Fridays?" Could I say, "Read *The Snow Goose* by Gallico and drop in to show gratitude on Christmas?" There was nothing I could say. With a bird, just-born is the equivalent of a human adolescent. There is a definite loss of communication.

"Come on, crazies," said Le Granf. "Clarette is oozing oil."

Polite at the end, the Nagle and I offered firsts at the door. We were subdued. Le Granf started his rubber band motor.

"Wait," I said, climbing out, running back to the nursery where two shells lay open like broken worlds.

"Moron. Come on," said Le Granf.

I put my Hikhoff on the ground, facing the trees.

At Goose Bay I said to Le Granf, "Monsieur, you are a reindeer's udder." Nothing.

I said, "Sir, you are an abortion." Puzzlement.

I said, "Pierre, your missing arm should goose the devil." Double take.

I said, "Laval, you are a lousy pilot with a greasy plane."

He hit me on the head. I hated to use Le Granf that way, but I needed the jolt. I felt better, much better, purged. It was the Nagle who picked me up.

"Nagle, what do you plan to do now?" I said. "Myself, I plan to go some place where a pineapple can grow. Someplace where the sun is the size of a dinner plate. I am going to get salt water in my mouth."

Still reeling, I thought, *who needs me most?*

E. MOONISH SYRACUSE, NEW YORK OFFER PLUS-PLUS IN SALUBRIOUS CLIMATE STOP ALL EXPENSES STOP PLENTY HONEY STOP PLEASE REPLY COLLECT STOP LOVE STOP HAROLD NORTH

After cabling, I went with the Nagle for a drink. While the drinks were being brewed, I excused myself, left for the john and read FINALLY under an open bulb.

Dear Harold,

Bless you and keep you. Also, thank you. Harold, enclosed is a check for $1000. Write poems. Also, here is my recipe for a grand roast Glak:

Take Glak, place in pan, cover with butter and garlic salt. Add paprika, and pepper. Line pan with roasting potatoes and tender on-

ions. Place in pre-heated range 450 degrees. Cook 30 minutes per pound. Serve hot. Suggest lively Gumpolskierchner '59 for a sparkle.

Best regards,
David Hikhoff

"It was delicious, delicious," I yelled to Hikhoff. "Boy, you have some weird sense of humor."

Hikhoff, roller of RRR's, chamber of guts, juggler of opposites, galloping ghost, A.E.I.O.U. now sleep well.

So it was that I entered my *puerperium,* which is gynecological for the time of recovery after delivering, the time of post-partum elation. Of life after birth.

———————————◆———————————

Mike Resnick is such a jolly, pleasant, unassuming soul that it's almost difficult to think of him as a writer. Even the way he puts his name on his books, the simple and prosaic "Mike Resnick" instead of "Michael Q.L. Resnick, Esq." or some such goes a ways toward showing what kind of man, and writer, he is. Upon meeting him one searches in vain for the signs of torment, of a diseased childhood or fractured sensibility that one tends to associate with successful authors.

Clearly this is someone wholly content with life, whose daily work is a litany of bliss and ease, devoid of worries, fears, or concerns. Except for one thing. Mike Resnick *is* a writer, and as such is prey to all the torments and terrors and horrors that travel hand in hand with that agonizing, miserable, misbegotten profession. It's just that on Mike it doesn't show as much as it does on some others.

But it's all still there. Even in passing, as in . . .

———————————◆———————————

Beibermann's Soul

MIKE RESNICK

WHEN BEIBERMANN WOKE up on Wednesday morning, he discovered that his soul was missing.

"This can't be," he muttered to himself. "I know I had it with me when I went to bed last night."

He thoroughly searched his bedroom and his closet and his office, and even checked the kitchen (just in case he had left it there when he got up around midnight for a peanut butter sandwich), but it was nowhere to be found.

He questioned Mrs. Beibermann about it, but she was certain it had come back from the cleaner's the previous day.

"I'm sure it will turn up, wherever it is," she said cheerfully.

"But I need it *now,*" he protested. "I am a literary artist, and what good is an artist without a soul?"

"I've always thought that some of the most successful writers we know had no souls," offered Mrs. Beibermann, thinking of a number of her husband's colleagues.

"Well, *I* need it," he said adamantly. "I mean, it's all very well to remove it when one is taking a shower or working in the garden, but I absolutely must have it before I can sit down to work."

So he continued searching for it. He went up to the attic and looked for it amid a lifetime's accumulation of memorabilia. He took his flashlight down to the basement and hunted through a thicket of broken chairs and sofas that he planned someday to give to the Salvation Army. Then, just to be on the safe side, he called the restaurant where he and his agent had eaten the previous evening to see if he had inadvertently left it there. But by midday he was forced to admit that it was indeed lost, or at the very least thoroughly misplaced.

"I can't wait any longer," he told his wife. "It's not as if I am a best-selling author. I have deadlines to meet and bills to pay. I must sit down to work."

"Shall I place a notice in the classified section of the paper?" she asked. "We could offer a reward."

"Yes," he said. "And report it to the police as well. They must stumble across lost and mislaid souls all the time." He walked to his office door, turned to his wife, and sighed dramatically. "In the meantime, I suppose I'll have to try to do without it."

So he closed the office door, sat down, and began to work. Ideas (though not entirely his own) flowed freely, concepts (slightly tarnished but still workable) easily manifested themselves, characters (neatly labeled and ready to perform) popped up as he needed them. In fact, the ease with which he achieved his day's quota of neatly typed pages surprised him, although he had the distinct feeling that there was something *missing,* some element that could be supplied only by his misplaced soul.

Still, he decided, staring at what he had thus far accomplished, a lifetime's mastery of technique could hide a lot of faults. So he did a little of this, and a little of that, made a correction here, inserted some literary pyrotechnics there. He imbued it with a certain fashionable eroticism to impress his audience and a certain trendy obtuseness to bedazzle the critics, and finally he emerged and showed the finished product to his wife.

"I don't like it," said Mrs. Beibermann.

"I thought it was rather good," said Beibermann petulantly.

"It *is* rather good," she agreed. "But you never settled for rather good before."

Beibermann shrugged. "It's got a lot of style to it," he said. "Maybe no one else will see what's missing."

And indeed, no one else *did* see what was missing. His agent loved it, his public loved it, and most of all, his editor loved it. Beibermann deposited an enormous check in his bank account and went back to work.

"But what about your soul?" asked his wife.

"Oh, make sure the police are still looking for it, by all means," replied Beibermann. "But in the meantime, we must eat—and technique is not, after all, to be despised."

His next three projects brought higher advances and still more critical acclaim. By now he had also created a public *persona*—articulate, worldly, with just a hint of the sadness of one who had suffered too much for his Art—and while he still missed his soul, he had to admit that his new situation in the world was not at all unpleasant.

"We have enough money now," announced his wife one day. "Why don't we take a vacation? Surely your soul will be found by then—and even if it isn't, perhaps we can get you a new one. I understand they can make one up in three days in Hong Kong."

"Don't be silly," he said irritably. "My work is more popular than ever, I'm finally making good money, this is hardly the time for a vacation, and weren't you a lot thinner when I married you?"

He began sporting a goatee and a hairpiece after his next sale, and started working out in the neighborhood gymnasium, so that he wouldn't feel awkward and embarrassed when sweet young things accosted him for autographs at literary luncheons. He borrowed a number of surefire jokes and snappy comebacks and made the circuit of the television talk shows, and even began work on his autobiography, changing only those facts that seemed dull or mundane.

And then, on a cold winter's morning, a police detective knocked at his front door.

"Yes?" said Beibermann, puffing a Turkish cigarette through a golden holder, and eyeing him suspiciously.

The detective pulled out a worn, tattered soul and held it up.

"This just turned up in a pawnshop in Jersey," said the detective. "We have every reason to believe that it might be yours."

"Let me just step into the bathroom and try it on," said Beibermann, taking it from him.

Beibermann walked to the bathroom and locked the door behind him. Then he carefully unfolded the soul, smoothing it out here and there, and trying not to wince at its sorry condition. He did not try it on, however—it was quite dirty and shopworn, and there was no way to know who had been wearing it. Instead, he began examining it thoroughly, looking for telltale signs—a crease here, a worn spot there, most of them left over from his college days—and came to the inescapable conclusion that he was, indeed, holding his own soul.

For a moment his elation knew no bounds. Now, at last, he could go back to producing works of true Art.

Then he stared at himself in the mirror. He'd have to go back to living on a budget again, and of course there'd be no more spare time, for he was a meticulous craftsman when he toiled in the service of his art. Beibermann frowned. The innocent young things would seek someone else's autograph, the television hosts would flock to a new best-seller, and the only literary luncheon he would attend would be for some *other* author.

He continued staring at the New Improved Beibermann, admiring the well-trimmed goatee, the satin ascot, the tweed smoking jacket, the world-weary gaze from beneath half-lowered eyelids. Then, sighing deeply, he unlocked the door and walked back to the foyer.

"I'm sorry," he said as he handed the neatly folded soul back to the detective, "but this isn't mine."

"I apologize for taking up the valuable time of a world-famous man like yourself, sir," said the detective. "I could have sworn this was it."

Beibermann shook his head. "I'm afraid not."

"Well, we'll keep plugging away, sir."

"By all means, officer," said Beibermann. He lowered his voice confidentially. "I trust that you'll be *very* discreet, though; it wouldn't do for certain critics to discover that my soul was missing." He passed a fifty dollar bill to the detective.

"I quite understand, sir," said the detective, grabbing the bill and stuffing it into a pocket of his trenchcoat. "You can depend on me."

Beibermann smiled a winning smile. "I knew I could, officer."

Then he returned to his office and went back to work.

* * *

He had been dead and buried for seven years before anyone suggested that his work lacked some intangible factor. A few revisionist critics agreed, but nobody could pinpoint what was missing.

Mrs. Beibermann could have told them, of course—but she had taken an around-the-world cruise when Beibermann left her for the second of his seven wives, met and married a banker who was far too busy to discuss Art, and spent the rest of her life raising orchids, avoiding writers, and redecorating her house.

There was a time when our civilization wasn't sensitive to the point of implosion. When people used words now shunned in polite society. When human beings with incapacitating injuries were referred to as crippled instead of physically handicapped or deaf rather than hearing impaired. When Raymond Chandler employed such terms heads dropped closer to print, as if expecting to find the solution to confusion and mystery buried deep within the smudged letters themselves. When Damon Runyon used them readers threw back their heads and laughed. Same terms, different reactions. Words with power, with effect, with guts.

Now all we get are polite euphemisms, usually delivered with an aggravatingly smarmy sense of superiority. Perhaps some sensibilities are now spared that would otherwise be bruised, but there is also honesty in pain. Ted Cogswell was not a prolific writer, or a best-selling one, but he was honest, bless 'im. And honesty there is aplenty in . . .

Thimgs

THEODORE R. COGSWELL

" . . . AND THE GROUND *was frozen solid. It took them two hours before they reached Hawkins' coffin.*

" 'See,' grunted the coroner as he threw back the lid, 'he's still there. I told you you were seeing things.'

" 'I've got to be sure,' said Van Dusen thickly, and grabbing a smoking lantern from beside the grave, he thrust it down into the open casket.

"A shrill scream tore through the night air and he slumped over—

dead! Instead of the heavy features of the man he had killed, Reginald Van Dusen saw HIMSELF!"

There was a sudden ripple of discordant music from the loudspeaker and then the unctuous voice of The Ghoul broke in.

"The coroner called it suicide. And in a way I suppose it was . . ." His voice trailed off in a throaty chuckle. *"The moral? Only this, dear friends, if you should ever be walking through a strange part of town and come upon a little shop you never saw before, especially a little shop with a sign in the window that says* SHOTTLE BOP, WE SELL THRINGS, *or something equally ridiculous, remember* THE CASE OF THE CLUTTERED COFFIN *and run, don't walk, to the nearest morgue. HA HA HA HA HA."*

As the maniacal laughter trailed away, the background music surged up and then skittered out of hearing to make way for the announcer. He only managed to get three words out before Albert Blotz, owner, manager, and sole agent of World Wide Investigations, reached over and turned off the little radio that stood on the windowsill beside his desk.

"Boy," he said, "that was really something. Eh, Janie?"

The little crippled girl behind the typist's desk at the other side of the dingy office looked up.

"What?"

"The program. Wasn't it something?"

"Beats me," she said. "I wasn't listening. Somebody has to get some work done around here." She pulled a letter out of her correspondence basket and waved it in the air. "What about this Harris letter? It's been sitting here for a month. After spending the guy's dough the least you can do is write him an answer."

The fat man looked blank. "Harris? Who's he?"

"The fellow in Denver who wanted you to investigate everybody in New York who had had a big and unexpected windfall within the past year."

Blotz snorted impatiently. "That nut! Aw, tell him anything."

"Give me a for-instance."

"Tell him . . ." Blotz leaned heavily back in his chair and stared at the ceiling. "Tell him that World Wide Investigations assigned its best operatives to the case and that in sixteen cases out of twenty . . . No, better make it twenty-nine out of thirty-four . . . That way he'll really feel he's getting his money's worth."

"All right, in twenty-nine out of thirty-four cases what?"

"Don't rush me." Blotz pulled a bottle of cheap blend out of his drawer and eyed the remaining inch regretfully.

"You know the doctor said your heart wouldn't take much more of that."

The fat man shrugged and tossed the liquor down. As his eyes wandered around the office in search of inspiration, they came to rest on the radio.

"That's it!" he exclaimed.

"What's it?"

"The Ghoul! For once crime pays somebody but the actors and the script writers. Tell Harris that in whatever it was out of whatever it was cases, the individuals concerned visited small shops they had never noticed before and were sold objects whose nature they refused to reveal by a strange old man."

Janie looked up from her shorthand pad. "Is that all?"

"No, we need a clincher." He thought for a minute. "How's this? In each case when they went back and tried to find the shop it had disappeared."

"You ought to try writing radio scripts yourself."

"Too much work," said Blotz. "I like the mail order detective business better." He looked regretfully at the empty bottle and then back at Janie. "While you're at it you might as well tell that yokel that for five bills World Wide will find the shop for him and buy him one of those dingbats."

Janie's lips tightened. "Doesn't your conscience ever bother you?"

Blotz let out a nasty laugh. "If it weren't for the suckers I'd have to work for a living. This way it's a breeze. Some old dame in Podunk hasn't heard from her kid since he took off for the big city and gets worried about him. He doesn't answer her letters and then one day she sees my ad in the Podunk *Gazette* and sends me fifty bucks to go look for him. How come you asked?"

"Because mine bothers me. Every day I work here I feel dirtier."

Blotz grinned. "Then quit."

"I've been thinking of that. At least I'd be able to sleep nights."

"But you wouldn't be eating so regular. Face it, kid—nobody is going to hire a gimpy sparrow like you unless he's a big-hearted guy like me. And there ain't many around."

Janie looked from him to the pair of worn crutches that leaned against the wall.

"Yeah," she said as she started punching out the letter to Harris. "Yeah, there sure ain't."

Mr. Blotz's pulse was finally back to normal but he still couldn't tear his eyes away from the crisp green slip of paper that bore the magic figures $500.00 and the name of a Denver bank.

"He bit," he said in an awed voice. "He really bit. May wonders, and suckers, never cease." He rubbed his fat hands together nervously. "I'd better get this to the bank and cash it before something happens."

Half an hour later he was back, carefully stacking bottles of bonded bourbon into his desk drawers. When they were arranged to his satisfaction, he leaned back and hoisted his feet on the desk.

"Take a letter to Harris."

Janie obediently took out her shorthand pad.

"Usual heading. Eh . . . oh, something like this. 'Pursuant to your instructions, my agents in all the major cities have been instructed to check for little shops they don't remember having seen before. They are to be especially alert for basement stores with dusty signs in the window with wordings like WE SELL THRINGS or SHOTTLE BOP. Upon discovery they are to enter immediately. If a small aged man appears from the rear of the shop and presses them to buy something, they are to do so. Once they leave they are to make careful note of the shop's location and walk around the block. If when they return the shop has disappeared, they are immediately to send their purchase to you.'"

Blotz paused, took a bottle out of his drawer, and uncapped it. "Put something in about unexpectedly heavy expenses at the end. If we play this right we may be able to tap him again. In the meantime we'd better have something ready to send him just in case."

"What kind of a something?" asked Janie.

"Who cares? Go over on Third and prowl some of those junk shops. Pick up something small—that'll keep the postage down—and old."

The little secretary pulled herself painfully to her feet, draped a threadbare coat over her humped back, and took her crutches from beside her typing desk.

"Just don't go over a dollar," added Blotz quickly.

She started toward the door and then turned and stood blinking at him through thick lensed glasses that made her eyes appear twice their normal size.

"Well?" he barked.

"I haven't got a dollar."

With a pained expression on his face he fumbled in an old coin purse. He reluctantly pulled out a quarter, then another, and then finally another.

"Here," he said, "see what you can do for seventy-five cents."

Blotz was deep in his bottle when Janie finally came hobbling back and placed a small paper-wrapped package on his desk.

"Any change?" he asked.

She shook her head. "It was funny," she ventured. "I mean after what you said about shottles and thrings—"

"Well, open it up," he interrupted. "Let's see what Harris is getting for his money."

"—all this shop had in front," she went on hesitantly, "was just one sign. It said: THIMGS."

"Poor bastard that owns it, I guess. Some people have funny names," said Blotz. "Go on—open it."

With fingers that trembled slightly she tore off the brown paper wrapping. Inside was a small corroded brass cylinder that on first glance looked like an old plumbing fixture.

"You paid seventy-five cents for that?" said Blotz in annoyance. "They saw you coming, kid." He picked it up and turned it over in his hand. On second look he realized that there was more to it than he had first thought. Through the heavy green patina he could make out a series of strange characters. At one end was a knob that seemed to be made out of a slightly different metal than the cylinder proper.

"I give up, what is it?" he asked.

Janie shuddered. "I wish I knew," she said. "I wish I knew."

Blotz frowned and took hold of the knob. He was about to twist it when a sudden thought occurred to him. It might explode or do something equally unpleasant.

"Here, you try it," he said to Janie. "It seems to be stuck."

She reached out a trembling hand and then jerked it back. "I'm afraid. The man in the shop said—"

"Take it!" he barked. "When I tell you to do something, you do it. And no back talk!"

In frightened obedience she took the cylinder and twisted the knob. For a moment nothing happened, and then with an odd flickering she vanished. Before Blotz had a chance to react properly to the sudden emptiness of the office, she was back. At least a not very reasonable facsimile was.

She might have passed for her sister, there was a strong family resemblance, but the pathetic twist in her spine was gone and so was its accompanying hump. She was thirty pounds heavier, and all the pounds were in the right places. She was—and the realization hit Blotz like a hammer blow as he stood gaping at her—one of the most beautiful things he had ever seen.

The first thing she did was to pull off her thick-lensed glasses and throw them in the wastebasket. The first thing Blotz did was to grab a bottle out of his desk. He took several long gulps, shook his head, and shuddered.

"It's when you're half drunk that things get twisty," he mumbled. "I'm just going to sit here with my eyes shut until I'm drunk enough to get back to normal." He counted to twenty slowly as the fireball in his stomach expanded and trickled a semi-sense of well being through his extremities. Then, as the nightmare slowly dispelled, he let out a long sigh of relief and opened his eyes.

She was still there!

There was a strange smile on her face that he didn't like.

"Where . . . ? What . . . ?" Blotz's vocal cords stopped operating and he just sat there and quivered. She laid the little bronze cylinder down on the desk in front of him.

"Here," she said softly. "You can go there too if you want to."

"Where?" whispered Blotz.

"I don't know. It's someplace else, a tremendous place with rooms filled with whirring machines. There was a man there and he asked what I wanted and I told him. So he did a little re-editing and here I am."

"Magic," said Blotz hoarsely. "Black magic, that's what it is. But . . ." His voice trailed off.

"But you don't believe in magic. Is that what you were going to say?" She didn't wait for an answer. "But I do. People like me have to. It's the only way we can keep going. But magic has a funny way of working. Do you know what I was thinking after the little man asked me what I wanted?"

Blotz moistened his thick lips and shook his head as if hypnotized.

"I was thinking that in spite of the way things look, there's just one thing you can always count on."

"Yeah?"

"People always end up getting what they got coming."

Blotz let out a half-hysterical laugh. "Then where's mine? Why does a guy with my brains have to scrabble out a living with a two-bit outfit like this?" He raved on for a minute and then got control of himself. The liquor helped. After he'd taken a couple more gulps from his bottle he still couldn't look what had happened squarely in the face, but with the abatement of the first shock came a gradual return of the old sense of mastery that had made him hire Janie in the first place, rather than some less experienced but more feminine—and amiable—typist.

As an awareness of the physical changes that had taken place began to grow, he found his eyes sliding greedily over her. The change hadn't extended to her dress. The garment that had been more than adequate covering for the twisted and scrawny little body she had occupied up until a few minutes before threatened to split at the thrusting of the rich new curves that strained against it.

"You know, Janie," he said slowly, "seeing as it was my money that got you what you got, that kind of makes me the copyright owner." Grabbing hold of the edge of his desk, he pulled himself to his feet and lurched toward her. When he put one flabby arm around her, she didn't pull away. Emboldened, he let his hand slip down and begin to fumble with the buttons on her blouse.

"I wouldn't do that if I were you," she said in a strange voice.

"But you ain't me. That's what makes it so nice for both of us."

His fumbling fingers had managed to unfasten the first button and his thick lips began to march like twin slugs over the soft curve of her shoulder.

She acted as if he were still on the other side of the room.

"It took more courage than I thought I had in me but I asked him to give me just what I deserved."

"Him? Oh, yeah. Well that's me, baby," said Blotz thickly as he went to work on the second button.

"You could have been," she said in the same distant voice. "That was the chance I was taking."

The second button was obstinate. Blotz gave an impatient yank that caused the worn fabric to rip in his hands. As if aware of them for the first time, she shrugged herself free. As Blotz grunted and grabbed for her, he felt a sudden wrenching, stabbing pain lance through his chest, and then with no transition at all he found himself falling. He slumped against the desk, and as his plump fingers scrabbled against the smooth surface, trying to secure a hold that would keep him from plummeting down into darkness, they touched the worn bronze cylinder. As he slid

on down, face purple and eyeballs bulging, more through instinct than
conscious volition he found and twisted the serrated knob at one end.
There was an immediate release, a translation into someplace else. He
was standing again and the pain was gone, but except for a tiny glowing
spot in front of him, it was darker than he had ever known before.

"Janie," he whimpered. "Janie."

His voice echoed metallically from distant walls. He turned to run
but there was no place to run to, only the darkness. He had a sudden
vision of unseen pits and crevasses, and froze where he stood. And then,
unable to stand his own immobility, he inched cautiously toward the tiny
spot of light, testing the whatever-it-was under his feet with each sliding
step.

At last he was able to touch it, a cold luminous circle set in a smooth
steel wall at chest height. As he moved his arm toward it, the hand that
still held the bronze cylinder jerked forward of its own volition, pulling
his arm with it, and plunged into the glowing circle. There was a clicking
of relays and then glaring overhead lights went on.

He had been wise to check his footing. He was standing on a catwalk
that arched dizzily over a several-acre expanse of strange whirring ma-
chinery. There were no guard rails, only a narrow tongue of metal that
stretched out from some spot lost in the murky distance until it reached
the smooth metal wall before which he stood. Then with a whining
sound, a door opened in front of him. An invisible force pushed him
through and he found himself in a great vault-like room whose walls
were covered with countless tiny winking lights and bank upon bank of
intricate controls. As the door clanged shut behind him, a little ball of
shimmering light bounced across the floor toward him, expanded, wa-
vered, and then suddenly took the shape of a harassed-faced little man
with burning, deep-set eyes and a long white beard.

"Well," he said impatiently, "out with it!"

Blotz didn't say anything for a minute. He couldn't. When he finally
got partial control of his vocal cords all that came out was an almost
incoherent series of who's, what's and how's. The little man interrupted
him with an impatient gesture.

"Stop sputtering," he said testily. "I'm tired of sputtering. This may
be new to you but it isn't to me. You're the four-hundred-and-thirty-six-
thousand-three-hundred-and-fifty-ninth mortal to get hold of one of the
keys, and you're also the four-hundred-and-thirty-six-thousand-three-
hundred-and-fifty-ninth sputterer. Damn the M.W. boys, anyway!"

"M.W.?" Blotz was sparring for enough time to get his own thinking organized. What steadied him was the thought that, fantastic as all this was, Janie had been here before him, and Janie had somehow managed to snag herself a jackpot. His first job was to find out enough about the situation to angle it around to his own advantage.

"Mysterious Ways. It's a special department in the home office that specializes in making life more complicated for the Guardians. I'm a Guardian," the little man added gloomily.

"After Reward and Punishment switched their records section over to completely automatic operation, somebody in M.W. came up with the bright idea that humans should still have some sort of a chance for personal attention. So they made up a few widgets like the one you got hold of and scattered them around at random." He gave a dry cough. "Not that you've got much when you do get hold of one. All that comes with it is the right to a little personal re-editing of your future—and even that is controlled by the Prime Directive."

Blotz's eyes narrowed slightly. So he had a right to something. He had something coming that they had to give him. He thought of Janie's sudden metamorphosis and he licked his thick lips.

"The girl that was here before me," he asked eagerly. "Is what happened to her what you call re-editing?"

The little man nodded.

"And I got a right to the same? I mean, you can make me look the way I'd like to instead of the way I do?"

There was another nod. "But—"

"No *buts*," interrupted Blotz rudely. "I want what I got a right to. You get to work on that tape of mine and fix it so I'll have as much on the ball on the male side as Janie has on the female. And toss in a nice fat bankroll while you're at it. Me, I like to travel first-class." He thought for a moment and then held up a restraining hand. "But don't start tinkering until I give you the word. It ain't every day that a guy gets a chance to rebuild himself from the ground up, and I want to be sure that I get all the little details just right."

"But," continued the Guardian as if the interruption had never occurred, "re-editing in your case wouldn't have much point. The heart attack you were having just before the key brought you here was a signal, a warning that the tape which has been recording the significant events of your life has just about reached its end. A few minutes after you return, the automatic rewind will cut in and then your spool will be removed from the recorder and sent over to Reward and Punishment for processing."

Blotz had always considered himself an atheist—more in self-defense than anything else. The thought of a superior something someplace taking personal note of each of his antisocial actions for purposes of future judgment was one that he had never cared to contemplate. He much preferred the feeling of immunity that came with the belief that man is simply an electrochemical machine that returns to its original components when it finally wears out.

But now! The little man's casual reference to something coming after was disturbing enough to almost override the shock caused by the announcement of his imminent death.

"What's processing?" he asked uneasily. "What are they going to do to me?"

Instead of answering, the Guardian walked over to a control panel and punched a series of buttons. A moment later a large screen over his head lit up.

"The playback starts here."

The screen flickered and then steadied to show a hospital delivery room and a writhing woman strapped to a table.

"What's all this got to do with me?"

"R&R have to start your processing someplace. This is what's planned for your next run-through. In your case I imagine some special arrangements have been made."

They had been. When Blotz started making little mewling noises, the little man reached forward and turned a knob. The screen went dark.

"Had enough?" he asked.

"Yeah," said the other thickly, "but I got to know." He shuddered. "Go ahead and hit the high spots. Nothing could be worse than what I just saw."

The Guardian did. There were things that could be worse. Much worse.

"Why?" whispered Blotz when it was finally over. "Why?"

"Because the ethical universe is just as orderly as the physical one. For each action there is an equal and contrary—though delayed—reaction."

Blotz fought frantically against the hysteria that threatened to engulf him. Always in the past there had been something that could be twisted to his advantage. The present had to be the same. There had to be an angle here. There had to be! Desperately he ran over the events of the past quarter hour, trying to find something that didn't fit the pattern as the little man had presented it.

The re-editing! There had to be something in the re-editing!

"Look," he stammered. "You *can* change things. You did for Janie. Why can't you go back over my tape and take out all the really bad things?"

"Because the past can't be changed," said the little man impatiently. "The re-editing that you have a right to applies only to the future. And as I've already pointed out, yours is so limited that any adjustment I might make would have very little meaning."

Blotz took a deep breath and held it. He couldn't afford to panic. Not now. But where was the angle? Given that the past couldn't be changed. Given that once he returned to Earth he had only a half a minute of life left. What then? How could a tape be kept from ending?

Say he'd bugged a bedroom to collect evidence for a divorce case and say he didn't want to miss recording a single squeak. Maybe if he. . . .

Of course!

"I've got a little job for you," he said in a voice that quivered slightly in spite of his best efforts to control it. "I want you to do some splicing."

The little man looked at him in obvious bewilderment.

"Splicing?"

Blotz was still shaky but he was beginning to enjoy himself. "That's what I said. It just occurred to me that if you spliced a second tape on to the end of the one that's just about finished, I could keep on living." He gestured toward the blank screen. "And after your little preview, keeping on living is what I want most to do. The splicing, it can be done, can't it?"

"Can? Of course it can. But I'm not about to," he added angrily. "To begin with, your old body's worn out and I'd have to hunt you up a new one."

"So what? The thing I want to hang on to is the *me*, the part that does the feeling and thinking, the part that *knows*." A snarl came into his voice. "And don't tell me you won't. You've got to!" He waved the bronze cylinder under the little man's nose. "I came up with the brass ring, Buster, and I got a free ride coming."

He stopped suddenly and a look of awe came over his face. "A free ride? And why only one, when I can keep on swapping horses?" He laughed exultantly. "Why, if you keep on splicing? Listen, here's the word. Every time the tape that's running through the recorder is about to reach its end, I want a new one patched on. And make sure that each body I get is well-heeled, healthy, and handsome. Like I said before, I like to travel first class."

The little man seemed on the verge of tears. "It's not a good idea," he said. "It's not a good idea at all. I can barely keep up with my work as it is, and if I have to—"

"But you do have to," said Blotz viciously. "Whether you like it or not, I've just beat the system. Me, little Al Blotz, the guy that used to have to work penny-ante swindles just to keep eating. But no more! What was chalked up against me before is peanuts compared to what's coming. And you know why? Because Reward and Punishment can't process me until my tape comes to an end. And it ain't ever. Never!"

"But—"

"Get going!"

The Guardian threw up his hands in defeat. "It's going to make a lot of extra work for me," he said mournfully, "but if you in—"

"Sure I insist," said Blotz, holding resolutely onto the cylinder. "You can tell Reward and Punishment to go process itself. I got it made."

The little machine that kept track of Mr. Blotz's actions hesitated momentarily when it came to the splice, and then gave a loud click and began to record on the new section of tape.

CLICK!

He woke to something heavy pressing on his chest and an angry buzzing. Blotz—no longer Blotz as far as externals went—opened sleepy eyes and blinked up at the ugly wedge-shaped head that was reared back ready to strike.

"Why didn't you tell me you were expecting company, Carl?" There was a note of savage enjoyment in the soft voice from the other side of the campfire.

Blotz wanted to beg, to plead with the other to save him, but he didn't dare risk the slightest lip movement. The snake was angry. One little motion and it would strike.

"I was going to kill you, Carl," the quiet voice went on. "I was going to damn my immortal soul to save the world from you. But now I don't have to. I'm just a spectator. Sometime before too long you're going to have to move. When you do it will be horrible, but it won't last more than a few hours. That's more than you granted the others. Remember my sister, Carl? And how long it took?"

The involuntary movement that was the prelude to agony was accompanied by a momentary feeling of relief. At least before too long it would be over. But with the final convulsion there came a

CLICK!

He was strangling. With a convulsive kick he brought himself to the surface and spat out a mouthful of blood-tinged salt water. To his left small bits of debris bobbed up and down in the oil slick that marked the spot where his cabin cruiser had gone down. He paddled in an aimless circle, unable to strike out because of the splintered rib that lanced into one lung. Almost an hour passed before the first black dorsal fin came circling curiously in.

The Guardian yawned as he looked around for another bit of tape to splice on to the one that was almost finished. Young, healthy, handsome —there were enough odd ends around so that Blotz would never have to worry about dying, never in a million years.

Not dying, that was something else.

CLICK!

We live in liberated times, when women no longer must be married to be considered whole. At least, that's what the media, and the psychologist-writers, and the feel-good analysts all say. And to a large extent that's certainly true, and all to the good.

But it's not a universal sediment, as a professor of social geology might say. There are still plenty of single ladies who devoutly wish they were otherwise, not because they feel incomplete without a man in their lives but because it is better not to be lonely than to be. Trouble is, men today are often confused about their roles. The times and traditions, they are still a-changin'. Respectable heterosexual pickings, as many women will tell you these days, tend to the slim.

Standards of male and female beauty also change. Dustin Hoffman and Al Pacino, after all, are not Clark Gable and Cary Grant. So how important in these "sensitive" times are looks, anyway?

Ms. Lipshutz and the Goblin

MARVIN KAYE

LIPSHUTZ, DAPHNE A., Ms. (age: 28; height: 5′ 2″; weight: 160 lbs.; must wear corrective lenses), had frizzy brown hair, buck teeth, and an almost terminal case of acne. Though her mother frequently reassured her she had a Very Nice Personality, that commodity seemed of little value in Daphne's Quest for The Perfect Mate.

According to Daphne A. (for Arabella) Lipshutz, The Perfect Mate must be 30, about 5′ 9″ in height, weigh approximately 130 pounds, have wavy blond hair (1st preference), white teeth, a gentle smile and peaches-and-cream complexion. He must like children and occasional sex, or if necessary, the other way around.

Daphne's Quest for The Perfect Mate was hampered by her job as an interviewer (2nd grade) for the State of New York, Manhattan division of the Labor Department's Upper West Side office of the Bureau of Unemployment. The only men she met there were sour-stomached married colleagues, or the people she processed for unemployment checks, "and them," her mother cautioned, "you can do without. Who'd buy the tickets, tip the cabbie, shmeer the headwaiter, pick up the check?"

Ms. Lipshutz worked in a dingy green office around the corner from a supermarket. To get there, she had to take a southbound bus from The Bronx, get off at 90th and Broadway and walk west past a narrow, dark alley. Next to it was a brick building with a doorway providing access to steep wooden stairs that mounted to her office. The stairs were worn smooth and low in the middle of each step by innumerable shuffling feet. Daphne noticed that unemployed feet frequently shuffle.

Late one October afternoon, just before Hallowe'en, Ms. Lipshutz was about to take her final coffee-break of the day when an unusual personage entered the unemployment bureau and approached her window. He was six feet eight inches tall and thin as a breadstick. There were warts all over his body, and the color of his skin was bright green.

Ms. Lipshutz thought he looked like the Jolly Green Pickle or an elongated cousin of Peter Pain. He was certainly the ugliest thing she'd ever set her soulful brown eyes on.

Leaning his pointy elbows on her window-shelf, the newcomer glanced admiringly at her acne-dimpled face and asked whether he was in the correct line. He addressed her as Miss.

Bridling, Daphne told him to address her as *Ms*. The tall green creature's eyebrows rose.

"Miz?" he echoed, mystified. "What dat?"

"I am a liberated woman," she said in the clockwork rhythm of a civil servant or a missioned spirit. Her vocal timbre was flat and nasal, pure Grand Concourse. "I do not like to be called Miss. If I were married—" (here she betrayed her cause with a profound sigh) "—I would not call myself Mrs. So please call me Ms."

The green one nodded. "Me once had girlfriend named Miz. Shlubya Miz. She great big troll. You troll?"

"This," said Ms. Lipshutz, "is an immaterial conversation. Please state your name and business."

"Name: Klotsch."

"Would you repeat that?" she asked, fishing out an application form and poising a pencil.

"Klotsch."

"First or last?"

"Always!"

Unusual names were common at the unemployment office, and so was unusual stupidity. Ms. Lipshutz patiently explained she wanted to know whether Klotsch was a first or last name.

"Only name. Just Klotsch."

"How do you spell it? Is that C as in Couch?"

"K as in Kill!" Klotsch shouted. "Kill-LOTSCH!"

"Kindly lower your voice," she said mechanically. "I presume you wish to apply for unemployment checks?"

Spreading his warty hands, the big green thing grinned. "Klotsch not come to count your pimples, Miz."

Not realizing the remark was meant flirtatiously, Daphne, who was extremely sensitive about her acne, took offense. "That was a cruel thing to say!"

"How come?" Klotsch was puzzled.

"Me no understand. Klotsch like pimples. You lots cuter than Shlubya the troll!"

Daphne, not very reassured, found it wise to retreat into the prescribed formulae of the State of New York for dealing with an unemployment insurance applicant.

"Now," she began. "Mister Klotsch—"

He waved a deprecatory claw. "No Mister."

"I beg your pardon?"

"You liberated, so okay, Klotsch liberated, too. If you Miz, me *Murr.*"

"I see," she said primly, unable to determine whether she was being made fun of. Inscribing Klotsch's name on Form NYS204-A, Ms. Lipshutz requested his address.

"Not got."

"You are a transient?"

He shook his shaggy head. "Me are a goblin."

"No, no, Murr Klotsch, we are not up to Employment History yet. Simply state your address."

"Me don't got. Landlady kick me out of cave."

"Oh, dear. Couldn't you pay your rent?"

"Ate landlord," Klotsch glumly confessed.

Daphne suddenly noticed that Klotsch had two lower incisors which protruded three inches north of his upper lip. Civic conscience aroused, she told him eating his landlord was a terrible thing to do.

"Telling me! Klotsch sick three days."

"Do you go round eating people all the time?"

The goblin drew himself erect, his pride hurt. "Klotsch no eat people! Only landlords!"

Ms. Lipshutz conceded the distinction. Returning to the form, she asked Klotsch for his last date of employment.

He sighed gloomily. "October 31st, 1877."

Time to be firm: "The unemployment relief act, Murr Klotsch, does *not* cover cases prior to 1932."

"So put down 1932," he suggested. In an uncharacteristic spirit of compromise, Daphne promptly complied. (It was eight minutes before five o'clock.)

"Place of previous employment?"

"Black Forest."

"Is that in New York?"

"Is Germany."

"You may not be aware that the State of New York does not share reciprocity with overseas powers."

Klotsch thought about it briefly, then raised a crooked talon in recollection. "Once did one-night gig in Poughkeepsie."

"Check." She wrote it down. "Previous employer's name."

"Beelzebub."

Ms. Lipshutz stuck pencil and application in Klotsch's paws. "Here —*you* tackle that one!" While he wrote, she studied him, deciding that, after all, Klotsch wasn't *so* bad looking. He had a kind of sexy expression in his big purple eye.

"And where does this Mist—uh, Murr Beelzebub conduct his business?"

The goblin shrugged. "Usually hangs around Times Square."

"Then he does not maintain a permanent place of business?"

"Oh, yeah: further south." Klotsch shook his large head, scowling. "He no good boss, got all goblins unionized. Me no like. Klotsch work for self."

Ms. Lipshutz muttered something about scabs. Klotsch, misunderstanding, beamed toothily. "Klotsch got plenty scabs. You like?"

Eye on the clock (four of five), Ms. Lipshutz proceeded with her routine. "Have you received any recent employment offers?"

"Just Beelzebub."

"Do you mean," she inquired with the frosty, lofty disapproval of an accredited representative of the State of New York, "that you have refused a job offer?"

"Me no going to shovel coal!" Klotsch howled, eyes glowing like the embers he disdained.

Ms. Lipshutz understood. "So long as the position was not in your chosen professional line." She ticked off another question on the form. "That brings us, Murr Klotsch, to the kind of work you are seeking. What precisely do you do?"

He replied in a solemn guttural tone. "Me goblin."

"What does that entail?"

By way of demonstration, Klotsch uttered a fearful yell, gnashed his teeth and dashed up and down the walls. He panted, snorted, whistled, screamed, swung from the light fixtures and dripped green on various desks. Ms. Lipshutz's colleagues paid no attention. Worse things happen in Manhattan.

Gibbering his last gibber, Klotsch returned to Ms. Lipshutz's window. "That my Class A material. You like?"

"Interesting," she conceded. "Did you get much call for that sort of thing?"

"Plenty work once! Double-time during day! Klotsch used to frighten farmers, shepherds, even once in a while, genuine hero." He sighed, shrugging eloquently. "But then scare biz go down toilet. They bust me down to kids, then not even them. Too many other scary things nowadays, goblins outclassed."

She nodded, not without hasty sympathy (two of five). "And have you ever considered changing your profession?"

"Got plenty monsters already on TV, movies, comics."

"What about the armed services?"

Klotsch shook his big green head. "All the best jobs already got by trolls."

Ms. Lipshutz sighed. She would have liked to assist Klotsch, but it was 4:59 and she did not want to miss the 5:03 bus. Setting his form aside for processing the following day, she asked him to return in one week.

The hapless goblin shambled out without another word.

* * *

Ms. Lipshutz hurried on her coat and hat, locked up her desk, pattered swiftly down the old stairs to catch the 5:03.

Turning east, she heel-clicked toward Broadway. There was a dark alleyway separating the corner supermarket from the building that housed the unemployment bureau. As she passed it, a great green goblin leaped out at her, whoofling, snorting and howling in outrageous menace.

Daphne nearly collapsed with laughter. She snickered, tittered, chortled and giggled for nearly a minute before gaining sufficient self-control to speak. "Murr Klotsch . . . it's you!"

His face was sad and long. "Miz no scared, she laugh."

"Oh . . . oh, *no!*" Daphne consolingly reached out her hand and touched him. "Murr Klotsch . . . I was so, *so* frightened!"

"Then why you laugh?"

"I was positively . . . uh . . . hysterical with fear!"

The goblin grinned shyly, hopefully. "No kidding?"

"Truly," she declared firmly, coyly adding, "I don't believe my heart will stop pounding until I've had a drink."

So she missed the 5:03 and Klotsch took her to a nearby Chinese restaurant where the bartender mixed excellent zombies. Just as her mother always warned, Daphne was stuck paying the bar bill. But somehow, she didn't mind.

Ms. Daphne Arabella Lipshutz (age: 28½; weight: 110 lbs., wears contact lenses) wedded Klotsch the following spring despite her mother's protests that she surely could have found a nice Jewish goblin somewhere.

"And what about the children?" she shrilled. "Suppose they resemble their father?"

Daphne shrugged. "He's not bad once you get used to him."

With the combined aid of his wife and the New York State Department of Labor, Klotsch found work in an amusement park fun house, where he made such a hit that a talent scout caught his act and signed him up. Since then, the goblin has made several horror films, appears on TV talk shows (as guest host on one of them), endorses a brand of green toothpaste and is part owner of a line of Hallowe'en masks. The couple moved to the suburbs, where Mrs. Lipshutz often visits her illustrious son-in-law.

The only unfortunate result of their marriage is that it has worked wonders with Daphne's complexion. But Klotsch is too considerate to mention his disappointment.

This is a lesson story. It doesn't start out that way, and it doesn't read that way. It doesn't strike you until it's over that George Effinger isn't being funny-funny ha-ha in "Unferno." That's because it *is* funny. Why, it's as downright amusing as Hell can be.

It's not that complicated, really. One of those mistake-in-transportation stories. We've seen them before. Poor schnook ends up in a place where he doesn't belong and has to cope. I've written some myself. Inevitably, he or she ends up coping, and in the coping lies the story.

The central character in "Unferno" copes too. Methodically, bewilderingly, but he copes. Nothing so surprising about that, is there?

That's what's so shocking.

Unferno

GEORGE ALEC EFFINGER

MORTON ROSENTHAL WAS A SMALL, mousy man who, in another story, had murdered his wife and ground her into hamburger. We'd better get a good look at him here while he's still vaguely connected to his earthly form; he'd just died, you see, and he was standing before a battered wooden desk, understandably dazed and bewildered. If they were still producing new episodes of "Alfred Hitchcock Presents," Morton Rosenthal would be played by John Fiedler. If you know who John Fiedler is, you have an immediate and rather complete image of Morton Rosenthal; if you don't know, John Fiedler played one of Dr. Hartley's patients on "The Bob Newhart Show," the henpecked Mr. Peterson. But they're not making "Alfred Hitchcock Presents" anymore, or that "Bob Newhart Show," either, and Morton Rosenthal himself was dead, too. He hadn't adjusted to it yet—he had never been a brilliant person. For thirty-five years he'd been a butcher, a competent, honest, and hardworking butcher; but he'd been pretty much of a washout as a human being. He would have made a terrific porcupine, and he had the stuff to have been a truly first-rate weasel. But you get the idea.

"You got that?" asked the angel with the deep voice.

Rosenthal just blinked. The angel drummed his fingers on the desk, looking virtuous but as nearly impatient as an angel can look. "No," said Rosenthal at last.

"Fill out the card. We got a whole crowd of people waiting behind you."

"Sorry," muttered Rosenthal. He really hated causing any inconvenience.

" 'S all right," said the angel. "Number thirty-four?" A fat black woman raised her hand timidly and walked slowly and painfully to the desk. Rosenthal looked at the card he held in one hand, the pencil he held in the other. He didn't remember receiving either. He didn't even remember coming here. He didn't remember—

—dying. His eyes opened wide. He was dead, really *dead*. "Oh, my God," he said to himself. He knew what being dead meant; it meant that everyone who had ever lived would know every little humiliating thing about him. They were all waiting for him here, especially Rose, his USDA prime-cut wife. He was in for it now. His mouth got very dry and his ears started to ring. He had never felt so guilty in his life, and he knew that this was absolutely the worst place he could be to be guilty. They had their coldly methodical ways of adding up your score, he figured; and he sensed, too, that it was just about half an hour too late to try to get by on charm. He didn't yet have any idea how closely this Afterlife matched the various versions he'd heard about or imagined on Earth, but it didn't make much difference: there weren't many of them that welcomed uxoricides with open arms.

The card. Rosenthal looked down at the card. The first question on it was: *How long has it been since your last confession?*

Talk about shocked! Rosenthal just stared at it uncomprehendingly. Slowly, like sewage backing up in the pipes of his old Brooklyn apartment, meaning attached itself to the separate letters, then to entire words, and at last to the question as a whole. They wanted to know how long it had been since he'd "been to confession." Rosenthal knew he was really getting off on the wrong foot here, and there didn't seem to be any way to make himself more acceptable. He went up to the desk and waited until the angel finished giving the same set of instructions to a freckled little boy. The angel glanced up. "You're not number forty-six, are you?"

"No," admitted Rosenthal. "I was number thirty-three. You want to know how long it's been since my last confession, and I'm not even Catholic."

The angel sighed. "Sorry about that, mate," he said. "Give me back that card, then go over to desk R. Tell the angel your name and she'll punch you up on her terminal. Actually, you've saved yourself some time this way."

"Is that good?" asked Rosenthal.

"Probably not," said the angel.

"Look, I'm really sorry." Rosenthal was now banking heavily on the forgiveness-and-mercy angle.

The angel smiled sadly. "You people *always* try that one. Well, we'll see how sorry you can be. Go over to desk R."

None of that sounded good to Rosenthal. He was about ready to throw up by the time he found desk R. There was a crowd there, too, and he took a number and waited. His feet and legs were getting tired. He didn't know where he was, exactly—it was like God's equivalent of the Atlanta airport, where everybody had to go before they could go where they were *supposed* to go—but they didn't have chairs for the transients, only for the employees. There was no way to tell how long he'd been waiting, either. Nobody wanted to get into a conversation; everybody just stood around and stared at the ground or at the card or form he was holding. Everyone looked guilty. Everyone *was* guilty. So when his number was called, Rosenthal went quickly to the desk, faced an angel with green eyes, and put on a pleasant expression. His stomach was knotted tighter than when the IRS had called him in for audits. Rosenthal suspected that everyone here was in the same boat with him, so if he looked even a little more co-operative by comparison, it couldn't hurt. He forced himself to smile. "Hello," he said, "they sent me over here because I'm not a Catholic and—"

"Name?" asked the angel.

"Rosenthal, Morton M."

"M or N?" she asked.

"M," said Rosenthal. "As in 'Mary.'" He tried to smile winningly again.

"Your middle name is Mary?" she said dubiously.

"No," said Rosenthal, feeling like he was trapped in a Kafka story, "my middle initial is M as in 'Mary.' My middle name is Mendel."

"Social Security Number?"

It took some thought to remember it in this context, but he told her. "Just a moment," said the angel, entering the data.

"The other angel said this would be quicker, but he didn't explain what that meant. I mean, do you *have* to be Catholic to get into Heaven? That sounds a little, forgive me, unfair, if you know what I mean. I always thought if you just did your best, you know, lived a good life—"

Suddenly, as Rosenthal's luck would have it, there was a great uproar, a raising of voices in song and cheers, a tumult never heard on Earth, a celebration that gladdened the heart and elevated the spirit. Rosenthal turned to stare in wonder and glimpsed, far in the heavenly distance, what appeared to be troops of angels, legions of angels, great armies of angels marching, while all around yet more angels greeted them and welcomed them with an immeasurable outpouring of joy. The angel with the green eyes at desk R rose from her seat and put a hand to her throat. "My goodness," she whispered.

"What is it?" asked Rosenthal. As they drew nearer, the columns of angels seemed ragged and dirty, their wings ruffled, their pennons torn, their lances bent. What place were they returning from, and what great battle had they fought? "What is it?" asked Rosenthal again.

"I'm not sure," said the angel. She looked at him briefly, then back at the astonishing sight, then at her computer terminal. "I really want to join the jubilation, but my duty is to deal with you first."

"I'm really sorry about that," said Rosenthal. "I hope it won't—"

"Hey, mister," said the angel in an outraged voice, "you don't *have* to be Catholic to get into Heaven. You were just given the wrong card; but this says you murdered your wife! So what are you giving me a song-and-dance for?" She raised one angelic hand, slowly closing all the fingers but the index, and jabbed down at a button on her desk. "You go straight to Hell, buster," she said, evidently glad to get rid of him.

Everything went black, and Rosenthal felt as if he were moving in every direction at once. There was a kind of loud, thunderish noise, like at the beginning of *Finnegans Wake*. He realized that now he'd probably never find out what was going on in Heaven just before he left; it hadn't yet occurred to him that very soon he'd have more immediate problems to occupy his attention.

Well, not *very* soon. Travel-time Heaven to Hell, including recovery period, is nine days and nights (according to legend); that's how long it takes for the first coherent thoughts to begin to work their way into the mind, thoughts of lost bliss and eternal pain. After Rosenthal had lain nine days and nights confounded, he began to get his senses back; it was like supernatural jet lag. Hell was hot; but, of course, that came as no surprise. He'd expected fire and brimstone, though he had no clear idea what brimstone was. He thought brimstone was a tool of some kind, maybe used in the hat business to flatten out brims. He thought brimstone was a kind of inconvenience, as in "she weighted him down like a brimstone around the neck." As it turned out, he was wrong. Brimstone is an old word for sulfur and, when combined with fire, is very unpleasant to have to lie around in. Rosenthal climbed out of the fire and brimstone as soon as he could, and sat down on a hot rock to think and clear his head.

His first realization was that he was now naked. He hadn't felt naked in Heaven; he'd simply been unaware. Now he *was* aware, and he didn't like being naked. It made him feel very vulnerable. Hell does that to you: it breaks down your confidence, it makes you feel vulnerable. And there certainly are a great number of things to be vulnerable to in Hell, as well. It's a very carefully planned place, like a gigantic anti-amusement park. Rosenthal sat on the rock, feeling it scorching his skin, and looked out across the burning lake of sulfur. Noxious clouds of gas wafted through the gloom; the heat was intolerable; and however Rosenthal shifted position, he found no relief from the torment. He shrugged. That was the idea, he supposed, but he didn't have to like it. He stood up again on one foot until he couldn't bear it any longer, then hopped to the other foot, then sat down, then stood up again—this was going to be a hell of a way to spend eternity. At least there were no devils with pitchforks poking at him—

—no devils at all in sight. There *should* have been, Rosenthal thought. Devils would have made a nice symmetry with the angels he'd seen in Heaven. As a matter of fact, search as he might, Rosenthal neither saw nor heard another being of any sort, anywhere. No damned souls, no gleeful demons—he appeared to be all alone. Maybe that was his punishment, maybe he was supposed to wander around this immense and awful place alone forever. He shrugged again; he thought he could handle that, if that was the worst of it. He decided to take the measure of his prison, because that was the appropriate thing to do at this point in an adventure. You pace your cell, you catalogue whatever objects your jailer permits you to have, you seek weaknesses where you know there are none, you tap on walls and try to communicate.

Rosenthal skipped from one foot to the other, wanting to see what was in the direction opposite of the lake of burning sulfur.

He came to a plain that seemed to burn with solid fire, as the lake had burned with liquid fire. This was the very same plain to which Satan swam, where he and Beelzebub first realized their miserable fate, according to Milton. Of course, Rosenthal didn't know anything about that; he'd never heard of *Paradise Lost,* and the only Milton he knew was his dead wife's brother, supposedly a bigshot in the *schmatte* trade who always had a million reasons why his mother should stay with Rosenthal and his wife because this *macher-schmacher* Milton had all his money tied up in his spring collection or he was too busy wheeling and dealing to worry about the old lady or something. Rosenthal made a wry face; Milton would learn a thing or two when he died. There was something in there about honoring your father and mother, Rosenthal recalled. He wished he could be there when some angel asked Milton about *his* last confession.

Rosenthal, just as others before him, began slowly to comprehend the immensity of punishment. It was hot. It was gloomy—all the flames cast "no light, but rather darkness visible" (as Milton put it). It stank. It reminded Rosenthal very much of the apartment on Second Avenue he'd lived in as a child, where his own parents had stayed until they'd succumbed to old age. He had never been able to persuade them to move— uptown, to Florida, anywhere but Second Avenue. His father had once waved an arm that took in all of that small, cabbage-reeking apartment and said, "There's nothing either good or bad, but thinking makes it so." Rosenthal didn't know what the hell the old man had meant. He just knew his mother and father wouldn't leave that apartment if Eddie Cantor himself came back from the dead to talk to them about it.

Rosenthal hopped from one foot to the other. "Goddamn it," he shouted in agony, "I wish my goddamn feet would stop burning!" And just like that, his feet stopped burning.

"Hey," said Rosenthal. He took a couple of steps around the fiery plain, testing. He was surprised, a little puzzled. The soles of his feet had cooled, or rather they had toughened so that it no longer tortured him quite so much to stand in one place. He looked down at himself and was not pleased by what he saw: his skin had become tough and leathery and the color of old, scuffed shoes. He was as ugly as—pardon the expression —homemade sin. After a moment's thought, however, he shrugged. "So nu," he said, "if I have to look like the outside of a football, I'll look like the outside of a football. At least I won't die from hopping around." He learned that he could walk anywhere, sit anywhere, even lie down and rest for short periods without too much discomfort. There was always *some* pain after a while; but, naturally, this was Hell. You couldn't expect miracles.

He pushed his luck—what could he lose? "I don't like being naked, either," he said. "What if somebody should come by?" And just like that, he was wearing some kind of scratchy, rough, ill-fitting, foul-smelling robe. "Feh," he said, but at least he had clothes.

He headed across the murky plain, hoping that moving around a little would air out his robe. He chewed his lip and thought. "How about something to drink?" he said. And just like that, he had a mug filled with something that tasted exactly like his Uncle Sammy's homemade wine. Once his Uncle Sammy had tipped over ten gallons of that wine in his basement, and he never had a roach problem down there again. It was the worst stuff in the world. Rosenthal swallowed it, grimacing; hell, what could you expect, Manischewitz Concord Grape?

His eyes opened wider as he realized that life in Hell might not be so terrible, if he had some kind of unseen delivery service to take care of his wants. As a matter of fact, as he considered one thing and another, it was almost comfortable. It wasn't so bad as he had imagined; it wasn't much worse than getting stuck on the subway at rush hour, except here he didn't have all those sweaty, obnoxious people jammed in his face. He had privacy and leisure and, if it hadn't been Hell and if he hadn't still suffered every moment, he would have had peace. He heard his mother's voice saying, a million times, "You can't have everything, Morty. You can't have everything."

After he accepted the tolerable nature of his situation, he grew bewildered. After all, he had been cast out of Heaven (or, at least, Heaven's front office). He had been sent to Hell; he shouldn't be in such a good mood. Sure, the darkness and the stench and the scorching still unsettled him. Let's be truthful—if he paid any close attention to the panorama of desolation around him, he began to quake with dread and despair. Still, he shouldn't have it so good. He shouldn't have been able to wish up his tough, blackened hide and clothes and his Uncle Sammy's godawful wine. He should have been denied everything. But he wasn't about to bring that to anybody's attention.

Rosenthal shuffled across the incandescent plain until he thought he saw a wall in the distance, looming ominously through the smoky dimness. "Then there's an end to Hell," he said. That notion cheered him a little. He had no way of knowing how much time had passed as he walked; he became neither hungry nor tired, and his surroundings did not change a single detail from eon to eon. He may have walked hours or days or years—he could not say. At last, however, he came to the blackfaced cliff that bordered the plain. It rose up straight and formidable like the shaft of a great well. Rosenthal guessed that this barrier surrounded the whole of the plain with the burning lake in the center. Although the cliff slanted slightly away from the true vertical, it was still too steep and sheer for Rosenthal to climb. He stood gazing upward into the hazy heights, lost in thought, until he was startled by the sound of a voice behind him. The voice was terrified. "*Mama!*" it screamed.

Rosenthal turned and saw a young, fat, pimply girl with straggly brown hair and broad, coarse features. She was the kind of unhappy girl Rosenthal always used to see in the company of a tall, lithe blond beauty who knew better how to fit into a sweater. Here was the drab companion sundered from her attractive friend, helpless now and alone. She was bent over, trying vainly to hide her flabby nakedness. It was an impossible task; it would have been an impossible task with the aid of an army-surplus canvas tent, and all she had to cover herself with were her hands and forearms. Perhaps out of pity, perhaps out of something less generous, Rosenthal turned his back on her.

"I'm freezing!" she cried.

Rosenthal didn't turn around. "Freezing? This is Hell, stupid. It's hot as hell around here."

"I'm *freezing!* I've *been* freezing ever since I fell into that lake of ice."

Lake of ice. Rosenthal had to think about that, now: *What* lake of ice? A lake like that didn't have a snowball's chance of lasting a minute in this place. "You're cold?" he asked. He still hadn't turned around; remembering what that girl looked like, he was prepared to spend the rest of eternity like that.

"Of *course* I'm cold! Aren't *you?*"

"I haven't been this hot since I was in Phoenix in 1950," said Rosenthal. "And at least in Phoenix a person can sit down inside a little without having to worry about getting heat stroke."

"I don't understand," said the girl, frightened. "I'm so cold and you're complaining of the heat."

"I came out of a lake of fire and you came out of a lake of ice," said Rosenthal, shrugging. "This is Hell. If you wanted things easy to understand, you shouldn't have died."

"Listen—" she began.

Rosenthal got tired of carrying on a conversation with his face to the rocky wall. He turned around and the girl dropped to her dimpled knees. "Jesus!" she cried, startled by his appearance.

"You'll forgive me," said Rosenthal, "you've got the wrong boy."

"You . . . you . . ." She couldn't get her mouth to form more words.

"*What,* girl? You're wasting my time."

She tried covering herself again, doing no better on the second attempt. She looked like she was on the verge of fainting. "*You* must be the devil! You're all . . . all leathery and awful and . . ." Her voice trailed away and she *did* faint.

Rosenthal rolled his eyes upward. "She thinks I'm the devil," he muttered. He watched her plop on the ground and lie there for a little while; then she started to wake up.

Her eyelids fluttered, and then she opened them. "Oh, my *God,*" she whispered.

"Wrong again."

"Satan."

Rosenthal had a flash of inspiration. If she thought he was the devil, what the hell? "So what's wrong?" he asked solicitously.

She gave him a horrified look. "What are you going to do with me?" she asked.

"Not a damn thing. I'm busy."

"I fell for nine days and landed in that lake of ice, pulled myself out and walked all the way here, but you're not going to *do* anything?"

He gave her a trial leer. "Are you disappointed? You have any suggestions?"

She shuddered. "No, Your Majesty," she said weakly.

"You don't have to be afraid of me, sweetheart. Why are you here?"

"You don't know, Your Majesty?"

"And if it's all the same, you can stop with that Your Majesty business, too. No, I *don't* know. What do you think I am, all-knowing or something?"

It was her turn to be confused. "They said I broke the First Commandment."

"Uh huh. Which one is that? I forget."

"Listen," said the plump girl, "can I have something to wear? I'm still freezing."

"You're still naked," said Rosenthal, leering again. He was getting the hang of it.

"Well, yeah, that too."

"Wish for it. Just wish for some clothes."

The girl looked dubious, but did as she was told. "I wish I had something nice to wear," she said in a quavery voice.

Nothing happened. No nice outfit appeared, not even a cruddy poodle skirt and a blouse with a Peter Pan collar. "How about that," marveled Rosenthal.

"What's the joke?" asked the girl.

"Nothing," he said. "I want a robe for this girl here," he said in a loud voice. And just like that, she had a robe. It was every bit as disgusting as his.

"Thank you, O Satan," she said meekly. She slipped, somewhat disconsolately, into the filthy garment.

"Okay," said Rosenthal, "we still got business. You were telling me about your commandment."

The girl nodded. "It's the one about worshiping false idols. They said I was paying too much attention to this graven image. They said I was the first one to get busted on that rap in a couple of hundred years." She added that with a defiant touch of pride. "They asked me if I wanted to repent my words and deeds. I said no. They hit the button, and I ended up here."

Rosenthal shook his head. "I would have gone along with them. They never gave me a chance to repent. Bing bang, here I am."

"Yes, sir."

"So what kind of graven image were you worshiping?"

"I had this kind of shrine set up in my locker at school—I went to Ste. Nitouche's Academy in Arbier, Louisiana—pictures of Dick, you know?"

"Dick?" He said it differently; apparently he misunderstood her.

"The lead singer for Tuffy and the Tectonics. Up in Heaven they said I had crossed the fine line between music appreciation and idolatry. *I* said they could never make me deny my love. They gave me until the count of ten, but I was loyal; then it was *look out for that first step.*"

"You picked Hell over Heaven on account of somebody called Tuffy and the Tectonics? I wouldn't have done that for Martha Tilton with the Andrews Sisters thrown in."

For the first time, she looked a little doubtful about it. "Maybe it was a mistake," she said.

"What's your name, sweetheart?" asked Rosenthal.

"Rosalyn."

He smiled wanly. "Nu, my wife's name was Rose," he said.

"Your wife, O Prince of Darkness?"

"Never mind. Well, you're here for some punishment, right?" She nodded fearfully. "Give me twenty pushups, right now," he said.

"Twenty pushups?" It was doubtful that she could manage even one. Getting down, with the aid of gravity, would probably be simple enough; getting back up was another matter.

"Twenty, *shiksa*, or I'll think up something even worse."

She got down in pushup position and tried her best, but she failed to do one decent pushup. "The nuns said Hell would be unimaginably terrible. I'd rather have little ugly devils with pitchfolks," she said, gasping for breath.

"Very sad, very sad," said Rosenthal, clucking his tongue. "The kids of today."

"Where *are* the devils and everybody?" Rosalyn asked.

"What, you think you're special or something? You think all of Hell is going to turn out to welcome you? This is a big operation, sweetheart. I can't spare any more demons to shape you up. We have our hands full as it is."

"How do I rate your individual attention?"

Rosenthal laughed. "I haven't heard of anybody breaking Number One in a long time, either," he said. He'd always been a good liar; he'd been a lousy murderer, but he'd always been a terrific liar.

"And the penalty for breaking the First Commandment is twenty pushups?"

"Hey, you and I are just getting started here. We have all the rest of forever to kill. Who knows what I'll think up next?" He looked around at the base of the cliff and kicked together a little pile of black pebbles. "Here, pull up your robe and kneel on these for a while. See how you like *that*."

"The nuns used to make us do this," said Rosalyn. "It's not so bad."

"Try it for a couple of hundred million years, *then* we'll talk."

Rosalyn gave him a sideways glance. "Why are you being so easy on me?" she asked.

"I like you. Can I help it? I like you is all."

"I'm not that kind of girl. You *know* I'm not that kind of girl."

"Listen, Rosalyn, sweetheart, you're in *Hell* now, grow up. What, you think if you do something wrong, God won't like it? God isn't *watching* anymore, Rosalyn, you've paid in advance. I'm not saying I'm entertaining ideas like that, I'm just saying you're not in some fancy Catholic girls' school in Louisiana anymore."

"You're the Arch-Enemy, the Great Tempter," she said.

Rosenthal was losing patience with this thick-skulled, fat-faced *zhlub*. "*Tempter-schmempter!*" he cried. "What do I have to tempt for, you're *already* in goddamn Hell!"

"It could be worse," she offered.

"You tell me how."

She shifted uneasily on the sharp pebbles. "I could have bat-winged things with horns pouring molten lead down my throat. I could have scaly fiends flaying the flesh off my bones while spiders crawled all over me and snakes and lizards chewed at my eyeballs. Lots of things."

"You got some good ideas, *bubeleh*," said Rosenthal. He genuinely admired her imagination; of course, a lot of the credit had to go to her Catholic school upbringing. Still, he saw that she might be valuable to have around. "There's always a place in the organization for somebody with ideas."

"You mean—"

He raised a hand, admonishing her. "I'm not promising anything, you can't hold me to it. I'm just saying that sometimes there's an opening every quintillion years or so, and I like to surround myself with bright people. You could work your way out of the class of tortur*ees* and into the tortur*ers*. It's still unpleasant; but unless you have a crazy thing for pain, you'll find I'm sure that it's better all the way around to be on the staff."

"What do I have to do?"

Rosenthal shrugged airily. "Well, you have to flatter me a lot and praise me and tell me how wonderful I am and generally carry on as if I was the hottest thing going down here. I like that kind of thing; the nuns probably told you about that. And you have to do everything I tell you."

"We're back to that again." She made a face.

"So what's so terrible? You were saving yourself for this Tuffy or something?"

"For Dick. There wasn't really any Tuffy. It was just the name of the group."

"Why don't you try some situps? I think I'm getting an idea." He watched her puff and wheeze her way through fifteen or twenty situps, he wasn't really paying close attention. She gave him a pleading look; he was feeling satanic, so he said, "Come on, come on, do a few more. I'm being generous, you know. You could end up back in the ice, frozen up to your *pupik* until, well, until Hell freezes over." He gave a good, demonic laugh and watched her pitiful eyes grow even bigger.

His idea was that he had to learn what she expected from the devil, if he hoped to pull off this impersonation. Eternity is a long time to bluff your way through any role, and Rosenthal suspected that he couldn't keep handing out mere rise-and-shine exercises. For the first time in his life—existence, rather—he felt his lack of imagination. Plaguing Rosalyn with the gruesome punishments she expected would have the additional benefit of entertaining him. The long haul was going to be pretty dull for him otherwise.

"Isn't that enough?" she whined.

"Huh? Oh, sure, knock it off for now. Listen, Rosalyn, I'll tell you what: because I'm giving you my personal supervision and because I *like* you, I'm going to do something I shouldn't do: I'm going to take it easy on you. *Wait* a minute, let me explain. I really shouldn't do this—you wouldn't believe it, but they keep an eye on me, too. They don't like that I should take it easy on somebody. After all, you're here for hard labor, not for two weeks in the Catskills. I get a little leeway, so I'm going to make you this offer. I want you to flatter me and treat me nice and tell me I'm wonderful and whatever else crosses your mind. In return, I'll just inflict the kind of tortures you expected with no awful *shticklech* that you'd be afraid to tell your mother about."

"Just the regular tortures? Like in the paintings?"

Rosenthal didn't have any idea what she had in mind, but he'd find out. "Like in the paintings," he said.

"You promise?"

"If you'll take my word for it."

"You're the devil. You want me to worship you," she said with some distaste.

"Oy, is that so bad? You were ready to worship this hoo-ha of a juvenile delinquent—"

"Don't you talk about my Dick that way!" She was furious. "*He* could sing. *He* could play the guitar *and* the tambourine."

"*He's* not here—yet. In the meantime, you could do worse than worship me, lots worse. Believe me."

She started to say something, then decided against it. "I'll give it a try," she said.

"Good girl. I don't expect anything fancy, no slaughtered oxen or anything. Sincerity counts with me."

"Okay, I'll wait then, until I really feel it."

"You do that. In the meantime, I wish I had some molten lead." And just like that, he had molten lead. He also had an awful inspiration for what to do with it. He laughed satanically the whole time he did it; he was growing into the part.

Just before all the molten lead was used up, a thin baritone voice called out to him. The man didn't sound so fearful as Rosalyn had. "Try tilting her upper body back a little more," the man said.

"So fine, that's just what I need now, a *kibitzer*," said Rosenthal. "You're not here to help. Your puny *aroysgevorfineh* soul's here to get its own share of the hot lead, smartie. Take a number, I'll be right with you."

"*Grüss Gott!* A Jew!"

Rosenthal gave the man a long, chilly, intimidating stare. "Watch it, *bubie*, remember who you're dealing with. I can appear a million different ways and I can speak a million different languages. So what are you, some kind of Nazi?"

"Yes," said the man. He was tall and skinny and young, with a sloppily trimmed beard; he looked more like the devil than Rosenthal did. He seemed perfectly unconcerned about being naked.

"Ai-yi-*yi*." Rosenthal wondered if *he* was torturing these people, or if they'd been sent to torture *him*. "And stop *grüssing Gott* around here, you're too late for that. And it gives me a pain, too."

"Sorry," said the man.

"Name?"

"Friedman, Lamar S."

"Friedman? Aha."

"My family's Lutheran."

"Of course it is. Offense?"

"Generally good, but I could have used more depth up the middle."

"What the hell does that mean?"

"Sorry," Friedman said, "I did some high school football coaching. Want to know why I'm here? I committed an unforgivable sin."

"Mmneh," said Rosenthal noncommittally. "Why? Your team choke in the big game?"

Friedman laughed dryly. "Hardly. I was jilted by my fiancée."

Rosenthal thought about the twenty-nine years of wedded horror he had escaped from.

"You're a fool, Friedman," he said.

"You're saying she wasn't worth it. You never even *met* her. She was some dish."

"Dishes get filthy, they crack, they break, or else they sit in the cupboard and cockroaches crawl all over them. They're not worth having your *kishkas* pumped full of boiling lead."

Friedman blanched. "Maybe you're right," he said, staring at Rosalyn, who was loudly, raucously, and unashamedly writhing, blaspheming, imploring, and hemorrhaging. It was already getting tedious, Rosenthal thought.

"You were telling me about your sin," said Rosenthal. "To be honest, you never got close to telling me about your sin, but let's pretend that you did."

Friedman couldn't take his eyes off the hideous sight of young Rosalyn in agony. "I broke the Second Commandment," he said, all his cockiness now gone. "That's what they told me in Heaven."

"The Second Commandment," said Rosenthal. "Which one's that?"

Friedman glanced at him briefly, but quickly looked back at Rosalyn. Her shrieks filled the silence of the empty hell. Friedman acted as if he hadn't heard Rosenthal's question.

"So which one is Number Two?" asked Rosenthal again.

Friedman looked very queasy. "That's the one about blasphemy and cursing. I took the name of the Lord in vain."

"That's what they sent you to Hell for? Did they give you a chance to repent?"

"Well, yeah."

"So what happened?"

Friedman's eyes squeezed shut. "I thought they were making a big deal over nothing. I didn't think they'd nail me for something like that. And I guess I was trying to act tough."

"You didn't repent?"

"I told them I didn't have anything to repent for, I never killed nobody, I never stole anything."

Rosenthal shook his head in disbelief. "You let them trip you on Number Two. They *are* worse than the IRS."

"At least the IRS will take a check, you can halfway dicker with them. Now I'm in Hell." He looked again at Rosalyn; made the connection that the same thing or something similar would soon be happening to him, too; and passed out.

"Some Nazi," muttered Rosenthal, looking down at Friedman. "I wish Rosalyn would stop suffering. I wish she'd be healed, too, and completely forget the whole molten-lead incident." And just like that, she was standing beside him in the same bewildered but untortured shape in which she'd arrived.

"What happened?" she asked. "Who's that?"

"Some Nazi."

"What are we going to do with him?"

"We?" asked Rosenthal. "*We?*"

Rosalyn scratched her oily scalp for a few seconds. "Weren't you offering me some kind of partnership or something?"

"*Bubkes!*" said Rosenthal. "Nobody's partners with me. I take on help now and then, but I *own* this place. I don't need *partners,* I need *servants.* Period."

"Whatever. What do you want me to do?"

Rosenthal smiled. "I want you should work on the new arrivals."

"I don't know if I can do that."

"Sure you can. You've got *great* ideas. You've got all those plaid-skirted Ste. Nitouche's Academy horror stories you can use; and when you use all those up, you can make up brand-new ones of your very own. You can have complete freedom to express yourself. You can develop your creativity. Who knows? You may find a God-given gift you never even knew you had."

"I didn't expect such a nice reception in Hell," she said. She was still dubious.

Rosenthal was glad she didn't remember anything at all about her own recent anguish. "I want you to start on Mr. Friedman here."

"How will I do it?"

Rosenthal klopped his forehead with the heel of one hand. "I'm a fool," he said. "I wish Rosalyn had enough power to wish up torments for Mr. Friedman and whoever else comes along, but not enough power to hinder or harm me in any way." And just like that, Rosalyn became second-in-command in Hell. She woke Friedman up and took him off across the plain. Rosenthal was once again alone.

Some time later, as Rosenthal was wandering along the base of the obsidian cliff looking for an end to his boredom, he saw a growing spark of light high up above his head. It looked like a bright star, but it quickly became a burning moon, then a blazing sun. The light was too intense for Rosenthal to watch directly. He muttered a curse and averted his eyes, wondering what was happening now. Even in Hell you couldn't get any peace and quiet. It was always something.

The light, whatever its source, flared brighter and spread further and further through the gloom. Something was approaching Rosenthal that was going to be awfully impressive when it got there. "I wish I could look at it without feeling like I got jabbed in the eye." And just like that, he had a pair of polarized sunglasses in his hand. He put them on.

He saw a gigantic callused hand. The hand, at least as big as Shea Stadium, was ill-formed and badly manicured. It was attached to an arm so huge that it rose into the shadows out of sight. Rosenthal shuddered, imagining how vast the entire body must be, judging by the size of this grotesque hand. He didn't want to know whose hand it was. It was reaching down into the very pit of Hell like you'd reach down into the garbage disposal to retrieve a spoon; and in the hand was the brilliant passenger.

It was an angel—an angel with a flaming sword, yet. "Ai-yi-yi," muttered Rosenthal. He felt an intense fear, although he was sure that there was nothing more Heaven could do to him. He was already in Hell, what could be worse? He had the paralyzing suspicion that very soon he was going to find out, God forbid.

The hand set the angel down on the floor of Hell and lifted itself back up into the gloom overhead. The angel looked up and waved. "Thanks, Antaeus," he called. "I'll let you know when I'm finished here."

Rosenthal just stood where he was. The sight of an angel in full glory, evidently on official business, was awesome. It made the clerk-angels he'd seen soon after his death almost drab. The angel of the flaming sword sighted Rosenthal and raised a hand. "Peace be with you," called the angel.

"So nu? That's why you brought a flaming sword?"

The angel smiled. "Never mind that, it just goes with the job. Personally, I think a badge or a nice cap would be better than shlepping this thing around, but it does make some impression."

"And to what do I owe the pleasure?"

"I am Orahamiel, an angel of the order of Virtues, which is a few orders above Archangel. Virtues are the bestowers of grace, and we're also those angels men refer to as 'guardian angels.'"

"That's nice," said Rosenthal. "Well, I have work to do, so if you need anything—"

"Mr. Rosenthal," said Orahamiel sternly, "we must talk."

His own name sounded odd in Rosenthal's ears. He had long since forgotten that he had ever been Morton Rosenthal; he had assumed the role of devil, and he was brought up short by this recollection of his earthly existence. "How do *I* come to have this little chat with my *op-stairsiker*?"

"There seems to have been a minor mistake made in the handling of your case, Mr. Rosenthal. I've been sent to correct it."

Rosenthal looked down at his tough, blackened skin that even yet did not fully protect him from the incendiary fury of Hell. He gave a humorless laugh. "You people take your time," he said.

Orahamiel pretended to study his flaming sword. "Errors do not often happen in Heaven," he said. "As a matter of fact, your damnation was the very first such error in memory. We're all sorry as h— I mean, sorry as we could be about it. I know that hardly makes up for the misery you've suffered here; but I hope you'll listen to the remarkable story I have to tell, and then accept our apology."

Rosenthal was more bitter now than he'd ever been, because it had all been "a mistake." Pain and suffering were inevitable, he supposed; but nothing in the world is as hard to bear as *unnecessary* pain. "You must miss being in Heaven," he said. "You must sure be on somebody's list, to get stuck with a lousy job like this, coming down to Hell when everybody else is still up there hymning and everything."

Orahamiel looked surprised. "Why, this is Heaven," he said, "nor am I out of it. I mean, it doesn't make any difference where I am—if I have to carry a message to Hotzeplotz and back—I'm still in the presence of God."

"You're in Hell now, not Hotzeplotz."

"Look," said the Virtue, spreading wide his wings, "not so much as a singed feather."

"Mmneh," admitted Rosenthal. "So you were saying?"

"Do you mind if I lean this sword against the rocks and we sit down? This is a longish story."

"Sitting hurts," said Rosenthal.

"I can relieve your pain while we sit," said Orahamiel.

"Then we'll sit."

They made themselves comfortable at the foot of the towering rocks; miraculously, Rosenthal didn't feel the slightest discomfort. It was like the sun coming out after a long, grim, and dreary day. The angel began his story. "You see, there was an interruption while your case was being processed—"

"I remember some big *tummel*. The angel who was looking at my records got up and wanted to see what was happening."

Orahamiel nodded. "Well, you'll never guess what it was all about!"

"Probably not!" agreed Rosenthal.

"You just had the unbelievably *shlimm mazel* to appear in Heaven at the *precise moment* when Satan and all his fallen angels decided to repent and ask God's forgiveness. That's what all the fuss was about. They were being welcomed back into Heaven."

Rosenthal stared at the angel, then looked around the vast, frightening solitude of Hell. "That's why I was all by myself? I thought maybe being alone was my punishment, but—"

"There was always a tradition—an unofficial tradition, sometimes labeled heresy, but that was just your human theologians limiting the grace of God—in the three Middle Eastern religions that someday the devil would get fed up with Hell. All that kept him here was his pride. If he asked for mercy, God in His infinite benevolence would grant it. Satan was once a seraph, you know, and he's been given back his old rank and privileges, and nobody in all the choirs sings praises more loudly now than he."

"While Morton Rosenthal, poor shmuck of a butcher, sits on his *tuchis* and takes his place."

"You were supposed to be asked if you repented your crimes," said Orahamiel. "Even at that last minute, if you repented, you'd have been welcomed into Heaven, too. Your angel was distracted a little by the sudden reappearance of the fallen ones. You weren't given due process."

Rosenthal shrugged. "To err is human," he said.

"But not angelic. Now, Mr. Rosenthal, I ask you: do you repent?"

Rosenthal started to respond, but closed his mouth and thought for a moment. At last he said, "Do I get a little something in the way of reparation?"

The Virtue frowned. "We're not in the reparation game, Mr. Rosenthal."

"You're telling me you don't pay for your mistakes?"

"We're making you quite a generous offer. I've come all the way to Hell to take you back to Heaven with me."

"But you won't give me anything for the physical and mental distress you've caused me. I get a better deal than that from some *momzer* who sideswipes my car. I'm sorry, but it's true."

"It isn't smart to try to bargain with Heaven, Mr. Rosenthal."

"Ha! I've got you over a barrel and you know it. You just won't admit you're wrong."

Orahamiel looked stern again. "We could see who has whom over a barrel very easily. I'll just leave you here in the darkness and wait for you to come to your senses."

"You just do that. You can't push people around like this. There's such a thing as justice, you know."

"Your choice is between Heaven and Hell. Now you must choose."

When put that baldly, the proposition made Rosenthal hesitate. "If I stay here—"

Orahamiel was astonished. "How could anyone even *consider* staying here, in preference to returning to Heaven?"

"You forget, I was never really *in* Heaven. I don't know what I'm missing."

The angel thought that over. "Yes, Satan's punishment was the denial of the beatific vision, and his memory of the bliss he'd lost."

"I never had it to lose in the first place. This Hell isn't much worse than what I was used to when I was still alive."

"And I suppose you'd rather reign in Hell than serve in Heaven, that old business again?"

Rosenthal really didn't want to commit himself, but he'd come too far to back down. "I guess so," he said.

"Your answer was anticipated. Now I must learn if you plan to pursue a course of subversion against the human race, as Satan did before you."

Rosenthal's shoulders slumped. "What do you think I am?" he asked hotly, insulted.

"Well," said Orahamiel, "if this is what you wish, I'll leave you to your new kingdom, such as it is."

"You do that, see if I care," said Rosenthal. He was bluffing, although his mind was telling him to fall to his knees and beg for another chance. He thought about his wife, Rose, whom he'd murdered, waiting to greet him in Heaven. He shuddered and hardened his heart, determined that he would make the best of it in Hell, instead. Especially if he was the new *gontser macher* around here.

"That kind of reasoning is just Satan's error of pride, all over again," said the angel, reading Rosenthal's thoughts. He just shook his head, got to his feet, and gathered up his flaming sword. "Last chance," he said.

"Thanks, but no thanks."

Orahamiel shrugged. "Go figure," he said sadly. He called to Antaeus. As the gigantic hand cut through the darkness lower and lower, Rosenthal looked away. Across the great plain he saw six more sinners approaching, probably Commandments Three through Eight. They'd all been given the opportunity to repent, and they'd all in their foolishness refused. He turned his back so that he wouldn't have to watch Orahamiel rising up toward Heaven. "Home is where the heart is," said the devil, disgusted by the reeking, foul place he'd chosen, disgusted by the newly arriving lost souls, disgusted by his own stubbornness. The terrified damned inched nearer, accompanied, he now saw, by Rosalyn. "Oy," he murmured.

Many fantasy tales are set in bars, perhaps because bars by their very nature give rise to the telling of tales and spinning of yarns. Except that the bar in this story is no more. Which in no way limits its usefulness or, inevitably, its clientele.

It's an easygoing little story Roger Zelazny spins here. Nothing of very much import. The fate of mankind, the destruction of ecosystems . . . mere background material for matters of true magnitude.

Like chess. And beer.

You'll like the characters who populate this bar. Readers who are also habitual imbibers may even find some of them familiar. Perhaps that's why they seem so natural in this setting. It's their very ordinariness that makes them so much fun to be around. Clearly Roger Zelazny thought so, as he played around with . . .

Unicorn Variations

ROGER ZELAZNY

A BIZARRERIE OF FIRES, cunabulum of light, it moved with a deft, almost dainty deliberation, phasing into and out of existence like a storm-shot piece of evening; or perhaps the darkness between the flares was more akin to its truest nature—swirl of black ashes assembled in prancing cadence to the lowing note of desert wind down the arroyo behind buildings as empty yet filled as the pages of unread books or stillnesses between the notes of a song.

Gone again. Back again. Again.

111

Power, you said? Yes. It takes considerable force of identity to manifest before or after one's time. Or both.

As it faded and gained it also advanced, moving through the warm afternoon, its tracks erased by the wind. That is, on those occasions when there were tracks.

A reason. There should always be a reason. Or reasons.

It knew why it was there—but not why it was *there*, in that particular locale.

It anticipated learning this shortly, as it approached the desolation-bound line of the old street. However, it knew that the reason may also come before, or after. Yet again, the pull was there and the force of its being was such that it had to be close to something.

The buildings were worn and decayed and some of them fallen and all of them drafty and dusty and empty. Weeds grew among floorboards. Birds nested upon rafters. The droppings of wild things were everywhere, and it knew them all as they would have known it, were they to meet face to face.

It froze, for there had come the tiniest unanticipated sound from somewhere ahead and to the left. At that moment, it was again phasing into existence and it released its outline which faded as quickly as a rainbow in hell, that but the naked presence remained beyond subtraction.

Invisible, yet existing, strong, it moved again. The clue. The cue. Ahead. *A gauche.* Beyond the faded word SALOON on weathered board above. Through the swinging doors. (One of them pinned alop.)

Pause and assess.

Bar to the right, dusty. Cracked mirror behind it. Empty bottles. Broken bottles. Brass rail, black, encrusted. Tables to the left and rear. In various states of repair.

Man seated at the best of the lot. His back to the door. Levi's. Hiking boots. Faded blue shirt. Green backpack leaning against the wall to his left.

Before him, on the tabletop, is the faint, painted outline of a chessboard, stained, scratched, almost obliterated.

The drawer in which he had found the chessmen is still partly open.

He could no more have passed up a chess set without working out a problem or replaying one of his better games than he could have gone without breathing, circulating his blood or maintaining a relatively stable body temperature.

It moved nearer, and perhaps there were fresh prints in the dust behind it, but none noted them.

It, too, played chess.

It watched as the man replayed what had perhaps been his finest game, from the world preliminaries of seven years past. He had blown up after that—surprised to have gotten even as far as he had—for he never could perform well under pressure. But he had always been proud of that one game, and he relived it as all sensitive beings do certain turning points in their lives. For perhaps twenty minutes, no one could have touched him. He had been shining and pure and hard and clear. He had felt like the best.

It took up a position across the board from him and stared. The man completed the game, smiling. Then he set up the board again, rose and fetched a can of beer from his pack. He popped the top.

When he returned, he discovered that White's King's Pawn had been advanced to K4. His brow furrowed. He turned his head, searching the bar, meeting his own puzzled gaze in the grimy mirror. He looked under the table. He took a drink of beer and seated himself.

He reached out and moved his Pawn to K4. A moment later, he saw White's King's Knight rise slowly into the air and drift forward to settle upon KB3. He stared for a long while into the emptiness across the table before he advanced his own Knight to his KB3.

White's Knight moved to take his Pawn. He dismissed the novelty of the situation and moved his Pawn to Q3. He all but forgot the absence of a tangible opponent as the White Knight dropped back to its KB3. He paused to take a sip of beer, but no sooner had he placed the can upon the tabletop than it rose again, passed across the board and was upended. A gurgling noise followed. Then the can fell to the floor, bouncing, ringing with an empty sound.

"I'm sorry," he said, rising and returning to his pack. "I'd have offered you one if I'd thought you were something that might like it."

He opened two more cans, returned with them, placed one near the far edge of the table, one at his own right hand.

"Thank you," came a soft, precise voice from a point beyond it.

The can was raised, tilted slightly, returned to the tabletop.

"My name is Martin," the man said.

"Call me Tlingel," said the other. "I had thought that perhaps your kind was extinct. I am pleased that you at least have survived to afford me this game."

"Huh?" Martin said. "We were all still around the last time that I looked—a couple of days ago."

"No matter. I can take care of that later," Tlingel replied. "I was misled by the appearance of this place."

"Oh. It's a ghost town. I backpack a lot."

"Not important. I am near the proper point in your career as a species. I can feel that much."

"I am afraid that I do not follow you."

"I am not at all certain that you would wish to. I assume that you intend to capture that pawn?"

"Perhaps. Yes, I do wish to. What are you talking about?"

The beer can rose. The invisible entity took another drink.

"Well," said Tlingel, "to put it simply, your—successors—grow anxious. Your place in the scheme of things being such an important one, I had sufficient power to come and check things out."

" 'Successors'? I do not understand."

"Have you seen any griffins recently?"

Martin chuckled.

"I've heard the stories," he said, "seen the photos of the one supposedly shot in the Rockies. A hoax, of course."

"Of course it must seem so. That is the way with mythical beasts."

"You're trying to say that it was real?"

"Certainly. Your world is in bad shape. When the last grizzly bear died recently, the way was opened for the griffins—just as the death of the last aepyornis brought in the yeti, the dodo the Loch Ness creature, the passenger pigeon the sasquatch, the blue whale the kraken, the American eagle the cockatrice—"

"You can't prove it by me."

"Have another drink."

Martin began to reach for the can, halted his hand and stared.

A creature approximately two inches in length, with a human face, a lion-like body and feathered wings was crouched next to the beer can.

"A mini-sphinx," the voice continued. "They came when you killed off the last smallpox bacillus."

"Are you trying to say that whenever a natural species dies out a mythical one takes its place?" he asked.

"In a word—yes. Now. It was not always so, but you have destroyed the mechanisms of evolution. The balance is now redressed by those others of us, from the morning land—we, who have never truly been endangered. We return, in our time."

"And you—whatever you are, Tlingel—you say that humanity is now endangered?"

"Very much so. But there is nothing that you can do about it, is there? Let us get on with the game."

The sphinx flew off. Martin took a sip of beer and captured the Pawn.

"Who," he asked then, "are to be our successors?"

"Modesty almost forbids," Tlingel replied. "In the case of a species as prominent as your own, it naturally has to be the loveliest, most intelligent, most important of us all."

"And what are you? Is there any way that I can have a look?"

"Well—yes. If I exert myself a trifle."

The beer can rose, was drained, fell to the floor. There followed a series of rapid rattling sounds retreating from the table. The air began to flicker over a large area opposite Martin, darkening within the glowing framework. The outline continued to brighten, its interior growing jet black. The form moved, prancing about the saloon, multitudes of tiny, cloven hoofprints scoring and cracking the floorboards. With a final, near-blinding flash it came into full view and Martin gasped to behold it.

A black unicorn with mocking, yellow eyes sported before him, rising for a moment onto its hind legs to strike a heraldic pose. The fires flared about it a second longer, then vanished.

Martin had drawn back, raising one hand defensively.

"Regard me!" Tlingel announced. "Ancient symbol of wisdom, valor and beauty, I stand before you!"

"I thought your typical unicorn was white," Martin finally said.

"I am archetypical," Tlingel responded, dropping to all fours, "and possessed of virtues beyond the ordinary."

"Such as?"

"Let us continue our game."

"What about the fate of the human race? You said—"

". . . And save the small talk for later."

"I hardly consider the destruction of humanity to be small talk."

"And if you've any more beer . . ."

"All right," Martin said, retreating to his pack as the creature advanced, its eyes like a pair of pale suns. "There's some lager."

Something had gone out of the game. As Martin sat before the ebon horn on Tlingel's bowed head, like an insect about to be pinned, he realized that his playing was off. He had felt the pressure the moment he had seen the beast—and there was all that talk about an imminent doomsday. Any run-of-the-mill pessimist could say it without troubling him, but coming from a source as peculiar as this . . .

His earlier elation had fled. He was no longer in top form. And Tlingel was good. Very good. Martin found himself wondering whether he could manage a stalemate.

After a time, he saw that he could not and resigned.

The unicorn looked at him and smiled.

"You don't really play badly—for a human," it said.

"I've done a lot better."

"It is no shame to lose to me, mortal. Even among mythical creatures there are very few who can give a unicorn a good game."

"I am pleased that you were not wholly bored," Martin said. "Now will you tell me what you were talking about concerning the destruction of my species?"

"Oh, that," Tlingel replied. "In the morning land where those such as I dwell, I felt the possibility of your passing come like a gentle wind to my nostrils, with the promise of clearing the way for us—"

"How is it supposed to happen?"

Tlingel shrugged, horn writing on the air with a toss of the head.

"I really couldn't say. Premonitions are seldom specific. In fact, that is what I came to discover. I should have been about it already, but you diverted me with beer and good sport."

"Could you be wrong about this?"

"I doubt it. That is the other reason I am here."

"Please explain."

"Are there any beers left?"

"Two, I think."

"Please."

Martin rose and fetched them.

"Damn! The tab broke off this one," he said.

"Place it upon the table and hold it firmly."

"All right."

Tlingel's horn dipped forward quickly, piercing the can's top.

". . . Useful for all sorts of things," Tlingel observed, withdrawing it.

"The other reason you're here . . ." Martin prompted.

"It is just that I am special. I can do things that the others cannot."

"Such as?"

"Find your weak spot and influence events to exploit it, to—hasten matters. To turn the possibility into a probability, and then—"

"*You* are going to destroy us? Personally?"

"That is the wrong way to look at it. It is more like a game of chess. It is as much a matter of exploiting your opponent's weaknesses as of exercising your own strengths. If you had not already laid the groundwork I would be powerless. I can only influence that which already exists."

"So what will it be? World War III? An ecological disaster? A mutated disease?"

"I do not really know yet, so I wish you wouldn't ask me in that fashion. I repeat that at the moment I am only observing. I am only an agent—"

"It doesn't sound that way to me."

Tlingel was silent. Martin began gathering up the chessmen.

"Aren't you going to set up the board again?"

"To amuse my destroyer a little more? No thanks."

"That's hardly the way to look at it—"

"Besides, those are the last beers."

"Oh." Tlingel stared wistfully at the vanishing pieces, then remarked, "I would be willing to play you again without additional refreshment . . ."

"No thanks."

"You are angry."

"Wouldn't you be, if our situations were reversed?"

"You are anthropomorphizing."

"Well?"

"Oh, I suppose I would."

"You could give us a break, you know—at least, let us make our own mistakes."

"You've hardly done that yourself, though, with all the creatures my fellows have succeeded."

Martin reddened.

"Okay. You just scored one. But I don't have to like it."

"You are a good player. I know that . . ."

"Tlingel, if I were capable of playing at my best again, I think I could beat you."

The unicorn snorted two tiny wisps of smoke.

"Not *that* good," Tlingel said.

"I guess you'll never know."

"Do I detect a proposal?"

"Possibly. What's another game worth to you?"

Tlingel made a chuckling noise.

"Let me guess: You are going to say that if you beat me you want my promise not to lay my will upon the weakest link in mankind's existence and shatter it."

"Of course."

"And what do I get for winning?"

"The pleasure of the game. That's what you want, isn't it?"

"The terms sound a little lopsided."

"Not if you are going to win anyway. You keep insisting that you will."

"All right. Set up the board."

"There is something else that you have to know about me first."

"Yes?"

"I don't play well under pressure, and this game is going to be a terrific strain. You want my best game, don't you?"

"Yes, but I'm afraid I've no way of adjusting your own reactions to the play."

"I believe I could do that myself if I had more than the usual amount of time between moves."

"Agreed."

"I mean a lot of time."

"Just what do you have in mind?"

"I'll need time to get my mind off it, to relax, to come back to the positions as if they were only problems. . . ."

"You mean to go away from here between moves?"

"Yes."

"All right. How long?"

"I don't know. A few weeks, maybe."

"Take a month. Consult your experts, put your computers onto it. It may make for a slightly more interesting game."

"I really didn't have that in mind."

"Then it's time that you're trying to buy."

"I can't deny that. On the other hand, I will need it."

"In that case, I have some terms. I'd like this place cleaned up, fixed up, more lively. It's a mess. I also want beer on tap."

"Okay. I'll see to that."

"Then I agree. Let's see who goes first."

Martin switched a black and a white pawn from hand to hand beneath the table. He raised his fists then and extended them. Tlingel leaned forward and tapped. The black horn's tip touched Martin's left hand.

"Well, it matches my sleek and glossy hide," the unicorn announced.

Martin smiled, setting up the white for himself, the black pieces for his opponent. As soon as he had finished, he pushed his Pawn to K4.

Tlingel's delicate, ebon hoof moved to advance the Black King's Pawn to K4.

"I take it that you want a month now, to consider your next move?"

Martin did not reply but moved his Knight to KB3. Tlingel immediately moved a Knight to QB3.

Martin took a swallow of beer and then moved his Bishop to N5. The unicorn moved the other Knight to B3. Martin immediately castled and Tlingel moved the Knight to take his Pawn.

"I think we'll make it," Martin said suddenly, "if you'll just let us alone. We do learn from our mistakes, in time."

"Mythical things do not exactly exist in time. Your world is a special case."

"Don't you people ever make mistakes?"

"Whenever we do they're sort of poetic."

Martin snarled and advanced his Pawn to Q4. Tlingel immediately countered by moving the Knight to Q3.

"I've got to stop," Martin said, standing. "I'm getting mad, and it will affect my game."

"You will be going, then?"

"Yes."

He moved to fetch his pack.

"I will see you here in one month's time?"

"Yes."

"Very well."

The unicorn rose and stamped upon the floor and lights began to play across its dark coat. Suddenly, they blazed and shot outward in all directions like a silent explosion. A wave of blackness followed.

Martin found himself leaning against the wall, shaking. When he lowered his hand from his eyes, he saw that he was alone, save for the knights, the bishops, the kings, the queens, their castles and both the kings' men.

He went away.

* * *

Three days later Martin returned in a small truck, with a generator, lumber, windows, power tools, paint, stain, cleaning compounds, wax. He dusted and vacuumed and replaced rotted wood. He installed the windows. He polished the old brass until it shone. He stained and rubbed. He waxed the floors and buffed them. He plugged holes and washed glass. He hauled all the trash away.

It took him the better part of a week to turn the old place from a wreck back into a saloon in appearance. Then he drove off, returned all of the equipment he had rented and bought a ticket for the Northwest.

The big, damp forest was another of his favorite places for hiking, for thinking. And he was seeking a complete change of scene, a total revision of outlook. Not that his next move did not seem obvious, standard even. Yet, something nagged . . .

He knew that it was more than just the game. Before that he had been ready to get away again, to walk drowsing among shadows, breathing clean air.

Resting, his back against the bulging root of a giant tree, he withdrew a small chess set from his pack, set it up on a rock he'd moved into position nearby. A fine, mist-like rain was settling, but the tree sheltered him, so far. He reconstructed the opening through Tlingel's withdrawal of the Knight to Q3. The simplest thing would be to take the Knight with the Bishop. But he did not move to do it.

He watched the board for a time, felt his eyelids dropping, closed them and drowsed. It may only have been for a few minutes. He was never certain afterwards.

Something aroused him. He did not know what. He blinked several times and closed his eyes again. Then he reopened them hurriedly.

In his nodded position, eyes directed downward, his gaze was fixed upon an enormous pair of hairy, unshod feet—the largest pair of feet that he had ever beheld. They stood unmoving before him, pointed toward his right.

Slowly—very slowly—he raised his eyes. Not very far, as it turned out. The creature was only about four and a half feet in height. As it was looking at the chessboard rather than at him, he took the opportunity to study it.

It was unclothed but very hairy, with a dark brown pelt, obviously masculine, possessed of low brow ridges, deep-set eyes that matched its hair, heavy shoulders, five-fingered hands that sported opposing thumbs.

It turned suddenly and regarded him, flashing a large number of shining teeth.

"White's pawn should take the pawn," it said in a soft, nasal voice.

"Huh? Come on," Martin said. "Bishop takes knight."

"You want to give me black and play it that way? I'll walk all over you."

Martin glanced again at its feet.

". . . Or give me white and let me take that pawn. I'll still do it."

"Take white," Martin said, straightening. "Let's see if you know what you're talking about." He reached for his pack. "Have a beer?"

"What's a beer?"

"A recreational aid. Wait a minute."

Before they had finished the six-pack, the sasquatch—whose name, he had learned, was Grend—had finished Martin. Grend had quickly entered a ferocious midgame, backed him into a position of swindling security and pushed him to the point where he had seen the end and resigned.

"That was one hell of a game," Martin declared, leaning back and considering the ape-like countenance before him.

"Yes, we Bigfeet are pretty good, if I do say it. It's our one big recreation, and we're so damned primitive we don't have much in the way of boards and chessmen. Most of the time, we just play it in our heads. There're not many can come close to us."

"How about unicorns?" Martin asked.

Grend nodded slowly.

"They're about the only ones can really give us a good game. A little dainty, but they're subtle. Awfully sure of themselves, though, I must say. Even when they're wrong. Haven't seen any since we left the morning land, of course. Too bad. Got any more of that beer left?"

"I'm afraid not. But listen, I'll be back this way in a month. I'll bring some more if you'll meet me here and play again."

"Martin, you've got a deal. Sorry. Didn't mean to step on your toes."

He cleaned the saloon again and brought in a keg of beer which he installed under the bar and packed with ice. He moved in some bar stools, chairs and tables which he had obtained at a Goodwill store. He hung red curtains. By then it was evening. He set up the board, ate a light meal, unrolled his sleeping bag behind the bar and camped there that night.

The following day passed quickly. Since Tlingel might show up at any time, he did not leave the vicinity, but took his meals there and sat about working chess problems. When it began to grow dark, he lit a number of oil lamps and candles.

He looked at his watch with increasing frequency. He began to pace. He couldn't have made a mistake. This was the proper day. He—

He heard a chuckle.

Turning about, he saw a black unicorn head floating in the air above the chessboard. As he watched, the rest of Tlingel's body materialized.

"Good evening, Martin." Tlingel turned away from the board. "The place looks a little better. Could use some music . . ."

Martin stepped behind the bar and switched on the transistor radio he had brought along. The sounds of a string quartet filled the air. Tlingel winced.

"Hardly in keeping with the atmosphere of the place."

He changed stations, located a Country & Western show.

"I think not," Tlingel said. "It loses something in transmission."

He turned it off.

"Have we a good supply of beverage?"

Martin drew a gallon stein of beer—the largest mug that he could locate, from a novelty store—and set it upon the bar. He filled a much smaller one for himself. He was determined to get the beast drunk if it were at all possible.

"Ah! Much better than those little cans," said Tlingel, whose muzzle dipped for but a moment. "Very good."

The mug was empty. Martin refilled it.

"Will you move it to the table for me?"

"Certainly."

"Have an interesting month?"

"I suppose I did."

"You've decided upon your next move?"

"Yes."

"Then let's get on with it."

Martin seated himself and captured the Pawn.

"Hm. Interesting."

Tlingel stared at the board for a long while, then raised a cloven hoof which parted in reaching for the piece.

"I'll just take that bishop with this little knight. Now I suppose you'll be wanting another month to make up your mind what to do next."

Tlingel leaned to the side and drained the mug.

"Let me consider it," Martin said, "while I get you a refill."

Martin sat and stared at the board through three more refills. Actually, he was not planning. He was waiting. His response to Grend had been Knight takes Bishop, and he had Grend's next move ready.

"Well?" Tlingel finally said. "What do you think?"

Martin took a small sip of beer.

"Almost ready," he said. "You hold your beer awfully well."

Tlingel laughed.

"A unicorn's horn is a detoxicant. Its possession is a universal remedy. I wait until I reach the warm glow stage, then I use my horn to burn off any excess and keep me right there."

"Oh," said Martin. "Neat trick, that."

". . . If you've had too much, just touch my horn for a moment and I'll put you back in business."

"No, thanks. That's all right. I'll just push this little pawn in front of the queen's rook two steps ahead."

"Really . . ." said Tlingel. "That's interesting. You know, what this place really needs is a piano—rinkytink, funky . . . Think you could manage it?"

"I don't play."

"Too bad."

"I suppose I could hire a piano player."

"No. I do not care to be seen by other humans."

"If he's really good, I suppose he could play blindfolded."

"Never mind."

"I'm sorry."

"You are also ingenious. I am certain that you will figure something out by next time."

Martin nodded.

"Also, didn't those old places used to have sawdust all over the floors?"

"I believe so."

"That would be nice."

"Check."

Tlingel searched the board frantically for a moment.

"Yes. I meant 'yes'. I said 'check'. It means 'yes' sometimes, too."

"Oh. Rather. Well, while we're here . . ."

Tlingel advanced the Pawn to Q3.

Martin stared. That was not what Grend had done. For a moment he considered continuing on his own from here. He had tried to think of

Grend as a coach up until this point. He had forced away the notion of crudely and crassly pitting one of them against the other. Until P-Q3. Then he recalled the game he had lost to the sasquatch.

"I'll draw the line here," he said, "and take my month."

"All right. Let's have another drink before we say good night. Okay?"

"Sure. Why not?"

They sat for a time and Tlingel told him of the morning land, of primeval forests and rolling plains, of high craggy mountains and purple seas, of magic and mythic beasts.

Martin shook his head.

"I can't quite see why you're so anxious to come here," he said, "with a place like that to call home."

Tlingel sighed.

"I suppose you'd call it keeping up with the griffins. It's the thing to do these days. Well. Till next month . . ."

Tlingel rose and turned away.

"I've got complete control now. Watch!"

The unicorn form faded, jerked out of shape, grew white, faded again, was gone, like an afterimage.

Martin moved to the bar and drew himself another mug. It was a shame to waste what was left. In the morning, he wished the unicorn were there again. Or at least the horn.

It was a gray day in the forest and he held an umbrella over the chessboard upon the rock. The droplets fell from the leaves and made dull, plopping noises as they struck the fabric. The board was set up again through Tlingel's P-Q3. Martin wondered whether Grend had remembered, had kept proper track of the days . . .

"Hello," came the nasal voice from somewhere behind him and to the left.

He turned to see Grend moving about the tree, stepping over the massive roots with massive feet.

"You remembered," Grend said. "How good! I trust you also remembered the beer?"

"I've lugged up a whole case. We can set up the bar right here."

"What's a bar?"

"Well, it's a place where people go to drink—in out of the rain—a bit dark, for atmosphere—and they sit up on stools before a big counter, or else at little tables—and they talk to each other—and sometimes there's music—and they drink."

"We're going to have all that here?"

"No. Just the dark and the drinks. Unless you count the rain as music. I was speaking figuratively."

"Oh. It does sound like a very good place to visit, though."

"Yes. If you will hold this umbrella over the board, I'll set up the best equivalent we can have here."

"All right. Say, this looks like a version of that game we played last time."

"It is. I got to wondering what would happen if it had gone this way rather than the way that it went."

"Hmm. Let me see . . ."

Martin removed four six-packs from his pack and opened the first.

"Here you go."

"Thanks."

Grend accepted the beer, squatted, passed the umbrella back to Martin.

"I'm still white?"

"Yeah."

"Pawn to King six."

"Really?"

"Yep."

"About the best thing for me to do would be to take this pawn with this one."

"I'd say. Then I'll just knock off your knight with this one."

"I guess I'll just pull this knight back to K2."

". . . And I'll take this one over to B3. May I have another beer?"

An hour and a quarter later, Martin resigned. The rain had let up and he had folded the umbrella.

"Another game?" Grend asked.

"Yes."

The afternoon wore on. The pressure was off. This one was just for fun. Martin tried wild combinations, seeing ahead with great clarity, as he had that one day . . .

"Stalemate," Grend announced much later. "That was a good one, though. You picked up considerably."

"I was more relaxed. Want another?"

"Maybe in a little while. Tell me more about bars now."

So he did. Finally, "How is all that beer affecting you?" he asked.

"I'm a bit dizzy. But that's all right. I'll still cream you the third game."

And he did.

"Not bad for a human, though. Not bad at all. You coming back next month?"

"Yes."

"Good. You'll bring more beer?"

"So long as my money holds out."

"Oh. Bring some plaster of paris then. I'll make you some nice footprints and you can take casts of them. I understand they're going for quite a bit."

"I'll remember that."

Martin lurched to his feet and collected the chess set.

"Till then."

"Ciao."

Martin dusted and polished again, moved in the player piano and scattered sawdust upon the floor. He installed a fresh keg. He hung some reproductions of period posters and some atrocious old paintings he had located in a junk shop. He placed cuspidors in strategic locations. When he was finished, he seated himself at the bar and opened a bottle of mineral water. He listened to the New Mexico wind moaning as it passed, to grains of sand striking against the windowpanes. He wondered whether the whole world would have that dry, mournful sound to it if Tlingel found a means of doing away with humanity, or—disturbing thought—whether the successors to his own kind might turn things into something resembling the mythical morning land.

This troubled him for a time. Then he went and set up the board through Black's P-Q3. When he turned back to clear the bar he saw a line of cloven hoofprints advancing across the sawdust.

"Good evening, Tlingel," he said. "What is your pleasure?"

Suddenly, the unicorn was there, without preliminary pyrotechnics. It moved to the bar and placed one hoof upon the brass rail.

"The usual."

As Martin drew the beer, Tlingel looked about.

"The place has improved, a bit."

"Glad you think so. Would you care for some music?"

"Yes."

Martin fumbled at the back of the piano, locating the switch for the small, battery-operated computer which controlled the pumping mechanism and substituted its own memory for rolls. The keyboard immediately came to life.

"Very good," Tlingel stated. "Have you found your move?"

"I have."

"Then let us be about it."

He refilled the unicorn's mug and moved it to the table, along with his own.

"Pawn to King six," he said, executing it.

"What?"

"Just that."

"Give me a minute. I want to study this."

"Take your time."

"I'll take the pawn," Tlingel said, after a long pause and another mug.

"Then I'll take this knight."

Later, "Knight to K2," Tlingel said.

"Knight to B3."

An extremely long pause ensued before Tlingel moved the Knight to N3.

The hell with asking Grend, Martin suddenly decided. He'd been through this part any number of times already. He moved his Knight to N5.

"Change the tune on that thing!" Tlingel snapped.

Martin rose and obliged.

"I don't like that one either. Find a better one or shut it off!"

After three more tries, Martin shut it off.

"And get me another beer!"

He refilled their mugs.

"All right."

Tlingel moved the Bishop to K2.

Keeping the unicorn from castling had to be the most important thing at the moment. So Martin moved his Queen to R5. Tlingel made a tiny, strangling noise, and when Martin looked up smoke was curling from the unicorn's nostrils.

"More beer?"

"If you please."

As he returned with it, he saw Tlingel move the Bishop to capture the Knight. There seemed no choice for him at that moment, but he studied the position for a long while anyhow.

Finally, "Bishop takes bishop," he said.

"Of course."

"How's the warm glow?"

Tlingel chuckled.

"You'll see."

The wind rose again, began to howl. The building creaked.

"Okay," Tlingel finally said, and moved the Queen to Q2.

Martin stared. What was he doing? So far, it had gone all right, but —He listened again to the wind and thought of the risk he was taking.

"That's all, folks," he said, leaning back in his chair. "Continued next month."

Tlingel sighed.

"Don't run off. Fetch me another. Let me tell you of my wanderings in your world this past month."

"Looking for weak links?"

"You're lousy with them. How do you stand it?"

"They're harder to strengthen than you might think. Any advice?"

"Get the beer."

They talked until the sky paled in the east, and Martin found himself taking surreptitious notes. His admiration for the unicorn's analytical abilities increased as the evening advanced.

When they finally rose, Tlingel staggered.

"You all right?"

"Forgot to detox, that's all. Just a second. Then I'll be fading."

"Wait!"

"Whazzat?"

"I could use one, too."

"Oh. Grab hold, then."

Tlingel's head descended and Martin took the tip of the horn between his fingertips. Immediately, a delicious, warm sensation flowed through him. He closed his eyes to enjoy it. His head cleared. An ache which had been growing within his frontal sinus vanished. The tiredness went out of his muscles. He opened his eyes again.

"Thank—"

Tlingel had vanished. He held but a handful of air.

"—you."

"Rael here is my friend," Grend stated. "He's a griffin."

"I'd noticed."

Martin nodded at the beaked, golden-winged creature.

"Pleased to meet you, Rael."

"The same," cried the other in a high-pitched voice. "Have you got the beer?"

"Why—uh—yes."

"I've been telling him about beer," Grend explained, half-apologetically. "He can have some of mine. He won't kibitz or anything like that."

"Sure. All right. Any friend of yours . . ."

"The beer!" Rael cried. "Bars!"

"He's not real bright," Grend whispered. "But he's good company. I'd appreciate your humoring him."

Martin opened the first six-pack and passed the griffin and the sasquatch a beer apiece. Rael immediately punctured the can with his beak, chugged it, belched and held out his claw.

"Beer!" he shrieked. "More beer!"

Martin handed him another.

"Say, you're still into that first game, aren't you?" Grend observed, studying the board. "Now, *that* is an interesting position."

Grend drank and studied the board.

"Good thing it's not raining," Martin commented.

"Oh, it will. Just wait a while."

"More beer!" Rael screamed.

Martin passed him another without looking.

"I'll move my pawn to N6," Grend said.

"You're kidding."

"Nope. Then you'll take that pawn with your bishop's pawn. Right?"

"Yes . . ."

Martin reached out and did it.

"Okay. Now I'll just swing this knight to Q5."

Martin took it with the Pawn.

Grend moved his Rook to K1.

"Check," he announced.

"Yes. That *is* the way to go," Martin observed.

Grend chuckled.

"I'm going to win this game another time," he said.

"I wouldn't put it past you."

"More beer?" Rael said softly.

"Sure."

As Martin poured him another, he noticed that the griffin was now leaning against the treetrunk.

After several minutes, Martin pushed his King to B1.

"Yeah, that's what I thought you'd do," Grend said. "You know something?"

"What?"

"You play a lot like a unicorn."

"Hm."

Grend moved his Rook to R3.

Later, as the rain descended gently about them and Grend beat him again, Martin realized that a prolonged period of silence had prevailed. He glanced over at the griffin. Rael had tucked his head beneath his left wing, balanced upon one leg, leaned heavily against the tree and gone to sleep.

"I told you he wouldn't be much trouble," Grend remarked.

Two games later, the beer was gone, the shadows were lengthening and Rael was stirring.

"See you next month?"

"Yeah."

"You bring my plaster of paris?"

"Yes, I did."

"Come on, then. I know a good place pretty far from here. We don't want people beating about *these* bushes. Let's go make you some money."

"To buy beer?" Rael said, looking out from under his wing.

"Next month," Grend said.

"You ride?"

"I don't think you could carry both of us," said Grend, "and I'm not sure I'd want to right now if you could."

"Bye-bye then," Rael shrieked, and he leaped into the air, crashing into branches and treetrunks, finally breaking through the overhead cover and vanishing.

"There goes a really decent guy," said Grend. "He sees everything and he never forgets. Knows how everything works—in the woods, in the air—even in the water. Generous, too, whenever he has anything."

"Hm," Martin observed.

"Let's make tracks," Grend said.

"Pawn to N6? Really?" Tlingel said. "All right. The bishop's pawn will just knock off the pawn."

Tlingel's eyes narrowed as Martin moved the Knight to Q5.

"At least this is an interesting game," the unicorn remarked. "Pawn takes knight."

Martin moved the Rook.

"Check."

"Yes, it is. This next one is going to be a three flagon move. Kindly bring me the first."

Martin thought back as he watched Tlingel drink and ponder. He almost felt guilty for hitting it with a powerhouse like the sasquatch behind its back. He was convinced now that the unicorn was going to lose. In every variation of this game that he'd played with Black against Grend, he'd been beaten. Tlingel was very good, but the sasquatch was a wizard with not much else to do but mental chess. It was unfair. But it was not a matter of personal honor, he kept telling himself. He was playing to protect his species against a supernatural force which might well be able to precipitate World War III by some arcane mind-manipulation or magically induced computer foulup. He didn't dare give the creature a break.

"Flagon number two, please."

He brought it another. He studied it as it studied the board. It was beautiful, he realized for the first time. It was the loveliest living thing he had ever seen. Now that the pressure was on the verge of evaporating and he could regard it without the overlay of fear which had always been there in the past, he could pause to admire it. If something *had* to succeed the human race, he could think of worse choices . . .

"Number three now."

"Coming up."

Tlingel drained it and moved the King to B1.

Martin leaned forward immediately and pushed the Rook to R3.

Tlingel looked up, stared at him.

"Not bad."

Martin wanted to squirm. He was struck by the nobility of the creature. He wanted so badly to play and beat the unicorn on his own, fairly. Not this way.

Tlingel looked back at the board, then almost carelessly moved the Knight to K4.

"Go ahead. Or will it take you another month?"

Martin growled softly, advanced the Rook and captured the Knight.

"Of course."

Tlingel captured the Rook with the Pawn. This was not the way that the last variation with Grend had run. Still . . .

He moved his Rook to KB3. As he did, the wind seemed to commence a peculiar shrieking, above, amid the ruined buildings.

"Check," he announced.

The hell with it! he decided. I'm good enough to manage my own endgame. Let's play this out.

He watched and waited and finally saw Tlingel move the King to N1.

He moved his Bishop to R6. Tlingel moved the Queen to K2. The shrieking came again, sounding nearer now. Martin took the Pawn with the Bishop.

The unicorn's head came up and it seemed to listen for a moment. Then Tlingel lowered it and captured the Bishop with the King.

Martin moved his Rook to KN3.

"Check."

Tlingel returned the King to B1.

Martin moved the Rook to KB3.

"Check."

Tlingel pushed the King to N2.

Martin moved the Rook back to KN3.

"Check."

Tlingel returned the King to B1, looked up and stared at him, showing teeth.

"Looks as if we've got a drawn game," the unicorn stated. "Care for another one?"

"Yes, but not for the fate of humanity."

"Forget it. I'd given up on that a long time ago. I decided that I wouldn't care to live here after all. I'm a little more discriminating than that.

"Except for this bar." Tlingel turned away as another shriek sounded just beyond the door, followed by strange voices. "What is that?"

"I don't know," Martin answered, rising.

The doors opened and a golden griffin entered.

"Martin!" it cried. "Beer! Beer!"

"Uh—Tlingel, this is Rael, and, and—"

Three more griffins followed him in. Then came Grend, and three others of his own kind.

"—and that one's Grend," Martin said lamely. "I don't know the others."

They all halted when they beheld the unicorn.

"Tlingel," one of the sasquatches said. "I thought you were still in the morning land."

"I still am, in a way. Martin, how is it that you are acquainted with my former countrymen?"

"Well—uh—Grend here is my chess coach."

"Aha! I begin to understand."

"I am not sure that you really do. But let me get everyone a drink first."

Martin turned on the piano and set everyone up.

"How did you find this place?" he asked Grend as he was doing it. "And how did you get here?"

"Well . . ." Grend looked embarrassed. "Rael followed you back."

"Followed a jet?"

"Griffins are supernaturally fast."

"Oh."

"Anyway, he told his relatives and some of my folks about it. When we saw that the griffins were determined to visit you, we decided that we had better come along to keep them out of trouble. They brought us."

"I—see. Interesting . . ."

"No wonder you played like a unicorn, that one game with all the variations."

"Uh—yes."

Martin turned away, moved to the end of the bar.

"Welcome, all of you," he said. "I have a small announcement. Tlingel, awhile back you had a number of observations concerning possible ecological and urban disasters and lesser dangers. Also, some ideas as to possible safeguards against some of them."

"I recall," said the unicorn.

"I passed them along to a friend of mine in Washington who used to be a member of my old chess club. I told him that the work was not entirely my own."

"I should hope so."

"He has since suggested that I turn whatever group was involved into a think tank. He will then see about paying something for its efforts."

"I didn't come here to save the world," Tlingel said.

"No, but you've been very helpful. And Grend tells me that the griffins, even if their vocabulary is a bit limited, know almost all that there is to know about ecology."

"That is probably true."

"Since they have inherited a part of the Earth, it would be to their benefit as well to help preserve the place. Inasmuch as this many of us are already here, I can save myself some travel and suggest right now that we find a meeting place—say here, once a month—and that you let me have your unique viewpoints. You must know more about how species become extinct than anyone else in the business."

"Of course," said Grend, waving his mug, "but we really should ask the yeti, also. I'll do it, if you'd like. Is that stuff coming out of the big box music?"

"Yes."

"I like it. If we do this think tank thing, you'll make enough to keep this place going?"

"I'll buy the whole town."

Grend conversed in quick gutturals with the griffins, who shrieked back at him.

"You've got a think tank," he said, "and they want more beer."

Martin turned toward Tlingel.

"They were your observations. What do you think?"

"It may be amusing," said the unicorn, "to stop by occasionally." Then, "So much for saving the world. Did you say you wanted another game?"

"I've nothing to lose."

Grend took over the tending of the bar while Tlingel and Martin returned to the table.

He beat the unicorn in thirty-one moves and touched the extended horn.

The piano keys went up and down. Tiny sphinxes buzzed about the bar, drinking the spillage.

---◆---

Joan Rivers made a movie *(Rabbit Test)* about the subject of this story some time ago. The movie is all but forgotten. Joan Rivers, who has turned out to be a pretty good interviewer, is not.

There's a lot to say on the subject, but in the movie, as in most stories dealing with same, it's said by others and not the subject most concerned. Daniel Dern addresses that imbalance in the cheerful, easygoing, no-problem-here style of . . .

---◆---

Yes Sir That's My

DANIEL P. DERN

I TRY TO imagine, amid our early-morning tussling, what it must be like, in her body, how it feels, to have foreign flesh pushed within me; how strange it is, that in pressing two bodies so close together another body could be formed and plucked from me. And that would be the meaning of it all, a meaning so clear that all attempts to subvert it would seem distasteful, no matter how necessary. And I would stay home and cook and wash dishes while she went out to hustle nine to five (assuming rotation rather than revolution) and the moon would go round the earth and I would feel mysterious and burbling (so they say); but I'll never understand, all I can do is hold her tight as one of us bucks above the other, and smile, feeling that I *do* understand something, and that I must pretend the rest. Or make do, accepting that there are some things I will never understand.

We drift back to sleep, and then the alarm is going off, *brrp, barrupp,* ho, time to get up. I blink hard, tap the switch for silence, and walk my fingers up the arm across my chest to her neck, chin, nose. Her face tells

135

me she has cramps, slight ones; I kiss her gently and place my palms below her stomach for a moment, then turn her on her side and rub her back, paying special attention to the diagonals behind her kidneys, where the warmth is most needed. We get up, and in the shower she pinches my waist; *you're getting fat,* she says, so I promise to skip lunch and jog, which satisfies her. Then, as we clear away breakfast and she leafs through her papers for the morning's appointments, she curses and snaps the briefcase shut, biting her upper lip between the teeth.

What's wrong? I ask. She has to go to the clinic, some special test they want her to take, a urine sample, sugar levels, whatever. *Can I help?* I offer. She goes and dials a number on the phone, chews on a nail while they leave her holding. I put the dishes away and knot my tie. *Yes,* she tells me; I can bring it in for her. In fact, they want my sample, too, while I'm there. One moment. She shuffles through the shelves. Here, this will do. Hang on.

Lawyers—even bright-eyed, red-haired, long-nosed lawyers—have to start their days early. Especially when they're just out of law school, as my wife is, and don't own or run the office, which she doesn't. Us photographers have it easier. No model is going to show her body, much less her face, before ten, and all the adfolks I know believe it's immoral to start drinking before ten-thirty. So all I have to do, unless there's work left over from the day before, is know what to set up and check over my equipment and hope it's merely another long day in the studio and not some bright sales maven's idea of inspiration to make me go out on location chasing long-legged dreams in this New York's most unlikely folly of a cold, cold winter. Never mind my solidified sinuses and blue-tinged fingers—do you know what those subfreezing temperatures do to my *film?* Not to mention my shutters? Give me a CIA special Besseler Topcon Super D and I'll shoot your frozen beauties; just spare, if you will, my poor gray Hasselblad.

So while she makes ready to go off to help honest, outraged prostitutes bring suit against the police department in arresting sellers while ignoring purchasers—tort for tart, she calls it—I hunt up a book to accompany me to the clinic, knowing there will be a wait. "Feel better?" I ask as she leaves. She nods. "See you tonight."

Her family's got this hyperglycemia habit; we check her every so often but luckily haven't nabbed her metabolism yet. She shows traces, however, so she eats real careful. Me, I got my own worries. Now they find another new test, or it's a golden oldie, or maybe they just want to keep us worried, whatever the reason, off I go, maybe we'll learn something new today.

The doctor's office is typically clogged; squalling rug rats quiver in their mothers' laps; lizard-skinned septuagenarians sit motionlessly; I twiddle a *Reader's Digest,* taking two and three readings to decode each joke. Vaguely I remember my first visits as a child: brown block toys, the bristling smell I now know to be ammonia, the anticipation of pain. My eyes take in the paragraph once again; I know there is humor in there, but it evades me with Middle-American cunning.

A starch-white nurse gargles my name.

I quickstep down the hallway and return with filled bottle and vial, extract from my pocket the home brew. Tests, yes, mumble check babble the doctor mutters, see you at pay the next week call you. Still cringing from the shot my childhood memories awaited, I rebundle and trudge off.

It's a problem day, they keep sending models with skin tones half a zone off, too dark, too light, I'm tempted to send them back saying, not cooked enough, another turn on the spit please. Finally we slide the last film back off and call it a day. That's all girls see you tomorrow and don't break that smile.

The phone is ringing when I unboot in the doorway; I ignore it, knowing you never make it in time. Settling back with a light drink and heavy novel, I brood over Eleanor of Aquitaine until another car rattles in the driveway.

She is perturbed, I can tell; I start tea and gentle her as she uncloaks. *The doctor called,* she recites, *they want me in for testing.*

I hold her and ask, *did they say why;* she shakes her head. Tea, news, dinner, work, wine, shower, and bed. I hold her again and whisper not to worry. She cries out as she clutches me, and in relaxing, weeps.

The look upon her face next evening is stranger still: *They thought I was pregnant, but I'm not; they want to see you tomorrow at ten.*

Penetration, relaxation, penetration, relaxation—whose arrogance is it to classify this act "invasion"? For every woman demanding *out, out,* is there not a male whose inner voice screams, *keep it in, don't let anything escape,* and then roll away before feeling becomes a fact. Lock it in, lock it out; it is the violation of surfaces that distresses. I cannot imagine what it would be to have her squirt inside me, fill me and lie by my side empty and drained. Nor the inexhaustible transport of her release; this jealously will never be reconciled. What soft, bleary smile might I drift with after such elevation, and the warm knowing shit-eating grin that would mist my eyes till noon?

I cannot know, only cause; rod and tongue march around her flesh like Jericho horns until she crumbles.

The office is still fey; they pluck fluids from me, prod me, ray me, invade me, with stiff lights and cold devices up every orifice, and gather like flies to prognose.

It is evident, it is impossible, I am *enceinte*.

A blessed event! Will it be a boy or a girl? Shall I knit booties and crave pickles? What are the rules in such circumstances? *Man Expecting,* tabloids would hawk. *Hubby Takes Turn—Mom Stays Mum.* Men's faces grow pale; women guffaw. They have to be carried; their deep laughter overcomes them. The rich chortling echoes down the hallways and explodes in amazed whispers. I sit there, stomach twisting; I am not amused.

Ectopic pregnancy, they chant. *Parthogenetic reproduction, reverse ovarian drift.* Not impossible, not odd. Perfectly explainable. Nature not putting all her eggs in one basket. *Liberoparous hominem. Homo anticipatus.* Their professional mumbo-jumbo permits them to gloss over the miraculous with blasé jargon, but I am not fooled. They are staggered and still reeling from the blow; all their fancy words are just a mask for their fright. I loosen my belt thoughtfully; I've got love in my tummy.

How do I tell her? Am I going to be a father or a mother? Will she be suspicious, suspect another woman? Is she willing to accept this child? My God, suppose she refuses—am I prepared to sacrifice this flesh of my flesh, say yes to the silver knife and sucking tube? Not with my child you don't!

Then again, this could be more than a mild disruption in my life: by what right would the church and others decide what I will do with my body?

Thoughts avalanche faster than I can cope: what about my job, my career? Is it all right for me to work, can I get paternity leave?

I wonder if my medical plan will cover the hospital bills. And will my dry breasts blossom in time to suckle my child?

First she is amused, then startled, then shocked. As she slowly believes, her emotions do a tango. The lawyer's cool surfaces, mixed with spousely concern. Unbelief returns; she cannot grasp the truth. Jealously. Confusion. Love. Fear. Joy. Humor. Concern. Doubt. She proves equal to the situation; she is no more capable of accepting it than I am.

We sit and think.

A strange, loving look suffuses her features. Never before has she been gentle in this way. It is a deep loving we make late that evening, almost irrelevant to pleasure. I hold her close and weep.

My belly is swelling; we have abandoned tobacco, alcohol, aspirin. Loose trousers hide my precious paunch; even so, I get comments—*Too much beer, old fellow? Better get to work on those pounds, boy.*

I banter back and look chagrined. Conveniently, the clinic has maintained my delicate condition *entre nous* and *sub rosa* and no doubt *oy vey iz mir,* but I still fear someone will discover me.

Is it embarrassment or the inevitable pursuit by the media and fanatics that encourages my furtiveness? It is not yet too late for this all to turn out a bad dream, or at least a creative tumor.

No one could be more loving, more supportive than that bright-eyed, red-haired, long-nosed lawyer who is my wife. "The entire legal establishment is prepared to defend you," she assures you. "At least, I pledge myself without cost in your cause, no matter how prolonged. So long, Mom, and all that. Here is a list of precedents I have made up for you already."

Spencer Tracy never received so magnanimous an offer from his legal-minded screenmate Kate; happy am I to have such a wife, to care for the swelling life within me.

*   *   *

The doctors are very puzzled.

"It's not a parthen," they declare. "It's clearly got both your chromosomes. Confess, sly scoundrel, how did you do it? Did Johns Hopkins pull this fast one? What perverse position did your wife and you employ that fatal night? Talk, or we shall publish!"

I stay silent, aware of my rights. Their bluster cannot budge me. I know they are relieved that Christmas will come only once this year.

She is gentle with me now, allowing me the bottom in all but our most energetic moments. Even so, my tongue is more convenient. We do not go out much; our evenings are preoccupied with reading and talk. We have much to discuss; all these years she has been a woman and I have failed to take interest except in the obvious. Suddenly I am very concerned; the rights of mothers, Lamaze and painless birth, proper nutrition, obligations to the state—I find I am less alert to the outside world than I used to be; my mind drifts at unlikely moments and fills with thoughts of sky.

To hide our fear, we joke: will she join me in the delivery room, or pace frantically outside, choking on cigars?

Someone has told the papers, the mercenary scoundrel. Peace is a forgotten concept; the household, the driveway, the entire block is littered with newssneaks. Our phone sounds like an ice cream truck. Our mailbox is overrun; indeed, the mailman has taken to doing our house as an entire bag drop. Luckily, no one has yet been violent.

The church is rather off-balance. Hurrah!

I can feel movement already. My body feels light in spite of its new bulk; I rest my hands on my hairy navel and wonder whether some mistake has not been made. Surely the noble doctors could not be wrong?

Perhaps the women never really did it at all, it is only a lie spread and carefully maintained by some mysterious power structure. It is as likely as my being the only one.

The thought does not console me.

* * *

Spring has exploded: the air is overpoweringly sweet. Birds sing, worms turn, leaves unroll . . . I feel a mysterious kinship with the earth, and cautious of my cargo I take to our garden.

Sitting in the class together, my wife and I attract strange glances, but everyone is too polite to talk to us. *I don't mind,* I would say, *come, do you believe in breast-feeding.* But beneath their distance I know I frighten them, so we do not press for company. *One, two, one, two,* we all chant together. *Breathe. Breathe. Relax.*

You have given your fellow men another tool for oppressing us, an angry woman writes. *Now you don't need us at all.* Uncertain, I ponder this. But: *You are a brave man,* another letter says, *to share our burden with us. I wish you well.*

I answer as many of these letters as I am able; their encouragement strengthens me. The others, the distressed mudslingers, I skim for originality and then feed to the trash.

Business is booming, I can report. Vicarious notoriety has brought flush times to the law firm. Multi-digit offers from institutions and periodicals cover our bulletin board. We contemplate the temptation, but steadfastly refuse to say, "Come on over."

I drink milk, take vitamins. Obviously I have not been to work in weeks; my condition is distracting when not downright encumbering, and I feel as if I am in front of the cameras instead of behind them. Well, that's what you get for not taking precautions. I wonder if she would have married me, had we been single when it happened.

Our parents, who have always pestered us to have children, do not appear satisfied by the recent development. There's no pleasing some people.

The companies are beginning to get obnoxious again; they view me as a viable sales gimmick. Entire new markets! Dolls! Sweatshirts! Advice to unwed fathers! Bah!

The only consolation I have is that *Pravda* has not yet announced the previously unpublicized case of a Russian man who gave birth to a healthy seven-pound boy—or maybe twins—back in 1962.

* * *

Well, we had to give in; Blue Cross would not spring for my obstetric expenses. We expect to win the lawsuit, but in the meantime the clinic's offer was our only hope of financial nonruin. We intend to get those hard-fisted bastards, however. Deny childbirth coverage on account of my sex, will they? I will relish watching them squirm in court. Let's hear it for the Equal Rights Amendment, brothers!

Buying a suitable nursing brassiere was quite an adventure.

It is a triumph worth crowing over. Single-handedly, I have thrown an entire medical research team into panic. Now that they've got me, they don't know what to do with me. Hi-ho, they're so confused! They'd love to be able to say, *there's been a mistake, it's only a strange growth,* but not after the X rays.

Actually, it began as a wart on my ass.

My art is suffering, I admit, but I realize I am not the first whose baby preempted a career.

When the child is two months old, I intend to go back to work full-time, if at all possible. Meanwhile, I am catching up on my reading.

I have accepted an invitation to speak before the upcoming Gay Rights Conference. My topic (by request): Male Mothers: A Viable Gay Alternative to Adoption.

Though uncertain how I feel about all this, I was too flattered to refuse.

The day has come. Swollen-bellied they cart me away, accompanied by a certain red-haired lawyer. The connection between my vast abdomen and a son or daughter seems tenuous even at this moment; it is hard to believe that another living creature is in there. I think Saul's a good name for a boy, although Minerva might be more appropriate. Though the prospect of being a househusband swaddled by mewling babes frightens me, the whole experience has been most enlightening. I wonder if my feelings are common.

They have the operating theatre all ready for me. Doctors circle like eager vultures. (A large fuss was needed to get my wife's permission to be with me.) TV cameras wait, ready to dolly in for the close-ups; should we have sold tickets to the intrigued M.D.? But viewing privileges were included in the deal we made.

It will have to be the knife. The one thing I lack is an egress; however the little bugger managed to sneak inside me, he or she forgot to provide for a graceful exit. For some reason, neither my wife nor I really worried about it; I guess I thought I would sprout a zipper in the final week, or something.

They assure me the caesarean is routine and I do not have to be afraid.

Since this is a high-class operation, well-funded, I get the luxury of an epidural. I would have insisted on a local rather than general anesthetic in any case. *I will not sleep through the birth of my child.* In their arrogant professional distance they assumed I would take a dive. And not know what they were doing to me? I will endure pain if I must, but I will be there and awake the whole time.

The insufferable *maleness* of the medical profession has never been more evident.

The nurses are all on my side. They have been good to me. Those who have children of their own have spent time chatting with me to put me at ease; they made sure I was comfortable and not worried. It was at their urging that I insisted on staying awake.

Trembling shakes my body; I grasp the sides of the table. Where are my rope handles!

A white-masked face nods; another needle sinks into my flesh. They wheel a device which sounds like a coffee percolator to my side.

Holding my hand, my wife stands by me. She tries to look calm and loving, but I can see the fear, the worry in her eyes.

In her place, would I have cared so well?

My guts buckle. I suck air and scream in pain. This is a mistake. They wave the gas tube in my face. *Are you sure?* they inquire.

Don't you dare, I threaten. My wife's hand tightens around my fingers. They back off.

Another pain. How the devil can I suffer contractions when I don't have a birth canal?

The entire event has been irregular that way.

The pains quicken. I moan softly. The doctors confer in whispers; then the head shaman steps near. He flexes his arms as if preparing to carve a holiday bird. They lift the white sheet from my body.

Somewhere below my monstrous belly hang my standard-issue male-type genitals. I have not seen them lately, being too fat in front for line-of-sight viewing, but since I can still urinate while standing, I assume that everything is still there. (Actually, I can still feel them when I wash.)

So I am cheered; some things have *not* changed . . .

I want ice cream.

Ahhh the metal is cold! Damn them! *Aieee!*

My hairless flesh prickles at their touch. (They shaved me yesterday —my belly, that is. They had the goodness to leave the pubic hair intact, as it was not in the way.)

They swab me down with antiseptics. The drying alcohol tingles. I imagine already hearing my child's cries.

A wave of love fills me, dulling the first incision's pain. I can tell I am bleeding.

The television lights shine on my skin. *Ladies, have you tried . . .* Unlike most commercial housewife illusions, my skin is not soft, but my wife still loves me.

In the later months of my pregnancy I was gleeful. I had never felt more handsome. But in the odd moments I found myself thinking, *Is she out with other women now? Other men? Do I look fat and ugly now?* Afraid, I did not mention these thoughts to my wife.

Under the bright-lit pain of parturition, my mask dissolves. I hear voices discussing me. I do not care.

My breath comes in chunks now: *a-haa, a-haa.* My diaphragm is rock-hard. They are peeling me apart like an orange.

My breasts throb. My body is being torn in two. *What are they doing to me?* Pain, incredible pain, the rush of voices, the measured beat of calm nurses ready with the instruments, oxygen shoved in my mouth, futile nausea, wrenching jolts that shake the table and rattle the trays. Shake, rattle and roll. My fingernails are ripping into my palms. *How can they stand it?* My eyes press shut in pain; my screams fill the room. No more strength now—*let it be over, please!* Hands explore me; fingers close like hooks in around the payload. My flesh parts and I feel the sucking as they lift the body from me, there is another wave of pain that blurs my eyes and I feel cold air inside me while I gasp above—and suddenly everything is silent, it is over.

In that still moment before they slap the baby into squalling life, I am overcome with emptiness; I am empty again and helpless to change it. *Put it back in!* I try to cry out, even as they begin to sew me up again, but I am too weak to speak. Reflex attempts to make me ignore my feelings, but they are too strong; reaching for my wife's hand, I begin to weep. Overcome with grief, joy, and loss, I let my tears mingle with the cries of my newborn child.

Ron Goulart has been doing funny for a long time now, though he tends to favor science-fiction over fantasy. Well, this isn't science-fiction. It's plain silly. The very *notion* is silly. It's as silly as silly can be. In this day and age. The very idea. Imagine. You just can't take something so obviously silly and make a decent story out of it. A flip one-liner, a quirky gag, sure. But a story? No way. There's no substance to it, no body, no meat, and besides, it's silly.

You can't rationalize it. It doesn't make any sense. It's too neat and easy. There's not enough work involved in the polishing. Trying to make a story out of the basic premise of "Please Stand By" is obviously an utter waste of time, and words, and paper, when there are so many more worthy subjects, so many more sage and subtle bits of satire that demand an author's attention.

Well, I can see that there's no point in beating you over the head with it, no way to get around it. The damn thing's in here, so I guess you're going to have to read it and see for yourself what I'm talking about. Then you'll understand. After you've stopped reading.

And laughing.

Please Stand By

RON GOULART

THE ART DEPARTMENT SECRETARY put her Christmas tree down and kissed Max Kearny. "There's somebody to see you," she said, getting her coat the rest of the way on and picking up the tree again.

Max shifted on his stool. "On the last working day before Christmas?"

"Pile those packages in my arms," the secretary said. "He says it's an emergency."

Moving away from his drawing board Max arranged the gift packages in the girl's arms. "Who is it? A rep?"

"Somebody named Dan Padgett."

"Oh, sure. He's a friend of mine from another agency. Tell him to come on back."

"Will do. You'll have a nice Christmas, won't you, Max?"

"I think the Salvation Army has something nice planned."

"No, seriously, Max. Don't sit around some cold bar. Well, Merry Christmas."

"Same to you." Max looked at the rough layout on his board for a moment and then Dan Padgett came in. "Hi, Dan. What is it?"

Dan Padgett rubbed his palms together. "You still have your hobby?"

Max shook out a cigarette from his pack. "The ghost detective stuff? Sure."

"But you don't specialize in ghosts only?" Dan went around the room once, then closed the door.

"No. I'm interested in most of the occult field. The last case I worked on involved a free-lance resurrectionist. Why?"

"You remember Anne Clemens, the blonde?"

"Yeah. You used to go out with her when we worked at Bryan-Josephs and Associates. Skinny girl."

"Slender. Fashion model type." Dan sat in the room's chair and unbuttoned his coat. "I want to marry her."

"Right now?"

"I asked her two weeks ago but she hasn't given me an answer yet. One reason is Kenneth Westerland."

"The animator?"

"Yes. The guy who created Major Bowser. He's seeing Anne, too."

"Well," said Max, dragging his stool back from the drawing board. "I don't do lovelorn work, Dan. Now if Westerland were a vampire or a warlock I might be able to help."

"He's not the main problem. It's if Anne says yes."

"What is?"

"I can't marry her."

"Change of heart?"

"No." Dan tilted to his feet. "No." He rubbed his hands together. "No, I love her. The thing is there's something wrong with me. I hate to bother you so close to Christmas, but that's part of it."

Max lit a fresh cigarette from the old one. "I still don't have a clear idea of the problem, Dan."

"I change into an elephant on all national holidays."

Max leaned forward and squinted one eye at Dan. "An elephant?"

"Middle-sized gray elephant."

"On national holidays?"

"More or less. It started on Halloween. It didn't happen again till Thanksgiving. Fortunately I can talk during it and I was able to explain to my folks that I wouldn't get home for our traditional Thanksgiving get-together."

"How do you dial the phone?"

"I waited till they called me. You can pick up a phone with your trunk. I found that out."

"Usually people change into cats or wolves."

"I wouldn't mind that," Dan said, sitting. "A wolf, that's accept-able. It has a certain appeal. I'd even settle for a giant cockroach, for the symbolic value. But a middle-sized gray elephant. I can't expect Anne to marry me when I do things like that."

"You don't think," said Max, crossing to the window and looking down at the late afternoon crowds, "that you're simply having hallucina-tions?"

"If I am they are pretty authentic. Thanksgiving Day I ate a bale of hay." Dan tapped his fingers on his knees. "See, the first time I changed I got hungry after a while. But I couldn't work the damned can opener with my trunk. So I figured I'd get a bale of hay and keep it handy if I ever changed again."

"You seemed to stay an elephant for how long?"

"Twenty-four hours. The first time—both times I've been in my apartment, which has a nice solid floor—I got worried. I trumpeted and stomped around. Then the guy upstairs, the queer ceramicist, started pounding on the floor. I figured I'd better keep quiet so nobody would call the cops and take me off to a zoo or animal shelter. Well, I waited around and tried to figure things out and then right on the nose at midnight I was myself again."

Max ground his cigarette into the small metal pie plate on his work-stand. "You're not putting me on, are you?"

"No, Max." Dan looked up hopefully. "Is this in your line? I don't know anyone else to ask. I tried to forget it. Now, though, Christmas is nearly here. Both other times I changed was on a holiday. I'm worried."

"Lycanthropy," said Max. "That can't be it. Have you been near any elephants lately?"

"I was at the zoo a couple of years ago. None of them bit me or even looked at me funny."

"This is something else. Look, Dan, I've got a date with a girl down in Palo Alto on Christmas Day. But Christmas Eve I can be free. Do you change right on the dot?"

"If it happens I should switch over right at midnight on the twenty-fourth. I already told my folks I was going to spend these holidays with Anne. And I told her I'd be with them."

"Which leaves her free to see Westerland."

"That son of a bitch."

"Major Bowser's not a bad cartoon show."

"Successful anyway. That dog's voice is what makes the show. I hate Westerland and I've laughed at it." Dan rose. "Maybe nothing will happen."

"If anything does it may give me a lead."

"Hope so. Well, Merry Christmas, Max. See you tomorrow night."

Max nodded and Dan Padgett left. Leaning over his drawing board Max wrote *Hex?* on the margin of his layout.

He listened to the piped in music play Christmas carols for a few minutes and then started drawing again.

The bale of hay crackled as Max sat down on it. He lit a cigarette carefully and checked his watch again. "Half hour to go," he said.

Dan Padgett poured some scotch into a cup marked Tom & Jerry and closed the venetian blinds. "I felt silly carrying that bale of hay up here. People expect to see you with a tree this time of year."

"You could have hung tinsel on it."

"That'd hurt my fillings when I eat the hay." Dan poured some more scotch and walked to the heater outlet. He kicked it once. "Getting cold in here. I'm afraid to complain to the landlady. She'd probably say —'Who else would let you keep an elephant in your rooms? A little chill you shouldn't mind.' "

"You know," said Max, "I've been reading up on lycanthropy. A friend of mine runs an occult bookshop."

"Non-fiction seems to be doing better and better."

"There doesn't seem to be any recorded case of were-elephants."

"Maybe the others didn't want any publicity."

"Maybe. It's more likely somebody has put a spell on you. In that case you could change into most anything."

Dan frowned. "I hadn't thought of that. What time is it?"

"Quarter to."

"A spell, huh? Would I have to meet the person who did it? Or is it done from a distance?"

"Usually there has to be some kind of contact."

"Say," said Dan, lowering his head and stroking his nose, "you'd better not sit on the bale of hay. Animals don't like people fooling with their food." He was standing with his feet wide apart, his legs stiff.

Max carefully got up and moved back across the room. "Something?"

"No," said Dan. He leaned far forward, reaching for the floor with his hands. "I just have an itch. My stomach."

Max watched as Dan scratched his stomach with his trunk. "Damn."

Raising his head, the middle-sized gray elephant squinted at Max. "Hell, I thought it wouldn't happen again."

"Can I come closer?"

Dan beckoned with his trunk. "I won't trample you."

Max reached out and touched the side of the elephant. "You're a real elephant sure enough."

"I should have thought to get some cabbages, too. This stuff is pretty bland." He was tearing trunkfuls of hay from the bale and stuffing them into his mouth.

Max remembered the cigarette in his hand and lit it. He walked twice around the elephant and said, "Think back now, Dan. To the first time this happened. When was it?"

"I told you. Halloween."

"But that's not really a holiday. Was it the day after Halloween? Or the night itself?"

"Wait. It was before. It was the day after the party at Eando Carawan's. In the Beach."

"Where?"

"North Beach. There was a party. Anne knows Eando's wife. Her name is Eando, too."

"Why?"

"His name is Ernest and hers is Olivia. E-and-O. So they both called themselves Eando. They paint those pictures of bug-eyed children you can buy in all the stores down there. You should know them, being an artist yourself."

Max grunted. "Ernie Carawan. Sure, he used to be a free-lance artist, specializing in dogs. We stopped using him because all his dogs started having bug-eyes."

"You ought to see Olivia."

"What happened at the party?"

"Well," said Dan, tearing off more hay. "I get the idea that there was some guy at this party. A little round fat guy. About your height. Around thirty-five. Somebody said he was a stage magician or something."

"Come on," said Max, "elephants are supposed to have good memories."

"I think I was sort of drunk at the time. I can't remember all he said. Something about doing me a favor. And a flash."

"A flash?"

"The flash came to him like that. I told him to—to do whatever he did." Dan stopped eating the hay. "That would be magic, though, Max. That's impossible."

"Shut up and eat your hay. Anything is possible."

"You're right. Who'd have thought I'd be spending Christmas as an elephant."

"That magician for one," said Max. "What's his name? He may know something."

"His name?"

"That's right."

"I don't know. He didn't tell me."

"Just came up and put a spell on you."

"You know how it is at parties."

Max found the phone on a black table near the bookshelves. "Where's the phone book?"

"Oh, yeah."

"What?"

"It's not here. The last time I was an elephant I ate it."

"I'll get Carawan's number from information and see if he knows who this wizard is."

Carawan didn't. But someone at his Christmas Eve party did. The magician ran a sandal shop in North Beach. His name was Claude Waller. As far as anyone knew he was visiting his ex-wife in Los Angeles for Christmas and wouldn't be back until Monday or Tuesday.

Max reached for the price tag on a pair of orange leather slippers. The beaded screen at the back of the shop clattered.

"You a faggot or something, buddy?" asked the heavyset man who came into the room.

"No, sir. Sorry."

"Then you don't want that pair of slippers. That's my faggot special. Also comes in light green. Who are you?"

"Max Kearny. Are you Claude Waller?"

Waller was wearing a loose brown suit. He unbuttoned the coat and sat down on a stool in front of the counter. "That's who I am. The little old shoemaker."

Max nodded.

"That's a switch on the wine commercial with the little old wine-maker."

"I know."

"My humor always bombs. It's like my life. A big bomb. What do you want?"

"I hear you're a magician."

"No."

"You aren't?"

"Not anymore. My ex-wife, that flat-chested bitch, and I have reunited. I don't know what happened. I'm a tough guy. I don't take any crap."

"I'd say so."

"Then why'd I send her two hundred bucks to come up here?"

"Is there time to stop the check?"

"I sent cash."

"You're stuck then, I guess."

"She's not that bad."

"Do you know a guy named Dan Padgett?"

"No."

"How about Ernie Carawan?"

"Eando? Yeah."

"On Halloween you met Dan Padgett and a girl named Anne Clemens at the party the Carawans gave."

"That's a good act. Can you tell me what it says on the slip of paper in my pocket?"

"Do you remember talking to Dan? Could you have put some kind of spell on him?"

Waller slid forward off the stool. "That guy. I'll be damned. I did do it then."

"Do what?"

"I was whacked out of my mind. Juiced out of my skull, you know. I got this flash. Some guy was in trouble. This Padgett it was. I didn't think I'd really done anything. Did I?"

"He turns into an elephant on national holidays."

Waller looked at his feet. Then laughed. "He does. That's great. Why'd I do that do you suppose?"

"Tell me."

Waller stopped laughing. "I get these flashes all the time. It bugs my wife. She doesn't know who to sleep with. I might get a flash about it. Wait now." He picked up a hammer from his workbench and tapped the palm of his hand. "This girl. The blonde girl. What's her name?"

"Anne Clemens."

"There's something. Trouble. Has it happened yet?"

"What's supposed to happen?"

"Ouch," said Waller. He'd brought the hammer down hard enough to start a bruise. "I can't remember. But I know I put a spell on your friend so he could save her when the time came."

Max lit a cigarette. "It would be simpler just to tell us what sort of trouble is coming."

Waller reached out behind him to set the hammer down. He missed the bench and the hammer smashed through the top of a shoe box. "Look, Kearny. I'm not a professional wizard. It's like in baseball. Sometimes a guy's just a natural. That's the way I am. A natural. I'm sorry, buddy. I can't tell you anything else. And I can't take the spell off your friend. I don't even remember how I did it."

"There's nothing else you can remember about what kind of trouble Anne is going to have?"

Frowning, Waller said, "Dogs. A pack of dogs. Dogs barking in the rain. No, that's not right. I can't get it. I don't know. This Dan Padgett will save her." Waller bent to pick up the hammer. "I'm pretty sure of that."

"This is Tuesday. On Saturday he's due to change again. Will the trouble come on New Year's Eve?"

"Buddy, if I get another flash I'll let you know."

At the door Max said, "I'll give you my number."

"Skip it," said Waller. "When I need it, I'll know it."

The door of the old Victorian house buzzed and Max caught the doorknob and turned it. The stairway leading upstairs was lined with brown paintings of little girls with ponies and dogs. The light from the door opening upstairs flashed down across the bright gilt frames on which eagles and flowers twisted and curled together.

"Max Kearny?" said Anne Clemens over the stair railing.

"Hi, Anne. Are you busy?"

"Not at the moment. I'm going out later. I just got home from work a little while ago."

This was Wednesday night. Max hadn't been able to find Anne at home until now. "I was driving by and I thought I'd stop."

"It's been several months since we've seen each other," said the girl as Max reached the doorway to her apartment. "Come in."

She was wearing a white blouse and what looked like a pair of black leotards. She wasn't as thin as Max had remembered. Her blonde hair was held back with a thin black ribbon.

"I won't hold you up?" Max asked.

Anne shook her head. "I won't have to start getting ready for a while yet."

"Fine." Max got out his cigarettes and sat down in the old sofa chair Anne gestured at.

"Is it something about Dan, Max?" The single overhead light was soft and it touched her hair gently.

"In a way."

"Is it some trouble?" She was sitting opposite Max, straight up on the sofa bed.

"No," said Max. "Dan's got the idea, though, that you might be in trouble of some sort."

The girl moistened her lips. "Dan's too sensitive in some areas. I think I know what he means."

Max held his pack of cigarettes to her.

"No, thanks. Dan's worried about Ken Westerland, isn't he?"

"That's part of it."

"Max," said Anne, "I worked for Ken a couple of years ago. We've gone out off and on since then. Dan shouldn't worry about that."

"Westerland isn't causing you any trouble?"

"Ken? Of course not. If I seem hesitant to Dan it's only that I don't want Ken to be hurt either." She frowned, turning away. She turned back to Max and studied him as though he had suddenly appeared across from her. "What was I saying? Well, never mind. I really should be getting ready."

"If you need anything," said Max, "let me know."

"What?"

"I said that—"

"Oh, yes. If I need anything. Fine. If I'm going to dinner I should get started."

"You studying modern dance?"

Anne opened the door. "The leotards. No. They're comfortable. I don't have any show business leanings." She smiled quickly. "Thank you for dropping by, Max."

The door closed and he was in the hall. Max stood there long enough to light a cigarette and then went downstairs and outside.

It was dark now. The street lights were on and the night cold was coming. Max got in his car and sat back, watching the front steps of Anne's building across the street. Next to his car was a narrow empty lot, high with dark grass. A house had been there once and when it was torn down the stone stairs had been left. Max's eyes went up, stopping in nothing beyond the last step. Shaking his head and lighting a new cigarette he turned to watch Anne's apartment house.

The front of the building was covered with yards and yards of white wooden gingerbread. It wound around and around the house. There was a wide porch across the building front. One with a peaked roof over it.

About an hour later Kenneth Westerland parked his gray Mercedes sedan at the corner. He was a tall thin man of about thirty-five. He had a fat man's face, too round and plump-cheeked for his body. He was carrying a small suitcase.

After Westerland had gone inside Max left his car and walked casually to the corner. He crossed the street. He stepped suddenly across a lawn and into the row of darkness alongside Anne's building. Using a garbage can to stand on Max pulled himself up onto the first landing of the fire escape without use of the noisy ladder.

Max sat on the fire escape rail and, concealing the match flame, lit a cigarette. When he'd finished smoking it he ground out the butt against the ladder. Then he swung out around the edge of the building and onto the top of the porch roof. Flat on his stomach he worked up the slight incline. In a profusion of ivy and hollyhock, Max concealed himself and let his left eye look up into the window.

This was the window of her living room and he could see Anne sitting in the chair he'd been sitting in. She was wearing a black cocktail dress now and her hair was down, touching her shoulders. She was watching Westerland. The suitcase was sitting on the rug between Max and the animator.

Westerland had a silver chain held between his thumb and forefinger. On the end of the chain a bright silver medallion spun.

Max blinked and ducked back into the vines. Westerland was hypnotizing Anne. It was like an illustration from a pulp magazine.

Looking in again Max saw Westerland let the medallion drop into his suit pocket. Westerland came toward the window and Max eased down.

After a moment he looked in. Westerland had opened the suitcase. It held a tape recorder. The mike was in Anne's hand. In her other she held several stapled together sheets of paper.

Westerland pushed her coffee table in front of Anne and she set the papers on it. Her eyes seemed focused still on the spot where the spinning disc had been.

On his knees by the tape machine Westerland fitted on a spool of tape. After speaking a few words into the mike he gave it back to the girl. They began recording what had to be a script of some kind.

From the way Westerland used his face he was doing different voices. Anne's expression never changed as she spoke. Max couldn't hear anything.

Letting himself go flat he slid back to the edge of the old house and swung onto the fire escape. He waited to make sure no one had seen him and went to work on the window that led to the escape. It wasn't much work because there was no lock on it. It hadn't been opened for quite a while and it creaked. Max stepped into the hall and closed the window. Then he went slowly to the door of Anne's apartment and put his ear against it.

He could hear the voices faintly now. Westerland speaking as various characters. Anne using only one voice, not her own. Max sensed something behind him and turned to see the door of the next apartment opening. A big girl with black-rimmed glasses was looking at him.

"What is it?" she said.

Max smiled and came to her door. "Nobody home I guess. Perhaps you'd like to subscribe to the *Seditionist Daily*. If I sell eight more subscriptions I get a stuffed panda."

The girl poked her chin. "A panda? A grown man like you shouldn't want a stuffed panda."

Max watched her for a second. "It is sort of foolish. To hell with them then. It's not much of a paper anyway. No comics and only fifteen words in the crossword puzzle. Good night, miss. Sorry to bother you. You've opened my eyes." He went down the stairs as the door closed behind him.

What he'd learned tonight gave him no clues as to Dan's problem. But it was interesting. For some reason Anne Clemens was the voice of Westerland's animated cartoon character, Major Bowser.

By Friday, Max had found out that Westerland had once worked in night clubs as a hypnotist. That gave him no leads about why Dan Padgett periodically turned into an elephant.

Early in the afternoon Dan called him. "Max. Something's wrong."

"Have you changed already?"

"No, I'm okay. But I can't find Anne."

"What do you mean?"

"She hasn't showed up at work today. And I can't get an answer at her place."

"Did you tell her about Westerland? About what I found out the other night?"

"I know you said not to. But you also said I was due to save her from some trouble. I thought maybe telling her about Westerland was the way to do it."

"You're supposed to save her while you're an elephant. Damn it. I didn't want her to know what Westerland was doing yet."

"If it's any help Anne didn't know she was Major Bowser. And she thinks she went to dinner with Westerland on Wednesday."

"No wonder she's so skinny. Okay. What else did she say?"

"She thought I was kidding. Then she seemed to become convinced. Even asked me how much Westerland probably made off the series."

"Great," said Max, making heavy lines on his memo pad. "Now she's probably gone to him and asked him for her back salary or something."

"Is that so bad?"

"We don't know." Max looked at his watch. "I can take off right now. I'll go out to her place and look around. Then check at Westerland's apartment. He lives out on California Street. I'll call you as soon as I find out anything."

"In the meantime," said Dan, "I'd better see about getting another bale of hay."

There was no lead on Anne's whereabouts at her apartment, which Max broke into. Or at Westerland's, where he came in through the skylight.

At noon on Saturday Max was wondering if he should sit back and trust to Waller's prediction that Dan would save Anne when the time came.

He lit a new cigarette and wandered about his apartment. He looked through quite a few of the occult books he'd collected.

The phone rang.

"Yes?"

"This is Waller's Sandal Shop."

"The magician?"

"Right, buddy. This is you, Kearny?"

"Yes. What's happening?"

"I got a flash."

"So?"

"Go to Sausalito."

"And?"

"That's all the flash told me. You and your friend get over to Sausalito. Today. Before midnight."

"You haven't got any more details?"

"Sorry. My ex-wife got in last night and I've been too unsettled to get any full scale flashes." The line went dead.

"Sausalito?" said Dan when Max called him.

"That's what Waller says."

"Hey," said Dan. "Westerland's ex-wife."

"He's got one, too?"

"His wife had a place over there. I remember going to a party with Anne there once. Before Westerland got divorced. Could Anne be there?"

"Wouldn't Mrs. Westerland complain?"

"No, she's in Europe. It was in Herb Caen and—Max! The house would be empty now. Anne must be there. And in trouble."

* * *

The house was far back from the road that ran up through the low hills of Sausalito, the town just across the Golden Gate Bridge from San Francisco. It was a flat scattered house of redwood and glass.

Max and Dan had driven by it and parked the car. Max in the lead, they came downhill through a stretch of trees, descending toward the back of the Westerland house. It was late afternoon now and the great flat windows sparkled and went black and sparkled again as they came near. A high hedge circled the patio and when Max and Dan came close their view of the house was cut off.

"Think she's here?" Dan asked.

"We should be able to spot some signs of life," Max said. "I'm turning into a first class peeping tom. All I do is watch people's houses."

"I guess detective work's like that," said Dan. "Even the occult stuff."

"Hold it," said Max. "Listen."

"To what?"

"I heard a dog barking."

"In the house?"

"Yep."

"Means there's somebody in there."

"It means Anne's in there probably. Pretty sure that was Major Bowser."

"Hi, pals," said a high-pitched voice.

"Hello," said Max, turning to face the wide bald man behind them.

"Geese Louise," the man said, pointing his police special at them, "this sure saves me a lot of work. The boss had me out looking for you all day. And just when I was giving up and coming back here with my tail between my legs—well, here you are."

"Who's your boss?"

"Him. Westerland. I'm a full-time pro gunman. Hired to get you."

"You got us," said Max.

"Look, would you let me tell him I caught you over in Frisco? Makes me seem more efficient."

"We will," said Max, "if you'll let us go. Tell him we used karate on you. We can even break your arm to make it look good."

"No," said the bald man. "Let it pass. You guys want too many concessions. Go on inside."

Westerland was opening the refrigerator when his gunman brought Max and Dan into the kitchen.

"You brought it off, Lloyd," said Westerland, taking a popsicle from the freezer compartment.

"I studied those pictures you gave me."

"Where's Anne?" Dan asked.

Westerland squeezed the wrapper off the popsicle. "Here. We've only this minute finished a recording session. Sit down."

When the four of them were around the white wooden table Westerland said, "You, Mr. Kearny."

Max took out his pack of cigarettes and put them on the table in front of him. "Sir?"

"Your detective work will be the ruin of you."

"All I did was look through a few windows. It's more acrobatics than detection."

"Nevertheless, you're on to me. Your overprotective attitude toward Miss Clemens has caused you to stumble on one of the most closely guarded secrets of the entertainment industry."

"You mean Anne's being the voice of Major Bowser?"

"Exactly," said Westerland, his round cheeks caving as he sucked the popsicle. "But it's too late. Residuals and reruns."

Dan tapped the tabletop. "What's that mean?"

"What else? I've completed taping the sound track for episode 78 of Major Bowser. I have a new series in the works. Within a few months the major will be released to secondary markets. That means I don't need Anne Clemens anymore."

Dan clenched his fists. "So let her go."

"Why did you ever need her?" Max asked, looking at Westerland.

"She's an unconscious talent," said Westerland, catching the last fragment of the popsicle off the stick. "She first did that voice one night over two years ago. After a party I'd taken her to. She'd had too much to drink. I thought it was funny. The next day she'd forgotten about it. Couldn't even remember the voice. Instead of pressing her I used my hypnotic ability. I had a whole sketch book full of drawings of that damned dog. The voice clicked. It matched. I used it."

"And made $100,000," said Dan.

"The writing is mine. And quite a bit of the drawing."

"And now?" said Max.

"She knows about it. She has thoughts of marrying and settling down. She asked me if $5,000 would be a fair share of the profits from the major."

"Is that scale for 78 shows?" Max said.

"I could look it up," said Westerland. He was at the refrigerator again. "Lemon, lime, grape, watermelon. How's grape sound? Fine. Grape it is." He stood at the head of the table and unwrapped the purple popsicle. "I've come up with an alternative. I intend to eliminate all of you. Much cheaper way of settling things."

"You're kidding," said Dan.

"Animators are supposed to be lovable guys like Walt Disney," said Max.

"I'm a businessman first. I can't use Anne Clemens anymore. We'll fix her first and you two at some later date. Lloyd, put these detectives in the cellar and lock it up."

Lloyd grinned and pointed to a door beyond the stove. Max and Dan were made to go down a long flight of wooden stairs and into a room that was filled with the smell of old newspapers and unused furniture. There were small dusty windows high up around the beamed ceiling.

"Not a very tough cellar," Dan whispered to Max.

"But you won't be staying here," said Lloyd. He kept his gun aimed at them and stepped around a fallen tricycle to a wide oak door in the cement wall. A padlock and chain hung down from a hook on the wall. Lloyd slid the bolt and opened the door. "The wine cellar. He showed it to me this morning. No wine left, but it's homey. You'll come to like it."

He got them inside and bolted the door. The chains rattled and the padlock snapped.

Max blinked. He lit a match and looked around the cement room. It was about twelve feet high and ten feet wide.

Dan made his way to an old cobbler's bench in the corner. "Does your watch glow in the dark?" he asked as the match went out.

"It's five thirty."

"The magician was right. We're in trouble."

"I'm wondering," said Max, striking another match.

"You're wondering what the son of a bitch is going to do to Anne."

"Yes," Max said, spotting an empty wine barrel. He turned it upside down and sat on it.

"And what'll he do with us?"

Max started a cigarette from the dying match flames. "Drop gas pellets through the ceiling, fill the room with water, make the walls squeeze in."

"Westerland's trickier than that. He'll probably hypnotize us into thinking we're pheasants and then turn us loose the day the hunting season opens."

"Wonder how Lloyd knew what we looked like."

"Anne's got my picture in her purse. And one I think we all took at some beach party once."

Max leaned back against the dark wall. "This is about a middle-sized room, isn't it?"

"I don't know. The only architecture course I took at school was in water color painting."

"In six hours you'll be a middle-sized elephant."

Dan's bench clattered. "You think this is it?"

"Should be. How else are we going to get out of here?"

"I smash the door like a real elephant would." He snapped his fingers. "That's great."

"You should be able to do it."

"But Max?"

"Yeah?"

"Suppose I don't change?"

"You will."

"We only have the word of an alcoholic shoemaker."

"He knew about Sausalito."

"He could be a fink."

"He's a real magician. You're proof of that."

"Max?"

"Huh?"

"Maybe Westerland hypnotized us into thinking I was an elephant."

"How could he hypnotize me? I haven't seen him for years."

"He could hypnotize you and then make you forget you were."

"Dan," said Max, "relax. After midnight if we're still in here we can think up excuses."

"How do we know he won't harm Anne before midnight?"

"We don't."

"Let's try to break out now."

Max lit a match and stood up. "I don't think these barrel staves will do it. See anything else?"

"Legs off this bench. We can unscrew them and bang the door down."

They got the wooden legs loose and taking one each began hammering at the bolt with them.

After a few minutes a voice echoed in. "Stop that ruckus."

"The hell with you," said Dan.

"Wait now," said Westerland's voice. "You can't break down the door. And even if you could Lloyd would shoot you. I'm sending him down to sit guard. Last night at Playland he won four Betty Boop dolls at the shooting gallery. Be rational."

"How come we can hear you?"

"I'm talking through an air vent."

"Where's Anne?" shouted Dan.

"Still in a trance. If you behave I may let her bark for you before we leave."

"You louse."

Max found Dan in the dark and caught his arm. "Take it easy." Raising his voice he said, "Westerland, how long do we stay down here?"

"Well, my ex-wife will be in Rome until next April. I hope to have a plan worked out by then. At the moment, however, I can't spare the time. I have to get ready for the party."

"What party?"

"The New Year's Eve party at the Leversons'. It's the one where Anne Clemens will drink too much."

"What?"

"She'll drink too much and get the idea she's an acrobat. She'll borrow a car and drive to the Golden Gate Bridge. While trying out her act on the top rail she'll discover she's not an acrobat at all and actually has a severe dread of heights. When I hear about it I'll still be at the Leversons' party. I'll be saddened that she was able to see so little of the New Year."

"You can't make her do that. Hypnotism doesn't work that way."

"That's what you say now, Padgett. In the morning I'll have Lloyd slip the papers under the door."

The pipe stopped talking.

Dan slammed his fist into the cement wall. "He can't do it."

"Who are the Leversons?"

Dan was silent for a moment. "Leverson. Joe and Jackie. Isn't that the art director at BBDO? He and his wife live over here. Just up from Sally Stanford's restaurant. It could be them."

"It's a long way to midnight," said Max. "But I have a feeling we'll make it."

"We have to save Anne," said Dan, "and there doesn't seem to be anything to do but wait."

"What's the damn time, Max?"
"Six thirty."

"Must be nearly eight by now."
"Seven fifteen."
"I think I still hear them up there."

"Now?"
"Little after nine."

"Only ten? Is that watch going?"
"Yeah, it's ticking."

"Eleven yet, Max?"
"In five minutes."
"They've gone, I'm sure."
"Relax."

"Look," said Dan, when Max told him it was quarter to twelve, "I don't want to step on you if I change."

"I'll duck down on the floor by your feet. Your present feet. Then when you've changed I should be under your stomach."

"Okay. After I do you hop on my back."

At five to twelve Max sat down on the stone floor. "Happy New Year."

Dan's feet shuffled, moved farther apart. "My stomach is starting to itch."

Max ducked a little. In the darkness a darker shadow seemed to grow overhead. "Dan?"

"I did it, Max." Dan laughed. "I did it right on time."

Max edged up and climbed on top of the elephant. "I'm aboard."

"Hang on. I'm going to push the door with my head."

Max hung on and waited. The door creaked and began to give.

"Watch it, you guys!" shouted Lloyd from outside.

"Trumpet at him," said Max.

"Good idea." Dan gave a violent angry elephant roar.

"Jesus!" Lloyd said.

The door exploded out and Dan's trunk slapped Lloyd into the side of the furnace. His gun sailed into a clothes basket. Max jumped down and retrieved it.

"Go away," he said to Lloyd.

Lloyd blew his nose. "What kind of prank is this?"

"If he doesn't go," said Max, "trample him."

"Let's trample him no matter what," said Dan.

Lloyd left.

"Hell," said Dan. "How do I get up those stairs?"

"You don't," said Max, pointing. "See there, behind that stack of papers. A door. I'll see if it's open."

"Who cares. I'll push it open."

"Okay. I'll go find a phone book and look up Leversons. Meet you in the patio."

Dan trumpeted and Max ran up the narrow wooden stairs.

The elephant careened down the grassy hillside. All around now New Year's horns were sounding.

"Only two Leversons, huh?" Dan asked again.

"It's most likely the art director. He's nearest the bridge."

They came out on Bridgeway, which ran along the water.

Dan trumpeted cars and people out of the way and Max ducked down, holding onto the big elephant ears.

They turned as the road curved and headed them for the Leverson home. "It better be this one," Dan said.

The old two story house was filled with lighted windows, the windows spotted with people. "A party sure enough," said Max.

In the long twisted driveway a motor started. "A car," said Dan, running up the gravel.

Max jumped free as Dan made himself a road block in the driveway.

Red tail lights tinted the exhaust of a small gray Jaguar convertible. Max ran to the car. Anne Clemens jerked the wheel and spun it. Max dived over the back of the car and, teetering on his stomach, jerked the ignition key off and out. Anne kept turning the wheel.

Max caught her by the shoulders, swung around off the car and pulled her up so that she was now kneeling in the driver's seat.

The girl shook her head twice, looking beyond Max.

He got the door open and helped her out. The gravel seemed to slide away from them in all directions.

"Duck," yelled Dan, still an elephant.

Max didn't turn. He dropped, pulling the girl with him.

A shot smashed a cobweb pattern across the windshield.

"You've spoiled it for sure," cried Westerland. "You and your silly damn elephant have spoiled my plan for sure."

The parking area lights were on and a circle of people was forming behind Westerland. He was standing twenty feet away from Max and Anne.

Then he fell over as Dan's trunk flipped his gun away from him.

Dan caught up the fallen animator and shook him.

Max got Anne to her feet and held onto her. "Bring her out of this, Westerland."

"In a pig's valise."

Dan tossed him up and caught him.

"Come on."

"Since you're so belligerent," said Westerland. "Dangle me closer to her."

Max had Lloyd's gun in his coat pocket. He took it out now and pointed it up at the swinging Westerland. "No wise stuff."

Westerland snapped his fingers near Anne's pale face.

She shivered once and fell against Max. He put his arms under hers and held her.

Dan suddenly dropped Westerland and, trumpeting once at the silent guests, galloped away into the night.

As his trumpet faded a siren filled the night.

"Real detectives," said Max.

Both Anne and Westerland were out. The guests were too far away to hear him.

A bush crackled behind him and Max turned his head.

Dan, himself again, came up to them. "Would it be okay if I held Anne?"

Max carefully transferred her. "She should be fine when she comes to."

"What'll we tell the law?"

"The truth. Except for the elephant."

"How'd we get from his place here?"

"My car wouldn't start. We figured he'd tampered with it. We hailed a passing motorist who dropped us here."

"People saw the elephant."

"It escaped from a zoo."

"What zoo?"

"Look," said Max, dropping the gun back into his pocket, "don't be so practical about this. We don't have to explain it. Okay?"

"Okay. Thanks, Max."

Max lit a cigarette.

"I changed back in only an hour. I don't think it will happen again, Max. Do you?"

"If it would make you feel any better I'll spend the night before Lincoln's Birthday with you and Anne. How about it?"

"How about what?" said Anne. She looked up at Dan. "Dan? What is it?"

"Nothing much. A little trouble with Westerland. I'll explain."

Max nodded at them and went up the driveway to meet the approaching police. Somewhere in the night a final New Year's horn sounded.

Stories smell. No, that's too blunt. They have aromas, flavors. Some are redolent of the city, all smoke and noise and anxiety. Others have a corresponding country flavor, laid-back and grassy and full of prose that couldn't be ruffled by the most intrusive verb imaginable.

There are some that reek of the shore, long strings of adjectives crashing like heavy surf against immovable nouns. There are stories that speak of pained childhoods, and extensive travels, and inner twists of mind and fate.

Then there is elegance, a literary quality not much in vogue today. Light and fine as champagne and as difficult to lay down in bottles. Speaking of bottles, here is an *elegant* story about one, by perhaps the most elegant writer of short modern fantasy. Some stories grow on you. Those of John Collier, like the aforementioned champagne, merely bubble and get better with age.

Bottle Party

JOHN COLLIER

FRANKLIN FLETCHER DREAMED OF LUXURY in the form of tiger-skins and beautiful women. He was prepared, at a pinch, to forgo the tiger-skins. Unfortunately the beautiful women seemed equally rare and inaccessible. At his office and at his boardinghouse the girls were mere mice, or cattish, or kittenish, or had insufficiently read the advertisements. He met no others. At thirty-five he gave up, and decided he must console himself with a hobby, which is a very miserable second-best.

He prowled about in odd corners of the town, looking in at the windows of antique dealers and junk-shops, wondering what on earth he might collect. He came upon a poor shop, in a poor alley, in whose dusty window stood a single object: it was a full-rigged ship in a bottle. Feeling rather like that himself he decided to go in and ask the price.

The shop was small and bare. Some shabby racks were ranged about the walls, and these racks bore a large number of bottles, of every shape and size, containing a variety of objects which were interesting only because they were in bottles. While Franklin still looked about, a little door opened, and out shuffled the proprietor, a wizened old man in a smoking-cap, who seemed mildly surprised and mildly pleased to have a customer.

He showed Franklin bouquets, and birds of paradise, and the Battle of Gettysburg, and miniature Japanese gardens, and even a shrunken human head, all stoppered up in bottles. "And what," said Frank, "are those, down there on the bottom shelf?"

"They are not much to look at," said the old man. "A lot of people think they are all nonsense. Personally, I like them."

He lugged out a few specimens from their dusty obscurity. One seemed to have nothing but a little dried-up fly in it, others contained what might have been horse-hairs or straws, or mere wisps of heaven knows what; some appeared to be filled with grey or opalescent smoke. "They are," said the old man,"various sorts of genii, jinns, sibyls, demons, and such things. Some of them, I believe, are much harder, even than a full-rigged ship, to get into a bottle."

"Oh, but come! This is New York," said Frank.

"All the more reason," said the old man, "to expect the most extraordinary jinns in bottles. I'll show you. Wait a moment. The stopper is a little stiff."

"You mean there's one in there?" said Frank. "And you're going to let it out?"

"Why not?" replied the old man, desisting in his efforts, and holding the bottle up to the light. "This one——Good heavens! *Why not*, indeed! My eyes are getting weak. I very nearly undid the wrong bottle. A very ugly customer, that one! Dear me! It's just as well I didn't get that stopper undone. I'd better put him right back in the rack. I must remember he's in the lower right-hand corner. I'll stick a label on him one of these days. Here's something more harmless."

"What's in that?" said Frank.

"Supposed to be the most beautiful girl in the world," said the old man. "All right, if you like that sort of thing. Myself, I've never troubled to undo her. I'll find something more interesting."

"Well, from a scientific point of view," said Frank, "I—"

"Science isn't everything," said the old man. "Look at this." He held up one which contained a tiny, mummified, insect-looking object, just visible through the grime. "Put your ear to it," he said.

Frank did so. He heard, in a sort of whistling nothing of a voice, the words, "Louisiana Lad, Saratoga, four-fifteen. Louisiana Lad, Saratoga, four-fifteen," repeated over and over again.

"What on earth is that?" said he.

"That," said the old man, "is the original Cumaean Sibyl. Very interesting. She's taken up racing."

"Very interesting," said Frank. "All the same, I'd just like to see that other. I adore beauty."

"A bit of an artist, eh?" said the old man. "Believe me, what you really want is a good, all-around, serviceable type. Here's one, for example. I recommend this little fellow from personal experience. He's practical. He can fix you anything."

"Well, if that's so," said Frank, "why haven't you got a palace, tiger-skins, and all that?"

"I had all that," said the old man. "And he fixed it. Yes, this was my first bottle. All the rest came from him. First of all I had a palace, pictures, marbles, slaves. And, as you say, tiger-skins. I had him put Cleopatra on one of them."

"What was she like?" cried Frank.

"All right," said the old man, "if you like that sort of thing. I got bored with it. I thought to myself, 'What I'd like, really, is a little shop, with all sorts of things in bottles.' So I had him fix it. He got me the sibyl. He got me the ferocious fellow there. In fact, he got me all of them."

"And now he's in there?" said Frank.

"Yes. He's in there," said the old man. "Listen to him."

Frank put his ear to the bottle. He heard, uttered in the most plaintive tones, "Let me out. Do let me out. Please let me out. I'll do anything. Let me out. I'm harmless. Please let me out. Just for a little while. Do let me out. I'll do anything. Please——"

Frank looked at the old man. "He's there all right," he said. "He's there."

"Of course he's there," said the old man. "I wouldn't sell you an empty bottle. What do you take me for? In fact, I wouldn't sell this one at all, for sentimental reasons, only I've had the shop a good many years now, and you're my first customer."

Frank put his ear to the bottle again. "Let me out. Let me out. Oh, please let me out. I'll—"

"My God!" said Frank uneasily. "Does he go on like that *all* the time?"

"Very probably," said the old man. "I can't say I listen. I prefer the radio."

"It seems rather tough on him," said Frank sympathetically.

"Maybe," said the old man. "They don't seem to like bottles. Personally, I do. They fascinate me. For example, I——"

"Tell me," said Frank. "Is he really harmless?"

"Oh, yes," said the old man. "Bless you, yes. Some say they're tricky —eastern blood and all that—I never found him so. I used to let him out; he'd do his stuff, then back he'd go again. I must say, he's very efficient."

"He could get me anything?"

"Absolutely anything."

"And how much do you want for him?" said Frank.

"Oh, I don't know," said the old man. "Ten million dollars, perhaps."

"I say! I haven't got that. Still, if he's as good as you say, maybe I could work it off on the hire purchase system."

"Don't worry. We'll say five dollars instead. I've got all I want, really. Shall I wrap him up for you?"

Frank paid over his five dollars, and hurried home with the precious bottle, terrified of breaking it. As soon as he was in his room he pulled out the stopper. Out flowed a prodigious quantity of greasy smoke, which immediately solidified into the figure of a gross and fleshy Oriental, six feet six in height, with rolls of fat, a hook nose, a wicked white to his eye, vast double chins, altogether like a film-producer, only larger. Frank, striving desperately for something to say, ordered shashlik, kebabs, and Turkish delight. These were immediately forthcoming.

Frank, having recovered his balance, noted that these modest offerings were of surpassing quality, and set upon dishes of solid gold, superbly engraved, and polished to a dazzling brightness. It is by little details of this description that one may recognize a really first-rate servant. Frank was delighted, but restrained his enthusiasm. "Gold plates," said he, "are all very well. Let us, however, get down to brass tacks. I should like a palace."

"To hear," said his dusky henchman, "is to obey."

"It should," said Frank, "be of suitable size, suitably situated, suitably furnished, suitable pictures, suitable marbles, hangings, and all that.

I should like there to be a large number of tiger-skins. I am very fond of tiger-skins."

"They shall be there," said his slave.

"I am," said Frank, "a bit of an artist, as your late owner remarked. My art, so to speak, demands the presence, upon these tiger-skins, of a number of young women, some blonde, some brunette, some petite, some Junoesque, some languorous, some vivacious, all beautiful, and they need not be over-dressed. I hate over-dressing. It is vulgar. Have you got that?"

"I have," said the jinn.

"Then," said Frank, "let *me* have it."

"Condescend only," said his servant, "to close your eyes for the space of a single minute, and opening them you shall find yourself surrounded by the agreeable objects you have described."

"O.K.," said Frank. "But no tricks, mind!"

He closed his eyes as requested. A low, musical humming, whooshing sound rose and fell about him. At the end of the minute he looked around. There were the arches, pillars, marbles, hangings, etc. of the most exquisite palace imaginable, and wherever he looked he saw a tiger-skin, and on every tiger-skin there reclined a young woman of surpassing beauty who was certainly not vulgarly over-dressed.

Our good Frank was, to put it mildly, in an ecstasy. He darted to and fro like a honey-bee in a florist's shop. He was received everywhere with smiles sweet beyond description, and with glances of an open or a veiled responsiveness. Here were blushes and lowered lids. Here was the flaming face of ardour. Here was a shoulder turned, but by no means a cold shoulder. Here were open arms, and such arms! Here was love dissembled, but vainly dissembled. Here was love triumphant. "I must say," said Frank at a later hour, "I have spent a really delightful afternoon. I have enjoyed it thoroughly."

"Then may I crave," said the jinn, who was at that moment serving him his supper, "may I crave the boon of being allowed to act as your butler, and as general minister to your pleasures, instead of being returned to that abominable bottle?"

"I don't see why not," said Frank. "It certainly seems rather tough that, after having fixed all this up, you should be crammed back into that bottle again. Very well, act as my butler, but understand, whatever the convention may be, I wish you never to enter a room without knocking. And above all—no tricks."

The jinn, with a soapy smile of gratitude, withdrew, and Frank shortly retired to his harem, where he passed the evening as pleasantly as he had passed the afternoon.

Some weeks went by entirely filled with these agreeable pastimes, till Frank, in obedience to law which not even the most efficient jinns can set aside, found himself growing a little over-particular, a little blasé, a little inclined to criticize and find fault.

"These," said he to his jinn, "are very pretty young creatures, if you like that sort of thing, but I imagine they can hardly be first-rate, or I should feel more interest in them. I am, after all, a connoisseur; nothing can please me but the very best. Take them away. Roll up all the tiger-skins but one."

"It shall be done," said the jinn. "Behold, it is accomplished."

"And on that remaining tiger-skin," said Frank, "put me Cleopatra herself."

The next moment, Cleopatra was there, looking, it must be admitted, absolutely superb. "Hullo!" she said. "Here I am, on a tiger-skin again!"

"*Again?*" cried Frank, suddenly reminded of the old man in the shop. "Here! Take her back. Bring me Helen of Troy."

Next moment, Helen of Troy was there. "Hullo!" she said. "Here I am, on a tiger-skin again!"

"*Again?*" cried Frank. "Damn that old man! Take her away. Bring me Queen Guinevere."

Guinevere said exactly the same thing; so did Madame la Pompadour, Lady Hamilton, and every other famous beauty that Frank could think of. "No wonder," said he, "that that old man was such an extremely wizened old man! The old fiend! The old devil! He has properly taken the gilt off all the gingerbread. Call me jealous if you like; I will not play second fiddle to that ugly old rascal. Where shall I find a perfect creature, worthy of the embraces of such a connoisseur as I am?"

"If you are deigning to address that question to me," said the jinn, "let me remind you that there was, in that shop, a little bottle which my late master had never unstoppered, because I supplied him with it after he had lost interest in matters of this sort. Nevertheless it has the reputation of containing the most beautiful girl in the whole world."

"You are right," cried Frank. "Get me that bottle without delay."

In a few seconds the bottle lay before him. "You may have the afternoon off," said Frank to the jinn.

"Thank you," said the jinn. "I will go and see my family in Arabia. I have not seen them for a long time." With that he bowed and withdrew.

Frank turned his attention to the bottle, which he was not long in unstoppering.

Out came the most beautiful girl you can possibly imagine. Cleopatra and all that lot were hags and frumps compared with her. "Where am I?" said she. "What is this beautiful palace? What am I doing on a tigerskin? Who is this handsome young prince?"

"It's me!" cried Frank, in a rapture. "It's me!"

The afternoon passed like a moment in Paradise. Before Frank knew it the jinn was back, ready to serve up supper. Frank must sup with his charmer, for this time it was love, the real thing. The jinn, entering with the viands, rolled up his wicked eyes at the sight of so much beauty.

It happened that Frank, all love and restlessness, darted out into the garden between two mouthfuls, to pluck his beloved a rose. The jinn, on the pretence of serving her wine, edged up very closely. "I don't know if you remember me," said he in a whisper. "I used to be in the next bottle to you. I have often admired you through the glass."

"Oh, yes," said she. "I remember you quite well."

At that moment Frank returned. The jinn could say no more, but he stood about the room, inflating his monstrous chest, and showing off his plump and dusky muscles. "You need not be afraid of him," said Frank. "He is only a jinn. Pay no attention to him. Tell me if you really love me."

"Of course I do," said she.

"Well, say so," said he. "Why don't you say so?"

"I have said so," said she. "Of course I do. Isn't that saying so?"

This vague, evasive reply dimmed all Frank's happiness, as if a cloud had come over the sun. Doubt sprang up in his mind, and entirely ruined moments of exquisite bliss.

"What are you thinking of?" he would say.

"I don't know," she would reply.

"Well, you ought to know," he would say, and then a quarrel would begin.

Once or twice he even ordered her back into her bottle. She obeyed with a malicious and secretive smile.

"Why should she give that sort of smile?" said Frank to the jinn, to whom he confided his distress.

"I cannot tell," replied the jinn. "Unless she has a lover concealed in there."

"Is it possible?" cried Frank in consternation.

"It is surprising," said the jinn, "how much room there is in one of these bottles."

"Come out!" cried Frank. "Come out at once!"

His charmer obediently emerged. "Is there anyone else in that bottle?" cried Frank.

"How could there be?" she asked, with a look of rather overdone innocence.

"Give me a straight answer," said he. "Answer me yes or no."

"Yes or no," she replied maddeningly.

"You double-talking, two-timing little bitch!" cried Frank. "I'll go in and find out for myself. If I find anybody, God help him and you!"

With that, and with an intense effort of the will, he flowed himself into the bottle. He looked all around: there was no one. Suddenly he heard a sound above him. He looked up, and there was the stopper being thrust in.

"What are you doing?" cried he.

"We are putting in the stopper," said the jinn.

Frank cursed, begged, prayed, and implored. "Let me out!" he cried. "Let me out. Please let me out. Do let me out. I'll do anything. Let me out, do."

The jinn, however, had other matters to attend to. Frank had the infinite mortification of beholding these other matters through the glassy walls of his prison. Next day he was picked up, whisked through the air, and deposited in the dirty little shop, among the other bottles, from which this one had never been missed.

There he remained for an interminable period, covered all over with dust, and frantic with rage at the thought of what was going on in his exquisite palace, between his jinn and his faithless charmer. In the end some sailors happened to drift into the shop, and, hearing this bottle contained the most beautiful girl in the world, they bought it up by general subscription of the fo'c'sle. When they unstoppered him at sea, and found it was only poor Frank, their disappointment knew no bounds, and they used him with the utmost barbarity.

Time for a change of pace. So here's a story that's not fantasy at all. It's simply a childhood memoir, quite true to life. I know because I've lived the same scenario.

This isn't a story about witches. There are no witches, of course. Oh, there are women who talk like witches, and act like witches, and look like witches, and certainly on occasion are very much capable of bewitching one. But actual witch-craft? Not at all.

No, despite its title, this isn't a story about witches. It's about mothers, and children. Or is it that as we age our perceptions change? What is reality and what merely real in the mind's eye of a child? Who is to say?

Only the mothers know, and they ain't talking.

My Mother Was a Witch

WILLIAM TENN

I SPENT MOST OF MY BOYHOOD utterly convinced that my mother was a witch. No psychological trauma was involved; instead, this belief made me feel like a thoroughly loved and protected child.

My memory begins in the ragged worst of Brooklyn's Brownsville—also known as East New York—where I was surrounded by witches. Every adult woman I knew was one. Shawled conventions of them buzzed and glowered constantly at our games from nearby "stoops." Whenever my playmates swirled too boisterously close, the air turned black with angry magic: immense and complicated curses were thrown.

"May you never live to grow up" was one of the simpler, cheerier incantations. "But if you do grow up, may it be like a radish, with your

176

head in the ground and your feet in the air." Another went: "May you itch from head to foot with scabs that drive you crazy—but only after your fingernails have broken off so you can't scratch."

These remarks were not directed at me; my mother's counter-magic was too widely feared, and I myself had been schooled in every block and parry applicable to little boys. At bedtime, my mother spat thrice, forcing the Powers with whom she was in constant familiar correspondence to reverse curses aimed at me that day back on their authors' heads three-fold, as many times as she had spit.

A witch in the family was indeed a rod and a staff of comfort.

My mother was a Yiddish witch, conducting her operations in that compote of German, Hebrew, and Slavic. This was a serious handicap: she had been born a Jewish cockney and spoke little Yiddish until she met my father, an ex-rabbinical student and fervent Socialist from Lithuania. Having bagged him in London's East End on his way to America, she set herself with immediate, wifely devotion to unlearn her useless English in place of what seemed to be the prevailing tongue of the New World.

While my father trained her to speak Yiddish fluently, he cannot have been of much help to her and their firstborn in that superstitious Brooklyn slum. He held science and sweet reason to be the hope of the world; her casual, workaday necromancy horrified him. Nary a spell would he teach her: idioms, literary phrases and fine Yiddish poetry, by all means, but no spells, absolutely no spells.

She needed them. A small boy, she noted, was a prime target for malice and envy, and her new neighbors had at their disposal whole libraries of protective cantrips. Cantrips, at first, had she none. Her rank on the block was determined by the potency of her invocations and her ability—when invoked upon—to knock aside or deftly neutralize. But she sorely lacked a cursing tradition passed for generations from mother to daughter; she alone had brought no such village lore to the United States wrapped in the thick bedspreads and sewed into goosedown-stuffed pillows. My mother's only weapons were imagination and ingenuity.

Fortunately her imagination and ingenuity never failed her—once she had gotten the hang of the thing. She was a quick study too, learning instruments of the occult as fast as she saw them used.

"*Mach a feig!*" she would whisper in the grocer's as a beaming housewife commented on my health and good looks. Up came my fist, thumb protruding between forefinger and middle-finger in the ancient male gesture against the female evil eye. *Feigs* were my reserve equipment

when alone: I could make them at any cursers and continue playing in
the serene confidence that all unpleasant wishes had been safely pasteur-
ized. If an errand took me past threatening witch faces in tenement door-
ways, I shot *feigs* left and right, all the way down the street.

Still, my mother's best would hardly have been worth its weight in
used pentagrams if she had not stood up worthily to Old Mrs. *Mokkeh*.
Mokkeh was the lady's nickname (it is Yiddish for plague or pestilence)
and suggested the blood-chilling imprecations she could toss off with
spectacular fluency.

This woman made such an impression on me that I have never been
able to read any of the fiercer fairy tales without thinking of her. A tiny,
square female with four daughters, each as ugly and short as she, Mrs.
Mokkeh walked as if every firmly planted step left desolated territory
forever and contemptuously behind. The hairy wart on the right side of
her nose was so large that behind her back—only behind her back; who
knew what she'd wish on you if she heard you?—people giggled and said,
"Her nose has a nose."

But that was humor's limit; everything else was sheer fright. She
would squint at you, squeezing first one eye shut, then the other, her nose
wart vibrating as she rooted about in her soul for an appropriately crip-
pling curse. If you were sensible, you scuttled away before the plague that
might darken your future could be fully fashioned and slung. Not only
children ran, but brave and learned witches.

Old Mrs. *Mokkeh* was a kind of witch-in-chief. She knew curses and
spells that went back to antiquity, to the crumbled ghettoes of Babylon
and Thebes, and she reconstructed them in the most novel and terrible
forms.

When we moved into the apartment directly above her, my mother
tried hard to avoid a clash. Balls must not be bounced in the kitchen;
indoor running and jumping were strictly prohibited. My mother was
still learning her trade at this time and had to be cautious. She would
frequently scowl at the floor and bite her lips worriedly. "The *mokkehs*
that woman can think up!" she would say.

There came a day when the two of us prepared to visit cousins in the
farthest arctic regions of the Bronx. Washed and scrubbed until my skin
smarted all over, I was dressed in the good blue serge suit bought for the
High Holy Days recently celebrated. My feet were shod in glossy black
leather, my neck encircled by a white collar that had been ultimately
alloyed with starch. Under this collar ran a tie of brightest red, the
intense shade of the Evil Eye.

As we emerged from the building entrance upon the stone stoop, Mrs. *Mokkeh* and her eldest, ugliest daughter, Pearl, began climbing it from the bottom. We passed them and stopped in a knot of women chatting on the sidewalk. While my mother sought advice from her friends on express stops and train changes, I sniffed like a fretful puppy at the bulging market bags of heavy oilcloth hanging from their wrists. There was onion reek, and garlic, and the fresh miscellany of "soup greens."

The casual, barely noticing glances I drew did not surprise me; a prolonged stare at someone's well-turned-out child invited rapid and murderous retaliation. Staring was like complimenting—it only attracted the attention of the Angel of Death to a choice specimen.

I grew bored; I yawned and wriggled in my mother's grasp. Twisting around, I beheld the witch-in-chief examining me squintily from the top of the stoop. She smiled a rare and awesomely gentle smile.

"That little boy, Pearlie," she muttered to her daughter. "A darling, a sweet one, a golden one. How nice he looks!"

My mother heard her and stiffened, but she failed to whirl, as everyone expected, and deliver a brutal riposte. She had no desire to tangle with Mrs. *Mokkeh*. Our whole group listened anxiously for the Yiddish phrase customarily added to such a compliment if good will had been at all behind it—*a leben uff em*, a long life upon him.

Once it was apparent that no such qualifying phrase was forthcoming, I showed I had been well-educated. I pointed my free right hand in a spell-nullifying *feig* at my admirer.

Old Mrs. *Mokkeh* studied the *feig* with her narrow little eyes. "May that hand drop off," she intoned in the same warm, low voice. "May the fingers rot one by one and wither to the wrist. May the hand drop off, but the rot remain. May you wither to the elbow and then to the shoulder. May the whole arm rot with which you made a *feig* at me, and may it fall off and lie festering at your feet, so you will remember for the rest of your life not to make a *feig* at me."

Every woman within range of her lilting Yiddish malediction gasped and gave a mighty head-shake. Then stepping back, they cleared a space in the center of which my mother stood alone.

She turned slowly to face Old Mrs. *Mokkeh*. "Aren't you ashamed of yourself?" she pleaded. "He's only a little boy—not even five years old. Take it back."

Mrs. *Mokkeh* spat calmly on the stoop. "May it happen ten times over. Ten and twenty and a hundred times over. May he wither, may he rot. His arms, his legs, his lungs, his belly. May he vomit green gall and no doctor should be able to save him."

This was battle irrevocably joined. My mother dropped her eyes, estimating the resources of her arsenal. She must have found them painfully slender against such an opponent.

When she raised her eyes again, the women waiting for action leaned forward. My mother was known to be clever and had many well-wishers, but her youth made her a welterweight or at most a lightweight. Mrs. *Mokkeh* was an experienced heavy, a pro who had trained in the old country under famous champions. If these women had been in the habit of making book, the consensus would have been: even money she lasts one or two rounds; five to three she doesn't go the distance.

"Your daughter, Pearlie—" my mother began at last.

"Oh, momma, no!" shrieked the girl, suddenly dragged from noncombatant status into the very eye of the fight.

"Shush! Be calm," her mother commanded. After all, only green campaigners expected a frontal attack. My mother had been hit on her vulnerable flank—me—and was replying in kind. Pearl whimpered and stamped her feet, but her elders ignored this: matters of high professional moment were claiming their attention.

"Your daughter, Pearlie," the chant developed. "Now she is fourteen—may she live to a hundred and fourteen! May she marry in five years a wonderful man, a brilliant man, a doctor, a lawyer, a dentist, who will wait on her hand and foot and give her everything her heart desires."

There was a stir of tremendous interest as the kind of curse my mother was kneading became recognizable. It is one of the most difficult forms in the entire Yiddish thaumaturgical repertoire, building the subject up and up and up and ending with an annihilating crash. A well-known buildup curse goes, "May you have a bank account in every bank, and a fortune in each bank account, may you spend every penny of it going from doctor to doctor, and no doctor should know what's the matter with you." Or: "May you own a hundred mansions, and in each mansion a hundred richly furnished bedrooms, and may you spend your life tossing from bed to bed, unable to get a single night's sleep on one of them."

To reach a peak and then explode it into an avalanche—that is the buildup curse. It requires perfect detail and even more perfect timing.

"May you give your daughter Pearlie a wedding to this wonderful husband of hers, such a wedding that the whole world will talk about it for years." Pearlie's head began a slow submergence into the collar of her dress. Her mother grunted like a boxer who has been jabbed lightly and is now dancing away.

"This wedding, may it be in all the papers, may they write about it even in books, and may you enjoy yourself at it like never before in your whole life. And one year later, may Pearlie, Pearlie and her wonderful, her rich, her considerate husband—may they present you with your first grandchild. And, *masel tov*, may it be a boy."

Old Mrs. *Mokkeh* shook unbelievingly and came down a step, her nose wart twitching and sensitive as an insect's antenna.

"And this baby boy," my mother sang, pausing to kiss her fingers before extending them to Mrs. *Mokkeh*, "what a glorious child may he be! Glorious? No. Magnificent! Such a wonderful baby boy no one will ever have seen before. The greatest rabbis coming from all over the world only to look upon him at the *bris*, so they'll be able to say in later years they were among those present at his circumcision ceremony eight days after birth. So beautiful and clever he'll be that people will expect him to say the prayers at his own *bris*. And this magnificent first grandson of yours, just one day afterward, when you are gathering happiness on every side, may he suddenly, in the middle of the night—"

"Hold!" Mrs. *Mokkeh* screamed, raising both her hands. "Stop!"

My mother took a deep breath. "And why should I stop?"

"Because I take it back! What I wished on the boy, let it be on my own head, everything I wished on him. Does that satisfy you?"

"That satisfies me," my mother said. Then she pulled my left arm up and began dragging me down the street. She walked proudly, no longer a junior among seniors, but a full and accredited sorceress.

Harlan Ellison is a very funny guy, but he reserves most of his humor for his conversations and his nonfiction. His stories tend to deal with subjects more somber, with the exposition and dissection of privacies less amusing in nature.

It's a delight to see what a truly fine writer can do with an old idea, how he can twist it around, give it a fresh new coat of adverbs, make it seem original and different. Sometimes you're sure it's impossible. Then you read it and realize it's not. Punchlines too are all very well and good, but if they're not supported by a well-crafted *story*, then what you have written is material for a stand-up comic, not a book.

Here's story *and* punchline.

Djinn, No Chaser

HARLAN ELLISON

"WHO THE HELL ever heard of Turkish Period?" Danny Squires said. He said it at the top of his voice, on a city street.

"Danny! People are staring at us; lower your voice!" Connie Squires punched his bicep. They stood on the street, in front of the furniture store. Danny was determined not to enter.

"Come on, Connie," he said, "let's get away from these junk shops and go see some inexpensive modern stuff. You know perfectly well I don't make enough to start filling the apartment with expensive antiques."

Connie furtively looked up and down the street—she was more concerned with a "scene" than with the argument itself—and then moved in toward Danny with a determined air. "Now listen up, Squires. *Did* you

182

or did you *not* marry me four days ago, and promise to love, honor and cherish and all that other good jive?"

Danny's blue eyes rolled toward Heaven; he knew he was losing ground. Instinctively defensive, he answered, "Well, sure, Connie, but—"

"Well, then, I am your wife, and you have not taken me on a honeymoon—"

"I can't *afford* one!"

"—have not taken me on a honeymoon," Connie repeated with inflexibility. "Consequently, we will buy a little furniture for that rabbit warren you laughingly call our little love nest. And *little* is hardly the term: that vale of tears was criminally undersized when Barbara Fritchie hung out her flag.

"So to make my life *bearable*, for the next few weeks, till we can talk Mr. Upjohn into giving you a raise—"

"Upjohn!" Danny fairly screamed. "You've got to stay away from the boss, Connie. Don't screw around. He won't give me a raise, and I'd rather you stayed away from him—"

"Until then," she went on relentlessly, "we will decorate our apartment in the style I've wanted for years."

"Turkish Period?"

"Turkish Period."

Danny flipped his hands in the air. What was the use? He had known Connie was strong-willed when he'd married her.

It had seemed an attractive quality at the time; now he wasn't so sure. But he was strong-willed too; he was sure he could outlast her. Probably.

"Okay," he said finally, "I suppose Turkish Period it'll be. What the hell *is* Turkish Period?"

She took his arm lovingly, and turned him around to look in the store window. "Well, honey, it's not *actually* Turkish. It's more Mesopotamian. You know, teak and silk and . . ."

"Sounds hideous."

"So you're starting up again!" She dropped his arm, her eyes flashing, her mouth a tight little line. "I'm really ashamed of you, depriving me of the few little pleasures I need to make my life a blub, sniff, hoohoo . . ."

The edge was hers.

"Connie . . . Connie . . ." She knocked away his comforting hand, saying, "You beast." That was too much for him. The words were so obviously put-on, he was suddenly infuriated:

"Now, goddammit!"

Her tears came faster. Danny stood there, furious, helpless, outmaneuvered, hoping desperately that no cop would come along and say, "This guy botherin' ya, lady?"

"Connie, okay, okay, we'll *have* Turkish Period. Come on, come on. It doesn't matter what it costs, I can scrape up the money somehow."

It was not one of the glass-brick and onyx emporia where sensible furniture might be found (if one searched hard enough and paid high enough and retained one's senses long enough as they were trying to palm off modernistic nightmares in which no comfortable position might be found); no, it was not even one of those. This was an antique shop.

They looked at beds that had canopies and ornate metalwork on the bedposts. They looked at rugs that were littered with pillows, so visitors could sit on the floors. They looked at tables built six inches off the deck, for low banquets. They inspected incense burners and hookahs and coffers and giant vases until Danny's head swam with visions of the courts of long-dead caliphs.

Yet, despite her determination, Connie chose very few items; and those she did select were moderately-priced and quite handsome . . . for what they were. And as the hours passed, and as they moved around town from one dismal junk emporium to another, Danny's respect for his wife's taste grew. She was selecting an apartment full of furniture that wasn't bad at all.

They were finished by six o'clock, and had bills of sale that totaled just under two hundred dollars. Exactly thirty dollars less than Danny had decided could be spent to furnish the new household . . . and still survive on his salary. He had taken the money from his spavined savings account, and had known he must eventually start buying on credit, or they would not be able to get enough furniture to start living properly.

He was tired, but content. She'd shopped wisely. They were in a shabby section of town. How had they gotten here? They walked past an empty lot sandwiched in between two tenements—wet-wash slapping on lines between them. The lot was weed-overgrown and garbage-strewn.

"May I call your attention to the depressing surroundings and my exhaustion?" Danny said. "Let's get a cab and go back to the apartment. I want to collapse."

They turned around to look for a cab, and the empty lot was gone.

In its place, sandwiched between the two tenements, was a little shop. It was a one-storey affair, with a dingy facade, and its front window completely grayed-over with dust. A hand-painted line of elaborate script on the glass-panel of the door, also opaque with grime, proclaimed:

MOHANADUS MUKHAR, CURIOS.

A little man in a flowing robe, wearing a fez, plunged out the front door, skidded to a stop, whirled and slapped a huge sign on the window. He swiped at it four times with a big paste-brush, sticking it to the glass, and whirled back inside, slamming the door.

"No," Danny said.

Connie's mouth was making peculiar sounds.

"There's no insanity in my family," Danny said firmly. "We come from very good stock."

"We've made a visual error," Connie said.

"Simply didn't notice it," Danny said. His usually baritone voice was much nearer soprano.

"If there's crazy, we've both got it," Connie said.

"Must be, if you see the same thing I see."

Connie was silent a moment, then said, "Large seagoing vessel, three stacks, maybe the Titanic. Flamingo on the bridge, flying the flag of Lichtenstein?"

"Don't play with me, woman," Danny whimpered. "I think I'm losing it."

She nodded soberly. "Right. Empty lot?"

He nodded back, "Empty lot. Clothesline, weeds, garbage."

"Right."

He pointed at the little store. "Little store?"

"Right."

"Man in a fez, name of Mukhar?"

She rolled her eyes. "Right."

"So why are we walking toward it?"

"Isn't this what always happens in stories where weird shops suddenly appear out of nowhere? Something inexorable draws the innocent bystanders into its grip?"

They stood in front of the grungy little shop. They read the sign. It said:

BIG SALE! HURRY! NOW! QUICK!

"The word *unnatural* comes to mind," Danny said.

"Nervously," Connie said, "she turned the knob and opened the door."

A tiny bell went tinkle-tinkle, and they stepped across the threshold into the gloaming of Mohanadus Mukhar's shop.

"Probably not the smartest move we've ever made," Danny said softly. The door closed behind them without any assistance.

It was cool and musty in the shop, and strange fragrances chased one another past their noses.

They looked around carefully. The shop was loaded with junk. From floor to ceiling, wall to wall, on tables and in heaps, the place was filled with oddities and bric-a-brac. Piles of things tumbled over one another on the floor; heaps of things leaned against the walls. There was barely room to walk down the aisle between the stacks and mounds of things. Things in all shapes, things in all sizes and colors. Things. They tried to separate the individual items from the jumble of the place, but all they could perceive was stuff . . . things! Stuff and flotsam and bits and junk.

"Curios, effendi," a voice said, by way of explanation.

Connie leaped in the air, and came down on Danny's foot.

Mukhar was standing beside such a pile of tumbled miscellany that for a moment they could not separate him from the stuff, junk, things he sold.

"We saw your sign," Connie said.

But Danny was more blunt, more direct. "There was an empty lot here; then a minute later, this shop. How come?"

The little man stepped out from the mounds of dust-collectors and his little nut-brown, wrinkled face burst into a million-creased smile. "A fortuitous accident, my children. A slight worn spot in the fabric of the cosmos, and I have been set down here for . . . how long I do not know. But it never hurts to try and stimulate business while I'm here."

"Uh, yeah," Danny said. He looked at Connie. Her expression was as blank as his own.

"Oh!" Connie cried, and went dashing off into one of the side-corridors lined with curios. "This is perfect! Just what we need for the end table. Oh, Danny, it's a dream! It's absolutely the *ne plus ultra*!"

Danny walked over to her, but in the dimness of the aisle between the curios he could barely make out what it was she was holding. He drew her into the light near the door. It had to be:

Aladdin's lamp.

Well, perhaps not that *particular* person's lamp, but one of the ancient, vile-smelling oil burning jobs: long thin spout, round-bottom body, wide, flaring handle.

It was algae-green with tarnish, brown with rust, and completely covered by the soot and debris of centuries. There was no contesting its antiquity; nothing so time-corrupted could fail to be authentic. "What the hell do you want with that old thing, Connie?"

"But Danny, it's so *per*-fect. If we just shine it up a bit. As soon as we put a little work into this lamp, it'll be a beauty." Danny knew he was defeated . . . and she'd probably be right, too. It probably would be very handsome when shined and brassed-up.

"How much?" he asked Mukhar. He didn't want to seem anxious; old camel traders were merciless at bargaining when they knew the item in question was hotly desired.

"Fifty drachmae, eh?" the old man said. His tone was one of malicious humor. "At current exchange rates, taking into account the fall of the Ottoman Empire, thirty dollars."

Danny's lips thinned. "Put it down, Connie; let's get out of here."

He started toward the door, dragging his wife behind him. But she still clutched the lamp; and Mukhar's voice halted them. "All right, noble sir. You are a cunning shopper, I can see that. You know a bargain when you spy it. But I am unfamiliar in this time-frame with your dollars and your strange fast-food native customs, having been set down here only once before; and since I am more at ease with the drachma than the dollar, with the shekel than the cent, I will cut my own throat, slash both my wrists, and offer you this magnificent antiquity for . . . uh . . . twenty dollars?" His voice was querulous, his tone one of wonder and hope.

"Jesse James at least had a horse!" Danny snarled, once again moving toward the door.

"Fifteen!" Mukhar yowled. "And may all your children need corrective lenses from too much tv-time!"

"Five; and may a hundred thousand syphilitic camels puke into your couscous," Danny screamed back over his shoulder.

"Not bad," said Mukhar.

"Thanks," said Danny, stifling a smile. Now he waited.

"Bloodsucker! Heartless trafficker in cheapness! Pimple on the fundament of decency! Graffito on the subway car of life! Thirteen; my last offer; and may the gods of ITT and the Bank of America turn a blind eye to your venality!" But *his* eyes held the golden gleam of the born haggler, at last, blessedly, in his element.

"Seven, not a penny more, you Arabic anathema! And may a weighty object drop from a great height, flattening you to the niggardly thickness of your soul." Connie stared at him with open awe and admiration.

"Eleven! Eleven dollars, a pittance, an outright theft we're talking about. Call the security guards, get a consumer advocate, gimme a break here!"

"My shadow will vanish from before the evil gleam of your rapacious gaze before I pay a penny more than six bucks, and let the word go out to every wadi and oasis across the limitless desert, that Mohanadus Mukhar steals maggots from diseased meat, flies from horse dung, and the hard-earned drachmae of honest laborers. Six, fuckface, and that's it!"

"My death is about to become a reality," the Arab bellowed, tearing at the strands of white hair showing under the fez. "Rob me, go ahead, rob me; drink my life's blood! Ten! A twenty dollar loss I'll take."

"Okay, okay." Danny turned around and produced his wallet. He pulled out one of the three ten dollar bills still inside and, turning to Connie, said, "You sure you want this ugly, dirty piece of crap?" She nodded, and he held the bill naked in the vicinity of the little merchant. For the first time Danny realized Mukhar was wearing pointed slippers that curled up; there was hair growing from his ears.

"Ten bucks."

The little man moved with the agility of a ferret, and whisked the tenner from Danny's outstretched hand before he could draw it back. "Sold!" Mukhar chuckled.

He spun around once, and when he faced them again, the ten dollars was out of sight. "And a steal, though Allah be the wiser; a hot deal, a veritable steal, blessed sir!"

Danny abruptly realized he had been taken. The lamp had probably been picked up in a junkyard and was worthless. He started to ask if it was a genuine antique, but the piles of junk had begun to waver and shimmer and coruscate with light. "Hey!" Danny said, alarmed, "What's this now?"

The little man's wrinkled face drew up in panic. "Out! Get out, quick! The time-frame is sucking back together! Out! Get out now if you don't want to roam the eternities with me and this shop . . . and I can't afford any help! Out!"

He shoved them forward, and Connie slipped and fell, flailing into a pile of glassware. None of it broke. Her hand went out to protect herself and went right through the glass. Danny dragged her to her feet, panic sweeping over him . . . as the shop continued to waver and grow more indistinct around them.

"Out! Out! Out!" Mukhar kept yelling.

Then they were at the door, and he was kicking them—literally planting his curl-slippered foot in Danny's backside and shoving—from the store. They landed in a heap on the sidewalk. The lamp bounced from Connie's hand and went into the gutter with a clang. The little man stood there grinning in the doorway, and as the shop faded and disappeared, they heard him mumble happily, "A clear nine-seventy-five profit. What a lemon! You got an Edsel, kid, a real lame piece of goods. But I gotta give it to you; the syphilitic camel bit was inspired."

Then the shop was gone, and they got to their feet in front of an empty, weed-overgrown lot.

A lame piece of goods?

"Are you asleep?"

"Yes."

"How come you're answering me?"

"I was raised polite."

"Danny, talk to me . . . come on!"

"The answer is no. I'm not going to talk about it."

"We have to!"

"Not only don't we *have* to, I don't *want* to, ain't *going* to, and shut up so I can go to sleep."

"We've been lying here almost an hour. Neither of us can sleep. We *have* to discuss it, Danny."

The light went on over his side of the bed. The single pool of illumination spread from the hand-me-down daybed they had gotten from Danny's brother in New Jersey, faintly limning the few packing crates full of dishes and linens, the three Cuisinarts they'd gotten as wedding gifts, the straight-back chairs from Connie's Aunt Medora, the entire bare and depressing reality of their first home together.

It would be better when the furniture they'd bought today was delivered. Later, it would be better. Now, it was the sort of urban landscape that drove divorcees and aging bachelors to jump down the airshaft at Christmastime.

"I'm going to talk about it, Squires."

"So talk. I have my thumbs in my ears."

"I think we should rub it."

"I can't hear you. It never happened. I deny the evidence of my senses. It never happened. I have these thumbs in my ears so I cannot hear a syllable of this craziness."

"For god's sake, Squires, I was *there* with you today. I saw it happen, the same as you. I saw that weird little old man and I saw his funky shop come and go like a big burp. Now, neither of us can deny it!"

"If I could hear you, I'd agree; and then I'd deny the evidence of my senses and tell you . . ." He took his thumbs from his ears, looking distressed. ". . . tell you with all my heart that I love you, that I have loved you since the moment I saw you in the typing pool at Upjohn, that if I live to be a hundred thousand years old I'll never love any one or any thing as much as I love you this very moment; and then I would tell you to fuck off and forget it, and let me go to sleep so that tomorrow I can con myself into believing it never happened the way I know it happened.

"Okay?"

She threw back the covers and got out of bed. She was naked. They had not been married that long.

"Where are you going?"

"You know where I'm going."

He sat up in the daybed. His voice had no lightness in it. "Connie!"

She stopped and stared at him, there in the light.

He spoke softly. "Don't. I'm scared. Please don't."

She said nothing. She looked at him for a time. Then, naked, she sat down cross-legged on the floor at the foot of the daybed. She looked around at what little they had, and she answered him gently. "I have to, Danny. I just have to . . . if there's a chance; I have to."

They sat that way, reaching across the abyss with silent imperatives, until—finally—Danny nodded, exhaled heavily, and got out of the daybed. He walked to one of the cartons, pulled out a dustrag, shook it clean over the box, and handed it to her. He walked over to the window ledge where the tarnished and rusted oil lamp sat, and he brought it to her.

"Shine the damned thing, Squires. Who knows, maybe we actually got ourselves a 24 carat genie. Shine on, oh mistress of my Mesopotamian mansion."

She held the lamp in one hand, the rag in the other. For a few minutes she did not bring them together. "I'm scared, too," she said, held her breath, and briskly rubbed the belly of the lamp.

Under her flying fingers the rust and tarnish began to come away in spots. "We'll need brass polish to do this right," she said; but suddenly the ruin covering the lamp melted away, and she was rubbing the bright skin of the lamp itself.

"Oh, Danny, look how nice it is, underneath all the crud!" And at that precise instant the lamp jumped from her hand, emitted a sharp, gray puff of smoke, and a monstrous voice bellowed in the apartment:

AH-HA! It screamed, louder than a subway train. AH-HA!

FREE AT LAST! FREE—AS FREE AS *I'LL* EVER BE—AFTER TEN THOUSAND YEARS! FREE TO SPEAK AND ACT, MY WILL TO BE KNOWN!

Danny went over backward. The sound was as mind-throttling as being at ground zero. The window glass blew out. Every light bulb in the apartment shattered. From the carton containing their meager chinaware came the distinct sound of hailstones as every plate and cup dissolved into shards. Dogs and cats blocks away began to howl. Connie screamed —though it could not be heard over the foghorn thunder of the voice— and was knocked head over ankles into a corner, still clutching the dust-rag. Plaster showered in the little apartment. The window shades rolled up.

Danny recovered first. He crawled over a chair and stared at the lamp with horror. Connie sat up in the corner, face white, eyes huge, hands over her ears. Danny stood and looked down at the seemingly innocuous lamp.

"Knock off that noise! You want to lose us the lease?"

CERTAINLY, OFFSPRING OF A WORM!

"I said: stop that goddam bellowing!"

THIS WHISPER? THIS IS NAUGHT TO THE HURRICANE I SHALL LOOSE, SPAWN OF PARAMECIUM!

"That's it," Danny yelled. "I'm not getting kicked out of the only apartment in the city of New York I can afford just because of some loudmouthed genie in a jug . . ."

He stopped. He looked at Connie. Connie looked back at him.

"Oh, my god," she said.

"It's real," he said.

They got to their knees and crawled over. The lamp lay on its side on the floor at the foot of the daybed.

"Are you really in there?" Connie asked.

WHERE ELSE WOULD I BE, SLUT!

"Hey, you can't talk to my wife that way—"

Connie shushed him. "If he's a genie, he can talk any way he likes. Sticks and stones; namecalling is better than poverty."

"Yeah? Well, *nobody* talks to my—"

"Put a lid on it, Squires. I can take care of myself. If what's in this lamp is even half the size of the genie in that movie you took me to the Thalia to see . . ."

"*The Thief of Bagdad* . . . 1939 version . . . but Rex Ingram was just an actor, they only made him *look* big."

"Even so. As big as he was, if this genie is only *half* that big, playing macho overprotective chauvinist hubby—"

SO HUMANS CONTINUE TO PRATTLE LIKE MONKEYS EVEN AFTER TEN THOUSAND YEARS! WILL NOTHING CLEANSE THE EARTH OF THIS RAUCOUS PLAGUE OF IN-SECTS?

"We're going to get thrown right out of here," Danny said. His face screwed up in a horrible expression of discomfort.

"If the cops don't beat the other tenants to it."

"Please, genie," Danny said, leaning down almost to the lamp. "Just tone it down a little, willya?"

OFFSPRING OF A MILLION STINKS! SUFFER!

"You're no genie," Connie said smugly. Danny looked at her with disbelief.

"He's no genie? Then what the hell do you *think* he is?"

She swatted him. Then put her finger to her lips.

THAT IS WHAT I AM, WHORE OF DEGENERACY!

"No you're not."

I AM.

"Am not."

AM

"Am not."

AM SO, CHARNEL HOUSE HARLOT! WHY SAY YOU NAY?

"A genie has a lot of power; a genie doesn't need to shout like that to make himself heard. You're no genie, or you'd speak softly. You *can't* speak at a decent level, because you're a fraud."

CAUTION, TROLLOP!

"Foo, you don't scare me. If you were as powerful as you make out, you'd tone it way down."

is this better? are you convinced?

"Yes," Connie said, "I think that's more convincing. Can you keep it up, though? That's the question."

forever, if need be.

"And you can grant wishes?" Danny was back in the conversation.

naturally, but not to you, disgusting grub of humanity.

"Hey, listen," Danny replied angrily, "I don't give a damn what or *who* you are! You can't talk to me that way." Then a thought dawned on him. "After all, I'm your master!"

ah! correction, filth of primordial seas. there are some djinn who are mastered by their owners, but unfortunately for you i am not one of them, for i am not free to leave this metal prison. i was imprisoned in this accursed vessel many ages ago by a besotted sorcerer who knew nothing of molecular compression and even less of the binding forces of the universe. he put me into this thrice-cursed lamp, far too small for me, and i have been wedged within ever since. over the ages my good nature has rotted away. i am powerful, but trapped. those who own me cannot request anything and hope to realize their boon. i am unhappy, and an unhappy djinn is an evil djinn. were i free, i might be your slave; but as i am now, i will visit unhappiness on you in a thousand forms!

Danny chuckled. "The hell you will. I'll toss you in the incinerator."

ah! but you cannot. once you have bought the lamp, you cannot lose it, destroy it or give it away, only sell it. i am with you forever, for who would buy such a miserable lamp?

And thunder rolled in the sky.

"What are you going to do?" Connie asked.

do? just ask me for something, and you shall see!

"Not me," Danny said, "you're too cranky."

wouldn't you like a billfold full of money?

There was sincerity in the voice from the lamp.

"Well, sure, I want money, but—"

The djinn's laughter was gigantic, and suddenly cut off by the rain of frogs that fell from a point one inch below the ceiling, clobbering Danny and Connie with small, reeking, wriggling green bodies. Connie screamed and dove for the clothes closet. She came out a second later, her hair full of them; they were falling in the closet, as well. The rain of frogs continued and when Danny opened the front door to try and escape them, they fell in the hall. He slammed the door—he realized he was still naked—and covered his head with his hands. The frogs fell, writhing, stinking, and then they were knee-deep in them, with little filthy, warty bodies jumping up at their faces.

what a lousy disposition i've got! the djinn said, and then he laughed.
And he laughed again, a clangorous peal that was silenced only when the
frogs stopped, disappeared, and the flood of blood began.

It went on for a week.

They could not get away from him, no matter where they went.
They were also slowly starving: they could not go out to buy groceries
without the earth opening under their feet, or a herd of elephants chasing
them down the street, or hundreds of people getting violently ill and
vomiting on them. So they stayed in and ate what canned goods they had
stored up in the first four days of their marriage. But who could eat with
locusts filling the apartment from top to bottom, or snakes that were
intent on gobbling them up like little white rats?

First came the frogs, then the flood of blood, then the whirling dust
storm, then the spiders and gnats, then the snakes and then the locusts
and then the tiger that had them backed against a wall and ate the chair
they used to ward him off. Then came the bats and the leprosy and the
hailstones and then the floor dissolved under them and they clung to the
wall fixtures while their furniture—which had been quickly delivered (the
moving men had brought it during the hailstones)—fell through, nearly
killing the little old lady who lived beneath them.

Then the walls turned red hot and melted, and then the lightning
burned everything black, and finally Danny had had enough. He cracked,
and went gibbering around the room, tripping over the man-eating vines
that were growing out of the light sockets and the floorboards. He finally
sat down in a huge puddle of monkey urine and cried till his face grew
puffy and his eyes flame-red and his nose swelled to three times normal
size.

"I've got to get *away* from all this!" he screamed hysterically, drum-
ming his heels, trying to eat his pants' cuffs.

*you can divorce her, and that means you are voided out of the pur-
chase contract: she wanted the lamp, not you,* the djinn suggested.

Danny looked up (just in time to get a ripe Black Angus meadow
muffin in his face) and yelled, "I won't! You can't make me. We've only
been married a week and four days and I won't leave her!"

Connie, covered with running sores, stumbled to Danny and hugged
him, though he had turned to tapioca pudding and was melting. But
three days later, when ghost images of people he had feared all his life
came to haunt him, he broke completely and allowed Connie to call the

rest home on the boa constrictor that had once been the phone. "You can come and get me when this is over," he cried pitifully, kissing her poison ivy lips. "Maybe if we split up, he'll have some mercy." But they both doubted it.

When the downstairs buzzer rang, the men from the Home for the Mentally Absent came into the debacle that had been their apartment and saw Connie pulling her feet out of the swamp slime only with difficulty; she was crying in unison with Danny as they bundled him into the white ambulance. Unearthly laughter rolled around the sky like thunder as her husband was driven away.

Connie was left alone. She went back upstairs; she had nowhere else to go.

She slumped into the pool of molten slag, and tried to think while ants ate at her flesh and rabid rats gnawed off the wallpaper.

i'm just getting warmed up, the djinn said from the lamp.

Less than three days after he had been admitted to the Asylum for the Temporarily Twitchy, Connie came to get Danny. She came into his room; the shades were drawn, the sheets were very white; when he saw her his teeth began to chatter.

She smiled at him gently. "If I didn't know better, I'd swear you weren't simply overjoyed to see me, Squires."

He slid under the sheets till only his eyes were showing. His voice came through the covers. "If I break out in boils, it will definitely cause a relapse, and the day nurse hates mess."

"Where's my macho protective husband now?"

"I've been unwell."

"Yeah, well, that's all over. You're fit as a fiddle, so bestir your buns and let's get out of here."

Danny Squires' brow furrowed. This was not the tone of a woman with frogs in her hair. "I've been contemplating divorce or suicide."

She yanked the covers down, exposing his naked legs sticking out from the hem of the hospital gown. "Forget it, little chum. There are at least a hundred and ten positions we haven't tried yet before I consider dissolution. Now will you get out of that bed and *come on?*"

"But . . ."

". . . a thing I'll kick, if you don't move it."

Bewildered, he moved it.

* * *

Outside, the Rolls-Royce waited with its motor running. As they came through the front doors of the Institute for the Neurologically Flaccid, and Connie helped Danny from the discharge wheelchair, the liveried chauffeur leaped out and opened the door for them. They got in the back seat, and Connie said, "To the house, Mark." The chauffeur nodded, trotted briskly around and climbed behind the wheel. They took off to the muted roar of twin mufflers.

Danny's voice was a querulous squeak. "Can we afford a rented limo?"

Connie did not answer, merely smiled, and snuggled closer to him.

After a moment Danny asked, "What house?"

Connie pressed a button on the console in the armrest and the glass partition between front and back seats slid silently closed. "Do me a favor, will you," she said, "just hold the twenty questions till we get home? It's been a tough three days and all I ask is that you hold it together for another hour."

Danny nodded reluctantly. Then he noticed she was dressed in extremely expensive clothes. "I'd better not ask about your mink-trimmed jacket, either, right?"

"It would help."

He settled into silence, uneasy and juggling more than just twenty unasked questions. And he remained silent until he realized they were not taking the expressway into New York. He sat up sharply, looked out the rear window, snapped his head right and left trying to ascertain their location, and Connie said, "We're not going to Manhattan. We're going to Darien, Connecticut."

"Darien? Who the hell do we know in Darien?"

"Well, Upjohn, for one, lives in Darien."

"Upjohn!?! Ohmigod, he's fired me and sent the car to bring me to him so he can have me executed! I *knew* it!"

"Squires," she said, "Daniel, my love, Danny heart of my heart, will you just kindly close the tap on it for a while! Upjohn has nothing to do with us any more. Nothing at all."

"But . . . but we live in New York!"

"Not no more we don't."

* * *

Twenty minutes later they turned into the most expensive section in Darien and sped down a private road.

They drove an eighth of a mile down the private road lined with Etruscan pines, beautifully maintained, and pulled into a winding driveway. Five hundred yards further, and the drive spiraled in to wind around the front of a huge, luxurious, completely tasteful Victorian mansion. "Go on," Connie said. "Look at your house."

"Who lives here?" Danny asked.

"I just told you: *we* do."

"I thought that's what you said. Let me out here, I'll walk back to the nuthouse."

The Rolls pulled up before the mansion, and a butler ran down to open the car door for them. They got out and the servant bowed low to Connie. Then he turned to Danny. "Good to have you home, Mr. Squires," he said. Danny was too unnerved to reply.

"Thank you, Penzler," Connie said. Then, to the chauffeur, "Take the car to the garage, Mark; we won't be needing it again this afternoon. But have the Porsche fueled and ready; we may drive out later to look at the grounds."

"Very good, Mrs. Squires," Mark said. Then he drove away.

Danny was somnambulistic. He allowed himself to be led into the house, where he was further stunned by the expensive fittings, the magnificent halls, the deep-pile rugs, the spectacular furniture, the communications complex set into an entire wall, the Art Deco bar that rose out of the floor at the touch of a button, the servants who bowed and smiled at him, as if he belonged there. He was boggled by the huge kitchen, fitted with every latest appliance; and the French chef who saluted with a huge ladle as Connie entered.

"Wh-where did all this *come* from?" He finally gasped out the question as Connie led him upstairs on the escalator.

"Come on, Danny; you know where it all came from."

"The limo, the house, the grounds, the mink-trimmed jacket, the servants, the Vermeer in the front hall, the cobalt-glass Art Deco bar, the entertainment center with the beam television set, the screening room, the bowling alley, the polo field, the Neptune swimming pool, the escalator and six-strand necklace of black pearls I now notice you are wearing around your throat . . . all of it came from the genie?"

"Sorta takes your breath away, don't it?" Connie said, ingenuously.

"I'm having a little trouble with this."

"What you're having trouble with, champ, is that Mas'úd gave you a hard time, you couldn't handle it, you crapped out, and somehow I've managed to pull it all out of the swamp."

"I'm thinking of divorce again."

They were walking down a long hall lined with works of modern Japanese illustration by Yamazaki, Kobayashi, Takahiko Li, Kenzo Tanii and Orai. Connie stopped and put both her hands on Danny's trembling shoulders.

"What we've got here, Squires, is a bad case of identity reevaluation. Nobody gets through *all* the battles. We've been married less than two weeks, but we've known each other for three years. You don't know how many times I folded before that time, and I don't know how many times you triumphed before that time.

"What I've known of you for three years made it okay for me to marry you; to think 'This guy will be able to handle it the times I can't.' That's a lot of what marriage is, to my way of thinking. I don't have to score every time, and neither do you. As long as the unit maintains. This time it was my score. Next time it'll be yours. Maybe."

Danny smiled weakly. "I'm not thinking of divorce."

Movement out of the corner of his eye made him look over his shoulder.

An eleven foot tall black man, physically perfect in every way, with chiseled features like an obsidian Adonis, dressed in an impeccably-tailored three-piece Savile Row suit, silk tie knotted precisely, stood just in the hallway, having emerged from open fifteen-foot-high doors of a room at the juncture of corridors.

"Uh . . ." Danny said.

Connie looked over her shoulder. "Hi, Mas'úd. Squires, I would like you to meet Mas'úd Jan bin Jan, a Mazikeen djinn of the ifrit, by the grace of Sulaymin, master of *all* the jinni, though Allah be the wiser. Our benefactor. My friend."

"How *good* a friend?" Danny whispered, seeing the totem of sexual perfection looming eleven feet high before him.

"We haven't known each other carnally, if that's what I perceive your squalid little remark to mean," she replied. And a bit wistfully she added, "I'm not his type. I think he's got it for Lena Horne." At Danny's semi-annoyed look she added, "For god's sake, stop being so bloody suspicious!"

Mas'úd stepped forward, two steps bringing him the fifteen feet intervening, and proffered his greeting in the traditional Islamic head-and-heart salute, flowing outward, a smile on his matinee idol face. "Welcome home, Master. I await your smallest request."

Danny looked from the djinn to Connie, amazement and copelessness rendering him almost speechless. "But . . . you were stuck in the lamp . . . bad-tempered, oh boy were you bad-tempered . . . how did you . . . how did she . . ."

Connie laughed, and with great dignity the djinn joined in.

"You were in the lamp . . . you gave us all this . . . but you said you'd give us nothing but aggravation! Why?"

In deep, mellifluous tones Danny had come to associate with a voice that could knock high-flying fowl from the air, the djinn smiled warmly at them and replied, "Your good wife freed me. After ten thousand years cramped over in pain with an eternal bellyache, in that most miserable of dungeons, Mistress Connie set me loose. For the first time in a hundred times ten thousand years of cruel and venal master after master, I have been delivered into the hands of one who treats me with respect. We are friends. I look forward to extending that friendship to you, Master Squires." He seemed to be warming to his explanation, expansive and effusive. "Free now, permitted to exist among humans in a time where my kind are thought a legend, and thus able to live an interesting, new life, my gratitude knows no bounds, as my hatred and anger knew no bounds. Now I need no longer act as a Kako-daemon, now I can be the sort of ifrit Rabbi Jeremiah bin Eliazar spoke of in Psalm XLI.

"I have seen much of this world in the last three days as humans judge time. I find it most pleasing in my view. The speed, the shine, the light. The incomparable Lena Horne. Do you like basketball?"

"But how? How did you *do* it, Connie? How? No one could get him out . . ."

She took him by the hand, leading him toward the fifteen-foot-high doors. "May we come into your apartment, Mas'úd?"

The djinn made a sweeping gesture of invitation, bowing so low his head was at Danny's waist as he and Connie walked past.

They stepped inside the djinn's suite and it was as if they had stepped back in time to ancient Basra and the Thousand Nights and a Night. Or into a Cornel Wilde costume epic.

But amid all the silks and hangings and pillows and tapers and coffers and brassware, there in the center of the foyer, in a Lucite case atop an onyx pedestal, lit from an unknown source by a single glowing spot of light, was a single icon.

"Occasionally magic has to bow to technology," Connie said. Danny

moved forward. He could not make out what the item lying on the black
velvet pillow was. "And sometimes ancient anger has to bow to common
sense."

Danny was close enough to see it now.

Simple. It had been so simple. But no one had thought of it before.
Probably because the last time it had been needed, by the lamp's previous
owner, it had not existed.

"A can opener," Danny said. "A can opener!?! A simple, stupid,
everyday can opener!?! That's all it took? I had a nervous breakdown, and
you figured out a can opener?"

"Can do," Connie said, winking at Mas'úd.

"Not cute, Squires," Danny said. But he was thinking of the dia-
mond as big as the Ritz.

Reading a story like this makes one want to toss out all the old history texts and let the fantasy and SF writing community have a go at re-doing them for the secondary-school market. Guaranteed you'd have more students interested in history, and that they wouldn't be bored.

Roman history is particularly fascinating, but all too often shrunken and curdled into an endless litany of Latin names and places and dates. The history that's fun to read is history that lives and breathes. "Up the Wall" doesn't merely breathe, it fairly vibrates with life. Whether it would be allowed in history texts, its contextual accuracy notwithstanding, is another matter entirely. Most such weighty tomes have perforce had all the life sucked out of them by "review committees," whose sole task in life it is to reduce all textbooks to the literary level of vanilla pudding.

"Up the Wall" adds some spice. It also leaves you wondering who you'd *really* like to have standing alongside you in a crisis.

Up the Wall

ESTHER M. FRIESNER

A GUST OF NORTHCOUNTRY air swept over the undulating hump of Hadrian's Wall, still bearing with it the chill of the sea. The northcountry was the hard country—even the starveling sheep had the grim air of failed philosophers—but worse land yet lay north of the wall, in wild Caledonia, if the word of tribal Celts and travelers could be believed. Two figures in the full finery of the Roman legions paced the earthworks as dusk came on. The last rays of the setting sun struck gold from the breast of the eagle standard jammed into the soil between them. In looks, in bearing, in the solemn silence folded in wings around them, they carried a taste of eternity.

It all would have been very heroic and poetical if the shorter man had not reached up under his tunic and *pteruges*, undone his *bracae*, and taken a long, reflective pee in the direction of Orkney. His comrade affected not to notice.

Rather by way of distraction than conversation, the taller fellow broke silence almost simultaneously with his mate's breaking wind. In a good, loud, carrying voice he declaimed, "Joy to the Ninth, Caius Lucius Piso! The days of the beast are numbered. It shall be today that the hero comes; I feel it. This morning all the omens were propitious." He had the educated voice and diction a senator's son might envy. His Latin was high and pure, preserved inviolate even here, at the northernmost outpost of the legions. He turned to his mate. "What news from the south?"

"News?" his companion echoed. Then he placed a stubby tongue between badly chapped lips and blew a sound that never issued from the wolf's-head bell of any bucina. "Sweet sodding Saturn, Junie, how the blazes would *I* have any more news from the friggin' south than you, stuck up here freezin' me cobblers off, waitin' on the relief—see if *them* buggers ever show up, bleedin' arse-lickers the lot of 'em, and everyone knows Tullius Cato's old lady's been slippin' into the commander's bedroll, so *he* never pulls the shit-shift, wish *my* girl'd show half as much support for me career, but that's women for you—only women ain't so much to your taste, now as I remember the barrack-room gab, are they, no offense taken, I hope?"

His Latin was somewhat less pure than that of his hawk-faced comrade-in-arms.

Junius Claudius Maro regarded the balding, podgy little man with a look fit to petrify absolutely that fellow's already chilled cobblers. "You presume too much upon our training days, Caius Lucius Piso. Were I to report the half of what you have just said, our beloved commander could order the flesh flayed from your bones." He settled the drape of his thick wool mantle more comfortably on his shoulders, then suffered a happy afterthought: "With a steel-tipped knout. However, for the love that is between us, I will say nothing." He looked inordinately pleased with himself.

"Right, then," said Caius Lucius Piso. His own afterthought bid him add: "Ta." He uprooted the Imperial eagle, hoisted it fishpole-wise over one shoulder, and casually commenced a westerly ramble. "I'll just be toddling on down the wall, eh? Have a bit of a lookabout? Keep one peeper peeled for this hero fella you say's coming, maybe kindle a light, start a little summat boiling on the guardroom fire, hot wine, the cup that cheers, just the thing what with a winter like we're like to have, judging by the misery as's crept into me bones. Bring you back a cuppa, Junie?" This last comment was flung back from a goodly distance down the wall, went unheard, and received no reply.

The nearest guardroom along that section of the wall where the ill-matched pair patrolled had once been a thing of pride, to judge by its size. It was large enough to have housed sheep, for whatever purpose. Years and neglect had done their damnedest to bring pride to a fall. Hares and foxes took it in turn to nest in the tumbledown sections of the derelict structure, but there was still a portion of the building with a make-do roof of old blankets and sod. In the lee of the October winds, surrounded by shadows, Caius Lucius Piso knelt to poke up the small peat fire in the pit.

The flame caught and flared, banishing darkness. Caius gasped as his small fire leaped in reflection on the iron helmet and drawn sword of the man hunkered on his hams in the dingy guardroom. The image of a slavering wild boar cresting his helmet seemed to leap out at the trembling Roman. Beneath the brim, two small, red, and nasty orbs glared. From porcine eyes to bristly snout, there was a striking family resemblance between boar crest and crest-wearer.

There was also the matter of the man's sword. Caius Lucius Piso's initial impression of that weapon had not been wrong. It was indeed as large, keen, and unsheathed as it had seemed at first glance. It was also leveled at the crouching Roman. The man snarled foreign words and raised the sword several degrees, sending ripples through his thickly-corded forearm muscles. Many of his teeth were broken, all were yellow as autumn crocus, and the stench emanating from him, body and bear-skin, was enough to strike an unsuspecting passer-by senseless. He looked like a man to whom filth was not just a way of life, but a religious calling.

Caius Lucius Piso knew a hero when he saw one.

"Oh, *shit*," he said.

"*That's* him?" Goewin knotted her fists on her hips and studied the new arrival. "*That's* our precious hero?"

"Hush now, dear, he'll hear you." Caius Lucius Piso made small dampening motions with his hands, but the lady of his hearth and heart was undaunted. She had been the one who'd taught him how to make that obnoxious tongue-and-lips blatting sound, after all.

"Hush yerself, you great cowpat. Who cares *does* he hear me? Stupid clod don't speak a *fly*speck of honest Gaelic." She smiled sweetly at the visitor, who stood beside the oxhide-hung doorway, arms crossed. He appeared to disapprove of everything he saw within the humble hut, and, without a word, somehow conveyed the message that he had sheathed his fearsome sword under protest.

"Who'd like a bit of the old nip-and-tuck with any ewe he fancies, then?" Goewin asked him, still smiling. "Whose Mum did it for kippers?"

"Goewin, for Mithra's sake, the man's a guest. *And* a hero! He's only biding under our roof until they're ready to receive him formally at headquarters."

"*Hind*quarters, you mean, if it's the Commander yer speaking of."

"Epona's east tit, woman, mind your tongue! If word gets back to the commander that you've been rude to his chosen hero . . ." Caius Lucius turned chalky at the thought.

"A *hero?*" Goewin cocked her head at the impassive presence guarding her doorway. "*Him?*" She clicked her tongue. "If *that's* the sort of labor we're down to bringing into Britain, just to take care of a piddling beast *you* lot could handle, weren't you such hermaphros, *well*—"

"That's not fair and you know it, Goewin. You can't call a monster big enough to carry off five legionaries any sort of piddler."

"Oh, pooh. 'Tisn't as if it carried all five off in one go. I've not seen it anymore than you have, but I know different. You Romans *always* exaggerate, as many a poor girl's learned to her sorrow on the wedding night or 'round the Beltaine fires. Probably no more'n a newt with glanders, but straightaway you lot bawl 'Dragon!' and off for help you run. Bunch of babes. And if *that* piece propping up the doorpost's the best you could drum up on the Continent—" She shrugged expressively. "This country's just going to ruin, Cai, that's all." She slouched over to grasp the stranger's impressive left bicep. "Look 'ee here. Shoddy goods, that is. Scrawnier than—"

There was a flicker of cold steel. The man's dagger was smaller than his sword, lighter, far handier, with a clean line that would never go out of style. It was almost the size of a Roman legionary's shortsword, but he handled it with more address. Presently it addressed Goewin's windpipe.

"*Ave*, all," said Junius, pulling back the oxhide and stepping unwittingly into the midst of this small domestic drama. "The commander is now prepared to greet our noble visitor with all due—"

The noble visitor growled something unintelligible and dropped his dagger point from Goewin's throat. Caius Lucius rather supposed that his guest disliked interruptions. Junius stared as the blade turned its attention to him.

"Now just a moment—" Junius objected in his flawless Latin.

A moment was all Caius Lucius wished. His wife was safe, but now his messmate was in danger. Dragon or no, and never mind that Junie Maro was the biggest prig the Glorious Ninth had ever spawned, the bonds of the legion still stood for *some*thing. While trying to remember precisely what, he picked up a small wine jug and belted the noble visitor smack on top of his iron boar.

Junius Claudius Maro looked down at the crumpled heap of clay shards, fur, and badly-tanned leather at his feet, then gave Caius Lucius a filthy glare by way of thanks for his life. "You *idiot*," he said.

"You're welcome, I'm sure," Caius replied. Sullen and bitter, he added, "Didn't kill 'im. Didn't even snuff his wick."

That much was true. The man was not unconscious, just badly dazed and grinning like a squirrel. Caius Lucius watched, astounded, as old Junie knelt beside the stunned barbarian and spoke to him in a strange, harsh tongue. Still half loopy, the man responded haltingly in kind, and before long the two of them were deep in earnest conversation punctuated by bellowing laughter.

"You—you *speak* that gibberish, Junie?" Caius Lucius ventured to ask when his comrade finally stood up.

"*Geatish*, not gibberish," Junius replied, wiping tears of hilarity from his eyes. "Gods, and to think I never believed the *pater* when he told me it's the only tongue on earth fit for telling a really *elegant* latrine joke! Later on, you must remind me to tell you the one about—but no. The pun won't translate, and, in any case, Ursus here says he's going to kill you in a bit. If our commander doesn't have you crucified first, for nearly doing in our dragon-slayer."

Caius Lucius gaped. "*Crucified?*"

His wife sighed. "Didn't me Mum just *warn* me you'd come to a bad end. Now I'll have to listen to the old girl's bloody I-told-you-so's 'til Imbolc. *Honestly*, Cai—!"

* * *

"Caius Lucius Piso, you are accused of damaging legion property."
The Commander of the Ninth slurped an oyster and gave the accused the
fish-eye. "This man has been brought into our service at great *personal*
expense to deal with our—ah—little problem, and you make free with his
cranial integrity." The commander grinned, never loath to let his audience know when he'd come up with an especially elegant turn of phrase.
Marcus Septimus, the commander's secretary, toady, and emergency catamite, applauded dutifully and made a note of it.

"Bashed him one on the conk, he did," Goewin piped up from the
doorway. "I *saw* 'im!"

Caius could not turn to give his wife the killing look she deserved.
He was compelled to stand facing his commander, head bowed, and hear
Goewin condemn him with one breath, then, with the second, titter.
"Oooh, Maxentius, you keep your hands to *yourself*, you horrid goat!
And me not even a widow yet!" Her pleased tone of voice belied her
harsh words. Obviously, Goewin did not believe in waiting until the last
minute to provide for her future.

Caius scuffed his already worn *perones* in the packed earthen floor of
the commander's hut, and tried to think of something besides death. It
didn't help to dwell on the thought of killing old Junie, for that specific
fantasy always veered over to the general theme of *thanatos*, which by
turns yanked his musings back to his own imminent fate. The commander was not happy, and all the way back to the first generation, the
Commanders of the Ninth had had a simple way of dealing with their
discontent.

"Right. Guilty. Crucify him," said the commander.

Junius looked smug. He stood at the commander's left hand while
the man he had dubbed Ursus sprawled on a bench to the right. He still
wore the boar's head helm, but now the eyes beneath the brim no longer
showed murderous rage. Instead they roved slowly around the hut, silently weighing the worth and transportability of every even vaguely
valuable item they spied. They only paused in their mercantile circuit
when Junius leaned around the back of the commander's chair to
whisper a translation of Caius' sentence in the barbarian's shaggy ear.

Something like a flint-struck spark kindled in the depth of those tiny
eyes. "NEVER!" Ursus bawled—and then all Hades broke loose.

Afterwards, Caius could not say whether he was more shocked by
the barbarian's reaction, or by the fact that he had understood the man's
exclamation precisely.

He quickly shelved linguistic musings in favor of survival. It really *was* an impressive tantrum the barbarian was throwing; he also threw the bench. Everyone in the commander's hut who could reach an exit, did so, in short order. The commander and all members of the makeshift tribunal held their ground, but only because they were cut off from the sole escape route by the rampaging dragon-slayer himself.

Ursus was on his feet, each clenched fist the size of a toddler's skull. He gave a fierce kick, knocking over a little tabouret bearing a bowl of windfalls and a silver wine jug with matched goblets. He picked up the fallen objects one by one and flung them at the hut's curved walls. Though his sword and dagger had perforce been laid aside before coming into the commander's presence, he still looked able to reduce the population barehanded *ad libitum*. Throughout this demonstration, he continued to chant, "Never, never, *never!*"

The commander's face resembled an adolescent cheese. His jowls shuddered as much as his voice when he inquired so very delicately of his guest, "What? *Never?*"

When Junius went to translate this into Geatish, the hero seized him by the throat and shook him until his kneecaps rattled. He pitched the Roman javelin-fashion at the open doorway of the commander's house. Unfortunately, he missed his aim by a handspan. Junius came up face-first against a doorpost and knocked one of the severed heads out of its niche. The commander's woman, a hutproud lady, fussed loudly as she dusted it off and tucked it back where it belonged.

Junius received no such attentions.

Ursus glowered at the fallen foe.

"Far though my fate has flung me,
Weary the whale-road wandering,
Still shall I no stupidity stomach,
Butt and baited of boobies!"

All this he spat at his retired translator. He used a sadly corrupt version of Latin, admixed higgledy-piggledy with a sprinkling of other tongues. Like most bastards, it had its charm, and was able to penetrate where purebreds could not follow. It took some concentration, but every man of the Ninth who heard Ursus speak so, understood him.

Caius took a tentative step towards his unexpected champion. "You haven't half got a bad accent, mate. For a bloody foreigner, I mean. Pick up the tongue from a trader, then?"

Ursus' eyes narrowed, making them nigh invisible. He motioned for Caius to approach, and when the little man complied, he grabbed him and hoisted him onto tip-toe by a knot of tunic.

"Hear me, O halfling halfblood,
Lees of the legion's long lingering
Here hard by Hadrian's human-reared hillock!
Your lowly life I love not.
Murder you might I meetly,
Yet you are young and useful.
Wise is the woman-born warrior
Dragons who dauntless dares;
Smarter the soul who sword-smites serpents
Carefully, in company of comrades."

Caius was still puzzling this out when Marcus Septimus inched up behind him and whispered, "I think he wants a sword-bearer or something to stand by while he does in the dragon for us."

"Want *my* opinion," Caius growled out of the corner of his mouth, "the bugger's just as scared as the rest of us. Sword-bearer, my arse! What he wants is *bait!*"

"We could still crucify you," Marcus suggested.

Caius got his hands up and delicately disengaged the barbarian's hold on his tunic. Once there was solid earth under his feet again, he said, "All right, Ursus. You've got me over the soddin' barrel. I'll go."

Everyone left in the hut smiled, including Junius, who had just rejoined the sentient.

Ursus clapped the little legionary on the shoulder and declaimed: "Victory velcomes the valiant!"

Marcus raised one carefully-plucked brow and clucked. " 'Velcomes?' Hmph. If they're going to come over here and take our coin, they might at *least* learn to speak our language properly!"

"Silly Geat," Junius agreed, rubbing his head.

Ursus was neither deaf nor amused, and his smattering of Latin was enough to parse personal remarks. He gathered up the two critics as lesser men might pick strawberries. Marcus cast an imploring glance at the commander, who was suddenly consumed by a passion to get to know his toenails better.

"Sagas they sing of swordsmen," Ursus informed them.
"Hymn they the homicidal.
Geats, though for glory greedy,
Shame think it not to share.
Wily, the Worm awaits us.
Guides will I guard right gladly!
And, should the shambler slay you,

Sorrow shall I sincerely."

Caius leered at the two wriggling captives. "In other words, gents, we've *all* been bloody drafted."

"Oh, I hate this, hate this, *hate this*," Marcus whined as they trudged along Hadrian's Wall, fruitlessly trying to keep pace with Ursus.

"Put a *caliga* in it, you miserable cow! It's not like he'd tapped *you* to be his weapons bearer." Caius gave Marcus an encouraging jab with the bundle of spears that had been wished on him by his new boss. "All *you've* got to do is lead him to the fen where the monster's skulking and take off once the fun starts. Shouldn't be too hard for you."

"We're all going to *die*," Marcus moaned. "The dragon will be all stirred up, and it will slay that great brute before you can say *hic ibat Simois*, and then it will come after *us*. I can't outrun a dragon! Not in *these* shoes."

At the head of the line where he marched beside Ursus, a spare eagle standard jouncing along on his shoulder, Junius overheard and gave them a scornful backwards glance. He said something that Caius did not quite catch, but which caused Marcus to make an obscene gesture.

"Soddin' ears going on me," Caius complained. "What'd he say, then?"

"*That*—" Marcus pursed his ungenerous mouth "—was *Greek*."

"Greek to *me*, all right," Caius agreed. "Junie always was a bloody show-off."

"He said we were both slackers and cowards, and when we get back and he tells the Commander how badly we've disgraced the Glorious Ninth in front of the hired help, we'll both be crucified."

"Not *that* again." Caius shifted the spears. "I'm fucking sick and tired of Junie and his thrice-damned crucifixions. Mithra, it's like a bally religion with him. What's he need to get off, then? A handful of sesterce spikes and a mallet?"

"He also said that he was going to warn Arctos to keep a weather eye on us so we don't bolt."

Caius flung down his bundle, exasperated. "*Now* who's been wished on us for this little deathmarch, eh? Bad enough we're to split two men's rations four ways—sod the commander for a stone-arsed miser—but who's this fifth wheel coming to join us?"

The clatter of falling spears made the rest of the party draw up short. Marcus was totally bewildered. "*What* fifth wheel?"

"This Arctos bastard who'll be baby-minding us, that's who!" Caius shouted.

Junius regarded the angry little man with disdain. "I will thank you to keep a civil tongue in your head when speaking of our *pro tempore* commander, Caius Lucius Piso." He then turned to the barbarian and added, "Do not kill him yet, O august Ursus. We still need him to carry the spears."

"Arctos *is* Ursus, Cai, old boy," Marcus whispered. "Greek, Latin, same meaning, same name. So sorry if I confused you. The drawbacks of a really good classical education." He tittered behind his hand.

"Sod off," Caius growled, gathering up the armory.

It was some three days later that the little group finally stepped off on the northern side of the Wall and reached their goal. Gray and brown and thoroughly uninviting, the fen stretched out before them. Mist lay thick upon the quaking earth. A few scraggly bushes, their branches stripped of foliage, clung to the banks of the grim tarn like the clutching hands of drowning men going under for the last time.

"—and the best freshwater fishing for miles about." Caius sighed as he viewed the haunt of their watery Nemesis. "If the commander wasn't half such a great glutton, we could leave the fish to the dragon and eat good boiled mutton like honest folk. But *no.* Off he goes, filling our ears with endless, colicky speeches about the honor of the Ninth and all that Miles Gloriosus codswallop, when the *truth* is that he just fancies a sliver of stuffed pike now and again. So in he brings this hero fella, and now our lives aren't worth a tench's fart."

"I heard that!" Junius called. "And when the commander finds out—"

"Junie, love, why don't you go nail your balls to a board?" Marcus Septimus remarked over-sweetly.

Caius patted the former secretary on the back. "You know, Marc, old dear, you're not a bad sort for a catamite."

The barbarian directed his helpers to pitch camp, which they did in swift, efficient, legion fashion. Despite their internal bickerings, proper training made them work well together. Even Marcus did not manage to get too badly underfoot. When the lone tent was pitched and dinner on the boil, Caius flopped down on the damp ground without further ceremony.

"Oh, me aching back! Mithra knows how many friggin' *milia pasuum* we've covered, and for what? Just so's we'd be on time to be ate tomorrow morning!"

A gaunt shadow fell across his closed eyes. "Get up, Caius Lucius Piso," Junius said, using the tip of his foot to put some muscle behind the order. "The food is ready and we can't find Ursus anywhere."

"Can't we now?" Caius did not bother to open his eyes. "Here's me heart, bleeding like a stuck pig over the news. Run off, has he? Jupiter, I never figured the big ox to have a fraction so much sense as *that*. Commander shouldn't't've paid him in advance."

"He was paid nothing." Junius' words were as dry as Goewin's onion tart. "Nor has he run off. Ursus is a *hero*."

"Says who? Himself?"

Junius tucked his hands tightly into the crooks of his elbows. "Our commander is not without his sources of information, nor would he engage such an important hireling blind. He heard nothing but the most sterling reports of our man's prowess at disposing of supernumerary monsters. Granted, the fellow's one of those Ultima Thule types who hails from where they've the better part of the year to work on polishing their lies for the spring trade, but even discounting a third of what they say he's done—"

Caius made that blatting sound again.

"In any case, our noble commander is not the sort to make a bad bargain, and were he to hear *you* so much as *implying* that he might, he would—"

"Yes, yes, I know, crucify me." Caius forced himself to stand. "I'll go fetch 'im, then, before you get yer hands all over calluses from nailing me up."

Caius didn't have far to go before he found his temporary leader. The barbarian squatted on a little hummock of high ground overlooking the fen, his sword jammed into a large, moldy-looking log some short distance away. His helmet was off, propped upside-down between his ankles, and his left hand kept dipping into it, then traveling to his mouth. Caius smelled a penetrating sweetness above the fetid reek of the marshland.

"Hail, heart-strong helper!" Ursus beamed at the little Roman. Viscous golden brown strands dripped from his beard and moustache.

"Hail yerself," Caius replied. He sauntered up the hummock and scrooched down beside the barbarian. "Got something good, have we?" He peered into the upended helm.

Ursus nodded cheerfully, his expression miraculously purged of any bloodlust. He jerked one thumb at the log, while with the other hand he shoved the helmet at Caius.

"Hollow this harvest's home,
Fallen the forest friend
Ages ago, several seasons spent.
Rotten and rent, core and root,
Toppled to turf the tall tree.
Gilded the gliding gladiators,
Plying their pleasant pastime,
Sweetness sun-gold instilling,
Honey they heap in hives.
Noisy their nest they name,
Daring and daunting dastards,
Stabbing with stings to startle
Thieves that their treasure try taking.
Came then the conquering caller,
Scorning their scabrous squabbles,
Their dire drones disdaining,
Helping himself to honey.
Right were the runes they wrought
When saw he first the sunlight,
Bidding the birthed boy Bee-wolf
Never another name know."

"Boy? Who gave birth to what boy hereabouts?" Caius' eyes darted about suspiciously.

The barbarian struck his own chest a fearsome thump.

"Oh." Caius dipped into the honey. Through gummy lips he added, "Going on about yerself, then, were you?"

The barbarian bobbed his head eagerly.

"Nice bit o' puffery, that. Bee-wolf, eh? That'd be yer common or garden variety bear, ain't it? So that's why Junie stuck you with Ursus, leave it to *him* not to have more imagination than a badger's bottom. Kind of a circumlocutionariatory way to go about naming a sprat, don't ask *me* why you'd want yer kid associated in decent folks' minds with a horrid great smelly beast what hasn't the brains of a turnip, though it does make for a tasty stew, especially *with* a turnip or two, gods know *I* hope you didn't smell like one from the minute you were born—a bear, I mean, not a turnip; *nor* a stew—but you can't bloody tell about foreigners, now can you? Never one word where twenty'll do, no offense taken, I hope?"

Bee-wolf nodded, still grinning. His find of wild honey had sweetened his temper amazingly well.

" 'Course, not that a name like that don't have its poetry to it, mate. A man needs a bit of poetry in his life now and again." Caius chewed up a fat hunk of waxy comb and spat dead bees into the fen with casual accuracy. " 'Mongst my Goewin's folk—Goewin's the jabbery little woman you came near to filleting with yer dagger—they keep a whole *stable* of bards plumped up just to natter on about how this chief slew that one and made off with his cattle. It's a wonder to me the poor beasties have a bit o' flesh left on their bones, the way those mad Celts keep peaching 'em back and forth, forth and back, always on the move. Savagery, *I* call it; not like us Romans. Compassionate, we are—one of the refinements of civilization. Cruelty to dumb brutes makes me want to spew."

Caius leaned forward, encouraged to this intimacy by the barbarian's continued calm. "Now if it were up to *me*," he confided, "I'd leave this poor soddin' dragon alone, I would. Live and let live, I say—that's the civilized way to go about it. It's not as though he's ate up more'n *five* of our men, after all, and we've just got guesses to go by even for that. Only one witness ever come back to tell us it *were* the dragon for certain as ate 'em, or even *was* they ate, and *that* man was our *signifer* Drusus Llyr, what no one knew his parents was first cousins 'til it was too late, and *he* died stark bonkers that very night. You want me considered opinion, them fellers went over the Wall, they did, fed up to their gizzards with the commander and the whole glorious Ninth fucking Legion." He drew a deep sigh. "Can't say as I blame 'em. Can't even rightly say as I wouldn't do the same."

Ursus looked puzzled.

"Came the commander's call.
Summoning my sword to serve him.
Nobly the Ninth he named,
Home and haven of heroes."

"Arr, that's just recruitment blabber." Caius waved it all aside. "Lot of fine talk, all of it slicker than goose shit, just to rope in the young men as are half stupid, half innocent, and t'other half ignorant, no offense meant. Once in a while he manages to gammon a few of the local brats into uniform, but mostly it's sons of the legion following in their Da's footsteps because a camp upbringing's ruined 'em for honest work stealing cattle. No, the Ninth's not what she used to be."

"When, I do wistful wonder,
Was this, thy lonesome legion
More than a muddle of men

Prowling the piddling plowlands,
Wandering the Wall's wide way?"

"Wozzat? Oh, I get yer. Well, truth to tell—" Caius leaned in even
closer and nearly rested his elbow in the honey "—I haven't the foggiest.
See, mate, *used* to be the Ninth was as fine a lot of pureblood Roman
soldiers as ever you'd fancy—and didn't our commander just! But then,
well . . . you know as how *things* have this narsty way of just . . .
happening, like?"

"Fate do I fear not.
Still, circumstances stun stalwarts.
Here, have more honey."

Caius did so. "Like I been saying, what with the wild upcountry folk
the Ninth was first sent here to deal with, always on the march, camp
here today, there tomorrow, try to keep the Celtic chieftains in line or
even learn to tell 'em *apart* one from the other, and what with the odd
carryings-on back home in dear old Roma Mater, inside the city, out in
the provinces, up 'crost the German frontier with them as must be yer
kissin' cousins, Saxons and Goths and that lot, *well*, in comes one rosy-
fingered dawn and gooses our then-commander with the fact that there
ain't no orders come through from Rome or even Londinium to tell us
arse from elbow. No *orders*, mate! You know what *that* means to a professional soldier and bureaucrat like our commander?"

"No, that knowledge I know not."

"Small wonder you would, you being a hero and all. Stand up for
yerself, do what you like, go where the fancy takes you. But *regular
army?* We don't dare take a *shit* without proper orders to wipe off with
after. So when there *wasn't* none coming through, we dug in where we
was, up by the Wall, took up with the local ladies, bred our boys to the
Legion and our girls to bribe any tribes we couldn't beat in a fair fight,
and we waited." Caius rested his face on one hand, forgetting it was the
one he'd been using to dip into Ursus' helmet. "We're still waiting, man
and boy, father to son, can't *tell* you how bloody long it's been."

The barbarian tilted his helmet and slurped out the last of the plun-
dered honey. He wiped his gooey whiskers on the back of an equally
hairy forearm, then said:

"Strangely this strikes me as scoop-skulled.
Why do you wait and wonder?
Beneath your brows lurk brains or bran?
Sit you thus centuries? Shitheads."

Caius made a hand-sign that translated across any number of cultures. "Look, mate, so long as our bleedin' commander, latest in a long line of Imperially-appointed shitheads, has got more than three like old Junie there to lick his tail and say *please, sir, what's for afters?* it's no use running off. There's precious little as *is* to keep the men occupied. Hunting down a deserter'd be a rare treat for any of 'em. And it's as much as me life's worth to speak up and say let's break camp and head south like sensible folk, try to scare up some news from Rome as isn't staler than week-old pig piss. See, so long as we're up *here*, our commander's the law. Go *south*, and he could find out that the only thing he's got a right to control is his own bladder, and not too strict a say over *that*. So if a man's fool enough to suggest a move off the Wall, 'Orders is orders,' he'd say, 'and traitors is traitors. And we of the Glorious Ninth know what to do with *traitors*, don't we, Junie, me proud beauty?' "

"Crudely crucify the creatures," Ursus supplied.

"You're not just talking through yer helmet there, mate," Caius agreed. "Speaking of which, it's in a proper mess. Give 'er here to me, and you go fetch that boar-sticker of yours out of the log. We'll have a proper wash-up—me for the helmet, you for the blade, before she rusts silly, doesn't anybody ever teach you barbarians respect for a good bit of steel?—then we'll go back to camp and get some oil for the pair of 'em. Supper's ready, and if we let it go to the bad, Junie'll be off crucifying us left and right again."

"Dares he the deed to do,
Sooner my sword shall steep its steel,
Blood-drinker, blade and brother,
Entirely in his entrails."

Caius took up the helmet, beaming. "You're a decent sort, Bee-wolf, for a bleedin' hero." He toddled down the slope to rinse out the helmet.

As he squatted to his task in the shallows, a tuneless ditty on his lips, a loud, wet, crunch hard by his right foot made him start and keel over into the murky water. The helmet went flying out over the fenland, landing with an echoing *plop* in a nearby pool.

Junius Claudius Maro leaned hard on the eagle standard and observed the helm's trajectory with a critical eye. "*Now* you shall not escape punishment, Caius Lucius Piso."

"*Punishment?*" Caius spluttered, scarcely feeling the cold water that seeped through his clothes. Rage kept him warm. "After *you* was the one as scared the *bracae* off me, sneaking up and chunking that whopping great standard into the sod like you was trying to spit me foot with it?" He picked himself up out of the shoreline muck and hailed the hummock. "Oi! Bee-wolf! You saw him do that, didn't you? You saw as it wasn't no fault of *mine* that your helmet—"

But Bee-wolf was not paying attention to the angry little Roman. He stood on the high ground, honey still gumming his beard, and stared out across the fen to the spot where his boar-crest helmet had gone down. He made no move to yank his sword free of the fallen log where it still stood wedged in the heart of the ruined beehive. Something in the barbarian's sudden pallor and paralysis stilled Caius' own tongue. From the corner of one eye, he saw that Junie was likewise rapt with terror. He did not *want* to see what had frightened them so, but, at last, look he did.

The fen bubbled. The slimy surface heaved. Slowly, seemingly as slender as a maiden's arm, a snaky form broke the face of the stagnant water. On and on it came, climbing every higher into the clear air, until Caius thought that there simply could *not* be any more to come without ripping reality wide open and sending all the world plunging down into the gods' own nightmares. He was only half aware of the eagle standard toppling over into the mud as Junie whirled and fled. This sudden movement galvanized the lazily rising length of serpentine flesh. The spade-shaped head darted within arm's length of Caius, ignoring the petrified little man as if he were part of the scenery. A maw lined with needlelike teeth gaped open, impossibly wide, and sharp jaws clamped shut around Junie, hauberk, shriek, and all.

"Oh, I *say!*" Caius exclaimed, as his comrade's scream knocked his own tongue free. Automatically, he stooped to retrieve the fallen standard, then turned to the hummock and bawled, "*There's* your bloody fen-monster, Bee-wolf, old boy! Do for 'er now while she's busy with poor Junie and you've got surprise on yer . . ." His words dribbled away.

The high ground was bare, the hero nowhere to be seen.

"*Coward!*" came Marcus' angry shout from the direction of camp. "You pusilanimous, recreant, craven, dastardly, caitiff—Oooooh, you *rabbit*, come back with Cai's *sword!*" The commander's secretary came stomping into sight of the fen just as the monster commenced reeling in a struggling Junie.

Caius heard Marcus' yips of shock blend nicely with Junie's continued screaming and blubbering. The dragon was imperturbable, allowing the bulk of his still-submerged and leisurely sinking body to drag his prize into the fen. Caius watched as span after span of sequentially decreasing neck slipped past him. It would not be long before Junie followed, down into the fen, without so much as a last *vale* for his old messmate.

"Bloody foreigners," Caius grumbled, and, raising the eagle standard high, he brought it crunching down as hard as he was able, just at the moment when the monster's head came by.

BONK.

The dragon froze, its wicked mouth falling open. Junius flopped out. He wasted no time in questioning deliverance, but hauled his body free. He was breathing hoarsely—no doubt he had a rib or two the worse for wear—but he was able to pull himself a little ways up the shore.

Caius smashed the beast in the head again with the eagle of the Ninth, putting all his weight in it. He and Junie looked at each other. "One bloody word out of you about damaging legion property, Junie," he shouted, "and it's back in the fen I'll toss you myself!"

"Not a word, not one!" Junie wheezed, pulling himself farther up the bank. Marcus came running down, holding his tunic well out of the mud, and tried to hoist the injured man without soiling himself. It was an impossible endeavor.

"Cai, leave that horrid creature alone and come here *right now* and help me with Junius!" he called. "Go on, let it be, it's had enough."

"Stop yer gob, will you?" Caius was panting with the effort of using the legion standard as a bludgeon, but he lofted it for a third blow anyhow. "If this bugger's just stunned, *I'm* nearest, and I'll be twigged if I'll be the tasty pud to tempt an invalid monster's palate when it comes to. Not just to keep *your* tunic clean, Missy Vestal!"

"Well, who died and made *us* Jupiter Capitolinus?" With a peeved sniff, Marcus slung Junie's arm around his neck, letting the mud slop where it would. "If you're still speaking to the *plebs*, Cai, we'll be back in camp." He hustled Junie out of sight without waiting to see the eagle descend for the third time.

The beast had been hissing weakly, but the final smash put paid to that. There was a sickening crunch that Caius felt all the way up his arms to his shoulders, and then it was no longer possible to tell where the monster's skull ended and the bogland began. Caius wiped his sweating brow, getting honey all over his face. "*That's* done," he said, "and damned if anyone'll credit it. Goewin won't, for one; not without proof, and that means the head." He felt for his sword, then remembered that not only had he left it in camp, but the barbarian had made off with it.

"Vesta's smoking hole!" He thrust the standard deep into the sodden ground, cradling it in the crook of one arm as he raised cupped hands to lips and bellowed, "Oi! Marcus! Fetch me back Junie's sword when yer at a loose end, there's a dear!" He waited. Not even an echo returned.

Caius called again, then another time, until he felt a proper fool. He left the standard rooted where it was and trudged back to the camp, only to find that all of it—tent, packs, gear, cookpots and dinner—was gone. In the failing light, he spied two rapidly retreating figures headed in the direction of the Wall.

"Plague rot 'em, lights and liver," Caius muttered. "Look at the buggers run! I never saw Junie move *that* fast, even when he wasn't chawed over by a dragon." He patted his legion dagger, still firmly tucked into his belt. "Well, old girl, it'll be a long saw, but you and me, we'll have that bleeder's head off right enough, even does it take us all night. After all, it's *my* dragon."

Caius' chest inflated with pride as he realized the full measure of his deed. "Didn't even need a sword to kill 'im," he told the air. "And if there's any man likes to fancy that means I did for the monster *bare-handed*, who's to tell the tale any different?" He was fairly swaggering by the time he returned to the scene of his triumph.

His mood of self-congratulation quickly soured to outrage when he beheld the tableau awaiting him at the fenside. The eagle had fallen again, knocked down by the hopeless struggle of a raggedy, gray-bearded relic who had the dragon by the narrowest bit of its neck and was obviously trying to yank the whole enormous carcass out of the water, hand over hand. The head, already pulpy, could not long stand such cavalier treatment. It squashed into splinters of bone and globs of unidentifiable tissue in the old man's grasp.

"Here, now!" Caius barked, rushing forward too late to preserve his trophy. He shouldered the gaffer aside, stared at what once might have been the full price of Goewin's respect—to say nothing of that of the commander and the Ninth—and burst into tears.

The old man cowered and wrung his hands, squeezing out little pips of blood and brain matter from between the palms. "Noble Chieftain, forgive this worthless fool for having dared to presume you had abandoned your lawful kill!" He spoke Gaelic, a dialect slightly different from Goewin's folk.

"Oh, you pasty old fiend, you've bally ruined *everything!*" Caius wailed, kicking the goo that had once been the dragon's head. "How am I ever going to prove I slew the beast without the head to show for it? I can't bloody well tow the whole fucking corpse down the Wall, can I now?"

"You might take a handful of the teeth with you, my lord," the old man suggested timidly, awed by Caius' passion.

"Oh, yes!" Caius did not bother to trim his sarcasm. "Dragon's teeth'll do, *won't* they? When every peddler the length and breadth of Britain's got *bags* full of such trumpery—grind 'em up and slip 'em in yer wine when yer woman wants cheering and you can't afford unicorn's horn on a legionary's pay—each and *all* culled from the mouths of any great fish luckless enough to wash up dead on the seacoast?" He gulped for breath, then spat, "Think the commander don't know *that* much? He's one of their biggest customers. You stupid *sod!*"

"High Chief, do but calm your wrath against me." The old man pointed a palsied finger at the pool that still concealed the bulk of the beast. "Together we can surely pull the monster's body onto land, and then you have but to cut out its heart and eat it and then—"

Caius stopped crying and frowned. "You off yer nut *entire*, or are you just senile? Eat a beastly dragon's *heart*? Whuffo?"

"Why, High Chief, then you shall be wiser than any wizard and understand the speech of all the birds of the air!" The old man flung his arms wide. He wore no more than a mantle of red deer hide, with a knot of anonymously colored cloth doing up his loins. His expansive gesture wafted the full power of his personal aroma right into Caius' face.

The legionary wiped his nose, then pinched it shut. "Is thad whad you was doing? Trying to beach this creature so as to ead id's heart and have yerself a chat with the birdies?" The old man nodded. Caius dropped his pinching fingers. "Mithra, what sort of cuckoo hatched you?"

The oldster hung his head. "My mother was a wise woman, my father I never knew. At my birth, the bards of our tribe tell that two dragons coupled in a field hereabouts and—"

"Right, right." Caius waved him silent. "Serve me right, asking for the straight story from a Celt," he said to himself. Aloud he added, "You one of them wizard fellers yerself, then? Or can't you afford decent clothes, just?"

A sly glint came into the old man's eye. When he smiled, Caius beheld a mouthful of the memories of decent teeth. "King and lord, you are as all-seeing as you are all-valiant. I am indeed privy to the occult forces of nature."

"Well, I knew there was summat of the privy about you," Caius riposted. He chortled over his own sally until he caught the look the old man was giving him. He decided to return to his wrathful pose; folk treated you with more honor if they feared you were going to send their conks down the same route he'd shown the dragon.

Thoughts of the beast forced him to consider the ruined trophy and his present position. Although he glared doom at the old man, in his heart he knew that he would not be able to afford the luxury of such a killing look when he faced his commander again.

Junie and Marcus, they'll make camp before I do, what with the time I'm wasting on this geezer and the thought of what I've got to say, he reflected. *Even with Junie banged up like he is, they'll stir their stumps to be first in line with the tale of what happened to the dragon. Think for a tick they'll make it truthful? Huh! That'd mean old Junie'd have to admit as he was near ate and saved by me.* Me! *He'd sooner—Well, he'd sooner crucify hisself, given there was a way to see that stunt through.*

Caius scraped his chin with fingers still sticky from the honey harvest and regarded the self-styled wizard thoughtfully. "Here," he said. "You called that great wallopin' beast me lawful kill, didn't yer?"

"Oh, aye, that I did, most awful lord."

"Saw the whole thing happen, did yer?"

The old man grinned like a death's head and nearly bobbed the head off his meager neck in agreement as he pointed to the paltry stand of scrub that had been his hiding place throughout the epic conflict.

"That's all right, then." Caius was better than satisfied. "You'll just nip along back to the legion camp with me and tell anyone as I points you at just exactly what happened here, how I stepped up bold to that 'ere dragon and—"

The old man's eyes rolled back in his head and he sank cross-legged to the ground. A horrid gurgling welled out of his throat as he tilted his face skywards. "Bold came the high king, master of men, open-handed to the least of his servants, and the golden eagle flew before him, symbol of his might and fame. Fled they all three, the cowards who had served him, leaving him lone to fight the unwholesome beast of the bogland. Terrible was his ire against the fainthearted. Cursing, he killed one man for his shameful act, striking him down like a dog—"

"Now just a minute, you old rattlebrain, I never killed no one but the *dragon!*"

The old man opened his eyes so sharply that Caius thought he heard a whipcrack. "Now you've made me lose the sacred thread of creation, O High Chief." He managed to make the highflown title sound like a synonym for *numbskull.*

"Arr, that don't signify. There wasn't half the truth in what you were saying—leave it to you Celts—and if the commander's not drunker than Silenus when he hears you out, he'll rule as *all* of what you have to say is pure horseshit."

An uneasy inspiration creased Caius' brow. "Excepting for the part as where you says I killed someone. Bee-wolf, curse him, *he's* gone. Who's to say what's become of him? That Junie and Marcus, they're clever as a brace of seaport whores, the pair of 'em. Shouldn't take 'em long to club together and tell the commander that *I* murdered the hero while *they* did for the dragon. Nodens' nuts, Junie's got the battle scars to prove it! And what've *I* got? What in bloody Hades have *I* got?" The gristle of reality stuck in his throat and he crumpled down beside the old man, sniveling.

"Does this mean that my noble lord will not help his sworn servant to cut out the dragon's heart?" the graybeard asked by way of comfort.

"Oh, go help yerself to the soddin' heart, you old fool!" Caius sobbed. "Can't you see I've me own troubles?"

"The burden of rule falls heavy on the uncounseled," the old man intoned with due solemnity. "Yet, by my head, I swear never to give you ill-considered advice, nor to let aught but wise words pour from my lips into your ears."

"You try pouring anything into *my* ears, grizzlepate, and I'll cosh you a good one!" Caius raised his fists to the darkening sky. "Oh gods, not even a place to lay me head tonight, and odds are it won't be many days before the commander sends out a patrol to hunt me down!"

"Over the dead bodies of your guardsmen, my lord." The old man looked grim but determined.

"Over—*what?*" Caius asked.

Even allowing for oral decoration and a useless genealogical sidebar tracing the ancestry of the dragon's last-but-one-victim, it did not take the old man too long to inform Caius that the beast had caused the death of his tribe's chieftain, a man of sterling character and many cattle. An upstart stripling named Llassar Llawr of the Lake Country had tried to avenge the chief's consumption, but he too had been dragged into the fen for his troubles.

"Is that why you were here, skulking about?" the Roman asked. "Waiting to see was anyone *else* fool enough to have a go at the monster, so's you could leap out and ask for a gob of heart did they succeed?"

"I was not *skulking*." The old man puffed up like an infected wound. "Wizards have no need to skulk. I was in trance, communing with the gods, awaiting a sign to foretell the coming of a hero to defeat the dragon and take the right of kingship over our tribe. Since the beast took the life of our lawful lord, it was only right that its death provide us with a replacement."

"So you were waiting for a hero?" Caius snorted. "Been there meself. Had one *on* me, I did, in fact, but he bolted." To himself he thought, *Wonder what did become of old Bee-wolf? Nothing too bad, I hope. Can't judge him too harsh, getting the monster sprung on him like that. How was he to know the beast wouldn't bide quiet 'til morning, then come be slaughtered all polite and planned? Luck to you, mate, wherever you are! Could be as you'll still make a hero, some day. Mithra knows there's fens aplenty in this wicked world, and maybe a dragon or two to be getting on with.*

To the old man he said, "I guess you'll have to make do with *me*, then. Kingship, eh? Well . . . it's bound to bring me no worse than the Glorious Ninth ever did, they can kiss me glorious bum goodbye, see if *I* care." He paused in his diatribe. " 'Course, there's Goewin . . ."

"This Goewin, is she your woman?" the old man asked.

Caius suddenly recalled Goewin's voice, alternately throwing him to the figurative lions during his trial and slyly encouraging Maxentius' advances. His mouth set hard. "Not any *more* she's not; not after all the slap-and-tickle she's no doubt been up to soon's as I got fairly out of sight. Just you tell me one thing: If I'm yer new chieftain, like you say, this don't mean I've got to be forever riding about, stealing other folks' cows, now does it? I'm strictly infantry, you know."

"You need lead no cattle-raids, my lord." The old man smiled beneficently, if a trifle smugly. "Not if you tell the tribesmen that your faithful servant and all-wise wizard has counseled you that the gods are against it." Softly he added, "I could be even *more* all-wise if you'd give me a hand with the dragon's heart, Noble Chief. Unless you'd like to eat it yourself . . . ?"

Caius gagged.

By the light of a hastily kindled fire, the two men managed to haul a length of the dragon's dead body onto the shore a little after nightfall. Caius made some exploratory excavations with his dagger in the region of the beast's chest, but quickly saw that this was a futile game as well as a messy one.

"Like a field mouse trying to rape a lion," he complained. "This job wants a man-sized blade. Bugger all, if only that Bee-wolf bastard hadn't run off with—"

Caius remembered something. He glanced up at the hummock,

where the departed barbarian's sword still stood at attention in the rotten log. "Hang on a mo', Grandda," he told the wizard. "Won't be gone but a shake."

The old man watched him ascend the high ground. The years, and the diet that had cost him most of his teeth, had been even less charitable to his eyes. The night, the wizard's nearsightedness, and the uncertain firelight all conspired to obscure just what happened next. The wizard wiped a small bit of rheum from his eyes, blinked, and looked again just in time to see Caius' hands close around one end of a long, thickish object standing upright in a second, far more massive, object. Just as the old man had mentally discounted a number of things those distant articles *might* be, Caius gave a heave and brandished something long and gleaming overhead with both hands.

There was only one possible object for a sane man to brandish in this fashion: a *sword*. As for what it had been sheathed *in* . . .

"A stone!" the wizard shouted. "He pulled the sword from a stone!"

By the time Caius came back down to the fire, the awe-smitten old man was groveling in the mud and gibbering about magical strength and miraculous proof of kingship.

"Say, O Highest of the High Chiefs," the wizard babbled. "Say what this, your humblest servant and counselor, shall name you before the tribe! Speak, and I shall fly swifter than the hunting merlin-hawk to spread your name among your waiting people!"

Caius rubbed his chin again. He was not sure what he had done to merit this, but he was not fool enough to question Fortuna's little pranks. "I am called Cai—" he began, then stopped. It would not take much for word to reach the Commander of someone with a Roman name jumped-up to chieftancy of a native tribe—not the way these Celts talked. It would take less time for the bastard to then dispatch the whole legion after him. The Glorious Ninth had gone to pot, true, but the strength of their old training still made them a bad enemy. Until Caius could give his new subjects the once-over and gauge their mettle as soldiers, he would do well to lay low.

"I mean, Cai, that's just me *milk*-name, as I was raised with," he said hastily. "What I'm *really* called is—" he cudgeled his brains for a moment, desperately trying to come up with a name that was not Roman and would not ring familiar in the Commander's ears.

He found one.

"—Arctos."

He settled down to clean his sword, completely forgetting his promise to cut out the dragon's heart.

"Lord," the old man prompted. "Lord, if you do not remove the beast's heart soon, it will lose all virtue."

"Sod off," said Arctos.

The old man scowled. "Bloody foreigners," he grumbled.

Still, it would make a good story.

Where do you get your ideas? That's what they always ask writers. If you're a writer, you already know the answer, and if you're not, you'll never have a clue. Sorry, but that's the way the galaxy spins.

Writers, and in particular writers of fantasy, should be able to make a good story out of anything. Out of the ordinary, the commonplace, the unspectacular. Any fool can build a story around dragons and elves and vampires. It takes a truly good writer to make one out of white bread, or a paperclip, or an ant or a rose.

Or something as plain, ordinary, and everyday as water.

Trouble With Water

HORACE L. GOLD

GREENBERG DID NOT deserve his surroundings. He was the first fisherman of the season, which guaranteed him a fine catch; he sat in a dry boat—one without a single leak—far out on a lake that was ruffled only enough to agitate his artificial fly. The sun was warm, the air was cool; he sat comfortably on a cushion; he had brought a hearty lunch; and two bottles of beer hung over the stern in the cold water.

Any other man would have been soaked with joy to be fishing on such a splendid day. Normally, Greenberg himself would have been ecstatic, but instead of relaxing and waiting for a nibble, he was plagued by worries.

This short, slightly gross, definitely bald, eminently respectable businessman lived a gypsy life. During the summer he lived in a hotel with kitchen privileges in Florida; and in both places he operated concessions.

For years now, rain had fallen on schedule every week end, and there had been storms and floods on Decoration Day, July 4th and Labor Day. He did not love his life, but it was a way of making a living.

He closed his eyes and groaned. If he had only had a son instead of his Rosie! Then things would have been mighty different—

For one thing, a son could run the hot dog and hamburger griddle, Esther could draw beer, and he would make soft drinks. There would be small difference in the profits, Greenberg admitted to himself; but at least those profits could be put aside for old age, instead of toward a dowry for his miserably ugly, dumpy, pitifully eager Rosie.

"All right—so what do I care if she don't get married?" he had cried to his wife a thousand times. "I'll support her. Other men can set up boys in candy stores with soda fountains that have only two spigots. Why should I have to give a boy a regular International Casino?"

"May your tongue rot in your head, you no-good piker!" she would scream. "It ain't right for a girl to be an old maid. If we have to die in the poorhouse, I'll get my poor Rosie a husband. Every penny we don't need for living goes to her dowry!"

Greenberg did not hate his daughter, nor did he blame her for his misfortunes; yet, because of her, he was fishing with a broken rod that he had to tape together.

That morning his wife opened her eyes and saw him packing his equipment. She instantly came awake. "Go ahead!" she shrilled—speaking in a conversational tone was not one of her accomplishments—"Go fishing, you loafer! Leave me here alone. I can connect the beer pipes and the gas for soda water. I can buy ice cream, frankfurters, rolls, sirup, and watch the gas and electric men at the same time. Go ahead—go fishing!"

"I ordered everything," he mumbled soothingly. "The gas and electric won't be turned on today. I only wanted to go fishing—it's my last chance. Tomorrow we open the concession. Tell the truth, Esther, can I go fishing after we open?"

"I don't care about that. Am I your wife or ain't I, that you should go ordering everything without asking me—"

He defended his actions. It was a tactical mistake. While she was still in bed, he should have picked up his equipment and left. By the time the argument got around to Rosie's dowry, she stood facing him.

"For myself I don't care," she yelled. "What kind of a monster are you that you can go fishing while your daughter eats her heart out? And on a day like this yet! You should only have to make supper and dress

Rosie up. A lot you care that a nice boy is coming to supper tonight and maybe take Rosie out, you no-good father, you!"

From that point it was only one hot protest and a shrill curse to finding himself clutching half a broken rod, with the other half being flung at his head.

Now he sat in his beautifully dry boat on an excellent game lake far out on Long Island, desperately aware that any average fish might collapse his taped rod.

What else could he expect? He had missed his train; he had had to wait for the boathouse proprietor; his favorite dry fly was missing; and, since morning, not a fish had struck at the bait. Not a single fish!

And it was getting late. He had no more patience. He ripped the cap off a bottle of beer and drank it, in order to gain courage to change his fly for a less sporting bloodworm. It hurt him, but he wanted a fish.

The hook and the squirming worm sank. Before it came to rest, he felt a nibble. He sucked in his breath exultantly and snapped the hook deep into the fish's mouth. Sometimes, he thought philosophically, they just won't take artificial bait. He reeled in slowly.

"Oh, Lord," he prayed, "a dollar for charity—just don't let the rod bend in half where I taped it!"

It was sagging dangerously. He looked at it unhappily and raised his ante to five dollars; even at that price it looked impossible. He dipped his rod into the water, parallel with the line, to remove the strain. He was glad no one could see him do it. The line reeled in without a fight.

"Have I—God forbid!—got an eel or something not kosher?" he mumbled. "A plague on you—why don't you fight?"

He did not really care what it was—even an eel—anything at all.

He pulled in a long, pointed, brimless green hat.

For a moment he glared at it. His mouth hardened. Then, viciously, he yanked the hat off the hook, threw it on the floor and trampled on it. He rubbed his hands together in anguish.

"All day I fish," he wailed, "two dollars for train fare, a dollar for a boat, a quarter for bait, a new rod I got to buy—and a five-dollar mortgage charity has got on me. For what? For you, you hat, you!"

Out in the water an extremely civil voice asked politely: "May I have my hat, please?"

Greenberg glowered up. He saw a little man come swimming vigorously through the water toward him: small arms crossed with enormous dignity, vast ears on a pointed face propelling him quite rapidly and efficiently. With serious determination he drove through the water, and, at the starboard rail, his amazing ears kept him stationary while he looked gravely at Greenberg.

"You are stamping on my hat," he pointed out without anger.

To Greenberg this was highly unimportant. "With the ears you're swimming," he grinned in a superior way. "Do you look funny!"

"How else could I swim?" the little man asked politely.

"With the arms and legs, like a regular human being, of course."

"But I am not a human being. I am a water gnome, a relative of the more common mining gnome. I cannot swim with my arms, because they must be crossed to give an appearance of dignity suitable to a water gnome; and my feet are used for writing and holding things. On the other hand, my ears are perfectly adapted for propulsion in water. Consequently, I employ them for that purpose. But please, my hat—there are several matters requiring my immediate attention, and I must not waste time."

Greenberg's unpleasant attitude toward the remarkably civil gnome is easily understandable. He had found someone he could feel superior to, and, by insulting him, his depressed ego could expand. The water gnome certainly looked inoffensive enough, being only two feet tall.

"What you got that's so important to do, Big Ears?" he asked nastily.

Greenberg hoped the gnome would be offended. He was not, since his ears, to him, were perfectly normal, just as you would not be insulted if a member of a race of atrophied being were to call you "Big Muscles." You might even feel flattered.

"I really must hurry," the gnome said, almost anxiously. "But if I have to answer your questions in order to get back my hat—we are engaged in restocking the Eastern waters with fish. Last year there was quite a drain. The bureau of fisheries is cooperating with us to some extent, but, of course, we cannot depend too much on them. Until the population rises to normal, every fish has instructions not to nibble."

Greenberg allowed himself a smile, an annoyingly skeptical smile.

"My main work," the gnome went on resignedly, "is control of the rainfall over the Eastern seaboard. Our fact-finding committee, which is scientifically situated in the meteorological center of the continent, coordinates the rainfall needs of the entire continent; and when they determine the amount of rain needed in particular spots of the East, I make it rain to that extent. Now may I have my hat, please?"

Greenberg laughed coarsely. "The first lie was big enough—about telling the fish not to bite. You make it rain like I'm President of the United States!" He bent toward the gnome slyly. "How's about proof?"

"Certainly, if you insist." The gnome raised his patient, triangular face toward a particularly clear blue spot in the sky, a trifle to one side of Greenberg. "Watch that bit of the sky."

Greenberg looked up humorously. Even when a small dark cloud rapidly formed in the previously clear spot, his grin remained broad. It could have been coincidental. But then large drops of undeniable rain fell over a twenty-foot circle; and Greenberg's mocking grin shrank and grew sour.

He glared hatred at the gnome, finally convinced. "So you're the dirty crook who makes it rain on week ends!"

"Usually on week ends during the summer," the gnome admitted. "Ninety-two percent of water consumption is on weekdays. Obviously we must replace that water. The week ends, of course, are the logical time."

"But, you thief!" Greenberg cried hysterically. "You murderer! What do you care what you do to my concession with your rain! It ain't bad enough business would be rotten even without rain, you got to make floods!"

"I'm sorry," the gnome replied, untouched by Greenberg's rhetoric. "We do not create rainfall for the benefit of men. We are here to protect the fish.

"Now please give me my hat. I have wasted enough time, when I should be preparing the extremely heavy rain needed for this coming week end."

Greenberg jumped to his feet in the unsteady boat. "Rain this week end—when I can maybe make a profit for a change! A lot you care if you ruin business. May you and your fish die a horrible, lingering death."

And he furiously ripped the green hat to pieces and hurled them at the gnome.

"I'm really sorry you did that," the little fellow said calmly, his huge ears treading water without the slightest increase of pace to indicate his anger. "We Little Folk have no tempers to lose. Nevertheless, occasionally we find it necessary to discipline certain of your people, in order to retain our dignity. I am not malignant; but, since you hate water and those who live in it, water and those who live in it will keep away from you."

With his arms still folded in great dignity, the tiny water gnome flipped his vast ears and disappeared in a neat surface dive.

Greenberg glowered at the spreading circles of waves. He did not grasp the gnome's final restraining order; he did not even attempt to interpret it. Instead he glared angrily out of the corner of his eye at the phenomenal circle of rain that fell from a perfectly clear sky. The gnome must have remembered it at length, for a moment later the rain stopped. Like shutting off a faucet, Greenberg unwillingly thought.

"Good-by, week-end business," he growled. "If Esther finds out I got into an argument with the guy who makes it rain—"

He made an underhand cast, hoping for just one fish. The line flew out over the water; then the hook arched upward and came to rest several inches above the surface, hanging quite steadily and without support in the air.

"Well, go down in the water, damn you!" Greenberg said viciously, and he swished his rod back and forth to pull the hook down from its ridiculous levitation. It refused.

Muttering something incoherent about being hanged before he'd give in, Greenberg hurled his useless rod at the water. By this time he was not surprised when it hovered in the air above the lake. He merely glanced red-eyed at it, tossed out the remains of the gnome's hat, and snatched up the oars.

When he pulled back on them to row to land, they did not touch the water—naturally. Instead they flashed unimpeded through the air, and Greenberg tumbled into the bow.

"Aha!" he grated. "Here's where the trouble begins." He bent over the side. As he had suspected, the keel floated a remarkable distance above the lake.

By rowing against the air, he moved with maddening slowness toward shore, like a medieval conception of a flying machine. His main concern was that no one should see him in his humiliating position.

At the hotel he tried to sneak past the kitchen to the bathroom. He knew that Esther waited to curse him for fishing the day before opening, but more especially on the very day that a nice boy was coming to see her Rosie. If he could dress in a hurry, she might have less to say—

"Oh, there you are, you good-for-nothing!"

He froze to a halt.

"Look at you!" she screamed shrilly. "Filthy—you stink from fish!"

"I didn't catch anything, darling," he protested timidly.

"You stink anyhow. Go take a bath, may you drown in it! Get dressed in two minutes or less, and entertain the boy when he gets here. Hurry!"

He locked himself in, happy to escape her voice, started the water in the tub and stripped from the waist up. A hot bath, he hoped, would rid him of his depressed feeling.

First, no fish; now, rain on week ends! What would Esther say—if she knew, of course. And, of course, he would not tell her.

"Let myself in for a lifetime of curses!" he sneered. "Ha!"

He clamped a new blade into his razor, opened the tube of shaving cream, and stared objectively at the mirror. The dominant feature of the soft, chubby face that stared back was its ugly black stubble; but he set his stubborn chin and glowered. He really looked quite fierce and indomitable. Unfortunately, Esther never saw his face in that uncharacteristic pose, otherwise she would speak more softly.

"Herman Greenberg never gives in!" he whispered between savagely hardened lips. "Rain on week ends, no fish—anything he wants; a lot I care! Believe me, he'll come crawling to me before I go to him."

He gradually became aware that his shaving brush was not getting wet. When he looked down and saw the water dividing into streams that flowed around it, his determined face slipped and grew desperately anxious. He tried to trap the water—by catching it in his cupped hands, by creeping up on it from behind, as if it were some shy animal, and shoving his brush at it—but it broke and ran away from his touch. Then he jammed his palm against the faucet. Defeated, he heard it gurgle back down the pipe, probably as far as the main.

"What do I do now?" he groaned. "Will Esther give it to me if I don't take a shave! But how? . . . I can't shave without water."

Glumly, he shut off the bath, undressed and stepped into the tub. He lay down to soak. It took a moment of horrified stupor to realize that he was completely dry and that he lay in a waterless bathtub. The water, in one surge of revulsion, had swept out onto the floor.

"Herman, stop splashing!" his wife yelled. "I just washed that floor. If I find one little puddle I'll murder you!"

Greenberg surveyed the instep-deep pool over the bathroom floor. "Yes, my love," he croaked unhappily.

With an inadequate washrag he chased the elusive water, hoping to mop it all up before it could seep through the apartment below. His washrag remained dry, however, and he knew that the ceiling underneath was dripping. The water was still on the floor.

In despair, he sat on the edge of the bathtub. For some time he sat in silence. Then his wife banged on the door, urging him to come out. He started and dressed moodily.

When he sneaked out and shut the bathroom door tightly on the floor inside, he was extremely dirty and his face was raw where he had experimentally attempted to shave with a dry razor.

"Rosie!" he called in a hoarse whisper. "Sh! Where's Mamma?"

His daughter sat on the studio couch and applied nail polish to her stubby fingers. "You look terrible," she said in a conversational tone. "Aren't you going to shave?"

He recoiled at the sound of her voice, which, to him, roared out like a siren. "Quiet, Rosie! Sh!" And for further emphasis, he shoved his lips out against a warning finger. He heard his wife striding heavily around the kitchen. "Rosie," he cooed, "I'll give you a dollar if you'll mop up the water I spilled in the bathroom."

"I can't Papa," she stated firmly. "I'm all dressed."

"Two dollars, Rosie—all right, two and a half, you blackmailer."

He flinched when he heard her gasp in the bathroom; but, when she came out with soaked shoes, he fled downstairs. He wandered aimlessly toward the village.

Now he was in for it, he thought; screams from Esther, tears from Rosie—plus a new pair of shoes for Rosie and two and a half dollars. It would be worse, though, if he could not get rid of his whiskers—

Rubbing the tender spots where his dry razor had raked his face, he mused blankly at a drugstore window. He saw nothing to help him, but he went inside anyhow and stood hopefully at the drug counter. A face peered at him through a space scratched in the wall case mirror, and the druggist came out. A nice-looking, intelligent fellow, Greenberg saw at a glance.

"What you got for shaving that I can use without water?" he asked.

"Skin irritation, eh?" the pharmacist replied. "I got something very good for that."

"No. It's just—Well, I don't like to shave with water."

The druggist seemed disappointed. "Well, I got brushless shaving cream." Then he brightened. "But I got an electric razor—much better."

"How much?" Greenberg asked cautiously.

"Only fifteen dollars, and it lasts a lifetime."

"Give me the shaving cream," Greenberg said coldly.

With the tactical science of a military expert, he walked around until some time after dark. Only then did he go back to the hotel, to wait outside. It was after seven, he was getting hungry, and the people who entered the hotel he knew as permanent summer guests. At last a stranger passed him and ran up the stairs.

Greenberg hesitated for a moment. The stranger was scarcely a boy, as Esther had definitely termed him, but Greenberg reasoned that her term was merely wish-fulfillment, and he jauntily ran up behind him.

He allowed a few minutes to pass, for the man to introduce himself and let Esther and Rosie don their company manners. Then, secure in the knowledge that there would be no scene until the guest left, he entered.

He waded through a hostile atmosphere, urbanely shook hands with Sammie Katz, who was a doctor—probably, Greenberg thought shrewdly, in search of an office—and excused himself.

In the bathroom he carefully read the directions for using brushless shaving cream. He felt less confident when he realized that he had to wash his face thoroughly with soap and water, but without benefit of either, he spread the cream on, patted it, and waited for his beard to soften. It did not, as he discovered while shaving. He wiped his face dry. The towel was sticky and black, with whiskers suspended in paste, and, for that, he knew, there would be more hell to pay. He shrugged resignedly. He would have to spend fifteen dollars for an electric razor after all; this foolishness was costing him a fortune!

That they were waiting for him before beginning supper, was, he knew, only a gesture for the sake of company. Without changing her hard, brilliant smile, Esther whispered: "Wait! I'll get you later—"

He smiled back, his tortured, slashed face creasing painfully. All that could be changed by his being enormously pleasant to Rosie's young man. If he could slip Sammie a few dollars—more expense, he groaned—to take Rosie out, Esther would forgive everything.

He was too engaged in beaming and putting Sammie at ease to think of what would happen after he ate caviar canapes. Under other circumstances Greenberg would have been repulsed by Sammie's ultra-professional waxed mustache—an offensively small, pointed thing—and his commercial attitude toward poor Rosie; but Greenberg regarded him as a potential savior.

"You open an office yet, Doctor Katz?"

"Not yet. You know how things are. Anyhow, call me Sammie."

Greenberg recognized the gambit with satisfaction, since it seemed to please Esther so much. At one stroke Sammie had ingratiated himself and begun bargaining negotiations.

Without another word, Greenberg lifted his spoon to attack the soup. It would be easy to snare this eager doctor. A *doctor*! No wonder Esther and Rosie were so puffed with joy.

In the proper company way, he pushed his spoon away from him. The soup spilled onto the tablecloth.

"Not so hard, you dope," Esther hissed.

He drew the spoon toward him. The soup leaped off it like a live thing and splashed over him—turning, just before contact, to fall on the floor. He gulped and pushed the bowl away. This time the soup poured over the side of the plate and lay in a huge puddle on the table.

"I didn't want any soup anyhow," he said in a horrible attempt at levity. Lucky for him, he thought wildly, that Sammie was there to pacify Esther with his smooth college talk—not a bad fellow, Sammie, in spite of his mustache; he'd come in handy at times.

Greenberg lapsed into a paralysis of fear. He was thirsty after having eaten the caviar, which beats herring any time as a thirst raiser. But the knowledge that he could not touch water without having it recoil and perhaps spill made his thirst a monumental craving. He attacked the problem cunningly.

The others were talking rapidly and rather hysterically. He waited until his courage was equal to his thirst; then he leaned over the table with a glass in his hand. "Sammie, do you mind—a little water, huh?"

Sammie poured from a pitcher while Esther watched for more of his tricks. It was to be expected, but still he was shocked when the water exploded out of the glass directly at Sammie's only suit.

"If you'll excuse me," Sammie said angrily, "I don't like to eat with lunatics."

And he left, though Esther cried and begged him to stay. Rosie was too stunned to move. But when the door closed, Greenberg raised his agonized eyes to watch his wife stalk murderously toward him.

Greenberg stood on the boardwalk outside his concession and glared blearily at the peaceful, blue, highly unpleasant ocean. He wondered what would happen if he started at the edge of the water and strode out. He could probably walk right to Europe on dry land.

It was early—much too early for business—and he was tired. Neither he nor Esther had slept; and it was practically certain that the neighbors hadn't either. But above all he was incredibly thirsty.

In a spirit of experimentation, he mixed a soda. Of course its high water content made it slop onto the floor. For breakfast he had surreptitiously tried fruit juice and coffee, without success.

With his tongue dry to the point of furriness, he sat weakly on a boardwalk bench in front of his concession. It was Friday morning, which meant that the day was clear, with a promise of intense heat. Had it been Saturday, it naturally would have been raining.

"This year," he moaned, "I'll be wiped out. If I can't mix sodas, why should beer stay in a glass for me? I thought I could hire a boy for ten dollars a week to run the hot-dog griddle; I could make sodas, and Esther could draw beer. All I can do is make hot dogs, Esther can still draw beer; but twenty or maybe twenty-five a week I got to pay a sodaman. I won't even come out square—a fortune I'll lose!"

The situation really was desperate. Concessions depend on too many factors to be anything but capriciously profitable.

His throat was fiery and his soft brown eyes held a fierce glaze when the gas and electric were turned on, the beer pipes connected, the tank of carbon dioxide hitched to the pump, and the refrigerator started.

Gradually, the beach was filling with bathers. Greenberg writhed on his bench and envied them. They could swim and drink without having liquids draw away from them as if in horror. They were not thirsty—

And then he saw his first customers approach. His business experience was that morning customers buy only soft drinks. In a mad haste he put up the shutters and fled to the hotel.

"Esther!" he cried. "I got to tell you. I can't stand it—"

Threateningly, his wife held her broom like a baseball bat. "Go back to the concession, you crazy fool. Ain't you done enough already?"

He could not be hurt more than he had been. For once he did not cringe. "You got to help me, Esther."

"Why didn't you shave, you no-good bum? Is that any way—"

"That's what I got to tell you. Yesterday I got into an argument with a water gnome—"

"A what?" Esther looked at him suspiciously.

"A water gnome," he babbled in a rush of words. "A little man so high, with big ears that he swims with, and he makes it rain—"

"Herman!" she screamed. "Stop that nonsense. You're crazy!"

Greenberg pounded his forehead with his fist. "I ain't crazy. Look, Esther. Come with me into the kitchen."

She followed him readily enough, but her attitude made him feel more helpless and alone than ever. With her fists on her plump hips and her feet set wide, she cautiously watched him try to fill a glass of water.

"Don't you see?" he wailed. "It won't go in the glass. It spills all over. It runs away from me."

She was puzzled. "What happened to you?"

Brokenly, Greenberg told of his encounter with the water gnome, leaving out no single degrading detail. "And now I can't touch water," he ended. "I can't drink it. I can't make sodas. On top of it all, I got such a thirst, it's killing me."

Esther's reaction was instantaneous. She threw her arms around him, drew his head down to her shoulder, and patted him comfortingly as if he were a child. "Herman, my poor Herman!" she breathed tenderly. "What did we ever do to deserve such a curse?"

"What shall I do, Esther?" he cried hopelessly.

She held him at arm's length. "You got to go to a doctor," she said firmly. "How long can you go without drinking? Without water you'll die. Maybe sometimes I am a little hard on you, but you know I love you—"

"I know, Mamma," he sighed. "But how can a doctor help me?"

"Am I a doctor that I should know? Go anyhow. What can you lose?"

He hesitated. "I need fifteen dollars for an electric razor," he said in a low, weak voice.

"So?" she replied. "If you got to, you got to. Go, darling. I'll take care of the concession."

Greenberg no longer felt deserted and alone. He walked almost confidently to a doctor's office. Manfully, he explained his symptoms. The doctor listened with professional sympathy, until Greenberg reached his description of the water gnome.

Then his eyes glittered and narrowed. "I know just the thing for you, Mr. Greenberg," he interrupted. "Sit there until I come back."

Greenberg sat quietly. He even permitted himself a surge of hope. But it seemed only a moment later that he was vaguely conscious of a siren screaming toward him; and then he was overwhelmed by the doctor and two interns who pounced on him and tried to squeeze him into a bag.

He resisted, of course. He was terrified enough to punch wildly. "What are you doing to me?" he shrieked. "Don't put that thing on me!"

"Easy now," the doctor soothed. "Everything will be all right."

It was on that humiliating scene that the policeman, required by law to accompany public ambulances, appeared. "What's up?" he asked.

"Don't stand there, you fathead," an intern shouted. "This man's crazy. Help us get him into this strait jacket."

But the policeman approached indecisively. "Take it easy, Mr. Greenberg. They ain't gonna hurt you while I'm here. What's all this about?"

"Mike!" Greenberg cried, and clung to his protector's sleeve. "They think I'm crazy—"

"Of course he's crazy," the doctor stated. "He came in here with a fantastic yarn about a water gnome putting a curse on him."

"What kind of curse, Mr. Greenberg?" Mike asked cautiously.

"I got into an argument with the water gnome who makes it rain and takes care of the fish," Greenberg blurted. "I tore up his hat. Now he won't let water touch me. I can't drink, or anything—"

The doctor nodded. "There you are. Absolutely insane."

"Shut up." For a long moment Mike stared curiously at Greenberg, Then: "Did any of you scientists think of testing him? Here, Mr. Greenberg." He poured water into a paper cup and held it out.

Greenberg moved to take it. The water backed up against the cup's far lips; when he took it in his hand, the water shot out into the air.

"Crazy, is he?" Mike asked with heavy irony. "I guess you don't know there's things like gnomes and elves. Come with me, Mr. Greenberg."

They went out together and walked toward the boardwalk. Greenberg told Mike the entire story and explained how, besides being so uncomfortable to him personally, it would ruin him financially.

"Well, doctors can't help you," Mike said at length. "What do they know about the Little Folk? And I can't say I blame you for sassing the gnome. You ain't Irish or you'd have spoke with more respect to him. Anyhow, you're thirsty. Can't you drink *anything*?"

"Not a thing," Greenberg said mournfully.

They entered the concession. A single glance told Greenberg that business was very quiet, but even that could not lower his feelings more than they already were. Esther clutched him as soon as she saw them.

"Well?" she asked anxiously.

Greenberg shrugged in despair. "Nothing. He thought I was crazy."

Mike stared at the bar. Memory seemed to struggle behind his reflective eyes. "Sure," he said after a long pause. "Did you try beer, Mr. Greenberg? When I was a boy my old mother told me all about elves and gnomes and the rest of the Little Folk. She knew them, all right. They don't touch alcohol, you know. Try drawing a glass of beer—"

Greenberg trudged obediently behind the bar and held a glass under the spigot. Suddenly his despondent face brightened. Beer creamed into the glass—and stayed there! Mike and Esther grinned at each other as Greenberg threw back his head and furiously drank.

"Mike!" he crowed. "I'm saved. You got to drink with me!"

"Well—" Mike protested feebly.

By late afternoon, Esther had to close the concession and take her husband and Mike to the hotel.

The following day, being Saturday, brought a flood of rain. Greenberg nursed an imposing hang-over that was constantly aggravated by his having to drink beer in order to satisfy his recurring thirst. He thought of forbidden icebags and alkaline drinks in an agony of longing.

"I can't stand it!" he groaned. "Beer for breakfast—phooey!"

"It's better than nothing," Esther said fatalistically.

"So help me, I don't know if it is. But, darling, you ain't mad at me on account of Sammie, are you?"

She smiled gently. "Poo! Talk dowry and he'll come back quick."

"That's what I thought. But what am I going to do about my curse?"

Cheerfully, Mike furled an umbrella and strode in with a little old woman, whom he introduced as his mother. Greenberg enviously saw evidence of the effectiveness of icebags and alkaline drinks, for Mike had been just as high as he the day before.

"Mike told me about you and the gnome," the old lady said. "Now I know the Little Folk well, and I don't hold you to blame for insulting him, seeing you never met a gnome before. But I suppose you want to get rid of your curse. Are you repentant?"

Greenberg shuddered. "Beer for breakfast! Can you ask?"

"Well, just you go to this lake and give the gnome proof."

"What kind of proof?" Greenberg asked eagerly.

"Bring him sugar. The Little Folk love the stuff—"

Greenberg beamed. "Did you hear that, Esther? I'll get a barrel—"

"They love sugar, but they can't eat it," the old lady broke in. "It melts in water. You got to figure out a way so it won't. Then the little gentleman'll know you're repentant for real."

"Aha!" Greenberg cried. "I knew there was a catch!"

There was a sympathetic silence while his agitated mind attacked the problem from all angles. Then the old lady said in awe: "The minute I saw your place I knew Mike had told the truth. I never seen a sight like it in my life—rain coming down, like the flood, everywhere else; but all around this place, in a big circle, it's dry as a bone!"

While Greenberg scarcely heard her, Mike nodded and Esther seemed peculiarly interested in the phenomenon. When he admitted defeat and came out of his reflected stupor, he was alone in the concession, with only a vague memory of Esther's saying she would not be back for several hours.

"What am I going to do?" he muttered. "Sugar that won't melt—" He drew a glass of beer and drank it thoughtfully. "Particular they got to be yet. Ain't it good enough if I bring simple sirup? That's sweet."

He puttered about the place, looking for something to do. He could not polish the fountain or the bar, and the few frankfurters broiling on the griddle probably would go to waste. The floor had already been swept. So he sat uneasily and worried his problem.

"Monday, no matter what," he resolved, "I'll go to the lake. It don't pay to go tomorrow. I'll only catch a cold because it'll rain."

At last Esther returned, smiling in a strange way. She was extremely gentle, tender and thoughtful; and for that he was appreciative. But that night and all day Sunday he understood the reason for her happiness.

She had spread word that, while it rained in every other place all over town, their concession was miraculously dry. So, besides a headache that made his body throb in rhythm to its vast pulse, Greenberg had to work like six men satisfying the crowd who mobbed the place to see the miracle and enjoy the dry warmth.

How much they took in will never be known. Greenberg made it a practice not to discuss such personal matters. But it is quite definite that not even in 1929 had he done so well over a single week end.

Very early Monday morning he was dressing quietly, not to disturb his wife. Esther, however, raised herself on her elbow and looked at him doubtfully.

"Herman," she called softly, "do you really have to go?"

He turned, puzzled. "What do you mean—do I have to go?"

"Well—" she hesitated. Then: "Couldn't you wait until the end of the season, Herman, darling?"

He staggered back a step, his face working in horror. "What kind of an idea is that for my own wife to have?" he croaked. "Beer I have to drink instead of water. How can I stand it? Do you think I *like* beer? I can't wash myself. Already people don't like to stand near me; and how will they act at the end of the season? I go around looking like a bum because my beard is too tough for an electric razor, and I'm all the time drunk—the first Greenberg to be a drunkard. I want to be respected—"

"I know, Herman, darling," she sighed. "But I thought for the sake of our Rosie— Such a business we've never done like we did this week end. If it rains every Saturday and Sunday, but not on our concession, we'll make a *fortune!*"

"Esther!" Herman cried, shocked. "Doesn't my health mean anything?"

"Of course, darling. Only I thought maybe you could stand it for—"

He snatched his hat, tie and jacket, and slammed the door. Outside, though, he stood indeterminedly. He could hear his wife crying, and he realized that, if he succeeded in getting the gnome to remove the curse, he would forfeit an opportunity to make a great deal of money.

He finished dressing more slowly. Esther was right, to a certain extent. If he could tolerate his waterless condition—

"No!" he gritted decisively. "Already my friends avoid me. It isn't right that a respectable man like me should always be drunk and not take a bath. So we'll make less money. Money isn't everything—"

And with great determination he went to the lake.

But that evening, before going home, Mike walked out of his way to stop in at the concession. He found Greenberg sitting on a chair, his head in his hands, and his body rocking slowly in anguish.

"What is it, Mr. Greenberg?" he asked gently.

Greenberg looked up. His eyes were dazed. "Oh, you, Mike," he said blankly. Then his gaze cleared, grew more intelligent, and he stood up and led Mike to the bar. Silently, they drank beer. "I went to the lake today," he said hollowly. "I walked all around it, hollering like mad. The gnome didn't stick his head out of the water once."

"I know." Mike nodded sadly. "They're busy all the time."

Greenberg spread his hands imploringly. "So what can I do? I can't write him a letter or send him a telegram; he ain't got a door to knock on or a bell for me to ring. How can I get him to come up and talk?"

His shoulders sagged. "Here, Mike. Have a cigar. You been a real good friend, but I guess we're licked."

They stood in an awkward silence. Finally Mike blurted: "Real hot, today. A regular scorcher."

"Yeah. Esther says business was pretty good, if it keeps up."

Mike fumbled at the cellophane wrapper. Greenberg said: "Anyhow, suppose I did talk to the gnome. What about the sugar?"

The silence dragged itself out, became intense and uncomfortable. Mike was distinctly embarrassed. His brusque nature was not adapted for comforting discouraged friends. With immense concentration he rolled the cigar between his fingers and listened for a rustle.

"Day like this's hell on cigars," he mumbled, for the sake of conversation. "Dries them like nobody's business. This one ain't, though."

"Yeah," Greenberg said abstractedly. "Cellophane keeps them—"

They looked suddenly at each other, their faces clean of expression.

"Holy smoke!" Mike yelled.

"Cellophane on sugar!" Greenberg choked out.

"Yeah," Mike whispered in awe. "I'll switch my day off with Joe, and I'll go to the lake with you tomorrow. I'll call for you early."

Greenberg pressed his hand, too strangled by emotion for speech. When Esther came to relieve him, he left her at the concession with only the inexperienced griddle boy to assist her, while he searched the village for cubes of sugar wrapped in cellophane.

The sun had scarcely risen when Mike reached the hotel, but Greenberg had long been dressed and stood on the porch waiting impatiently. Mike was genuinely anxious for his friend. Greenberg staggered along toward the station, his eyes almost crossed with the pain of a terrific hang-over.

They stopped at a cafeteria for breakfast. Mike ordered orange juice, bacon and eggs, and coffee half-and-half. When he heard the order, Greenberg had to gag down a lump in his throat.

"What'll you have?" the counterman asked.

Greenberg flushed. "Beer," he said hoarsely.

"You kidding me?" Greenberg shook his head, unable to speak. "Want anything with it? Cereal, pie, toast—"

"Just beer." And he forced himself to swallow it. "So help me," he hissed at Mike, "another beer for breakfast will kill me!"

"I know how it is," Mike said around a mouthful of food.

On the train they attempted to make plans. But they were faced by a phenomenon that neither had encountered before, and so they got nowhere. They walked glumly to the lake, fully aware that they would have to employ the empirical method of discarding tactics that did not work.

"How about a boat?" Mike suggested.

"It won't stay in the water with me in it. And you can't row it."

"Well, what'll we do then?"

Greenberg bit his lip and stared at the beautiful blue lake. There the gnome lived, so near to them. "Go through the woods along the shore, and holler like hell. I'll go the opposite way. We'll pass each other and meet at the boathouse. If the gnome comes up, yell for me."

"O.K.," Mike said, not very confidently.

The lake was quite large and they walked slowly around it, pausing often to get the proper stance for particularly emphatic shouts. But two hours later, when they stood opposite each other with the full diameter of the lake between them, Greenberg heard Mike's hoarse voice: "Hey, gnome!"

"Hey, gnome!" Greenberg yelled. "Come on up!"

An hour later they crossed paths. They were tired, discouraged, and their throats burned; and only fishermen disturbed the lake's surface.

"The hell with this," Mike said. "It ain't doing any good. Let's go back to the boathouse."

"What'll we do?" Greenberg rasped. "I can't give up!"

They trudged back around the lake, shouting halfheartedly. At the boathouse, Greenberg had to admit that he was beaten. The boathouse owner marched threateningly toward them.

"Why don't you maniacs get away from here?" he barked. "What's the idea of hollering and scaring away the fish? The guys are sore—"

"We're not going to holler any more," Greenberg said. "It's no use."

When they bought beer and Mike, on an impulse, hired a boat, the owner cooled off with amazing rapidity, and went off to unpack bait.

"What did you get a boat for?" Greenberg asked. "I can't ride in it."

"You're not going to. You're gonna walk."

"Around the lake again?" Greenberg cried.

"Nope. Look, Mr. Greenberg. Maybe the gnome can't hear us through all that water. Gnomes ain't hardhearted. If he heard us and thought you were sorry, he'd take his curse off you in a jiffy."

"Maybe." Greenberg was not convinced. "So where do I come in?"

"The way I figure it, some way or other you push water away, but the water pushes you away just as hard. Anyhow, I hope so. If it does, you can walk on the lake." As he spoke, Mike had been lifting large stones and dumping them on the bottom of the boat. "Give me a hand with these."

Any activity, however useless, was better than none, Greenberg felt. He helped Mike fill the boat until just the gunwales were above water. Then Mike got in and shoved off.

"Come on," Mike said. "Try to walk on the water."

Greenberg hesitated. "Suppose I can't?"

"Nothing'll happen to you. You can't get wet, so you won't drown."

The logic of Mike's statement reassured Greenberg. He stepped out boldly. He experienced a peculiar sense of accomplishment when the water hastily retreated under his feet into pressure bowls, and an unseen, powerful force buoyed him upright across the lake's surface. Though his footing was not too secure, with care he was able to walk quite swiftly.

"Now what?" he asked, almost happily.

Mike had kept pace with him in the boat. He shipped his oars and passed Greenberg a rock. "We'll drop them all over the lake—make it damned noisy down there and upset the place. That'll get him up."

They were more hopeful now, and the comments, "Here's one that'll wake him," and "I'll hit him right on the noodle with this one," served to cheer them still further. And less than half of the rocks had been dropped when Greenberg halted, a boulder in his hands. Something inside him wrapped itself tightly around his heart and his jaw dropped.

Mike followed his awed, joyful gaze. To himself, Mike had to admit that the gnome, propelling himself through the water with his ears, arms folded in tremendous dignity, was a funny sight.

"Must you drop rocks and disturb us at our work?" the gnome asked.

Greenberg gulped. "I'm sorry, Mr. Gnome," he said nervously. "I couldn't get you to come up by yelling."

The gnome looked at him. "Oh. You are the mortal who was disciplined. Why did you return?"

"To tell you that I'm sorry, and I won't insult you again."

"Have you proof of your sincerity?" the gnome asked quietly.

Greenberg fished furiously in his pocket and brought out a handful of sugar wrapped in cellophane, which he tremblingly handed to the gnome.

"Ah, very clever, indeed," the little man said, unwrapping a cube and popping it eagerly into his mouth. "Long time since I've had some."

A moment later Greenberg spluttered and floundered under the surface. Even if Mike had not caught his jacket and helped him up, he could almost have enjoyed the sensation of being able to drown.

I really don't believe in feminist fiction, and certainly not in the fields of fantasy and science-fiction. If a male writer can put us into the mind of a six-armed Legamoth from Canopus, he can sure as hell show us what Shirley McNulty from down the block is thinking. James Schmitz, for one, built a whole SF career on the antics of strong female protagonists (come to think of it, if you'd ever met Mrs. Schmitz, you'd understand why). Other male writers have done as well or better at putting themselves in the minds of members of the opposite sex, and of course the reverse is true.

On the other chromosome . . .

There are some stories that a man simply would not write. Not because being male renders him incapable of so doing, but just because he's unlikely to think of certain themes, or at least to approach them in as, well, personal a fashion.

After you read Nina Hoffman's story, you might want to think twice about approaching them at all.

Savage Breasts

NINA KIRIKI HOFFMAN

I WAS ONLY a lonely leftover on the table of Life. No one seemed interested in sampling me.

I was alone that day in the company cafeteria when I made the fateful decision which changed my life. If Gladys, the other secretary in my boss's office and my usual lunch companion, had been there, it might never have happened, but she had a dentist appointment. Alone with the day's entree, Spaghetti-O's, I sought company in a magazine I found on the table.

In the first blazing burst of inspiration I ever experienced, I cut out an ad on the back of the Wonder Woman comic book. "The Insult that Made a Woman Out of Wilma," it read. It showed a hipless, flat-chested girl being buried in the sand and abandoned by her date, who left her alone with the crabs as he followed a bosomy blonde off the page. Wilma eventually excavated herself, went home, kicked a chair, and sent away for Charlotte Atlas's pamphlet, "From Beanpole to Buxom in 20 days or your money back." Wilma read the pamphlet and developed breasts the size of breadboxes. She retrieved her boyfriend and rendered him acutely jealous by picking up a few hundred other men.

I emulated Wilma's example and sent away for the pamphlet and the equipment that came with it.

When my pamphlet and my powder-pink exerciser arrived, I felt a vague sense of unease. Some of the ink in the pamphlet was blurry. A few pages were repeated. Others were missing. Sensing that my uncharacteristic spurt of enthusiasm would dry up if I took the time to send for a replacement, I plunged into the exercises in the book (those I could decipher) and performed them faithfully for the requisite twenty days. My breasts blossomed. Men on the streets whistled. Guys at the office looked up when I jiggled past.

I felt like a palm tree hand-pollinated for the first time. I began to have clusters of dates. I was pawed, pleasured, and played with. I experienced lots of stuff I had only read about before, and I mostly loved it after the first few times. The desert I'd spent my life in vanished; everything I touched here in the center of the mirage seemed real, intense, throbbing with life. I exercised harder, hoping to make the reality realler.

Then parts of me began to fight back.

I reclined on Maxwell's couch, my hands behind my head, as he unbuttoned my shirt, unhooked my new, enormous, front-hook bra, and opened both wide. He kissed my stomach. He feathered kisses up my body. Suddenly my left breast flexed and punched him in the face. He was surprised. He looked at me suspiciously. I was surprised myself. I studied my left breast. It lay there gently bobbing like a Japanese glass float on a quiet sea. Innocent. Waiting.

Maxwell stared at my face. Then he shook his head. He eyed my breasts. Slowly he leaned closer. His lips drew back in a pucker. I waited, tingling, for them to flutter on my abdomen again. No such luck. Both breasts surged up and gave him a double whammy.

It took me an hour to wake him up. Once I got him conscious, he told me to get out! Out! And take my unnatural equipment with me. I collected my purse and coat and, with a last look at him as he lay there on the floor by the couch, I left.

In the elevator my breasts punched a man who was smoking a cigar. He coughed, choked, and called me unladylike. A woman told me I had done the right thing.

When I got home I took off my clothes and looked at myself in the mirror. What beautiful breasts. Pendulous. Centerfold quality. Heavy as water balloons. Firm as paperweights. I would be sorry to say good-bye to them. I sighed, and they bobbled. "Well, guys, no more exercise for you," I said. I would have to let them go. I couldn't let my breasts become a Menace to Mankind. I would rather be noble and suffer a bunch.

I took a shower and went to bed.

That night I had wild dreams. Something was chasing me, and I was chasing something else. I thought maybe I was chasing myself, and that scared me silly. I kept trying to wake up, but to no avail. When I finally woke, exhausted and sweaty, in the morning, I discovered my sheets twisted around my legs. My powder-pink exerciser lay beside me in the bed. My upper arms ached the way they did after a good workout.

At work, my breasts interfered with my typing. The minute I looked away from my typewriter keyboard to glance at my steno pad, my breasts pushed between my hands, monopolizing the keys and driving my Selectric to distraction. After an hour of trying to cope with this I told my boss I had a sick headache. He didn't want me to go home. "Mae June, you're such an ornament to the office these days," he said. "Can't you just sit out there and look pretty and suffering? More and more of my clients have remarked on how you spruce up the decor. If that clackety-clacking bothers your pretty little head, why, I'll get Gladys to take your work and hers and type in the closet."

"Thank you, sir," I said. I went back out in the front room and sat far away from everything my breasts could knock over. Gladys sent me vicious looks as she flat-chestedly crouched over her early-model IBM and worked twice as hard as usual.

For a while I was happy enough just to rest. After all that nocturnal exertion, I was tired. My chair wasn't comfortable, but my body didn't care. Then I started feeling rotten. I watched Gladys. She had scruffy hair that kept falling out of its bobby pins and into her face. She kept her fingernails short and unpolished and she didn't seem to care how carelessly she chose her clothes. She reminded me of the way I had looked two months earlier, before men started getting interested in me and giving me advice on what to wear and what to do with my hair. Gladys and I no longer went to lunch together. These days I usually took the boss's clients to lunch.

"Why don't you tell the boss you have a sick headache too?" I asked. "There's nothing here that can't wait until tomorrow."

"He'd fire me, you fool. I can't waggle my femininity in his face like you can. Mae June, you're a cheater."

"I didn't mean to cheat," I said. "I can't help it." I looked at her face to see if she remembered how we used to talk at lunch. "Watch this, Gladys." I turned back to my typewriter and pulled off the cover. The instant I inserted paper, my breasts reached up and parked on the typewriter keys. I leaned back, straightening up, then tried to type the date in the upper right-hand corner of the page. Plomp plomp. No dice. I looked at Gladys. She had that kind of look that says eyoo, ick, that's creepy, show it to me again.

I opened my mouth to explain about Wilma's insult and Charlotte Atlas when my breasts firmed up. I found myself leaning back to display me at an advantage. One of the boss's clients had walked in.

"Mae June, my nymphlet," said this guy, Burl Weaver. I had been to lunch with him before. I kind of liked him.

Gladys touched the intercom. "Sir, Mr. Weaver is here."

"Aw, Gladys," said Burl, one of the few men who had learned her name as well as mine, "why'd you haveta spoil it? I didn't come here for business."

"Burl?" the boss asked over the intercom. "What does he want?"

Burl strode over to my desk and pushed my transmit button. "I'd like to borrow your secretary for the afternoon, Otis. Any objections?"

"Why no, Burl, none at all." Burl is one of our biggest accounts. We produce the plastic for the records his company produces. "Mae June, you be good to Burl now."

Burl pressed my transmit button for me. I leaned as near to my speaker as I could get. "Yes, sir," I said. With tons of trepidation, I rose to my feet. My previous acquaintance with Burl had gone further than my acquaintance with Maxwell yesterday. Now that my breasts were seceding from my body, how could I be sure I'd be nice to Burl? What if I lost the company our biggest account?

With my breasts thrust out before me like dogs hot on a scent, I followed Burl out of the office, giving Gladys a misery-laden glance as I closed the door behind me. She gave me a suffering nod in return. At least there was somebody on my side, I thought, as Burl and I got on the elevator. I tried to cross my arms over my breasts, but they pushed my arms away. A familiar feeling of helplessness, one I knew well from before I sent away for that pamphlet, washed over me. Except this time I didn't feel my fate lay on the knees of the gods. No. My life was in the hands of my breasts, and they seemed determined to throw it away.

Burl waited until the elevator got midway between floors, then hit the stop button. "Just think, Mae June, here we are, suspended in mid-air," he said. "Think we can hump hard enough to make this thing drop? Wanna try? Think we'll even notice when she hits bottom?" With each sentence he got closer to me, until at last he was pulling the zip down the back of my dress.

I smiled at Burl and wondered what would happen next. I felt like an interested spectator at a sports event. Burl pulled my dress down around my waist.

"You sure look nice today, Mae June," he said, staring at my front, then at my lips. My breasts bobbled obligingly, and he looked down at them again. "Like you got little joy machines inside," he said, gently unhooking my bra.

Joy buzzers, I thought. Jolt city.

"You like me, don't you, Mae June? I can be real nice." He stroked me.

"Sure I like you, Burl."

"Would you like to work for me? I sure like you, Mae June. I'd like to put you in a nice little apartment on the top story of a real tall building with an elevator in it." As he talked, he kneaded at me like a kitten. "An express elevator. It would only stop at your floor and the basement. We could lock it from the inside. We could ride it. Up. Down. Up. Down. Hell, we could put a double bed in it. You'd like that, wouldn't you, Mae June?"

"Yes, Burl." When would my mammaries make their move?

He bent his head forward to pull down his own zipper, and they conked him. "Wha?" he said as he recoiled and collapsed gracefully to the floor. "How the heck did you do that, Mae June?"

I decided Burl had a harder head than Maxwell.

"Your hands are all snarled up in your dress. You been taking aikido or something?"

"No, Burl."

"Jeepers, if you didn't like me, you shoulda said something. I woulda left you alone."

"But I *do* like you, Burl. It's my breasts. They make their own decisions."

He lay on the floor and looked up at me. "That's the dumbest-assed thing I ever heard," he said. He rolled over and got to his feet. Then he came over, leaned toward me, and glared at my breasts. The left one flexed. He jumped back just in time. "Mae June, are you possessed?"

"Yes!" That must be it. The devil was in my breasts. I wondered what I had done to deserve such a fate. I wasn't even religious.

Burl made the sign of the cross over my breasts. Nothing happened. "That's not it," he said. "Maybe it's your subconscious. You hate men. Something like that. So how come this didn't happen last time, huh?" He began pacing.

"They were waiting to get strong enough. Oh, Burl, what am I going to do?"

"Get dressed. I think you better see a doctor, Mae June. Maybe we can get 'em tranquilized or something. I don't like the way they're sitting there, watching me."

I managed to hook my bra without too much trouble. Burl zipped me up and turned the elevator operational again. "Do you hate me?" I asked him on the way down.

"Course I don't hate you," he said, shifting a step further away from me. "You're real pretty, Mae June. Just as soon as you get yourself under control, you're gonna make somebody a real nice little something. I just don't want to take too many chances. Suppose what you've got is contagious? Suppose some of my body parts decide they don't like women? Let's be rational about this, huh?"

"I mean—you won't drop the contract with IPP, will you?"

"Shoot no. You worried about job security? I like that in a woman. You got sense. I won't complain. But I hope you got Blue Cross. You may have to get those knockers psychoanalyzed or something."

He offered to drive me to a doctor or the hospital. I told him I'd take the bus. He tried to get me to change my mind. He failed. I watched him drive away. Then I went home.

I picked up the powder-pink exerciser and took it to the window. My apartment was on the tenth floor. I was just going to drop the exerciser out the window when I looked down and saw Gladys's red coat wrapped around Gladys. My doorbell rang. I buzzed her into the building.

By the time she arrived at my front door I had collapsed on the couch, still holding the exerciser. "It's open," I called when she knocked. My arms were pumping the exerciser as I lay there. I thought about trying to stop exercising, but decided it was too much effort. "How'd you know I'd be home?" I asked Gladys as she came in and took off her coat.

"Burl stopped by the office."

"Did he say what happened?"

"No. He said he was worried about you. What *did* happen?"

"They punched him." I pumped the exerciser harder. "What am I going to do? I can't type, and now I can't even do lunch." I glared at my breasts. "You want us to starve?"

They were doing push-ups and didn't answer.

Gladys sat on a chair across from me and leaned forward, her gaze fixed on my new features. Her mouth was open.

My arms stopped pumping without me having anything to say about it. My left arm handed the exerciser to her. Her gaze still locked on my breasts, Gladys gripped the powder-pink exerciser and went to work.

"Don't," I said, sitting up. Startled, she fell against the chairback. "Do you want this to happen to you?"

"I—I—" She gulped and dropped the exerciser.

"I don't know what they want!" I stared at them with loathing. "It won't be long before the boss realizes I'm not an asset. Then what am I going to do?"

"You . . . you have a lot of career choices," said Gladys. "Like—have you ever considered mud wrestling?"

"What?"

"Exotic dancing?" She blinked. She licked her upper lip. "You could join the FBI, I bet. 'My breasts punched out spies for God and country.' You could sell your story to the *Enquirer*. 'Double-breasted Death.' Sounds like a slick detective movie from the Thirties. You could—"

"Stop," I said, "I don't want to hear any more."

"I'm sorry," she said after a minute. She got up and made tea.

We were sitting there sipping it when she had another brainstorm. "What do they want? You've been asking that yourself. What are breasts for, anyway?"

"Sex and babies," I said.

We looked at each other. We looked away. All those lunches and we had never talked about it. I bet she only knew what she read in books too.

She stared at the braided rug on the floor. "Were you . . . protected?"

I stared at the floor too. "I don't think so."
"They have tests you can do at home now."

I thought it was Burl's, so my breasts and I went to visit him. "You talk to them," I said. "If they think you're the father, maybe they won't beat you up anymore. Maybe they're just fending off all other comers."

Between the three of them they reached an arrangement. I moved into that penthouse apartment.

I shudder to think what they'll do when the baby comes.

All right, I can see you out there: sitting in your easy chairs, or in bed, or on the couch with the sound on the TV muted. Giggling and smiling, chuckling and wondering what's coming next. You're getting entirely too comfortable, you are. Not that I can hit you with a Lenny Bruce fantasy fable, because to the best of my knowledge, he never wrote one.

It's just not good to get *too* comfortable. I can't get violent with you, or nasty. This is, after all, an anthology of funny fantasy. So the best I can do is bring you another smile, another bit of humor.

Of course there are all kinds of smiles, and not all humor is light.

Or the Grasses Grow

AVRAM DAVIDSON

ABOUT HALFWAY ALONG the narrow and ill-paved county road between Crosby and Spanish Flats (all dips and hollows shimmering falsely like water in the heat till you get right up close to them), the road to Tickisall Agency branches off. No pretense of concrete or macadam—or even grading—deceives the chance or rare purposeful traveller. Federal, State, and County governments have better things to do with their money: Tickisall pays no taxes, and its handful of residents have only recently (and most grudgingly) been accorded the vote.

The sunbaked earth is cracked and riven. A few dirty sheep and a handful of scrub cows share its scanty herbage with an occasional sway-backed horse or stunted burro. Here and there a gaunt automobile rests in the thin shadow of a board shack, and a child, startled doubtless by the smooth sound of a strange motor, runs like a lizard through the dusty wastes to hide, and then to peer. Melon vines dried past all hope of fruit lie in patches next to whispery, tindery cornstalks.

And in the midst of all this, next to the only spring which never goes dry, are the only painted buildings, the only decent buildings in the area. In the middle of the green lawn is a pole with the flag, and right behind the pole, over the front door, the sign:

U. S. BUREAU OF INDIAN AFFAIRS
TICKISALL AGENCY
OFFICE OF THE SUPERINTENDENT

There were already a few Indians gathering around that afternoon, the women in cotton-print dresses, the men in overalls. There would soon be more. This was scheduled as the last day for the Tickisall Agency and Reservation. Congress had passed the bill, the President had signed it, the Director of the Bureau of Indian Affairs had issued the order. It was supposed to be a great day for the Tickisall Nation—only the Tickisalls, what was left of them, didn't seem to think so. Not a man or woman of them spoke. Not a child whimpered. Not a dog barked.

Before Uncle Fox-head sat a basket with four different kinds of clay, and next to the basket was a medicine gourd full of water. The old man rolled the clay between his moistened palms, singing in a low voice. Then he washed his hands and sprinkled them with pollen. Then he took up the prayer-sticks, made of juniper—(once there had been juniper trees on the Reservation, once there had been many trees)—and painted with the signs of Thunder, Sun, Moon, Rain, Lightning. There were feathers tied to the sticks—once there had been birds, too . . .

> *Oh, People-of-The-Hidden Places,*
> *Oh, take our message to The Hidden Places,*
> *Swiftly, swiftly, now . . .*

the old man chanted, shaking the medicine-sticks.

> *Oh, you, Swift Ones, People-with-no-legs,*
> *Take our message to The-People-with-no-bodies,*
> *Swiftly, swiftly, now . . .*

The old man's skin was like a cracked, worn moccasin. With his turkey-claw hand he took up the gourd rattle, shook it: West, South, Up, Down, East, North.

> *Oh, People-of-the-hollow Earth,*
> *Take our message to the hollow Earth,*
> *Take our song to our Fathers and Mothers,*
> *Take our cry to the Spirit People,*
> *Take and go, take and go,*
> *Swiftly, swiftly, now . . .*

The snakes rippled across the ground and were gone, one by one. The old man's sister's son helped him back to his sheepskin, spread in the shade, where he half-sat, half-lay, panting.

His great-nephews, Billy Cottonwood and Sam Quarterhorse, were talking together in English. "There was a fellow in my outfit," Cottonwood said, "a fellow from West Virginia, name of Corrothers. Said his grandmother claimed she could charm away warts. So I said my great-uncle claimed he could make snakes. And they all laughed fit to kill, and said, 'Chief, when you try a snow-job, it turns into a blizzard!' . . . Old Corrothers," he reflected. "We were pretty good buddies. Maybe I'll go to West Virginia and look him up. I could hitch, maybe."

Quarterhorse said, "Yeah, you can go to West Virginia, and I can go to L.A.—but what about the others? Where *they* going to go if Washington refuses to act?"

The fond smile of recollection left his cousin's lean, brown face. "I don't know," he said. "I be damned and go to Hell, if I know." And then the old pick-up came rattling and coughing up to the house, and Sam said, "Here's Newton."

Newton Quarterhorse, his brother Sam, and Billy Cottonwood, were the only three Tickisalls who had passed the physical and gone into the Army. There weren't a lot of others who were of conscripting age (or any other age, for that matter), and those whom TB didn't keep out, other ailments active or passive did. Once there had been trees on the Reservation, and birds, and deer, and healthy men.

The wash-faded Army suntans had been clean and fresh as always when Newt set out for Crosby, but they were dusty and sweaty now. He took a piece of wet burlap out and removed a few bottles from it. "Open these, Sam, will you, while I wash," he said. "Cokes for us, strawberry pop for the old people . . . How's Uncle Fox-head?"

Billy grunted. "Playing at making medicine snakes again. Do you suppose if we believed he could, he could?"

Newt shrugged. "So. Well, maybe if the telegrams don't do any good, the snakes will. And I'm damned sure they won't do no worse. That son of a bitch at the Western Union office," he said, looking out over the drought-bitten land. " 'Sending a smoke-signal to the Great White Father again, Sitting Bull?' he says, smirking and sneering. I told him, 'You just take the money and send the wire.' They looked at me like coyotes looking at a sick calf." Abruptly, he turned away and went to dip his handkerchief in the bucket. Water was hard come by.

The lip of the bottle clicked against one of Uncle Fox-head's few teeth. He drank noisily, then licked his lips. "Today we drink the white man's sweet water," he said. "What will we drink tomorrow?" No one said anything. "I will tell you, then," he continued. "Unless the white men relent, we will drink the bitter waters of The Hollow Places. They are bitter, but they are strong and good." He waved his withered hand in a semi-circle. "All this will go," he said, "and the Fathers and Mothers of The People will return and lead us to our old home inside the Earth." His sister's son, who had never learned English nor gone to school, moaned. "Unless the white men relent," said the old man.

"They never have," said Cottonwood, in Tickisall. In English, he said, "What will he do when he sees that nothing happens tomorrow except that we get kicked the Hell out of here?"

Newt said, "Die, I suppose . . . which might not be a bad idea. For all of us."

His brother turned and looked at him. "If you're planning Quarterhorse's Last Stand, forget about it. There aren't twenty rounds of ammunition on the whole reservation."

Billy Cottonwood raised his head. "We could maybe move in with the Apahoya," he suggested. "They're just as dirt-poor as we are, but there's more of them, and I guess they'll hold on to their land awhile yet." His cousins shook their heads. "Well, not for us. But the others . . . Look, I spoke to Joe Feather Cloud that last time I was at the Apahoya Agency. If we give him the truck and the sheep, he'll take care of Uncle Fox-head."

Sam Quarterhorse said he supposed that was the best thing. "For the old man, I mean. I made up *my* mind. I'm going to L.A. and pass for Colored." He stopped.

They waited till the new shiny automobile had gone by towards the Agency in a cloud of dust. Newt said, "The buzzards are gathering." Then he asked, "How come, Sam?"

"Because I'm tired of being an Indian. It has no present and no future. I can't be a white, they won't have me—the best I could hope for would be that they laugh: 'How, Big Chief'—'Hi, Blanket-bottom.' Yeah, I *could* pass for a Mexican as far as my looks go, only the Mexes won't have me, either. But the Colored will. And there's millions and millions of them—whatever price they pay for it, they never have to feel lonely. And they've got a fine, bitter contempt for the whites that I can use a lot of. 'Pecks,' they call them. I don't know where they got the name from, but, Damn! it sure fits them. They've been pecking away at us for over a hundred years."

They talked on some more, and all the while the dust never settled in the road. They watched the whole tribe, what there was of it, go by towards the Agency—in old trucks, in buckboards, on horses, on foot. And after some time, they loaded up the pick-up and followed.

The Indians sat all over the grass in front of the Agency, and for once no one bothered to chase them off. They just sat, silent, waiting. A group of men from Crosby and Spanish Flats were talking to the Superintendent; there were maps in their hands. The cousins went up to them; the white men looked out of the corners of their eyes, confidence still tempered—but only a bit—by wariness.

"Mr. Jenkins," Newt said to one, "most of this is your doing and you know how I feel about it—"

"You better not make any trouble, Quarterhorse," said another townsman.

Jenkins said, "Let the boy have his say."

"—but I know you'll give me a straight answer. What's going to be done here?"

Jenkins was a leathery little man, burnt almost as dark as an Indian. He looked at him, not unkindly, through the spectacles which magnified his blue eyes. "Why, you know, son, there's nothing personal in all this. The land belongs to them that can hold it and use it. It was made to be used. You people've had your chance, Lord knows—Well, no speeches. You see, here on the map, where this here dotted line is? The county is putting through a new road to connect with a new highway the state's going to construct. There'll be a lot of traffic through here, and this Agency ought to make a fine motel.

"And right along *here*—" his blunt finger traced "—there's going to be the main irrigation canal. There'll be branches all through the Reservation. I reckon we can raise some mighty fine alfalfa. Fatten some mighty fine cattle . . . I always thought, son, you'd be good with stock, if you had some good stock to work with. Not these worthless scrubs. If you want a job—"

One of the men cleared his sinus cavities with an ugly sound, and spat. "Are you out of your mind, Jenk? Here we been workin for years ta git these Indyins outa here, and you tryin ta make um stay . . ."

The Superintendent was a tall, fat, soft man with a loose smile. He said ingratiatingly, "Mr. Jenkins realizes, as I'm sure you do too, Mr. Waldo, that the policy of the United States government is, and always has been—except for the unfortunate period when John Collier was in charge of the Bureau of Indian Affairs—man may have *meant* well, but Lord! hopeless sentimentalist—well, our policy has always been: Prepare the Indian to join the general community. Get him off the reservation. Turn the tribal lands over to the *Individual*. And it's been done with other tribes, and now, finally, it's being done with this one." He beamed.

Newt gritted his teeth. Then he said, "And the result was always the same—as soon as the tribal lands were given to the individual red man they damn quick passed into the hand of the individual white man. That's what happened with other tribes, and now, finally, it's being done with this one. Don't you *know*, Mr. Scott, that we can't adapt ourselves to the system of individual land-ownership? That we just aren't strong enough by ourselves to hold onto real estate? That—"

"Root, hog, er die," said Mr. Waldo.

"Are men *hogs?*" Newt cried.

Waldo said, at large, "*Told* ya he w's a trouble-maker." Then, bringing his long, rough, red face next to Newt's, he said, "Listen, Indyin, you and all y'r stinkin relatives are through. If Jenkins is damnfool enough ta hire ya, that's his look-out. But if he don't, you better stay far, far away, because nobody likes ya, nobody wants ya, and now that the Guvermint in Worshennon is finely come ta their sentces, nobody is goin ta protec ya —you and y'r mangy cows and y'r smutty-nosed sheep and y'r blankets—"

Newt's face showed his feelings, but before he could voice them, Billy Cottonwood broke in. "Mr. Scott," he said, "we sent a telegram to Washington, asking to halt the break-up of the Reservation."

Scott smiled his sucaryl smile. "Well, that's your privilege as a citizen."

Cottonwood spoke on. He mentioned the provisions of the bill passed by Congress, authorizing the Commissioner of Indian Affairs to liquidate, at his discretion, all reservations including less than one hundred residents, and to divide the land among them.

"Mr. Scott, when the Treaty of Juniper Butte was made between the United States and the Tickisalls," Cottonwood said, "there were thousands of us. That treaty was to be kept 'as long as the sun shall rise or the grasses grow.' The Government pledged itself to send us doctors—it didn't, and we died like flies. It pledged to send us seed and cattle; it sent us no seed and we had to eat the few hundred head of stock-yard cast-offs they did send us, to keep from starving. The Government was to keep our land safe for us forever, in a sacred trust—and in every generation they've taken away more and more. Mr. Scott—Mr. Jenkins, Mr. Waldo, and all you other gentlemen—you knew, didn't you, when you were kind enough to loan us money—or rather, to give us credit at the stores, when this drought started—you knew that this bill was up before Congress, didn't you?"

No one answered him. "You knew that it would pass, and that turning our lands over to us wouldn't mean a darned thing, didn't you? That we already owed so much money that our creditors would take all our land? Mr. Scott, how can the Government let this happen to us? It made a treaty with us to keep our lands safe for us 'as long as the sun rises or the grasses grow.' Has the sun stopped rising? Has the grass stopped growing? We believed in you—we kept our part of the treaty. Mr. Scott, won't you wire Washington—won't you other gentlemen do the same? To stop this thing that's being done to us? It's almost a hundred years now since we made treaty, and we've always hoped. Now we've only got till midnight to hope. Unless—?"

But the Superintendent said, No, he couldn't do that. And Jenkins shook his head, and said, sorry; it was really all for the best. Waldo shrugged, produced a packet of legal papers. "I've been deppatized to serve all these," he said. "Soons the land's all passed over ta individj'l ownership—which is 12 P.M. tanight. But if you give me y'r word (whatever that's worth) not ta make no trouble, why, guess it c'n wait till morning. Yo go back ta y'r shacks and I'll be round, come morning. We'll sleep over with Scott f'r tanight."

Sam Quarterhorse said, "We won't make any trouble, no. Not much use in that. But we'll wait right here. It's still possible we'll hear from Washington before midnight."

The Superintendent's house was quite comfortable. Logs (cut by Indian labor from the last of the Reservation's trees) blazed in the big fireplace (built by Indian labor). A wealth of rugs (woven by Indians in the Agency school) decorated walls and floor. The card-game had been on for some time when they heard the first woman start to wail. Waldo looked up nervously. Jenkins glanced at the clock. "Twelve midnight," he said. "Well, that's it. All over but the details. Took almost a hundred years, but it'll be worth it."

Another woman took up the keening. It swelled to a chorus of heart-break, then died away. Waldo picked up his cards, then put them down again. An old man's voice had begun a chant. Someone took it up—then another. Drums joined it, and rattles. Scott said, "That was old Fox-head who started that just now. They're singing the death-song. They'll go on till morning."

Waldo swore. Then he laughed. "Let'm," he said. "It's their last morning."

Jenkins woke up first. Waldo stirred to wakefulness as he heard the other dressing. "What time is it?" he asked.

"Don't know," Jenkins said. "But it feels to me like gettin-up time. . . . You hear them go just a while back? No? Don't know how you could miss it. Singing got real loud—seemed like a whole lot of new voices joined in. Then they all got up and moved off. Wonder where they went . . . I'm going to have a look around outside." He switched on his flash-light and left the house. In another minute Waldo joined him, knocking on Scott's door as he passed.

The ashes of the fire still smoldered, making a dull red glow. It was very cold. Jenkins said, "Look here, Waldo—look." Waldo followed the flash-light's beam, said he didn't see anything. "It's the grass . . . it was green last night. It's all dead and brown now. Look at it . . ."

Waldo shivered. "Makes no difference. We'll get it green again. The land's ours now."

Scott joined them, his overcoat hugging his ears. "Why is it so cold?" he asked. "What's happened to the clock? Who was tinkering with the clock? It's past eight by the clock—it ought to be light by now.

Where did all the Tickisalls go to? What's happening? There's something in the air—I don't like the feel of it. I'm sorry I ever agreed to work with you, no matter what you paid me—"

Waldo said, roughly, nervously, "Shut up. Some damned Indyin sneaked in and must of fiddled with the clock. Hell with um. Govermint's on *our* side now. Soons it's daylight we'll clear um all out of here f'r good."

Shivering in the bitter cold, uneasy for reasons they only dimly perceived, the three white men huddled together alone in the dark by the dying fire, and waited for the sun to rise.

And waited . . . and waited . . . and waited. . . .

Like every successful form of fiction, fantasy is full of memorable characters. Harold Shea and Bilbo Baggins, Scheherazade and Sinbad stick in our minds long after the rest of the fictional fireworks may have faded. Usually they do so because they're strong personalities; great rugged heroes or utterly despicable villainesses. They move, they motivate, they thrust the story forward and keep us reading.

This is by way of suggesting that there are not many memorable failures in the lexicon of fantasy. Those who can't perform are usually accorded the same fate in our memories as a gigolo from Jersey afflicted with the same conundrum.

Which is what makes the occasional memorable failure all that more exceptional. So this anthology ends not with a bang, with a protagonist mighty-thewed (as E. Fudd might say), but with a whimper. More correctly, with a whimperer.

But a memorable one.

Snulbug

ANTHONY BOUCHER

"THAT'S A HELL of a spell you're using," said the demon, "if I'm the best you can call up."

He wasn't much, Bill Hitchens had to admit. He looked lost in the center of that pentacle. His basic design was impressive enough—snakes for hair, curling tusks, a sharp-tipped tail, all the works—but he was something under an inch tall.

Bill had chanted the words and lit the powder with the highest hopes. Even after the feeble flickering flash and the damp fizzling *zzzt*

261

which had replaced the expected thunder and lightning, he had still had hopes. He had stared up at the space above the pentacle waiting to be awe-struck until he had heard that plaintive little voice from the floor wailing, "Here I am."

"Nobody's wasted time and power on a misfit like me for years," the demon went on. "Where'd you get the spell?"

"Just a little something I whipped up," said Bill modestly.

The demon grunted and muttered something about people that thought they were magicians.

"But I'm not a magician," Bill explained. "I'm a biochemist."

The demon shuddered. "I land the damnedest cases," he mourned. "Working for that psychiatrist wasn't bad enough, I should draw a biochemist. Whatever that is."

Bill couldn't check his curiosity. "And what did you do for a psychiatrist?"

"He showed me to people who were followed by little men and told them I'd chase the little men away." The demon pantomimed shooing motions.

"And did they go away?"

"Sure. Only then the people decided they'd sooner have little men than me. It didn't work so good. Nothing ever does," he added woefully. "Yours won't either."

Bill sat down and filled his pipe. Calling up demons wasn't so terrifying after all. Something quiet and homey about it. "Oh, yes it will," he said. "This is foolproof."

"That's what they all think. People—" The demon wistfully eyed the match as Bill lit his pipe. "But we might as well get it over with. What do you want?"

"I want a laboratory for my embolism experiments. If this method works, it's going to mean that a doctor can spot an embolus in the blood stream long before it's dangerous and remove it safely. My ex-boss, that screwball old occultist Reuben Choatsby, said it wasn't practical—meaning there wasn't a fortune in it for him—and fired me. Everybody else thinks I'm wacky too, and I can't get any backing. So I need ten thousand dollars."

"There!" the demon sighed with satisfaction. "I told you it wouldn't work. That's out for me. They can't start fetching money on demand till three grades higher than me. I told you."

"But you don't," Bill insisted, "appreciate all my fiendish subtlety. Look— Say, what is your name?"

The demon hesitated. "You haven't got another of those things?"

"What things?"

"Matches."

"Sure."

"Light me one, please?"

Bill tossed the burning match into the center of the pentacle. The demon scrambled eagerly out of the now cold ashes of the powder and dived into the flame, rubbing himself with the brisk vigor of a man under a needle-shower. "There!" he gasped joyously. "That's more like it."

"And now what's your name?"

The demon's face fell again. "My name? You really want to know?"

"I've got to call you something."

"Oh, no you don't. I'm going home. No money games for me."

"But I haven't explained yet what you are to do. What's your name?"

"Snulbug." The demon's voice dropped almost too low to be heard.

"Snulbug?" Bill laughed.

"Uh-huh. I've got a cavity in one tusk, my snakes are falling out, I haven't got enough troubles, I should be named Snulbug."

"All right. Now listen, Snulbug, can you travel into the future?"

"A little. I don't like it much, though. It makes you itch in the memory."

"Look, my fine snake-haired friend. It isn't a question of what you like. How would you like to be left there in that pentacle with nobody to throw matches at you?" Snulbug shuddered. "I thought so. Now, you can travel into the future?"

"I said a little."

"And," Bill leaned forward and puffed hard at his corncob as he asked the vital question, "can you bring back material objects?" If the answer was no, all the fine febrile fertility of his spell-making was useless. And if that was useless, heaven alone knew how the Hitchens Embolus Diagnosis would ever succeed in ringing down the halls of history, and incidentally saving a few thousand lives annually.

Snulbug seemed more interested in the warm clouds of pipe smoke than in the question. "Sure," he said. "Within reason I can—" He broke off and stared up piteously. "You don't mean— You can't be going to pull that old gag again?"

"Look, baby. You do what I tell you and leave the worrying to me. You can bring back material objects?"

"Sure. But I warn you—"

Bill cut him off short. "Then as soon as I release you from that pentacle, you're to bring me tomorrow's newspaper."

Snulbug sat down on the burned match and tapped his forehead sorrowfully with his tail tip. "I knew it," he wailed. "I knew it. Three times already this happens to me. I've got limited powers, I'm a runt, I've got a funny name, so I should run foolish errands."

"Foolish errands?" Bill rose and began to pace about the bare attic. "Sir, if I may call you that, I resent such an imputation. I've spent weeks on this idea. Think of the limitless power in knowing the future. Think of what could be done with it: swaying the course of empire, dominating mankind. All I want is to take this stream of unlimited power, turn it into the simple channel of humanitarian research, and get me $10,000; and you call that a foolish errand!"

"That Spaniard," Snulbug moaned. "He was a nice guy, even if his spell was lousy. Had a solid, comfortable brazier where an imp could keep warm. Fine fellow. And he had to ask to see tomorrow's newspaper. I'm warning you—"

"I know," said Bill hastily. "I've been over in my mind all the things that can go wrong. And that's why I'm laying three conditions on you before you get out of that pentacle. I'm not falling for the easy snares."

"All right." Snulbug sounded almost resigned. "Let's hear 'em. Not that they'll do any good."

"First: This newspaper must not contain a notice of my own death or of any other disaster that would frustrate what I can do with it."

"But shucks," Snulbug protested. "I can't guarantee that. If you're slated to die between now and tomorrow, what can I do about it? Not that I guess you're important enough to crash the paper."

"Courtesy, Snulbug. Courtesy to your master. But I tell you what: When you go into the future, you'll know then if I'm going to die? Right. Well, if I am, come back and tell me and we'll work out other plans. This errand will be off."

"People," Snulbug observed, "make such an effort to make trouble for themselves. Go on."

"Second: The newspaper must be of this city and in English. I can just imagine you and your little friends presenting some dope with the Omsk and Tomsk *Daily Vuskutsukt*."

"We should take so much trouble," said Snulbug.

"And third: The newspaper must belong to this space-time continuum, to this spiral of the serial universe, to this Wheel of If. However you want to put it. It must be a newspaper of the tomorrow that I myself shall experience, not of some other, to me hypothetical, tomorrow."

"Throw me another match," said Snulbug.

"Those three conditions should cover it, I think. There's not a loophole there, and the Hitchens Laboratory is guaranteed."

Snulbug grunted. "You'll find out."

Bill took a sharp blade and duly cut a line of the pentacle with cold steel. But Snulbug simply dived in and out of the flame of his second match, twitching his tail happily, and seemed not to give a rap that the way to freedom was now open.

"Come on!" Bill snapped impatiently. "Or I'll take the match away."

Snulbug got as far as the opening and hesitated. "Twenty-four hours is a long way."

"You can make it."

"I don't know. Look." He shook his head, and a microscopic dead snake fell to the floor. "I'm not at my best. I'm shot to pieces lately, I am. Tap my tail."

"Do what?"

"Go on. Tap it with your fingernail right there where it joins on."

Bill grinned and obeyed. "Nothing happens."

"Sure nothing happens. My reflexes are all haywire. I don't know as I can make twenty-four hours." He brooded, and his snakes curled up into a concentrated clump. "Look. All you want is tomorrow's newspaper, huh? Just tomorrow's, not the edition that'll be out exactly twenty-four hours from now?"

"It's noon now," Bill reflected. "Sure, I guess tomorrow morning's paper'll do."

"OK. What's the date today?"

"August 21."

"Fine. I'll bring you a paper for August 22. Only I'm warning you: It won't do any good. But here goes nothing. Goodbye now. Hello again. Here you are." There was a string in Snulbug's horny hand, and on the end of the string was a newspaper.

"But hey!" Bill protested. "You haven't been gone."

"People," said Snulbug feelingly, "are dopes. Why should it take any time out of the present to go into the future? I leave this point, I come back to this point. I spent two hours hunting for this damned paper, but that doesn't mean two hours of your time here. People—" he snorted.

Bill scratched his head. "I guess it's all right. Let's see the paper. And I know: You're warning me." He turned quickly to the obituaries to check. No Hitchens. "And I wasn't dead in the time you were in?"

"No," Snulbug admitted. "Not *dead*," he added, with the most pessimistic implications possible.

"What was I, then? Was I—"

"I had salamander blood," Snulbug complained. "They thought I was an undine like my mother and they put me in the cold-water incubator when any dope knows salamandry is a dominant. So I'm a runt and good for nothing but to run errands, and now I should make prophecies! You read your paper and see how much good it does you."

Bill laid down his pipe and folded the paper back from the obituaries to the front page. He had not expected to find anything useful there—what advantage could he gain from knowing who won the next naval engagement or which cities were bombed?—but he was scientifically methodical. And this time method was rewarded. There it was, streaming across the front page in vast black blocks:

MAYOR ASSASSINATED
FIFTH COLUMN KILLS CRUSADER

Bill snapped his fingers. This was it. This was his chance. He jammed his pipe in his mouth, hastily pulled a coat on his shoulders, crammed the priceless paper into a pocket, and started out of the attic. Then he paused and looked around. He'd forgotten Snulbug. Shouldn't there be some sort of formal discharge?

The dismal demon was nowhere in sight. Not in the pentacle or out of it. Not a sign or a trace of him. Bill frowned. This was definitely not methodical. He struck a match and held it over the bowl of his pipe.

A warm sigh of pleasure came from inside the corncob.

Bill took the pipe from his mouth and stared at it. "So that's where you are!" he said musingly.

"I told you salamandry was a dominant," said Snulbug, peering out of the bowl. "I want to go along. I want to see just what kind of a fool you make of yourself." He withdrew his head into the glowing tobacco, muttering about newspapers, spells, and, with a wealth of unhappy scorn, people.

*   *   *

The crusading mayor of Granton was a national figure of splendid proportions. Without hysteria, red baiting, or strike-breaking, he had launched a quietly purposeful and well-directed program against subversive elements which had rapidly converted Granton into the safest and most American city in the country. He was also a persistent advocate of national, state, and municipal subsidy of the arts and sciences—the ideal man to wangle an endowment for the Hitchens Laboratory, if he were not so surrounded by overly skeptical assistants that Bill had never been able to lay the program before him.

This would do it. Rescue him from assassination in the very nick of time—in itself an act worth calling up demons to perform—and then when he asks, "And how, Mr. Hitchens, can I possibly repay you?" come forth with the whole great plan of research. It couldn't miss.

No sound came from the pipe bowl, but Bill clearly heard the words, "Couldn't it just?" ringing in his mind.

He braked his car to a fast stop in the red zone before the city hall, jumped out without even slamming the door, and dashed up the marble steps so rapidly, so purposefully, that pure momentum carried him up three flights and through four suites of offices before anybody had the courage to stop him and say, "What goes?"

The man with the courage was a huge bull-necked plainclothes man, whose bulk made Bill feel relatively about the size of Snulbug. "All right, there," this hulk rumbled. "All right. Where's the fire?"

"In an assassin's gun," said Bill. "And it had better stay there."

Bullneck had not expected a literal answer. He hesitated long enough for Bill to push him to the door marked MAYOR—PRIVATE. But though the husky's brain might move slowly, his muscles made up for the lag. Just as Bill started to shove the door open, a five-pronged mound of flesh lit on his neck and jerked.

Bill crawled from under a desk, ducked Bullneck's left, reached the door, executed a second backward flip, climbed down from the table, ducked a right, reached the door, sailed back in reverse, and lowered himself nimbly from the chandelier.

Bullneck took up a stand in front of the door, spread his legs in ready balance, and drew a service automatic from its holster. "You ain't going in there," he said, to make the situation perfectly clear.

Bill spat out a tooth, wiped the blood from his eyes, picked up the shattered remains of his pipe, and said, "Look. It's now 12:30. At 12:32 a redheaded hunchback is going to come out on that balcony across the street and aim through the open window into the mayor's office. At 12:33

His Honor is going to be slumped over his desk, dead. Unless you help me get him out of range."

"Yeah?" said Bullneck. "And who says so?"

"It says so here. Look. In the paper."

Bullneck guffawed. "How can a paper say what ain't even happened yet? You're nuts, brother, if you ain't something worse. Now go on. Scram. Go peddle your paper."

Bill's glance darted out the window. There was the balcony facing the mayor's office. And there coming out on it—

"Look!" he cried. "If you won't believe me, look out the window. See on that balcony? The redheaded hunchback? Just like I told you. Quick!"

Bullneck stared despite himself. He saw the hunchback peer across into the office. He saw the sudden glint of metal in the hunchback's hand. "Brother," he said to Bill, "I'll tend to you later."

The hunchback had his rifle halfway to his shoulder when Bullneck's automatic spat and Bill braked his car in the red zone, jumped out, and dashed through four suites of offices before anybody had the courage to stop him.

The man with the courage was a huge bull-necked plainclothes man, who rumbled, "Where's the fire?"

"In an assassin's gun," said Bill, and took advantage of Bullneck's confusion to reach the door marked MAYOR—PRIVATE. But just as he started to push it open, a vast hand lit on his neck and jerked.

As Bill descended from the chandelier after his third try, Bullneck took up a stand in front of the door, with straddled legs and drawn gun. "You ain't going in," he said clarifyingly.

Bill spat out a tooth and outlined the situation. "—12:33," he ended. "His Honor is going to be slumped over the desk dead. Unless you help me get him out of range. See? It says so here. In the paper."

"How can it? Gwan. Go peddle your paper."

Bill's glance darted to the balcony. "Look, if you won't believe me. See the redheaded hunchback? Just like I told you. Quick! We've got to—"

Bullneck stared. He saw the sudden glint of metal in the hunchback's hand. "Brother," he said, "I'll tend to you later."

The hunchback had his rifle halfway to his shoulder when Bullneck's automatic spat and Bill braked his car in the red zone, jumped out, and dashed through four suites before anybody stopped him.

The man who did was a bull-necked plainclothes man, who rumbled—

"Don't you think," said Snulbug, "you've had about enough of this?"

Bill agreed mentally, and there he was sitting in his roadster in front of the city hall. His clothes were unrumpled, his eyes were bloodless, his teeth were all there, and his corncob was still intact. "And just what," he demanded of his pipe bowl, "has been going on?"

Snulbug popped his snaky head out. "Light this again, will you? It's getting cold. Thanks."

"What happened?" Bill insisted.

"People!" Snulbug moaned. "No sense. Don't you see? So long as the newspaper was in the future, it was only a possibility. If you'd had, say, a hunch that the mayor was in danger, maybe you could have saved him. But when I brought it into now, it became a fact. You can't possibly make it untrue."

"But how about man's free will? Can't I do whatever I want to do?"

"Sure. It was your precious free will that brought the paper into now. You can't undo your own will. And, anyway, your will's still free. You're free to go getting thrown around chandeliers as often as you want. You probably like it. You can do anything up to the point where it would change what's in that paper. Then you have to start in again and again and again until you make up your mind to be sensible."

"But that—" Bill fumbled for words, "that's just as bad as . . . as fate or predestination. If my soul wills to—"

"Newspapers aren't enough. Time theory isn't enough. So I should tell him about his soul! People—" and Snulbug withdrew into the bowl.

Bill looked up at the city hall regretfully and shrugged his resignation. Then he folded his paper to the sports page and studied it carefully.

Snulbug thrust his head out again as they stopped in the many-acred parking lot. "Where is it this time?" he wanted to know. "Not that it matters."

"The racetrack."

"Oh—" Snulbug groaned, "I might have known it. You're all alike. No sense in the whole caboodle. I suppose you found a long shot?"

"Darned tooting I did. Alhazred at twenty to one in the fourth. I've got $500, the only money I've got left on earth. Plunk on Alhazred's nose it goes, and there's our $10,000."

Snulbug grunted. "I hear his lousy spell, I watch him get caught on a merry-go-round, it isn't enough, I should see him lay a bet on a long shot."

"But there isn't a loophole in this. I'm not interfering with the future; I'm just taking advantage of it. Alhazred'll win this race whether I bet on him or not. Five pretty hundred-dollar parimutuel tickets, and behold: The Hitchens Laboratory!" Bill jumped spryly out of his car and strutted along joyously. Suddenly he paused and addressed his pipe: "Hey! Why do I feel so good?"

Snulbug sighed dismally. "Why should anybody?"

"No, but I mean: I took a hell of a shellacking from that plug-ugly in the office. And I haven't got a pain or an ache."

"Of course not. It never happened."

"But I felt it then."

"Sure. In a future that never was. You changed your mind, didn't you? You decided not to go up there?"

"O.K., but that was after I'd already been beaten up."

"Uh-uh," said Snulbug firmly. "It was before you hadn't been." And he withdrew again into the pipe.

There was a band somewhere in the distance and the raucous burble of an announcer's voice. Crowds clustered around the $2 windows, and the $5 weren't doing bad business. But the $100 window, where the five beautiful pasteboards lived that were to create an embolism laboratory, was almost deserted.

Bill buttonholed a stranger with a purple nose. "What's the next race?"

"Second, Mac."

Swell, Bill thought. Lots of time. And from now on— He hastened to the $100 window and shoved across the five bills that he had drawn from the bank that morning. "Alhazred, on the nose," he said.

The clerk frowned with surprise, but took the money and turned to get the tickets.

Bill buttonholed a stranger with a purple nose. "What's the next race?"

"Second, Mac."

Swell, Bill thought. And then he yelled, "Hey!"

A stranger with a purple nose paused and said, " 'Smatter, Mac?"

"Nothing," Bill groaned. "Just everything."

The stranger hesitated. "Ain't I seen you someplace before?"

"No," said Bill hurriedly. "You were going to, but you haven't. I changed my mind."

The stranger walked away shaking his head and muttering how the ponies could get a guy.

Not till Bill was back in his roadster did he take the corncob from his mouth and glare at it. "All right!" he barked. "What was wrong this time? Why did I get on a merry-go-round again? I didn't try to change the future!"

Snulbug popped his head out and yawned a tuskful yawn. "I warn him, I explain it, I warn him again, now he wants I should explain it all over."

"But what did I do?"

"What did he do? You changed the odds, you dope. That much folding money on a long shot at a parimutuel track, and the odds change. It wouldn't have paid off at twenty to one, the way it said in the paper."

"Nuts," Bill muttered. "And I suppose that applies to anything? If I study the stock market in this paper and try to invest my $500 according to tomorrow's market—"

"Same thing. The quotations wouldn't be quite the same if you started in playing. I warned you. You're stuck," said Snulbug. "You're stymied. It's no use." He sounded almost cheerful.

"Isn't it?" Bill mused. "Now look, Snulbug. Me, I'm a great believer in Man. This universe doesn't hold a problem that Man can't eventually solve. And I'm no dumber than the average."

"That's saying a lot, that is," Snulbug sneered. "People—"

"I've got a responsibility now. It's more than just my $10,000. I've got to redeem the honor of Man. You say this is the insoluble problem. I say there *is* no insoluble problem."

"I say you talk a lot."

Bill's mind was racing furiously. How can a man take advantage of the future without in any smallest way altering that future? There must be an answer somewhere, and a man who devised the Hitchens Embolus Diagnosis could certainly crack a little nut like this. Man cannot refuse a challenge.

Unthinking, he reached for his tobacco pouch and tapped out his pipe on the sole of his foot. There was a microscopic thud as Snulbug crashed onto the floor of the car.

Bill looked down half-smiling. The tiny demon's tail was lashing madly, and every separate snake stood on end. "This is too much!" Snulbug screamed. "Dumb gags aren't enough, insults aren't enough, I

should get thrown around like a damned soul. This is the last straw. Give
me my dismissal!"

Bill snapped his fingers gleefully. "Dismissal!" he cried. "I've got it,
Snully. We're all set."

Snulbug looked up puzzled and slowly let his snakes droop more
amicably. "It won't work," he said, with an omnisciently sad shake of his
serpentine head.

It was the dashing act again that carried Bill through the Choatsby
Laboratories, where he had been employed so recently, and on up to the
very anteroom of old R. C.'s office.

But where you can do battle with a bull-necked guard, there is not a
thing you can oppose against the brisk competence of a young lady who
says, "I shall find out if Mr. Choatsby will see you." There was nothing
to do but wait.

"And what's the brilliant idea this time?" Snulbug obviously feared
the worst.

"R. C.'s nuts," said Bill. "He's an astrologer and a pyramidologist
and a British Israelite—American Branch Reformed—and Heaven
knows what else. He . . . why, he'll even believe in you."

"That's more than I do," said Snulbug. "It's a waste of energy."

"He'll buy this paper. He'll pay anything for it. There's nothing he
loves more than futzing around with the occult. He'll never be able to
resist a good solid slice of the future, with illusions of a fortune thrown
in."

"You better hurry, then."

"Why such a rush? It's only 2:30 now. Lots of time. And while that
girl's gone there's nothing for us to do but cool our heels."

"You might at least," said Snulbug, "warm the heel of your pipe."

The girl returned at last. "Mr. Choatsby will see you."

Reuben Choatsby overflowed the outsize chair behind his desk. His
little face, like a baby's head balanced on a giant suet pudding, beamed as
Bill entered. "Changed your mind, eh?" His words came in sudden soft
blobs, like the abrupt glugs of pouring syrup. "Good. Need you in K-39.
Lab's not the same since you left."

Bill groped for the exactly right words. "That's not it, R. C. I'm on
my own now and I'm doing all right."

The baby face soured. "Damned cheek. Competitor of mine, eh?
What you want now? Waste my time?"

"Not at all." With a pretty shaky assumption of confidence, Bill perched on the edge of the desk. "R. C.," he said, slowly and impressively, "what would you give for a glimpse into the future?"

Mr. Choatsby glugged vigorously. "Ribbing me? Get out of here! Have you thrown out— Hold on! You're the one— Used to read queer books. Had a grimoire here once." The baby face grew earnest. "What d'you mean?"

"Just what I said, R. C. What would you give for a glimpse into the future?"

Mr. Choatsby hesitated. "How? Time travel? Pyramid? You figured out the King's Chamber?"

"Much simpler than that. I have here"—he took it out of his pocket and folded it so that only the name and the date line were visible— "tomorrow's newspaper."

Mr. Choatsby grabbed. "Let me see."

"Uh-uh. Naughty. You'll see after we discuss terms. But there it is."

"Trick. Had some printer fake it. Don't believe it."

"All right. I never expected you, R. C., to descend to such unenlightened skepticism. But if that's all the faith you have—" Bill stuffed the paper back in his pocket and started for the door.

"Wait!" Mr. Choatsby lowered his voice. "How'd you do it? Sell your soul?"

"That wasn't necessary."

"How? Spells? Cantrips? Incantations? Prove it to me. Show me it's real. Then we'll talk terms."

Bill walked casually to the desk and emptied his pipe into the ash tray.

"I'm underdeveloped. I run errands. I'm named Snulbug. It isn't enough—now I should be a testimonial!"

Mr. Choatsby stared rapt at the furious little demon raging in his ash tray. He watched reverently as Bill held out the pipe for its inmate, filled it with tobacco, and lit it. He listened awe-struck as Snulbug moaned with delight at the flame.

"No more questions," he said. "What terms?"

"Fifteen thousand dollars." Bill was ready for bargaining.

"Don't put it too high," Snulbug warned. "You better hurry."

But Mr. Choatsby had pulled out his checkbook and was scribbling hastily. He blotted the check and handed it over. "It's a deal." He grabbed up the paper. "You're a fool, young man. Fifteen thousand!

Hmf!" He had it open already at the financial page. "With what I make on the market tomorrow, never notice $15,000. Pennies."

"Hurry up," Snulbug urged.

"Goodbye, sir," Bill began politely, "and thank you for—" But Reuben Choatsby wasn't even listening.

"What's all this hurry?" Bill demanded as he reached the elevator.

"People!" Snulbug sighed. "Never you mind what's the hurry. You get to your bank and deposit that check."

So Bill, with Snulbug's incessant prodding, made a dash to the bank worthy of his descents on the city hall and on the Choatsby Laboratories. He just made it, by stop-watch fractions of a second. The door was already closing as he shoved his way through at three o'clock sharp.

He made his deposit, watched the teller's eyes bug out at the size of the check, and delayed long enough to enjoy the incomparable thrill of changing the account from William Hitchens to The Hitchens Research Laboratory.

Then he climbed once more into his car, where he could talk with his pipe in peace. "Now," he asked as he drove home, "what was the rush?"

"He'd stop payment."

"You mean when he found out about the merry-go-round? But I didn't promise him anything. I just sold him tomorrow's paper. I didn't guarantee he'd make a fortune of it."

"That's all right. But—"

"Sure, you warned me. But where's the hitch? R. C.'s a bandit, but he's honest. He wouldn't stop payment."

"Wouldn't he?"

The car was waiting for a stop signal. The newsboy in the intersection was yelling "Uxtruh!" Bill glanced casually at the headline, did a double take, and instantly thrust out a nickel and seized a paper.

He turned into a side street, stopped the car, and went through this paper. Front page: MAYOR ASSASSINATED. Sports page: Alhazred at twenty to one. Obituaries: The same list he'd read at noon. He turned back to the date line. August 22. Tomorrow.

"I warned you," Snulbug was explaining. "I told you I wasn't strong enough to go far into the future. I'm not a well demon, I'm not. And an itch in the memory is something fierce. I just went far enough ahead to get a paper with tomorrow's date on it. And any dope knows that a Tuesday paper comes out Monday afternoon."

For a moment Bill was dazed. His magic paper, his fifteen-thousand-dollar paper, was being hawked by newsies on every corner. Small wonder R. C. might have stopped payment! And then he saw the other side. He started to laugh. He couldn't stop.

"Look out!" Snulbug shrilled. "You'll drop my pipe. And what's so funny?"

Bill wiped tears from his eyes. "I was right. Don't you see, Snulbug? Man can't be licked. My magic was lousy. All it could call up was you. You brought me what was practically a fake, and I got caught on the merry-go-round of time trying to use it. You were right enough there; no good could come of that magic.

"But without the magic, just using human psychology, knowing a man's weaknesses, playing on them, I made a syrup-voiced old bandit endow the very research he'd tabooed, and do more good for humanity than he's done in all the rest of his life. I was right, Snulbug. You can't lick Man."

Snulbug's snakes writhed into knots of scorn. "People!" he snorted. "You'll find out." And he shook his head with dismal satisfaction.

Afterword

———————————◆———————————

IT'S NOT MERELY fun to laugh: it's vitally necessary. Ask your doctor; he'll tell you so. It's critical to good health and long life. Fortunately, it goes down easy. Not everyone agrees on what's funny, of course. People have been trying to analyze humor and reduce it to easily quantifiable component parts since Grog made the first mammoth joke. I delight in their failure.

With two, you get eggroll. With *Smart Dragons, Foolish Elves*, you get smiles and stories, two for one, no extra charge, you should be so glad I'm not dunning you now. And if between the grins a story or two should happen to make you think a little, ponder then the meaning of life and what a sorry existence it would be devoid of laughter.

We memorialize the great writers, even deify them, but we hold closer to us those who make us laugh.